NATALIA BROTHERS

SOUL OF THE

AURAS OF NIGHT

CITY OWL
PRESS

SOUL OF THE UNBORN
Auras of Night: Book One

CITY OWL PRESS
www.cityowlpress.com

Cover Design by Tina Moss.
All stock photos licensed appropriately.

Edited by Yelena Casale.

For information on subsidiary rights, please contact the publisher at info@cityowlpress.com.

Print Edition ISBN: 978-1-944728-08-3
Digital Edition ISBN: 978-1-533770-07-3

Printed in the United States of America

To my family and friends

on both sides of the Atlantic.

-Natalia

PROLOGUE

Beneath a concrete bridge, the stream flowed under layers of ice and snow. A glow could be seen around the moon, if anyone in the village of Tishkino dared to abandon the shelter of goose-down pillows, thaw a peephole on frosted glass, and look at the blue pall of the sky. Under its vastness, the land sagged and shriveled, lying low like a wounded beast.

Leaving a winding pattern of footsteps, Terentey Malin made slow progress from the train station to the village, his parka unzipped, hat missing, and his bare fingers numb from gripping a half-empty bottle.

He cussed at the snow. He cried, mashing his mouth with a callused palm and smearing saliva across his chin. He choked on mouthfuls of vodka, his throat tight from sorrow.

In the hospital of the neighboring town of Kolieno, his newborn daughter, Katya, had lived and breathed and mewed like a kitten. Then she had died.

The doctor spoke of complications, using words Terentey didn't understand, patting his shoulder in a futile effort to comfort him. The reasons didn't matter. What mattered was if the girl had been stillborn, he would have taken her to the local witch, even if his wife tried to stop him. Prascovia had promised to help. But Katya, his precious angel, had entered the world alive. Now her tiny body lay in the morgue, and nothing could resurrect her, neither a prayer nor witchcraft.

Terentey lost his footing near the bridge, skidded, and rolled downhill to the stream. Dusty white flakes covered his coat, slipped under his collar, and nipped at his neck with icy teeth. Cursing, he crawled on all fours, unable to get up in the snowdrift or recover his bottle.

Murmurings under the arch interrupted his foul tirade. Like a woman crying over a loved one, a voice recited unintelligible words, hummed, whispered, and wept.

Terentey scooped a handful of snow to rub his face. A crusty slice bit his cheek, bringing the frozen world into focus. An old Tishkino tale spun in his head like a log caught under a waterfall. *Volkanoks*, "little wolves," mythical creatures living inside the bridge cried in human voices before devouring an unwary passerby.

Sweat covered Terentey's forehead. He jerked his sleeve to see his wristwatch. It was an hour after midnight.

Volkanoks' hunting time.

"*Bris.*" Terentey meant to shout to chase away the invisible menace as if it were a stray cat, but his throat produced a whimper. Gasps wheezed in and out at uneven intervals.

Twigs and dried grass snapped under his grasp. In the struggle to pull himself up the hill, he sensed movement behind him. He twisted and flopped onto his back. Sleek bodies with golden fur crept toward him.

A figure appeared on the bridge, swaying by the railing like a birch in the breeze. A black garment exposed only a semblance of a female face, pasty and carved with wrinkles.

"Prascovia?" Terentey whispered.

A twist of her brows reflected sorrow, until a sneer bared her uneven, triangular teeth. Her eyes shone violet, a feral gleam matching that of all the *volkanoks*.

No human ear heard Terentey's scream. Claws tore at his chest and face. Jaws found his throat. Salvation from pain came when his trachea was crushed, and his oxygen-deprived brain released his mind into nothingness.

CHAPTER ONE

The pleasure of Chris Waller's first morning in Moscow turned into annoyance when his younger cousin, Debra Alley, emerged from her hotel room carrying an overnight bag despite her promises not to stay in the village.

"Just in case all evening trains are canceled." Debra patted her bag.

"That would be convenient for you, wouldn't it?" Chris asked.

"Go pack your trunks. A couple days on a beach—doesn't it sound *mahvelous, dahling?*"

"We'll take that tour, have lunch, and I don't care what your friends decide to do next. You're returning with me to Moscow." Chris slapped at the elevator call button.

"If Moscow is all you want, then what's the point in you wasting any time on Vishenky?" Debra sounded sweeter than a wooing salesman.

"I'm glad you grasped the part about wasting my time."

"You're thirty-three, not ninety. Be adventurous."

"I was—when I signed up to chaperone you across the Atlantic. You mom said, quote-unquote, 'Promise me you'll watch her every step, breath, bite, and blink.'"

Chris understood Debra and her friends' desire to be on their own. Four college seniors, assisted by the English-speaking escort, Valya Svetlova, wouldn't get lost on their way to the village thirty miles from Moscow. The guide had rave recommendations from her visitors last year. *Vishenky's Legends and Supernatural Phenomena*, some countryside tour offered by the hotel—good luck with that. The whole thing irked Chris only because the airheads had the *Legends* on their list all along, but Debra didn't bother to tell him until last night. Maybe his overprotective Aunt Rita had a point when she had initially refused to pay for her daughter's trip to Russia.

"Playing babysitter in front of your students…." Debra clicked her tongue. "Must be embarrassing."

"Let me tell you about embarrassing. Your mother also asked me to make sure you don't lose your purse and check your room for a deadbolt lock. No food from street vendors, and, please, don't stay out after nine o'clock."

"And floss my teeth?"

"I was saving that detail until we joined your buddies."

"I'd kill you."

"Then stop being an ungrateful brat." Chris took hold of her skinny elbow, steadying Debra on the sinking floor of the high-speed elevator.

"Too bad your Beth is such a homebody," she cooed. "You two in Gorky Park—oh, so romantic, and off our backs." She turned sideways as a flock of silver-haired ladies invaded the cabin.

Beth Vogel. Another wave of jet lag swept over Chris, an exhausting brew of fatigue and restlessness that had kept him from getting any sleep. There was so much to see, to savor and appreciate, all meticulously selected and crammed into a seven-day trip. For the first time in weeks Beth wasn't on his mind. No, he wouldn't discuss their sudden breakup and endure Debra's tongue-in-cheek "Oh, how disappointing."

"You and Jessie Hunt," he said. "Enjoying your new friendship?" The girls had barely spoken a word to each other since the group had met at the check-in counter at Dulles International.

Debra turned away and studied the control panel, her shoulders positioned an inch higher.

The elevator slowed, stopped, and the doors slid open like symbolical curtains.

The entrance hall of the hotel reflected the same grandeur of the Soviet times as did the metro stations. Tiered chandeliers enticed a woman in a sari into snapping a quick picture as she rushed after her husband rolling his suitcase across the marble floor. Pointing fingers to the high ceiling, teenagers in matching green t-shirts tilted their heads back and giggled furtively, as if in awe of the frescoes that glorified the long-gone era.

Chris spotted Peter Moss and his standoffish girlfriend, Jessie Hunt, by the left wing of the curved staircase. Debra's childhood pal, Luke Higbee, was absent from the rendezvous point; his backpack, stuffed with camping gear, sat at Jessie's feet.

"You both decided to come," Peter said pleasantly, but his thin-lipped mouth twitched.

"I never said I wouldn't." Chris looked around. "Where's Higbee?"

Jessie rolled her eyes as Luke emerged from the gift shop. He shook a plastic bag where the red headdress of a doll peeked out. "A teakettle warmer. I'll tell my sister it's a hat." He tried to get a high five out of Jessie, but she ignored him, her pale eyes fixed on the hotel's entrance. Luke winked at Debra. "So, Deb, is Mr. Waller on board?"

"On board with what?" Chris asked.

Debra shrugged. "Guys, it was your idea. Don't put me in the middle."

"Well, somebody, it's now or never if you're going to bring this up at all," Jessie said. "Valya will be here any moment."

"Okay." Red blotches spread over Peter's cheekbones. "Mr. Waller, we want to ask you for a favor."

Chris turned his hand, palm up. "What?"

"Someone else went on this tour last summer."

"Your brother, yes. Deb told me."

"My half-brother." Peter moved a step toward Chris. "His last name is Ogden, not Moss. The guide has no way of knowing we're related, unless someone warns her."

Jessie raised her arm in front of her boyfriend as if to stop Peter's advancing. "Mr. Waller, please. We just don't want the guide to know how we found her. Maybe you could tell her the tour was your idea and Peter contacted her on your behalf."

"Why?" Chris asked.

"To confuse her." Luke extracted the souvenir doll out of the bag and pointed its pudgy hand at Chris. "You stumbled on Valya's website. Deb doesn't speak any Russian. Jessie will be my girlfriend. We've never heard about last summer's group or seen the footage they filmed."

"And I'm your kindergarten teacher," Chris said. "Why would the guide care who found her website?"

Peter studied Luke and his teakettle warmer as if debating what was more annoying, the doll or his buddy's perpetual grin. "If Valya hears that we saw my brother's film, she might change her program."

"So what?" Chris asked. "Don't you want to learn something new?"

A quick exchange of troubled glances told him that when the real story came out, he wouldn't like it.

"You won't have to lie if you skip the village," Luke said.

"I don't 'have to' anything," Chris assured him.

"Sir, do you believe in psychics?" Jessie asked. "Stuff like mind reading?"

Chris turned to Debra. "What's all this BS about?"

She pouted.

"The guide is like a performance artist, not a psychic," Luke said. "It would be interesting to see if she can read through a load of misinformation."

Chris stared at his cousin. "You told me this was a folklore tour."

"Among other things," Debra said. "Chris, really, you don't have to go. We'll be okay."

A day in a village, in the company of a "psychic" and this bunch of juveniles, seemed like a waste of time compared to the riches of Moscow museums. "See you later" would be a justified reply to Debra's suggestion.

"That's not what I promised your mother," Chris said instead. "And I won't lie about who found—"

"It's her," Jessie said.

A young woman strode across the lobby, a cell phone pressed to her ear, her eyes scanning the tourists congregated around the base of the staircase. For a second her glance met Chris's, but she looked away, searching for someone else.

"Valya Svetlova?" Peter called out.

Silence.

Dressed in beige slacks and a white blouse, with blushing cheeks and a braid streaming over her shoulder and down her chest, Valya could have been a poster girl for any Russian travel agency, except for the fact that not a hint of a smile touched her lips. Watching Valya's widening eyes, Chris thought the guide was startled by the sight of their group rather than glad her guests had arrived.

CHAPTER TWO

Too late for any last-minute qualms, I thought.

The great hotel thrust the tip of its starred steeple into an azure sky. Inside, the opulent, grand lobby appeared quiet after I had walked the noisy streets.

"Valya Svetlova?" A velvety voice riveted me.

The dark-haired speaker waited for my response, but these people couldn't be my visitors. Another man, in his early thirties, interrupted his conversation with his companions and studied me the way a cat would inspect a ferret—*smaller than me, but is it harmless?* He seemed too old to be a college student.

By a column, out of their sight, my friend Tamara Karpova raised her cell phone.

"Told you," her excited soprano sang into my ear. "They brought an extra person. Put Jessie in your room, and he can have hers."

"Thanks for the warning." I cut the connection. Late for work, my dutiful backup headed for the exit. I bravely approached the semicircle of my prospective guests.

"Good morning." The younger man, the one who had called out my name, smiled.

High cheekbones, onyx-colored eyes that could liquefy a rock, or at least raise a tide of heat to my face and neck. I recognized Peter Moss, my contact. His pictures, copious on Jessie Hunt's blog, hadn't truly revealed Peter's magnetism, maybe because his lips had never parted for the camera.

I smiled back. *"Vishenky's Legends and Supernatural Phenomena*: Are you brave enough to experience them?"

Holding a teakettle-warmer doll on his left hand like a puppet, Luke Higbee hit his shoulder in a mock salute. "You bet. Take us to your leader!"

"Did you come in peace?"

A grin stretched across Luke's full lips. I had just made his "my kind of gal" list.

This was my group, but for some reason they had brought an older man with them. Had Peter ever mentioned a fifth person? Could I have missed any of his emails? After my third sleepless night, my brain worked like the viscous substance inside a pitcher plant, where my thoughts were stuck and then drowned.

My guests' stay would be a brief one if they didn't consider me a trusted friend by nightfall. My only chance to attain that status and to delve into their secret yens was while Vishenky's energy still saturated every fiber of my body. I rushed to absorb everything at once—faces, moods, and those fleeting impulses that revealed bonds and antipathies within the group.

"I hope we'll hear something original," Jessie said. "You've done these tours before, right?"

Aggressive. Insecure from dating a domineering, gorgeous boyfriend?

"I assure you, I am fully qualified." I injected plenty of defensiveness into my amiable tone. "Tales are my specialty."

My approach failed. Jessie aimed her nose higher. The bleached curls that looked so messy on her photos were gone, replaced by stylish, uneven strands. The color of her eyes was incredible, pale gray, like weeks-old snow on a balmy spring day. I locked my gaze with hers. Nothing. Not even curiosity. My inability to register the usual array of human emotions demonstrated Jessie's tremendous willpower, making me wonder what she was hiding.

I felt a nudge of weakness in my diaphragm.

"Hold on, hold on…before we go…." Luke plopped the souvenir teakettle warmer on his head and thrust his camera into my hands.

"Would you take a picture?"

"Sure." I motioned for the group to cluster around him and fumbled with the buttons.

Debra Alley adjusted the doll's skirt over Luke's ears. "It looks great on you. You'd better keep it."

My Debra. She had no idea that a few lifetimes ago she and I shared the same ancestor. Her cropped, fluffy black hair left her neck exposed. As she raised a pale hand in a greeting, she reminded me of a silent movie star: deep, mesmerizing eyes, framed by black eyelashes, richly colored lips ready to unlock into a smile, and grace unmatched, with the utmost femininity revealed in each motion of her slim body. A modern girl, she wore a designer denim dress, but I pictured her dancing the Charleston.

Oh, Debra, if you only knew how much I hoped you were unique like me and Vishenky's portals would stir your dormant paranormal powers. A year ago, my mother's confession about the circumstances of my birth almost destroyed my world. The word "stillborn" had left her mouth, and knowing the implications, I had envisioned my name being deleted from the list of human species. If my every breath, every emotion, every desire was generated by a supernatural entity, where was my soul? Did I even have one? I had to have proof, once and for all, that it was my bloodline that gave me my supernatural abilities, not the energy that had chosen to inhabit an infant's corpse. I wasn't a puppet in someone's horror show with my strings pulled by a wicked director.

Now my emotions ran amok, and my heart scurried like a startled chipmunk. Before I lost control completely, I scanned the fifth member of the group, the older man I didn't know.

I had no trouble reading him. He hated standing here. He fervently detested Peter and my presence. His irritation boiled like magma, threatening to burst the surface of his polite demeanor. But the surface was sealed by unyielding self-control.

My preservation instincts set up no barbed wire in response. His combination of green eyes with wavy sandy-blond hair probably never failed to get a woman to like him at first sight, but I didn't think *I* could fall just for a nice face. And still, suddenly, I wanted to forget Debra, forget Vishenky, and drag this man from the gloominess of the hotel into the sunlight and to the lively boulevards and historic squares of my city. Let him absorb the view of the Cathedral of Christ the Savior from the Andreevsky Bridge. Make him listen to the beat of the new expressway that replaced the railroad across the Moscow River. Stun him with the sight of a sunset from my ninth-floor apartment over the Novodevichy Convent, at the hour when the glow of the last sunrays transformed the reflecting pond into a fairy tale of romantic twilight and ethereal shadows and—

I must have gone insane.

Vestiges of Vishenky's energy faded fast from my body. Peter spoke, but I didn't catch the meaning of his words. Above me, the painted images of joyful workers from the Soviet fifties swayed, and the rotund ceiling pushed its weight on my shoulders, gripping my head in a plaster clasp. Instead of throwing myself into the expected round of introductions, I summoned all my willpower to remain steady on my feet.

CHAPTER THREE

Something was off within the group.

Debra began to chatter after I had shoved the camera back to Luke and marched out of the hotel without a word of explanation. She babbled about the weather, traffic, pigeons, crowds, and a playful cocker spaniel biting its leash—anything around us. She wasn't just filling the pause left by my silence; she was trying to ingratiate herself with her unhappy companions.

Not how I had imagined our first encounter, but she was here and on her way to Vishenky, and I'd allow no one to interfere with my plan. I intended to rule this motley bunch by the time we stepped off the train.

I regained some of my bearings before the train left the station, thanks to the coffee Jessie bought for me while I purchased our tickets. I didn't dwell on the fact that her ice-gray eyes read me better than I read her.

The guys fussed over fitting their luggage, which I found excessive for one night, on the overhead shelves. The group settled in the compartments across the aisle, and I pushed the upper part of the smudged window open and rolled up the sleeves of my blouse, giving myself a few extra moments to decide how to proceed.

So tense and focused that my hands trembled, I picked a seat to face the man with whom I had yet to be acquainted. His stare dropped to my interlaced fingers then returned to my eyes.

No jacket for a cold evening on the river; no overnight bag, while Luke carried something the size of a pony in his backpack. Unlike the students, the man wasn't planning to stay in Vishenky.

On our ten-minute walk to the train station, I had managed to gauge his reaction to the labyrinth of the underground crossing, the apartment buildings and kiosks, and a cluster of gypsies huddling on an empty platform. I sensed his recognition, while Russia seemed an undiscovered concept to his younger companions.

There was something else in his reaction. A layer deeper, a shadow darker. Wisps of sadness drifted through his emotions like puffs of fog floating across a road between two fields.

"Has Moscow changed since your last visit?" I asked him.

"Yes," he said. "Twelve years is a long time."

My astounding insight left him unimpressed, but Debra's eyebrows moved. Across the aisle, Luke and Jessie leaned in my direction, smug "game-on" alertness mushrooming on their faces.

"But I had only stayed in Moscow for three days," the man added.

"Where else?" I asked.

"St. Petersburg."

I liked how he spoke, politely, softly, giving away no bad sentiments which I had earlier perceived in him at the hotel. "May I have your name?"

He regarded Peter, my email contact, with a quizzical glance. *That's right,* I thought, *Peter never mentioned you. Do you wonder now how I knew you'd been to Moscow before?*

"Chris Waller," the man said. "I teach political science."

"Russia is a good place for our studies," Peter chimed in.

I knew nothing about their plans to make this trip politically enlightening. I ignored Peter and focused on Chris. "What made you interested in Vishenky's folklore?"

"It's about Russian culture," Jessie informed me coldly, "our elective course. We're lucky Mr. Waller found you."

Seriously? He *found* me?

I kept my eyes on Chris. No pride for his diligent pupils; his glare fell on Jessie like a marble headstone.

What is it that you're not saying, Mr. Waller? What did they tell you to bring you here? Why are you letting your students lie?

"How often do you do these tours?" Chris asked me.

"Every July. My operation is tied to a natural phenomenon. I thought you knew." One lie, one truth, and then I fished to see his reaction.

"Maybe you could tell us more about yourself, Valya," Peter interrupted before Chris could elaborate on what he knew and what he didn't.

"Yeah, I have three questions," Luke announced.

"I'm twenty-three and single," I said. "What's your third question?"

I hit the mark. Luke and Debra chuckled. Chris's lips moved in a faint smile.

"Your favorite color?" Luke asked.

"Chartreuse." Dictionaries are full of magnificent words.

Luke scratched the back of his head in mock puzzlement. With his tousled hair cut short and eyes shining in exuberance, he had all the qualities of a puppy that had just rolled in grass and then jumped up suddenly, eager to greet its master. Puppies with unbounded energy and no discipline could be a challenge, but I knew the perfect incentive for training. I looked at Luke's chubby cheeks and untucked shirt. I was a good cook.

I pointed out an old brick water tower as we passed by. Then I recited my website pitch without adding anything new. I was offering a walking tour, plus lunch in a picturesque village. Some fascinating local stories. Plenty of room at my summer home. With my amazing group discount, for just twenty dollars more per person, they were invited to stay overnight and get a chance to witness an unusual phenomenon.

"You can decide for yourselves what you saw," I said.

"Sounds like fun," Debra said. "Your English is quite good. I like your accent."

"Do any of you speak Russian?" I asked.

"No," Debra said.

She didn't even blush. But Chris did, showing me he was aware Debra spoke my language fluently. By the way he clenched his jaw, I guessed he wasn't happy she had lied.

In fact, most of what the group had told me was a lie. They weren't ordinary tourists, folklore collectors who found me on the Internet. They didn't realize I had singled them out.

Panic scattered my thoughts. *Kenny Ogden and his team.*

I'd made a grave mistake twelve months ago. I had hosted another group, and that tour ended in disaster. I had dealt with the outcome and thought there would be no further consequences. But what if Debra and her friends knew my earlier guests?

Sweat moistened my palms. I unbuttoned the top of my blouse.

Chris watched me. More out of nervousness than with intent, I held his stare until he looked away.

I thought it was impossible, but what if Vishenky's secrets got out? If Kenny talked, and this crew believed him, they would be watching my every move. How soon would someone figure out that Debra was my target?

The remains of my confidence dissipated like the puff of a baby sparrow's breath.

CHAPTER FOUR

Chris caught an interesting view of the village of Vishenky from the train.

First, miles of industrial structures and bleak apartment buildings that crowded Moscow's outskirts were replaced with green fields interspersed with brightly painted country houses and modern boxy mansions. Then a mixed forest emerged on both sides of the railway as birches and junipers flashed by, blocking Chris's view for a few minutes.

When the wall of greenery parted, a stately white church with blue domes seemed to rotate on top of a hill as the train rode in a smooth arc around it. At the lowest level of the terrain, the snaking water surface glittered amid the verdant willows. A strip of rooftops followed the riverbed.

His younger cousin, Debra, leaned forward for a better view. "Quite scenic."

Valya's eyes lit up as she nodded at the window. "Vishenky."

Hallelujah. The spark of delight in the young woman's eyes gave Chris hope the guide might end her marathon of anxiety. During the thirty-minute train ride, Valya sat straight, her spine rigid. Her tightly interlocked fingers never loosened. She rarely made eye contact, but when she did, she stared with a feverish intensity that could ignite a wet log.

With a guide playing a psychic, Chris had expected to find a sly professional capable of entertaining while remaining in charge. He thought he'd detest her, a fake medium fooling gullible tourists. Instead, he wanted to help her.

Valya looked stunned when his cousin had lied about her Russian. After Debra blurted out, "No," Valya's shoulders slumped, and she sank into silence. At that moment, Chris began to grasp the cause of her predicament. The group was trying to confuse her, but she must have obtained some information from Jessie's blog or Peter's e-mails. That was why the idea of testing her "psychic powers" by misleading her had backfired. Rattled by Debra's dishonesty, the inexperienced, timid guide couldn't do her job.

What was the deal with Valya's tours, anyway? He should have asked about her at the hotel instead of trusting the accuracy of the information that Peter had given to Debra.

The train came to a stop. The doors slid open, and Chris squinted at the frenzied color palette of the countryside.

A short ride away, the Russian capital showed off the illustrious sight of the Kremlin rising above the Moscow River. He wasn't going to sacrifice an afternoon of browsing the streets and soaking up the mood and vibes of the dazzling city. He thought of a simple way to help the struggling guide. Then he'd grab Debra and flee the village.

CHAPTER FIVE

Surrounded by rye fields, the train station consisted of a platform and a ticket booth. Above the birch grove that sprawled between my raring-to-go group and Vishenky, the golden cross of the church sparkled in the blinding late-morning sun. The calm air smelled of cut grass and cornflowers. Only Luke's whistling disturbed the countryside's tranquility. Each trill sliced my sleep-deprived brain into pieces.

Jessie pulled off her khaki rain jacket and tied the sleeves around her waist. "I hope it doesn't get any hotter."

"No humidity compared to Virginia." For the first time, Chris sounded enthusiastic. "Very nice."

"Scattered clouds in the afternoon. A slight chance of thunderstorms." I had memorized the weather-channel talk in English. "Clear and cooler after sundown."

"Great forecast." Chris grinned, looking much too cute and no doubt knowing it. "Valya, you don't have to be so formal."

"I'm not," I said, riled not by his tone—it had been gracious all along—but by his patronizing encouragement. "This way." I strode along the platform, hurried by an irrational desire to put some distance between the station and us, as though my guests would jump on a train headed back to Moscow.

Maybe I should just explain to them that what happened to last summer's visitors wasn't entirely my fault. But was there really a link between the two groups? Or could the old paranoia have crawled from the catacombs of my subconscious, tainting my perception?

We crossed the railroad tracks. Instead of taking the dusty road that led straight to Vishenky, I turned onto a scenic trail that ran down a hill, weaved between isles of birches, and cut through a clover meadow. My guests' peculiar behavior on the train was forcing me to alter my plans. My first test, albeit spontaneous, waited for Debra in the grove ahead: a water well with a faint flow of energy from a portal. A portal into another world. The energy I craved. The force that infused my bloodstream with electric current, made me feel effervescent, alive.

My plan was simple. Exposed to the energy, Debra would exhibit supernatural skills. Her transformation would prove that our abilities stemmed solely from our genes. I wasn't a soulless monster destined to perish in another dimension.

I walked faster, ignoring Luke's puffing.

Debra's great-great-grandmother, Alexandra Gretishnikoff, had emigrated from Russia after the Bolshevik Revolution, and the last name, especially with this spelling, was rare. Thrilled I had found her, I was dying to call Debra and introduce myself, but without any urgency on her part, it could take years before she decided to meet the Russian side of the Gretishnikoff clan.

Fortunately for me, because of her friendship with Peter Moss, her name popped up on his girlfriend's blog.

Jessie Hunt, an odd but gifted blonde obsessed with paranormal phenomena, adored small and sleepy towns with chilling ghost tales. Her photo of a marble angel that appeared to drift in fog past ivy-covered decaying crypts had haunted my dreams for nights.

I left a comment pretending to be a German student who had just visited this incredible spooky village near Moscow. Jessie wanted to know more. My identity still concealed, I led her to the website explaining my tours. Then Peter Moss took charge, requesting a brochure to his home address.

Besides my flier, I also enclosed a sliver of a moisture-damaged mirror with instructions to drop it in a glass of water. The shard would turn into a transparent newt. Deprived of Vishenky's energy, the paranormal amphibian would then vanish in seconds.

Can I have another one? he quickly e-mailed.

If you take my tour, you can collect some in person, I wrote back.

He and his friends would love to do that, but travel to Moscow wasn't cheap. *Maybe in a year?*

I drowned my disappointment and impatience in Russian poetry and English grammar.

Then my cell phone rang one day. A group of aspiring journalists was traveling through Europe to make a documentary about paranormal sightings. They wanted to spruce up the story with Russian folklore.

"How did you find me?" I asked.

"You have a cool website," a young male voice said.

That troubled me. True, I had listed my phone number and email address as the means of contact, but I used the words "Moscow" and "Russian" only in the flyer, hoping the Internet search engines would overlook my site. Had Peter forwarded my info to someone else?

"Sorry, I screen my guests, and I'm currently full," I told the caller.

"Do you want me to post all over the Web that you're a fake?"

I wanted no publicity at all, good or bad, so I agreed. "I'll meet you at the airport," I said. They didn't know with whom they were dealing.

Two boys and a girl, all college freshmen, showed up.

Their documentary wasn't about poltergeists, Yeti, or UFOs. They investigated worldwide analogies in superstitions, ghost stories, and tactics of "crooks like me."

"I'll make you forget about Vishenky," I told them sweetly. "But first, I'll make you wonder how many of the stories you've recorded are true."

They laughed.

Their flight had arrived hours late, so they had slept on the train, and then we rushed to watch the phenomenon happening that evening. I didn't have the time to prep these skeptics for the encounter. I just told them to sit on a sheet of plastic, the material that kept the monsters away, and to stay put. But when the creature emerged from the portal, Kenny's girlfriend, Amanda, freaked out and ran. Her screams could have awakened a mummy in Cairo.

I used an arsenal of potions to treat Amanda's bitten hand, and cast a shroud to make the group unwilling to think or talk about Vishenky and me. Their footage of the creature, filmed in the dark with shaky hand-held cameras, would appear like any other pseudo-documentary. No one would believe it.

Even if Peter and his crew had seen Kenny's footage, I still couldn't understand the reason for their lies. And how did courteous but furtively annoyed Chris and his political science fit into the masquerade?

Who lied to whom?

A palm landed on my shoulder. "Hello-o, no daydreaming on the job," Luke's voice boomed in my ears. "Are we there yet?"

Our destination, the water well, sat in the ravine just twenty meters ahead.

"Almost." I studied Luke's face.

In his excited grin I saw my answers. Whether or not they knew something about me didn't seem to matter. Only Chris was unhappy about coming here. His presence, while pleasant in some ways, distracted me. His authority could jeopardize my influence on the group.

I'd have to get rid of him. Then I'd deal with the others.

CHAPTER SIX

A path wound through the multitude of white tree trunks rising from the sun-dappled carpet of vegetation. The pleasant earthy scent of fallen leaves and mushrooms wafted through the air, with a hint of something else, vanilla-sweet, a woodland flower Chris didn't know.

Their taciturn guide stopped on the trail. "Let's take a break."

"No one's tired," Chris said. "How far is it to the village?"

"There's a spring in the ravine. I'd like you to see it," Valya said.

"Let's get to your house."

"Break first," Peter ordered.

Chris paused to suppress his reply. He motioned instead toward an opening among the birches ahead. "Is that the way to the village?"

Valya nodded. "If you stay on the path."

"I'll meet you there," he said.

"Just don't cross the bridge."

"Why, it won't let me through without some special incantation?"

"Don't be silly, *Mr. Waller*," Debra cut in, emphasizing his last name, probably in an attempt to conceal their family ties from the guide. "The locals will sniff out a foreigner. Vishenky's grannies will think you're a spy."

Luke snorted and opened his mouth to comment.

"We'll meet in ten minutes," Valya interrupted. "Those of you who'd like to see the spring, it's right over here in the weeds." She marched in that direction as if hurrying to part with Chris.

Dammit, he thought. His frustration did nothing but impede his intention to help the guide.

The trail ran downhill, bringing him to a rickety wooden structure Valya had called a bridge. A number of its weary supporting pillars had collapsed into the river. They rested, stuck in muck, moss-covered above the surface and algae-wrapped below.

A bird screamed from the willow that leaned over the sandbar extending out from the bank. Another one screeched back.

Blop. By the time Chris turned his eyes to the water, he only saw an expanding circle of ripples. Then a foot-wide bubble rose to the surface and popped with another *blop* sound. Spooked, the birds tore through the branches. A few ripped leaves and brown feathers spiraled down onto the current.

Curious, Chris stepped onto the sandbar in the shade of the willow. Vishenky, as quaint as the clichéd depictions of carved eaves and cottage gardens, stretched out on the other side of the river, a perfect setting for storytelling. No wonder Debra, obsessed with her Russian roots, wanted to participate in the tour so badly.

Her mother's overprotective temperament was a joke only among those family members who didn't happen to sleep under her roof. At twenty-one, Debra was still Aunt Rita's baby, a concept that caused Chris's favorite cousin much embarrassment in front of her friends.

The trip to Russia magnified the old conflict. With problems of his own—a doomed relationship with yet another girlfriend—Chris never meant to play his cousin's chaperone. But on the last day of May, Debra broke into tears in his college office. "I told the guys I was going with them. How do I tell them, 'My mommy won't let me go'?"

Chris put down his paperwork and crossed to the open window where Debra stood sniffling. The sprinklers scattered misty droplets over a batch of red tulips next to a row of blooming azaleas. The breeze carried pollen, making Debra sneeze as it billowed the black strands of her hair. Chris gave her slim shoulders a brotherly squeeze and kissed the top of her head. Not taking his eyes off a mini-rainbow that had sprouted in a sunny patch above the lawn, he said, "Okay. I'll go with you."

Across Vishenky's river, the idyllic houses basked in the sun. The wind blew in tides through the uncut grass. A fine picture, worthy of seeing through a bus or train window on the way to some place more exciting.

A whiff of manure overpowered the waterfront smells of decaying vegetation and silt. At Chris's feet, two gray larvae crawled on the river bottom, their bodies half-hidden in the tubular homes built of tiny rocks and shells, a couple of strange things going about their peculiar lives.

This wasn't his world. Planting flowerbeds and tending his lawn was as close as he ever got to farming. He had fulfilled his promise to Aunt Rita. He had met the guide and escorted his cousin to the village. Once he checked out Valya's home, there was no reason for him to continue with the tour. Debra, even less country-living inclined, would most certainly follow him back to Moscow on the very next train. Chris just needed an appropriate excuse to leave, something that wouldn't make Valya, whose every smile and gesture were coronal mass ejections of vulnerability, more self-conscious.

Or should he stay and make sure the group behaved?

Ridiculous. She had chosen to run this tour. She needed to learn, and he shouldn't be interfering, and matter how hard it was to remain uninvolved.

Chris glanced around. Wildflowers and grass plumes generated a profusion of pollen, meaning allergies! A small lie, but it would salvage the rest of his day. The flamboyant Russian capital would have his undivided admiration before lunch.

Another pocket of gas escaped the river bottom, and the odor of silt grew stronger. Smaller bubbles fizzed in the wet sand, moving down the strip as if something alive and breathing crawled just below the surface. Chris walked along the growing line of froth, wondering what would happen when it reached the sandbar's end.

CHAPTER SEVEN

Looking for a secluded spot to pee, Debra descended the last flight of steps—packed dirt reinforced with rotting timber—leading to the bottom of the ravine. A crude, narrow bridge connected the stairs to the path going up the opposite slope. The air was much cooler here in the deep shade, where the rivulet flowing from the water well met a wider stream. Morning dew still coated thick, tall vegetation. Buzzing insects hung around the clusters of pasty flowers.

Unfortunately, Debra had company.

"Hey, Deb?" Peter called out, coming down the steps. "How could you not know that Chris was going to chaperone us everywhere?"

"Well, I didn't. Chris wanted to see Moscow. That's all I knew."

Peter's stare slid to her neck. Before she stopped herself, her hand flew up to her throat where her reddened skin revealed her embarrassment.

Flustered, Debra tested the sturdiness of the boards precariously nailed to the logs and walked to the middle of the bridge.

Peter followed. "As long as your cousin sticks around, this tour is a waste of time."

"So, Chris will stay for a few hours. What's the big deal?"

"His presence messes up the whole program."

Peter's bossiness was getting on her nerves. A slight shove, Debra fantasized, and he would stumble into the soggy, smelly muck. Feet wet, slacks ruined....He'd scream and curse, instead of criticizing her in his languid baritone for someone else's decisions.

She sighed. "How could Chris's presence mess up a simple folklore tour?"

Peter blinked several times and touched his forehead as if pondering a tricky algebra problem. A faint blush covered his tanned cheekbones.

"Oh my God," Debra said. "These 'ghost stories'…are they what…X-rated?"

His teeth grazed his bottom lip. He looked past her and said, "Yeahhhh."

"Why didn't you tell me?" Debra asked.

"Can you get rid of him?"

"You think Valya is too shy to talk about it in front of Chris? Because he's older?"

"Does she look comfortable to you?" Peter asked.

"She seems a bit tense, but…." Debra couldn't decide if Peter's problem with her cousin's presence was infuriating or comical. "I guess your Russian wallflower will have to toughen up or come up with a PG version. I have no authority to send Chris away."

"He's here because of you. Why don't you both leave?"

"Excuse me?"

"Deb, you're my friend. I like you. But this place is not for you."

"You're in my way. Move."

His fingers circled her wrist.

Startled, she tried to pull away. Peter held her arm at chest level. "Just leave with Chris. Please."

This bird of prey, with eyes like glimmering charcoals, wasn't the chivalrous man Debra knew. Welling tears of anger hazed her vision. She moved forward. "Asshole."

Peter released her wrist. He turned around, walked back to solid ground, and stepped aside, letting her stomp by.

Fuming, she hurried up the stairs, but he caught up with her. His arm slid around her waist. The smell of his cologne and body heat violated her senses. His lips brushed her ear. "Deb, wait."

She gasped and pushed him away.

He raised his arms. "What, now you're afraid of me?"

"I think you've lost your mind," Debra said. "Maybe I *should* tell Chris how much you want him out of here."

Peter blocked her path. A film of sweat glistened on his upper lip. "Listen to me. The tour is not X-rated. You haven't seen Kenny's film because there is no film. He deleted the footage. He wouldn't leave his room for a month. He's still in therapy, and still refuses to talk about Vishenky."

CHAPTER EIGHT

Debra took a step down, grasping the railing. "I don't understand. Did something happen to him on the tour?"

"We came here to find out."

"Is it just Kenny? What about his girlfriend?"

"Not a word. She wouldn't take my mother's calls. When they came home, my brother, Amanda, their buddy Ron, they all seemed fine. They spent two weeks watching the footage. Hungary, Poland, no problem. Then one evening I stopped by, and they stared at the screen as if they were hypnotized. Amanda had a notebook in her lap. The last entry was, 'Valya, Vishenky.'"

"Did you watch it?" Debra asked.

"Darkness, lots of screaming, Amanda's face, distorted, horrible, like she's about to die. Kenny wouldn't explain anything. But if I said, 'Vishenky,' he'd clam up. Lie down, curl up, and stare. It's the freakiest thing I've ever seen."

"What do your parents think?"

"Kenny's always been a drama queen, and my mother believes it was his breakup with Amanda."

"That sounds more plausible," Debra said.

Peter's eyebrows joined. "I was there right after they watched the footage. I don't give a damn if Jessie's the only one who believes me."

"Jessie, who also believes in ghosts and the Yeti. Great."

"You've met Valya. Would you say she's an ordinary tour guide?"

"Yes, she is. She's just nervous, and that's because we ganged up on her."

"You say nervous, and I say on edge. Mr. Waller's presence definitely bothers her. Why?"

"You tell me," Debra said, "because my logic will never catch up with Jessie's imagination."

Peter grimaced, hurt by her sarcasm. "What if Miss Valya runs some kind of unusual operation here? A horror show. Staged ghost stories. Something so unconventional, it's unsafe, but she doesn't care about the consequences. Maybe she thinks she can get away with anything."

"Because without Chris we're just a bunch of students? How long do you think her business would last if it were dangerous?"

Peter looked away, his black eyes scanning the other side of the ravine. "Business…right…My point is, you shouldn't be here. I thought it was a bad idea to invite you, but Jess insisted because you speak Russian. I should have never agreed."

"Thanks a lot." Debra rubbed her forearms. "I think it's ludicrous to even imagine that a visit to a simple little village could make your brother crazy. Did you tell him you were going to take Valya's tour?"

"It's impossible to keep something this big a secret when we live under one roof. He overheard us deciding on what we'd tell Valya. He walked into the room and said, 'She'll know. She'll know everything about you. Even if you pretend you're deaf and mute, she'll still know everything.'"

Debra huffed. "Definitely a drama queen. I can see Jessie believing him, but it's not something I'd ever expect from you."

"Be skeptical all you want, but not here. Deb, please, go, see the museums, go shopping. We'll catch up with you in three days. I promise we'll visit any gallery, any monastery, any church you want. We'll take pictures of every onion dome in the city. Just get yourself and Mr. Waller out of Vishenky. Please." Peter took her hand and squeezed her fingers as if to emphasize his point. "I don't want you here if things turn ugly."

Debra pulled her hand from his clasp. "For you or Valya?"

He paused, searching her face. "All I want is to find out what's really going on."

"I understand."

"Good." His gallantry back, Peter hooked her fingers to the crook of his elbow, pulling her up the stairs. Debra complied, her good humor lying in ashes like an English village after a Viking assault.

Before the spring water vanished into the forest of weeds, it filled a ringed concrete reservoir and spilled over the carved-out lip. Some would find the gurgling sound of the cascade melodious and soothing, but it only made Debra conscious of her full bladder.

"Find anything interesting?" Luke asked her, snapping Jessie's picture.

Debra shrugged.

"A crossing to the other side of the ravine," Peter said. "It must be a shortcut to the train station."

Jessie had created a head wreath out of the pasty flowers. Sitting on the thick rim of the well, she posed for Luke's camera with the sassiness of a nymph drifting in reverie, oblivious of the gnats swirling above her crow's-nest adornment.

Valya crouched on the other side of the well, her back pressed to the smooth surface, her eyes closed, her face an unemotional mask.

A little odd, yes, Debra thought, but not even close to Peter with his village conspiracy theory, or to Jessie, an aficionado of reincarnation and ghosts, a lunatic who wore Renaissance outfits "to honor the era of her past existence."

Jessie slid off the rim and walked by without a word.

Debra scooped spring water and spread her fingers, letting it run through. Maybe Peter was right. This tour wasn't for her. Maybe she should wake up Valya, find Chris, stop at the guide's house for a bathroom break and coffee, and head for Moscow.

Before Peter turned things ugly.

Jessie's husky laughter made Debra wince. Arms on Luke's and Peter's shoulders, Jessie tossed back her head in abandoned merriment. Adoration glowed in the guys' faces.

Debra grasped the well's rough rim. Reflections of tree branches swayed on the surface. On the bottom, sand particles hopped and sunk, pushed by the spring's jets.

How did it happen that a fake blonde with icy wide-set eyes had wedged her never-ending presence into the lives of the two men whom Debra considered her best friends? Why had the intelligent, no-nonsense Peter fallen for a weirdo who based her daily choices on horoscopes and premonitions?

"Not every friend is worth keeping," Valya said. "But some are worth fighting for."

Debra gripped the rim tighter and leaned to the left, craning her neck to see the orator. "What are you talking about?"

The guide looked up. "Loyalties. Who will stand by you at the end of the day?"

Goose bumps covered Debra's naked arms. "Do you have ears of an owl?"

"Eyes of an eagle. You've been uncomfortable since we left the hotel. Then you came back upset from a rendezvous with Peter."

Valya stretched out her hand. Debra pulled the guide to her feet, the slight palm hot against her chilled fingers.

"You're my guest," Valya said. "How can I help?"

A few minutes of rest had revived the strange Russian as if she were a droopy bud dipped in water now opening to its full might. No fidgeting. No shyness. An easy smile fitted the new Valya like a sword befitting a musketeer.

Comforting warmth spread through Debra's chest, a peculiar hunch, an irrational feeling rather than a coherent thought. She had a friend in Valya. A friend she could trust. A friend she *should* trust.

"Don't let Chris leave. He's not your real problem." The words gushed out before Debra processed her inexplicable yearning to act as Valya's confidant. She pressed her freezing fingertips to her eyelids. Her hullabaloo of emotions had to be a result of the sleepless transatlantic flight.

"Who is my problem?" Valya asked.

Kenny deleted the footage. He refuses to talk about Vishenky. Peter's words raced through Debra's head like a swarm of yellow jackets.

She forced herself to laugh. "Well, that's not what I meant. No one is a problem. I'm just saying, Mr. Waller...ask him to stay. Until tonight. For your stories. He's nice. You'll like him."

Valya's eyes searched hers. "Why does he want to leave?"

"Your tour, it's like going camping. Countryside, fresh air. He thinks we'll have more fun without him."

"Will you?" Valya asked.

"No. Just tell Mr. Waller that he should stay. He'll listen."

Valya arched an eyebrow.

"Hey, I'm not asking for dinosaur eggs for breakfast," Debra said. "Don't you want more business?"

"Right….What did you feel when you dipped your hands in the water?"

"It's very cold," Debra said, puzzled not as much by the question as by the intensity in Valya's voice. "But I didn't drink it, if that's what you're asking."

"No problem…It's your first time," the guide muttered, her posture deflated.

"Huh?"

"I mean, I'll tell you when something's dangerous to do in Vishenky." Valya picked up her purse from the ground and waved at the others. "Ready to go? Lots of things on the schedule for today."

Bathroom, then a cup of strong coffee, and things will then look clearer, Debra mused. "Who will stand by you at the end of the day?" Valya definitely had some cool ideas. Brain-dead from too much time with Jessie, Peter missed the mark about everyone and everything—especially the guide. If Chris hung around through the evening, his presence would prevent the trio from confronting Valya. By then, Debra would find a way to convince Peter that the whole story about his brother having a nervous breakdown because of Vishenky was nothing but a load of guano.

She let Luke and Jessie go by and stepped in front of Peter. "I'm staying."

CHAPTER NINE

The march to the spring must have ended in a coup. Debra had joined Valya to lead the procession, while Peter and his crew trudged a few paces behind. *Good for Debra*, Chris thought.

Valya walked to his shady refuge on the sandbar. "Enjoying the scenery?"

"Best view ever," he declared. Behind Valya, Debra shook her fist, demanding he tone down his sarcasm. "How old is the village?" Chris asked.

"The known history dates back to the sixteenth century," the guide said.

"Amazing how...." Chris faked a cough. "Excuse me. Too much pollen and I didn't bring anything for my allergies." He coughed again. "Valya, I'm sorry, but I'm afraid I have

to—"

"I've got antihistamines," Debra interrupted. "You're not leaving."

Baffled, Chris hesitated to protest. Debra stood so close to Valya, their shoulders almost touched. Both looked down at him like two stern elementary school teachers deciding the fate of a disruptive first-grader.

"It wasn't my fault," Chris said. "Luke did it."

"Did what?" Debra asked. Her expression clouded up with confusion, but Valya responded with a knowing smile.

"Then why did you run?" the guide asked.

"Sorry," Chris said. "It won't happen again."

Debra seized Valya's arm at the elbow. "Let's leave him to think about his behavior," she said, finally catching up with the quip.

She pulled the guide toward the bridge where the rest of the group stood lined up and waiting at the railing.

"Hey, these monstrous bubbles in the river," Chris said. "What causes them?"

"What are you talking about?" Valya tried to stop but Debra wouldn't let her.

Chris pointed at the spot where another release of gas produced heavy ripples on the surface. "That's from a single bubble. The farther they are from the bank, the larger they get."

Valya shook off his cousin. "For how long has it been going on?"

"Ten, maybe fifteen minutes. What is it?"

"Don't move." The guide slowly removed her purse from her shoulder and set it on the ground.

Two loud gulping sounds just to his left made Chris turn.

"I said, don't move." Valya crept through the knee-high grass like a bird-watcher intent on catching a glimpse of a rare specimen.

Chris smirked. Of course—it would be a part of her show to make things appear more mysterious than they really were. *And if I don't play along?* He headed for the bank.

Abandoning her caution, Valya sprinted forward. She used the willow's lower branch to hang on and set her knee against the leaning trunk. "Take my hand."

"Or what?" Chris asked.

"Now!"

"Listen, I don't—"

"Look! Look!" Debra shouted from the bridge.

"Now," Valya growled.

Compelled by the panic in his cousin's voice, Chris wrapped his fingers around Valya's wrist and placed his foot between two clumps of grass. Just as he shifted his weight, the ground sank beneath him.

The slender guide yanked him with a force that nearly took his shoulder out of its socket.

The strip of ground disappeared under the water, leaving only a tiny island of sand protruding two yards away from the bank.

"Quicksand? Here?" Chris asked, rubbing his shoulder.

Her cheeks red, Valya pressed the back of her hand to her forehead. "Yes. No. Are you okay?"

"Well, I nearly lost my arm, but—"

"Your arm is fine. Are *you* okay?"

"Yeah, I guess. It happened so fast."

Peter waved for his buddies to stay put and rushed to the bank. "What's going on here?" he asked Valya.

She rose on her tiptoes to peek at the river, but she didn't move closer to the bank's edge. "*Ondatra*, a freshwater rat—I'd have to look up the translation. It digs tunnels and sometimes they collapse."

"You could have warned us to stay away from the beach," Chris said.

The guide's eyes narrowed. "Would you listen?"

"It's a natural occurrence. Of course I'd listen."

"Aquatic rodents' burrows don't collapse like that." His jaw set, Peter walked up the willow trunk that stretched horizontally above the river. Using thin but resilient shoots for support, he leaned over the water and studied the surroundings.

On the bridge, Luke stomped his foot, laughing, and giving Chris a thumbs-up. "Mr. Waller, you were almost drowned by a rodent!"

"Shut up." Jessie put her hands on Luke's shoulders and steered him across the wobbly boards.

Peter gestured for Chris to come closer. "You must have stepped on top of some large underwater cavity. It's so deep I can't even see the bottom. You're lucky it didn't suck you in."

"Deep, but no whirlpool to suck you in," Valya said, "and no reason to exaggerate what could happen. Everyone's fine. I think we should go now."

She found her purse in the grass and headed for the bridge. Holding on to the weathered railing, Debra waited for her halfway across. Chris watched as an inaudible exchange followed, quick and simultaneous.

He pulled his camera from his shirt's pocket. The sight in front of him was fascinating. The two lovely women, petite against the tall mass of greenery behind them, chatted comfortably on the rickety carcass of a once-regal structure, their reflections blurred on the rippled river's surface below.

He snapped a shot, and the conversation on the bridge paused. Posing, Debra wrapped her arm around Valya's shoulders. Chris zoomed in and took another picture. Both girls wore charming, genuine smiles on the screen.

Peter jumped down from the willow trunk to the bank. "St. Basil fascinated humankind for generations, but human nature claims the title of the biggest wonder of the world."

"Every time," Chris said. "And what exactly are we talking about?"

"Deb has never warmed up to Jess, yet Valya won her over just like that." Peter snapped his fingers.

"I noticed. I wonder how she did it."

Debra waved. "Are you two coming?" she yelled.

"Well," Peter said, waving back, "we may as well cross this Rubicon and find out."

CHAPTER TEN

Vishenky's pastoral charm diminished with every step Chris took toward their destination. Ruts full of water and decomposing vegetation marred the surface of the road. Aged homes with remnants of multihued paint stood side-by-side with the new-century rivals of stucco, brick, and glass. Only a few fruit trees rose amongst the vast potato patches.

The front yards shared a common fence painted in different colors for each household. Old grandmas—*babushki*—uniformly dressed in navy-blue shirts and checkered skirts sat on the benches, enjoying the morning in the company of kids on tricycles. By the river, two women in washed-out summer dresses and headscarves turned over long rows of hay. They leaned on their rakes and watched, exchanging muffled observations as the group walked by.

"Here we are." Valya left the road and strolled up the path to the gate. "Shoo!" She clapped her hands to chase away a bunch of clucking brown chickens that were digging the holes in the dirt by the fence.

"Yours?" Luke asked.

"Neighbors'. Never leave the gate open. It's hard to get these guys out of the garden."

Valya's red brick house stood out with glass-enclosed verandas on two sides. Storing the warmth of the sunny morning, the larger one served as the front entry. Cheerful pink curtains hung on the wall-to-wall windows. A dining table and cupboard filled the space to the left, and a sofa and chair were crammed to the right. Bundles of dried flowers dangled from the rafters; an herbal fragrance permeated the air.

Chris walked to the center of the house.

This looked like the kitchen. *Or someone's surreal idea of one.*

There was just too much stuff, too many pieces of mismatched furniture squeezed into every corner and pushed against the walls. The kitchen boasted two cupboards, one from the seventies and another, primitively built and painted white, from some unidentifiable era. A round oilcloth-covered dining table served as a counter, and it held a cutting board, trivets, and a double hot plate. Crowding the area to the right was a freestanding brick stove with an iron top. Chris guessed it was used only as a source of heat, since there also was an antiquated gas stove. Two refrigerators, looking just as ancient, purred against the wall to the left.

Chris tapped Debra's shoulder and pointed at the foot-long metal cylinder with a plunger on the bottom hanging above a white ceramic basin. Two enameled buckets covered with lids sat on a short bench by the washstand.

"No running water," he said. "You wouldn't last here a day."

"You wanna bet?" Debra asked.

Catching Valya's glare, Chris didn't answer. If she was reading his reaction to the house, she clearly didn't like it.

Next to the lima-bean-green linen curtain that stretched from wall to wall behind the brick stove and defined the kitchen area, a wooden ladder leaned up against a panel-blocked opening in the ceiling.

"No stairs to the second floor?" Chris asked.

Valya laid both hands on a rung as if checking the ladder for sturdiness. "Remodeling never stops. That floor is unfinished."

"A perfect place to hide an evil twin," Luke said.

"If you only knew." Valya pulled back the green curtain. "Chris, you can have this room."

"I can barely breathe. I think I'd better go back to the hotel."

"When are you planning on heading out?" Peter inquired casually.

The look Debra sent her friend could have provided the village with electricity for a week. She unzipped her bag. "Let me find those antihistamines."

"Mr. Waller, why torture yourself?" Luke asked. "You felt fine in Moscow."

Valya pulled a slim booklet from her purse and scanned through the pages. "There's an afternoon break in the train schedule. Nothing until this evening."

"Sorry, looks like you're stuck," Debra said and then added, "*Mr. Waller.*"

Very much aware he had no say in the exchange, Chris resisted the urge to escort his cousin outside and demand she explain why his presence had become a necessity.

"Let's see the rest of the house," Jessie said.

Another doorway, set a step higher than the kitchen floor, led to a narrow hallway with two more doors. Chris saw the problem with the layout. The house was built room by room, at different times, without a master plan.

The guide directed Jessie to the smaller bedroom, while Debra was to stay in the converted living room with Valya. Luke and Peter were assigned the spacious back veranda.

Instead of paint or wallpaper, pictures from a decade-old calendar adorned the cement walls in every bedroom. But despite the shabby, rural antique-shop appearance, the house was welcoming. Chris understood why. With all the windows shut, a sweet aroma drifted through the rooms as if a pie had been taken out of the oven.

"What do I smell?" he asked.

"The guide," Luke whispered behind him.

"Wild strawberries. I made preserves this morning," Valya said. "Let me show you out back."

Chris looked at Debra and nodded toward the bedroom. She shook her head and slipped outside with the others.

She couldn't avoid him forever, for she would want coffee. Chris returned to the kitchen to set the ambush.

He peeked behind the linen curtain at the room that would be his if he stayed.

The window offered a view of the cloudless sky and a wild rose burgeoning in the sun. An iridescent vase with pink and lavender-blue flowers graced a round table, pretty against an ochre linen cloth. A vintage iron bed towered by the wall. Chris wondered if the bedding, probably river-washed and sun-dried, soaked up the smell of wild strawberries like the rest of the house.

A mirror in an ornate wooden frame hung in an odd spot, above the head of the bed. The frame's carvings depicted Venus flytraps, their fringed leaf apexes resembling human hands with spread, crooked fingers primed to catch prey. Chris walked to the foot of the bed and glanced at his reflection. A blurry gray figure drifted against the background as he moved. The relic mirror had lost most of its reflective properties and was merely a decoration.

The door to the kitchen rattled and Debra walked in, squinting after being in the sunlight. "A pump runs cold water from the river to the shower. No bathtub. An outhouse. I can't live in the Middle Ages. Ah." She brought the back of her hand to her forehead, demonstrating how a delicate flower like her could never survive in such a vulgar environment.

Chris loved the mischievous flicker in her eyes. "Too bad. I was going to let you stay."

"Of course, there are no trains to take us back to civilization."

"Liar."

"All right, all right, you win." She checked her watch. "The next one is in an hour. You really don't mind if I stay here overnight?"

Chris lowered his voice. "Valya is an amateur, and the place is a far cry from a chic B&B. I think it'll be quite an experience for you all. But you must stop lying to her. Why did you tell her you didn't speak Russian?"

"It shouldn't take her long to figure that out," Debra said. "Just like we didn't tell her you'd been to Russia before. How did she know?"

"Of course someone told her. Don't create additional problems for her. Valya's stressed. Imagine if you had to host this group."

"Your chivalry is touching, but the main problem is you, not us."

"Oh, really?"

"Tell me, Chris, who do you think bothers her, Luke with a teakettle warmer on his head or a grumpy professor who eyeballs her like a wolf?"

"That's ridiculous."

"Do you realize you've been staring at Valya non-stop? I've seen you lose your head over a woman, but I've never seen you lose your manners."

"Why would I—"

"Valya's very pretty."

"But it doesn't mean I—"

Debra raised her hand in an I-don't-want-to-hear-your-nonsense gesture.

Valya walked into the kitchen carrying a glass carafe. "Coffee will be ready in a few minutes."

"How did you know it's not my first visit to Russia?" Chris asked.

The guide filled the pot with water from one of the enameled buckets and put it on the table. "You bought soda at the train station. Where is your wallet?"

Chris pulled it from his jeans' pocket.

"Open it."

He did.

"People usually keep pictures here," Valya said. "Yours is half-full with foreign—how do you call these—coins?"

"Tokens."

"Metro tokens, right? This one is from Moscow, and the kind that has not been in use in ages."

Debra chuckled. "Well, Mr. Waller. Guess how much Valya has figured out from one peek in your wallet."

His travels. His collecting habits. His personal life, or the current lack of it.

Valya raised her hands. "Aw, 'peeking in someone's wallet' sounds awful. I should have claimed tremendous mind-reading skills." She was blushing, and she spoke too fast, a reluctant smile appearing on her lips but not lasting longer than a second.

"No, that's impressive," Chris said. "You're very observant."

"Let me ask you something, then. You don't have allergies, do you?"

"Sorry, I needed an excuse to leave. I'm really not into supernatural phenomena."

"But you're here."

"Actually, I never planned to stay. I just wanted to check the accommodations and make sure your tour was legit. It looks like you've got everything under control."

"Nothing but the authentic local folklore. As for the accommodations…." Valya looked around the room, as if trying to see it through her guests' eyes. "Not much I can do to make the house appealing. My mother is the official owner. And her brother, my uncle." Her upper lip moved, indicating a lack of affection for her relative. "He's not a fan of country living and doesn't come here too often. My parents love Vishenky, but whenever they buy new furniture for the city apartment, the old stuff ends up in this house. At least they didn't mind staying in Moscow while I host the group."

"The décor is fine," Chris said. "It gives the house character."

"Thank you. You have something exciting planned in Moscow?"

"Well…I've never been to Gorky Park."

"And here I am, trying to keep you in the village." Valya pointed at the artifact on the wall. "You know what's truly strange? This mirror shows clear reflections twice a day, just after sunrise and right before sunset. Too bad you'll miss it."

"You really want me to stay?"

"It's up to you, but a few hours in Vishenky might give you a whole new perspective on Gorky Park." Valya picked up the carafe. "Coffee and cherry pie, on the front veranda, in five minutes," she promised cheerfully on her way out of the room.

Debra's eyes twinkled. "Valya likes you."

"Is that so?"

"She smiles at you."

"And at Peter, and at Luke."

"Her voice is steel and iron when she talks to them. When she speaks to you, it's all peaches and cream. I think you're in trouble."

"Is this why *you* want me to stay?" Chris asked. "To get me into more trouble?"

"C'mon, would you have so much fun in Moscow? Luke will drive Valya nuts. Be a gentleman and save the defenseless maiden."

Debra had a point. Taming the jokester on her own would wear Valya out faster than if she had to manage a herd of minks.

One afternoon in the village wasn't going to ruin his trip. "Let's go save the maiden," Chris said.

"That's my favorite cousin." Debra headed for the door.

Chris followed her, thinking about what Laurie, his smart sister, told him once. "You need to learn to say no to the women in your life."

He never did.

CHAPTER ELEVEN

For my opening story I brought the group a kilometer away from the village to Zoya-and-Raya's dam, a messy formation of discarded metal bed frames, logs, and dirt. Without any open portals accessible at this hour, the only purpose of the outing was to hook my guests on my stories, preferably without alarming Chris. I didn't mind his presence for now, but by nightfall, I wanted his students to myself.

The site smothered an observer in a fairy-tale ambiance. Pond lilies covered the farthest side of the pool. In a sunny spot, minuscule fish hovered among the fuzzy stems of elodeas, the silver streaks of their bodies slicing the water like reflections from tiny mirrors. Wings whirring, dragonflies zigzagged above abundant forget-me-nots.

This was the place where Amanda, the girl from my last group, got hurt.

Not waiting for my narration, Peter walked the length of the dam and back, picked up a stick, and began to poke the river bottom in front of the overflow. Jessie hiked upriver. She jumped down on the narrow beach and examined the sand as if she'd lost a costly piece of jewelry. Hands in his pockets, Luke watched Peter's blond girlfriend from the bank.

Chris and Debra stayed by my side. I guessed both preferred to enjoy the pleasures of the great outdoors from a distance, or, unlike their fellow sightseers, they had no apparent agenda.

"How beautiful," Debra said. "I could sit here all day."

The warmth in her voice soothed the bruises from a cube of tension that swiveled in my rib cage.

"*Pahreet*," I said, nodding in the general direction of the meadow.

Her head went halfway down in a nod before Debra caught herself. She rubbed her chin against her shoulder. "What did you say?"

"Getting humid," I said.

Pahreet wasn't found in tourist phrase books. Her Russian had to be excellent.

Debra's isolation from her friends explained her harmless crush on Chris and her attempt to delay his departure from Vishenky. I understood her fondness of the man better than I wanted to. Before sunset, I had to make Debra feel the same comfort in my company that both of us found in his.

Pity I couldn't let Chris stay. Many adults hang on to their beliefs in UFOs and Bigfoot, but I sensed he wasn't one of them. Once the first paranormal creature made its grand appearance, I could handle a group of my peers, but I couldn't foretell the reaction from a levelheaded man like Chris.

I glanced at my handsome visitor. Chris responded with a friendly grin, but his acknowledged objective was unequivocal. He came to Vishenky to test my aptitude in hosting a tour. As long as I operated under his scrutiny, I had to manage my duties without a hitch.

Peter lost his interest in the stick and now gazed at the opposite bank behind the dam where the current left a meter of tree roots and brown soil exposed. A dislodged young willow bobbled in the flow, resisting being swept away.

"Peter, what are you looking for?" I yelled, tired of the holdup.

He spun around, waved, and marched to the bank, wearing a smile that would pacify a stadium of crazed soccer fans.

"Sorry," he said. "Hard to believe this pile of dirt can withstand such water pressure."

"Locals restore the dam every spring," I said. "But no matter how beautiful the weather is and how much everybody loves the river, this week you won't find any beachgoers in this spot. Not even Vishenky's teenagers, who fear nothing."

"Hey, Deb? Guess what really goes down after sunset," Luke

interrupted. A ruthless, wily glint lit up his eyes.

"I see you're dying to tell us," I said.

A casual response took quite an effort from my uncooperative vocal cords. I couldn't ignore the possibility that Luke would challenge my tour-guide cover, ask me who I really was—in front of Chris, in front of Debra.

Luke walked to the water's edge and stretched his arms, fingers wiggling. "It happened a hundred years ago. The sexy chicks from the village started to disappear. All blondes, by the way." He winked at Jessie. "One evening, an old hermit came here to do his laundry. Head wreaths made of black roses floated on the surface. Lots of them. And under the water—"

"Luke, shut up," Jessie said. "You're giving me the creeps."

"Me too," Debra said. "Let's drown him."

Jessie rubbed her palms. "Good idea."

"Not possible," Luke shouted. He grabbed the squealing girls by their waists and leaned out over the water. Laughing, Debra gasped for breath and begged for mercy.

"When Luke acts like this, look bored," Chris said to me. "It's the only thing that stops his antics."

"Hey, Higbee, quit acting like an idiot," Peter called out.

Luke pulled his captives away from the edge and set them free. He fell on his knees, growling and jerking his hands, no doubt his best interpretation of transforming into a werewolf.

"Food," I said. "Good food will work with Luke."

"What do you mean?" Chris asked.

"Bribing him. I'll gain his good behavior and cooperation through my cooking."

"You're not training a dog." Peter's black eyes failed to vaporize me but not for the lack of trying on his part.

Luke howled, ran in a circle on all fours, and pretended to pee on Jessie's sneakers.

"A puppy," I said. "Goofy, playful, and undisciplined."

Chris and Peter glanced at each other, at the commotion by the river, and chuckled.

"Higbee, c'mon, knock it off," Peter said.

Luke led his ladies back into our company.

Her cheeks scarlet, Debra asked, "So, what's the real story with this place?"

"According to Vishenky's legend, two toddlers disappeared from this beach in broad daylight. One minute the girls were playing in the shallows. The next, they were gone. The villagers searched the river, Osoka, for hours but never found the bodies."

As my silenced visitors watched the serene waters, a single cloud blotted out the sun. Suddenly, the little paradise looked gloomy.

"Like, this is a bitchin' site, dude," Luke tried to break the spell.

"The locals say that the girls, Zoya and Raya, were snatched by the underwater possum, an animal that hibernates deep beneath the riverbank. The creature comes to the surface and hunts once a year, in July."

"A giant, scraggly man-eating rat," Luke said. "Juicy."

Chris snapped his fingers, soundlessly, unendingly. I didn't think he realized it. That's right, Mr. Waller, no Russian Tsars' history, nothing educational to stick around for. I shouldn't have spared the group from images of chewed limbs and missing toes.

"Tonight, the possum will hunt," I continued. "Tomorrow, after the creature cleans its den, small bones will litter the river bottom behind the dam. Of course, the water is too deep to see anything."

"What's under the silt?" Debra asked.

"Clay and sand," I said. "Why?"

"Look at the overflow. It's shallow." Debra climbed up onto the narrow strip of the dam and balanced as she stomped the sedges. "There's not nearly enough space for the water to escape. The river has to have an underground flow. A small body could be sucked in and get stuck."

"Makes sense," Jessie said. "After a while, small bones would get carried out by the current. All it takes is one person to find them and invent a killer possum."

In comparison to her frosty demeanor toward Debra the whole morning, Jessie had turned into a paradigm of female solidarity.

Debra jumped onto the bank, into Luke's steadying embrace. "Warning signs would be all over the place back home. Here, they use a scary story to keep children away."

"Folklore and political science," Jessie said pointedly, as if to remind me the purpose of their visit she had proclaimed on the train. "Right, Professor Waller?"

"At least no one here thinks the story is true," Chris said.

Luke put his arm around my shoulders. "You know what would be totally cool? How about we camp here tonight? The stars, the moon, the river, wildlife roaming around."

"Are you nuts? I'm not camping here," Debra said. "Not after what Valya just told us."

"Be a chicken and stay at the house." Luke gripped my shoulders tighter. "Can we? Please?"

I smiled at Debra. "We can come back to the dam after dark, spend a couple of hours. No reason to stay here overnight."

"Sounds good," she said.

I climbed down to the water, knelt on the warm sand, and dampened my forehead and neck.

I'd have lured my guests back to the dam without Luke's request. My only opportunity to test Debra tonight, the portal here was of such strength that I could expose her to its energy from a distance. It would open at 11:24. The possum would appear at 11:28. Four minutes. Would I gain enough power to keep the scheming trio, Luke, Peter, and Jessie, out of harm's way?

Our second stop was supposed to be Vishenky's cemetery, but I changed my mind. I needed to show the conspirators how imperative their obedience to my command was for everyone's safety. Too bad I had left my plastic flyswatter at home. I was taking the group to the *Volkanoks'* bridge.

CHAPTER TWELVE

Debra wiped her burning forehead. After the endless succession of meadows and rye fields, another village had finally appeared on the hill ahead, but the clear sky promised no mercy from the midday sun.

Of course, Jessie marched alongside the guys like a perpetual motion machine.

"Another hundred yards, and I'll die," Debra complained to the guide.

"Me too," Valya confessed, "but this is the place."

A massive concrete bridge over a rapid stream lay before them. The colossal structure could carry a semi-truck. An iron masterpiece, the railing depicted a family of weasels, hopping, twisting, and dancing in a game.

Debra snapped a photo.

"This way." The guide motioned to the group to follow her to the bank.

While Luke insisted on carrying Jessie, Debra scrambled down the slope to catch up with Peter.

The great mind exhibited signs of immense absorption.

"Kenny's tape had to be a hoax," Debra said.

His look could've frozen the Caribbean, but he offered her a supporting hand.

Her courteous Peter, the brainiest friend she ever had. The only way to get him back was to rip apart the web of his girlfriend's nonsense.

"Your brother suffers from a mental disorder," Debra said. "The story he told you is a symptom. You can't seriously think his issues are Valya's fault."

"Something very creepy is happening here. Valya's tours have to be stopped."

"If the hotel received any complaints, they would have shut her down a long time ago."

Peter stopped and his face tightened with pain. "I'm begging you not to get involved. Valya doesn't deserve your sympathy."

Too flabbergasted to respond, Debra dropped his hand.

Peter hurried after the others, leaving her to stand on the slope alone.

The strenuous hike, the heat, Valya's pseudo folklore—Debra sighed, her frustration fermenting into resentment. Somewhere deep between Peter's ears flickered a speck of rationality. How could she fan it back into a bonfire?

At the foot of the bridge, patches of tall weeds stood at attention like troops protecting a classified site. Water dripped from the rough surface of the arch. Eddies licked the walls.

"Spoo-o-oky." Luke hurled a stone into the stream. A gulping sound accompanied the splash. Tiny birds raced through the brush on the opposite bank.

"Don't do that," Valya said. "The inhabitants of the bridge sleep during daylight. Be very, very quiet."

"Aha." Luke bobbed his head, but his grin pledged neither his understanding nor intent to cooperate.

"If you stand here on a quiet night…." Valya turned and looked under the arch. She inhaled slowly, as if any abrupt movement would wake up a horde of water possums, ghouls, ghosts, or whatever she planned to pass off as Russian myths. "Don't worry. There is no danger at this time of the day."

"That's good." Luke played with another stone, tossing it from hand to hand. "Because I didn't bring my possum repellent."

"If you stand here on a calm night," Valya said, "you'll hear moaning. Somebody is complaining, but you cannot grasp the words.

The locals say a reclusive predator lives inside the bridge. They call it *volkanok*. It's larger than a cat, has green fur with a golden shimmer, and it will kill you if you pass the bridge at one o'clock in the morning, when it hunts. Only a handful of people have seen this thing. Some of them have survived."

"How many?" Debra asked. "How many people have survived?"

"Six." Valya didn't hesitate with the answer. "A family."

"How do you know? I mean, what's the source of your stories? Are they written somewhere?"

"I interviewed Vishenky's oldest folks. Details differ. The story's core is the same. The bridge harbors *volkanoks* year-round because they escaped from another dimension and adjusted to our world." Valya leaned forward as if to tell the group a secret. "The bridge does make strange noises. Once I was here in December, when the stream froze. I could almost make out the words."

"These legends," Jessie said, "what timeframe are we talking about? World War Two? The Russian Revolution?"

"Early nineteen hundreds. Vishenky used to host fairs: merchants, circuses, carousels. Late one evening, a cart with the parents and four children was returning to Tishkino." Valya pointed at the village on the hill. "A wounded animal crawled on the road, crying like a baby. Larger than a cat, shimmering fur, nothing like they had seen before. The father wanted to finish off the creature, but his youngest son begged to let him tend the thing. By morning, the *volkanok* and the boy were gone."

"'Crying like a baby,'" Debra said, "It's always that, or a child's laugher."

"Totally." Luke mewed to corroborate the point.

Defying logic, the bridge responded. It was an echo, of course, but for a smidgeon of a second, the soft, pitiful whimper efficiently raised every hair on Debra's forearms.

"What was that?" Jessie asked.

Valya stared under the bridge. The goose bumps on her arms were real.

Peter took off his shoes. "I want to check out the arch."

"Out of the question," Valya said.

Wrong, wrong, wrong approach, Debra thought. Peter resented a commanding tone if the voice wasn't his.

"Why not?" Peter rolled up his pant legs.

"There can be junk and broken glass on the bottom."

"I'll be ve-e-ry careful."

"I cannot let you do this," Valya said in the same annoying authoritarian manner.

"But I don't need your permission." Peter climbed into the shallow stream and walked against the current, keeping close to the bank. The highest point of the arch was several feet above his head.

The water level reached his shins. Debra touched one of rocks on the bottom of the stream. Green slime made its surface slippery. Peter would be in for a cold bath if he stumbled.

"Wow, that's something," he called. "Thin pipes, cemented into the arch. At least two dozen. It's a strong draft here, so they are all howling. Unless you stand where I am, you won't hear them in the daytime because of too many other noises."

He placed his palm on the wall and lowered his head, listening.

Valya walked through the weeds to the arch. Her fingers on the concrete corner, the guide leaned over the rushing water and looked under the bridge. "I wouldn't touch anything," she yelled to Peter.

"Why would someone build a pipe organ into a country bridge?" Jessie asked.

"Air-conditioning for the fur-balls," Luke said. "Hey, Peter, are you too chicken to stick your finger in a pipe?"

"Don't," Jessie called.

Peter poked at the concrete. "It's just the wind."

"Let's wake the fuzzies." Luke hurled another rock.

CHAPTER THIRTEEN

Peter yelped and stumbled backward into the deeper water. He bent over his clasped hands.

"You okay?" Jessie asked.

"I'm bleeding," Peter yelled back. He waded from under the bridge.

"Happy now?" Valya asked Luke without much reproach.

Debra searched the guide's face. No frown. No flaring nostrils. No quivering lips. Valya's expression lacked any indications of alarm.

Blood smeared over his palms, Peter climbed out of the streambed. "Dammit. I think something bit me."

"Let me see." Chris tried to seize his hand, but Peter pulled back.

"Probably just a bad scratch," Debra said. "I hope you had your tetanus shot."

"Of course I did." Peter closed his eyes, furrows cutting his forehead. "God, it hurts."

Jessie unclenched Peter's grip and pressed his finger with a tissue. Two puncture wounds reddened on both sides of the fingertip.

Luke whistled. "Man, end of the line. You're marked. They'll hunt you down. Or you'll turn into a werewolf."

"Valya, what is it?" Chris asked.

"The ground beetle," she said. "One of the local species bites."

"So much blood from a bug bite?" Jessie pulled antibiotic ointment and bandages from her daypack.

The guide shrugged.

Peter sucked in air through his teeth as Jessie ministered to the wound.

"I warned you," Valya said.

"'Junk and broken glass'? You call that a warning?" Peter asked.

"Next time you'll listen."

His lips stretched in a thin smile. "Are you teaching me a lesson?"

Her body tall and straight, Valya pointed at the space in front of her. "Let's clarify some basics. This is my tour and I'm your guide. If you disobey my orders, then you have to face the consequences."

"No," Peter said. "We don't answer to you. You answer to us. From now on, I expect a full disclosure about where we're going and what we will see."

"You're kidding, right?" Debra asked.

Peter held up his bandaged hand. "I won't allow anything like this to happen again."

"And do I answer to you personally?" Valya asked.

"Consider me your boss," Peter said.

A quick smirk crossed the guide's face. "Very good. First of all, if we find a hornet's nest and I say, 'don't touch it,' it's your responsibility to ensure that no one does."

"Anything else?"

"Please remember, I'll end this tour if I deem your group unruly."

"Fine."

"Great. Then let's go back and have lunch."

Propelled by the promise of food, Luke raced to the road pulling Jessie behind. Nursing his hand, Peter followed. Valya used clumps of grass as steps.

Debra hesitated. The hill looked too steep. The tour had turned absurdly unorthodox.

Chris gestured toward the slope with a slight bow. "After you, my dear. Still want me to stick around and defend the innocent?"

She began to climb. "I want to find a glass vase and smash it on a rock."

"Ouch. Why?"

"Because, believe it or not, Peter used to be perfectly normal, and Valya could exercise some diplomacy."

"Do you want to leave?" Chris asked.

"After Miss V gloriously trapped Peter into taking charge? I can't wait to see what happens next."

Chris smiled. "Fooled us all, didn't she?"

"She's not a timid forest flower. Luke is Peter's problem now." Debra put her hand to her forehead to block out the glare as she looked at her cousin. "Do you think Valya wanted Peter to get hurt to prove her point?"

"I certainly hope she's not that cruel, but let me rephrase my question: Do you still feel comfortable staying here?"

"Absolutely," Debra said. "I just need you to do something for me. I can't figure out Peter's issues with Valya. Kenny, his brother, found her through the hotel. Ask at the front desk what they know about her tours."

"Good idea. I'll call you."

Grasshoppers crackled like a dozen faraway castanets. The afternoon sun beat down, and the breeze raised dust.

Crouching in the ditch on the side of the road, Valya harvested something in the grass.

"If this is lunch, I'm converting to cannibalism." Luke smelled the air in Jessie's direction. "Will you be my first course?"

Valya waved a bunch of ribbed glossy leaves. "*Podoroznik*. For Peter's finger. In case it hurts."

"Ribwort," Jessie said. "It grows everywhere. I saw a bunch around your house."

"Only the plants from around the *Volkanoks'* bridge will be effective."

"I assure you, I won't use your weeds," Peter said.

"In case you change your mind." Valya stuffed a cluster of leaves into a plastic bag. She rose to her feet but staggered, momentarily losing her balance as if under a spell of dizziness. Her light tan didn't mask her pallor.

"Are you feeling okay?" Chris asked.

The guide shrugged as she examined her witch doctor's supply. "Too much excitement when a new group comes. A sleepless night, it's hot, and I skipped breakfast."

Like two stray kittens under a porch, pity and guilt crawled into Debra's chest. "I'll help you with lunch."

A phantom of a smile moved the corners of Valya's mouth. "I just need to get out of the sun. The good thing is, from here on, the road to Vishenky is all downhill."

Her accent thickened as she got tired. Somehow, Valya's "downhill" sounded much like "down to hell."

CHAPTER FOURTEEN

Chris left after lunch.

I offered to walk him to the station and he said no, in a friendly way. "Get some rest," he added. I was washing my cooking pans on the river when I heard the muffled drone of a train coming to a stop and then accelerating toward Moscow. I normally noticed that sound only during sleepless predawn hours. Chris was gone.

Peter and his coven, Luke and Jessie, raided my tool shed, picked out three bicycles from the rusty collection my family had accumulated over generations, and rode out. The newest bike was mine, and I sent a mental thanks to my neighbor Gregory for restoring the others.

I set up a lawn chair for Debra under an apple tree, but I was too restless to keep her company. I had no enthusiasm for weeding squashes or watering the hothouse; potato bugs and cabbage worms could have the whole crop. I found my way to the kitchen and attempted to start dinner. I knocked down a salt shaker, spilled a box of matches, and broke my mother's favorite cup.

A runaway train of excruciating trials sped in my direction, but my mind remained fixated on the man I had known for less than a day.

I longed to close my eyes, and in an instant, it would be evening, and an open portal, and everything unfolding as intended. Then maybe tomorrow we all could go to Moscow. I'd play a different kind of guide, the one without worries about predatory creatures and covert agendas.

I'd see Chris.

To stop watching the seconds that crawled into eternity like sleepy ants on a cold autumn morning, I put on a swimsuit, walked to the river, and let the calm body of water caress, soothe, and nurture mine.

I had once felt this bubbly restlessness around a childhood friend. Dimitry died, and that loss put an emotional chastity belt on every relationship since.

The bond his death hadn't severed was the one I shared with the supernatural forces. The complications they bestowed upon me paled in comparison with the brightness the paranormal portals added to everything I experienced. I didn't rely on Vishenky for my physical survival, the way I depended on oxygen and protein. I needed it because its energy hurled color into my sky, flavor into my food, and passion into my emotions.

Long separations from the village robbed me of my vitality. Winters in Moscow are endless, and as a toddler, I would simply stop eating. I overheard too many of my mother's complaints to her brother about how only "fresh country air could keep that sickly girl strong." As soon as my parents brought me to the snowy train station, my appetite would miraculously recover. The majority of the portals opened in July, but Vishenky's enormous energy field alone was enough to resuscitate my interest in staying alive.

If life was drab, insipid, boring, the three-year-old Valya Svetlova refused to live it. Now, at twenty-three, I owned a miraculous realm always set to infuse my existence with excitement. My city routine— college, friends, dates—couldn't substitute for the anticipation of each new encounter, the pride of discovery, the buzz from dealing with the unknown. Vishenky had become my discreet addiction, my never-ending adventure. No roller coaster, drug, or love affair could match this thrill.

A large green dragonfly froze in midair like a miniature drone patrolling the river, and darted away. I drifted on my back, surrendering to Osoka's tranquil flow. The serene sky, bright blue and beautiful, swayed above me. In the corners of my vision, silvery waves rolled through the canopies of willows pushed by the gentle wind.

But I felt no inner peace.

This afternoon the paranormal didn't seem to matter. All I wanted was to see Chris again.

I reached the bank with a few strokes. As I hurried home to change out of my dripping swimsuit, I heard Lydia, the last woman in the village who still kept milk cows, calling my name from her house down the road. Ignoring her would result in a sudden shortage of milk, to my parents' displeasure.

Lydia waited for me in her dirt courtyard, trampled down by numerous hooves. The odor of manure blended with the bittersweet smell of hay piled on her late husband's pickup truck. One of Lydia's pudgy fists rested on her hip, the other clutched a basket covered with cheesecloth.

"Prascovia Serpina sent me eggs," she announced with the solemnity of a mafia don who had just received a dead fish.

I peeked under the cloth. Two baking-powder-white eggs rested on a layer of straw—Prascovia's favorites for spells. The old witch should know better than to bestow pearls of her craft on a neighbor. My hour of quiet had expired.

CHAPTER FIFTEEN

"Oh, thanks, I have been waiting for these," I lied.

Lydia wrinkled her forehead. "You two live next door. Why did she send the damn things to me?"

"Easier than catching me at home. I travel with my visitors, but I come for milk every day." As I spoke, it occurred to me how much sense such an arrangement would make. My property bordered Gregory's on one side and Prascovia's on the other, but the reclusive woman detested venturing outside in daylight. Prascovia indeed intended the eggs for me.

Lydia handed me the basket with a proper show of awe. The sender, Prascovia Kirillovna Serpina, was a certified witch in the villagers' opinion.

For once the superstitious folks were correct, but not about everything. She hadn't caused the unexplained death of chickens whose owner's goat had stripped clean Prascovia's young maple. She didn't turn into a cat on moonless nights and steal flowers from the fresh graves (I knew which creature did that). Her magic didn't instigate families' quarrels, neighbors' disputes, and kids' fights, no matter what the locals claimed.

However, Prascovia did cast spells, and the nature of an egg, its mystery of a life's starting point, made it irresistible for the woman's genius.

I knew something else about Prascovia. Vishenky's cemetery had been in use for centuries. Her name appeared on no less than three tombstones.

The thought sent goosebumps down my arms. It always did.

"You are shivering," Lydia said.

I pulled the sides of the cotton shirt I wore over my swimsuit tighter. "I took a dip in the river. Who delivered the basket?"

"Prascovia's grandson, Andrey. Stupid brat didn't tell me the eggs were for you." She smoothed her apron and her head scarf as if to assure herself that the contact with the foul objects had caused her no damage. "Who do you need them for?"

I wished I knew.

"A man," I improvised. "I am in love, and he left me. Maybe Prascovia's magic will lure him back."

Lydia's broad face broke into a grin. "About time!"

"What, that he left me?"

"That you have fallen for somebody. Go get him."

I had no idea my personal life caused our milk lady such a plethora of concerns.

Walking home, I tried to focus on the eggs. What was the witch up to now?

I wished I could call Prascovia my guardian or even a mentor, but her role in my life had always been uncertain.

She had presented me with my first plastic flyswatter—no explanation, no advice. I figured out on my own the importance of modern materials in deterring a few particularly bold creatures. In the years when I trusted her, Prascovia would intercept me on some forgotten path where I skulked in search of an adventure and give me a trinket—a beaded anklet, a strangely scented scarf—to keep me safe on my late-night exploration.

But Prascovia's magic hadn't protected her family from untimely losses. An offspring believed to be her daughter got pregnant in her late forties (father unknown) and died in childbirth, leaving Prascovia with an infant, Anna. I remembered the girl with the flowing flaxen hair, three years my senior, chasing me between haystacks in a game of tag.

Puberty earned her the nickname Ophelia. She was a fair-haired creature with blue eyes, slim waist, and shapely breasts, the envy of the teenage female population of Vishenky. But her mind disintegrated. She slept on the river bank. She walked the streets murmuring, braiding and unbraiding her hair, her eyes following something in the air around her. Boys avoided Anna despite her beauty.

Nonetheless....

At sixteen, she got pregnant. My neighbor, eighteen-year-old Gregory, confessed he was the father. I learned the meaning of "postpartum depression" when Anna disappeared and a small, reluctant search party found her headscarf on the bottom of the river.

Ophelia indeed. Her son, Andrey, was two weeks old.

While the young Gregory coped with his new role, my own life splintered under the weight of Dimitry's death. I paid little attention to my summer neighbors.

Then the rumors began to crawl from household to household like a swarm of cockroaches. Andrey, a healthy toddler, talked strangely, as if mixing his words, and for that, Gregory subjected his son to harsh punishments.

One evening, when Gregory's mother watched the boy, I overheard Andrey's whispers. My brain interpreted his tongue by the next morning. Mortified by the boy's words, I vowed to stay away from him and his family.

A few days later, reading on the back veranda, I heard Andrey's screams. I ran outside and forced my way through the prickly raspberry brush. The scene on the other side of the fence froze my vocal cords.

The three-year-old was curled on the ground, shrieking. Gregory struck his son with a belt, over and over and over, his face contorted with rage and maybe with grief. Tears streamed down his cheeks, but I didn't think he'd stop while the boy still breathed.

I burst through the old fence and rammed Gregory, slamming him into the stucco wall.

He squirmed on the ground beside his son and kept whispering, "I'm sorry." Blood dripped from his bitten lip.

"Andrey misses his mother, you idiot," I growled. "If you hurt him again, I'll know, and I will tell Prascovia, and she'll kill you."

I never told him about what I had overheard a few evening earlier. Andrey's actual words were, "I *see* my mother."

CHAPTER SIXTEEN

The impact had dislocated Gregory's shoulder and left a bloody mark above his ear. A week after the incident, he showed up at my doorstep, bandages wrapped around his head, his hair hanging over the cloth like tufts of mildewed straw.

"Will you let me talk?" he asked.

Filled with moral superiority, I let him in.

After half a bottle of vodka and an hour of rambling about his wifeless life and his wicked grandmother-in-law, Gregory gathered his courage. "Did you say anything to Prascovia?"

"No," I said, "and I won't, but you only get one chance. Don't give her a reason to make your son an orphan."

Gregory gazed at his glass as if meeting my eyes would shatter his resolve. "Have you ever heard the Legend of an Unborn?"

I shook my head.

"Then don't you threaten me." Another shot of vodka chased his warning.

Curiosity at odds with annoyance, I studied the drunken man hunched in a chair at my table, sweaty and unshaved, stinking up the veranda with cigarette smoke.

"From the bowels of Earth comes a buzzing swarm of Violet Lights," Gregory began, "so bright it burns your eyes. They spill over the land like a cloud of hungry locusts—no place to hide from their deadly glow. The planet succumbs to madness as humans and animals go blind. Under the smoldering blanket of chaos, the lights steal their spirits."

He paused, awaiting my response.

I wasn't sure how to react. I had never heard the story, and I didn't like it. *From the bowels of Earth*. That had to be a portal. The stolen spirits would be the life energy devoured by the entities, the otherworldly beings manifesting in our dimension as brilliant lights.

"How often does this mayhem happen?" I asked.

"All I know is that it's a cycle, like hatching cicadas."

"Who told you the legend?"

"Anna. Just before she disappeared."

"Oh." His dead mad wife.

"There's more," Gregory added quickly. "You've heard about the bog lights, right?"

"That's a common one. They lead a man lost in a swamp to his death."

"I'll tell you what you don't know. An experienced witch can trap such a light and put it in a stillborn baby. The infant will live. When he—or she—reaches a certain age, the witch will send the child into the world of Violet Lights, and that will stop them from coming to Earth. But not forever."

Gregory put out his cigarette, the pupils of his deep-set gray eyes fixed on mine like the muzzles of two gun barrels.

"You see, Valenteena," he said, using my proper first name to emphasize the importance of his tale, "Andrey was stillborn and resurrected by Prascovia. She has induced stillbirths in her family for generations. The last time the swarm was about to emerge, Prascovia would have sacrificed him, but Anna gave her life so our son could live."

Stillbirths? A sacrifice? This sounded over-the-top dramatic.

An actual tear moistened Gregory's hollow cheek. "Anna said you would believe me. That you would help me to raise Andrey."

"You're drunk. And she was wrong."

"You don't understand. It wasn't Anna's turn. She couldn't complete the cycle. The Violet Lights will return, and Andrey will have to walk through a portal to stop them. You'll be the one to bring him back."

The story was getting better and better. "And how would I do that?" I asked. "How do you 'complete the cycle'?"

Gregory waved his hand with exaggerated frustration and burped. "How the heck would I know? She didn't tell me everything. You figure this out." He nodded in the direction of Prascovia's house. "You're one of *them*."

I choked on the cookie I was nibbling. "I'm not one of *them*. My family doesn't practice witchcraft."

He sneered. "Your family…." He dug under his shirt and dropped a plastic-wrapped package on the table. "Here. Anna told me to give this to you when you turned sixteen."

The first thing I saw when I unwrapped the package was my family tree. Centuries ago, Prascovia had a sister, Antonina, and I was Antonina's descendant.

I could be "one of them."

Relishing my bewilderment, Gregory patted my hand. "It'll be okay. I'll be there for you whenever you need me. Just keep an eye on my boy. I won't betray you, like your friends did."

"Don't you dare," I growled.

"You and your Muscovite pals," Gregory spoke with alcohol-fueled disdain. "Always sneaked around, kept your secrets to yourselves. Turned up your noses on us, the locals."

"Yes, we played more badminton than soccer, but we never excluded anyone."

Gregory's throat generated a humorless chuckle. "Anna. You cast her out, too. Who was she for you? A simple girl from a village? Not enough smarts to be your friend? Here's something for you to chew on: She said you could have saved your precious Dimitry."

Dimitry Remizov, seventeen, the summer of his death. So talented, so funny, so romantic. The heart of our group. My childhood hero. My first love. And Gregory, a worthless drunken louse talking about my fallen friend in that obnoxious spite-laced tone.

I wished I could forget that conversation, for Gregory's sake. But today I stood in the hot sun, years older, millennia wiser, and my mouth was dry, my heart drummed an angry rhythm. Gripping the basket with the damn eggs, I fought an urge to smash them against Prascovia's maple. My hate for Gregory was returning, as searing as when it first set me ablaze on that hazy evening when he proclaimed his boundless devotion to my cause.

I fell on the bench in front of Prascovia's fence.

In her semi-incoherent letter, Anna defended her decision to enter the other universe. *You'll understand when you have a child,* she wrote. She urged me to participate in Andrey's upbringing. She begged me to stay away from Prascovia.

My best source of information about the occurrences, the diary of my great-great-grandmother Leontina Gretishnikoff, had never mentioned any homicidal violet swarms, but Anna's story sounded too disturbing to forget about it. I knew of only one person who could dispel my worries. Prascovia Serpina would tell me if there was some deadly cycle. If it existed, how often did the lethal phase occur? If Andrey had to walk into another dimension to stop it, what would I have to do to bring him back?

The witch sobbed when she spoke of Anna's demise. The young woman had been messed up in her head, and the childbirth pushed her over the edge. The Legend of an Unborn sounded exactly like a creation of her feverish mind.

I was a teenager who mistook her hunches and guesses for the right answers to paramount questions. Without Prascovia's careful protection, my well-meaning but clueless family would have destroyed me a long time ago. I saw no reason to doubt her tears. So I fulfilled my duty to Anna's boy as I saw it. Against Gregory's wishes, I had made sure Andrey stayed in contact with his Grandma.

Would I have done the same thing today?

I pushed my head against the planks of Prascovia's fence. Did the witch sense my presence at her doorstep? Had she guessed how much I missed her support?

Of course Prascovia knew. She had sent me her token, the eggs. It had been a year since a serpent of mistrust had poisoned my perception of Prascovia, but I remembered the sense of security I drew from her guidance.

Should I try to restore our brittle but important alliance?

Not yet. Debra Gretishnikoff Alley was my opportunity to resolve the worries that nagged me like horseflies on a beautiful white-sand beach. With Debra's assistance, I could handle Vishenky without Prascovia's patronage.

Drained but calmer, I rose from her bench and headed home.

An unfamiliar carry-on bag of black and navy blue lay under a chokeberry bush by the gate. I heard voices through the open window in the room that I shared with Debra, hushed but definitely sizzling in an argument. One of them brought heat to my cheeks. The voice belonged to Chris.

You had your chance to escape, Mr. Waller. Why did you come back?

CHAPTER SEVENTEEN

To seal Chris's fate, I picked up his bag. I went to the damp, fungus-smelling tool shed, where I deposited the basket with the eggs on the cool dirt floor. Then I carried his luggage inside the house and set it by his bed. As I tiptoed toward the sound of voices, a euphoric cloud billowed in my brain, a massive cumulus of serotonin.

Luke sat beside Jessie on my bed and held her hand. Peter propped himself against the door that led to the back veranda. Slumped in a chair, her lake-green eyes full of tears, Debra faced Chris standing in front of her.

"You're wrong," she said. "This means nothing."

"But we don't know who she is," Chris argued. His tone was soft, almost regretful.

Peter banged the back of his head on the door in a slow rhythm of exaggerated frustration. Debra was about to announce my presence when I stepped forward and put my hand on Chris's shoulder.

Burnt by the trying day, my paranormal perceptiveness bordered on zilch, but I captured a spark of his emotional aura. I detected his satisfaction, a kind of a feet-in-the-river-on-a-hot-summer-day contentment. After a morning of watching my guests, I knew why Chris was pleased to be back. An attraction between a student and a college professor was nothing novel.

"Greetings to Earthlings from the galaxy of Vishenky." Luke interpreted my gesture in a robotic voice. "Sir, you're lucky this was only 'hello.' You should see how they say 'good-afternoon.'"

No one laughed.

I sat on Debra's bed and leaned against my arm. The ribbed fabric of the bedspread bit into my palm. One exposure to an open portal, and the mold of jealousy boosted by the supernatural energy would suffocate my fondness for Chris and Debra faster than it took the sunlight to reach the Earth.

"How was Gorky Park?" I asked.

"No one knew about you at the hotel," Chris said, his frosty voice nothing like the purring he used with Debra.

"Why would they? I operate independently."

"But I thought...."

I crossed my legs to demonstrate my casual mood. "I find clients through my website. When somebody contacts me, I send out a flyer."

"Why did you claim you're affiliated with the hotel?" Chris asked.

"Who told you that?"

His eyes nailed Debra. She looked at Peter, her brow arched.

"I mention a few hotels," I said. "A tourist visa versus homestay visa; saves me from a lot of paperwork. Plus, you have a place to sleep if you do not like my accommodations."

"I guess I misunderstood," Peter said.

"I'm sick and tired of all your conspiracy theories." Debra pushed herself from the chair and stormed out of the room.

Chris made a move to follow her, glanced at me, stopped, and studied the floor for further guidance.

"What did she mean?" I asked Peter.

He lowered his head, shaking it and covering his eyes with his palm. "No idea. Blame it on jet lag."

"Do you mind if I talk to Chris alone?"

Peter bowed mockingly and held the back door for Jessie and Luke.

Waiting for Luke to finish the spectacle of fighting Jessie for his chance to squeeze through the doorway, I tried to figure out what to do with the man standing in the middle of my bedroom. I ached for his presence when Chris wasn't around. I could get hurt when he was.

The door's lock finally clicked.

"I brought your bag to your room," I told Chris.

Hands in his pockets, he nodded but didn't answer, now examining my great-grandfather's radio bulging between two windows.

"Why did you leave your stuff outside?" I asked.

"I wasn't sure what was going on. I wanted everyone to return to the hotel, but just in case you'd have a legit explanation, I brought a few things with me to stay, at least tonight."

"Under my chokeberry bush?"

A guilty grin wiped out his hard expression. "If you ran some shady business, I didn't want them to think that staying here was even an option."

When Chris said "them," he pointed not to the back veranda where I had sent Peter, Luke, and Jessie, but toward the kitchen, the way Debra had gone.

He drove Debra to tears. He wanted her to leave with him. If I hadn't interfered, he would have won. Next time he might succeed.

Keeping Chris in Vishenky shot to the top of my priorities.

CHAPTER EIGHTEEN

A vacation didn't have to be a rush through museums, Chris had to admit as he sank into a chair under an apple tree. In its dappled shade Debra pretended to doze with an upside-down book in her lap. A train whistling and whooshing by in the distance, the racket of grasshoppers, the tinny murmur of a waltz from a neighbor's radio created a lulling background buzz. A gust of wind brought parachutes of seeds and smells of hay and sage and made a spider web between tree roots quiver.

"Is this how we're going to spend the next two days?" Debra asked with her eyes closed. "With you hovering over me?"

"I can't hover over anyone else," Chris said.

"Valya wouldn't mind."

"I doubt it."

"The cousin I know would seek the good graces of a fine Russian maiden."

"The maiden seemed upset. Perhaps she didn't like my accusations of treachery."

Debra picked her wide-brimmed straw hat from the ground, tipped it over her ear, and leaned toward him. "*Dahling.* A woman will forgive a man's false accusations if he admits his faux pas. What a woman won't forgive is the man's indifference." She puffed an imaginary cigarette. "Tell me, love, did you really come back to save us from this dangerous Russian?"

"Well, if you insist. When they told me at the reception desk that they never heard about Valya's tours, I was glad I had an excuse to return to Vishenky."

Debra dropped her Bohemian show. "Were you? Honestly?"

"There you have it. Don't make me regret that I confessed."

"I won't say another word." A sly smile appeared on her lips. "Still think Valya is an amateur?"

Chris pulled a stem of grass and chewed the succulent part. "Hosting and coordinating a tour requires certain traits, like self-confidence, the right mix of toughness and flexibility, buoyancy. That's not Valya. Valya withdraws. She gets tired and shuts down like a mechanical toy running out of power. I don't think she has stamina for this kind of a job."

"Chris, you're ignoring an important fact."

"What's that?"

"No one has returned to Moscow for the night. Not even you."

CHAPTER NINETEEN

"We'll do as we planned," Peter said. "I want to see the dam at night."

"That wasn't my plan." Chris bit into a shortbread cookie covered with wild-strawberry jam. The red-purple substance with sprinkles of golden seeds had a tang of bitterness, the way a walnut differed from a pecan. Its heavenly aroma blended with the smell of smoldering pinecones heating water in a *samovar*, a Russian kettle. Abandoning the cozy veranda and wandering in the dark would be as amusing as giving a cat a bath.

"I'm so jet-lagged I could use a hike," Jessie said. "Luke?"

Luke tried to smear a drop of jam over Debra's nose. "I don't know. I'm busy here."

Debra pushed away his hand. "Why not? Another chance to drown this poor excuse for a human being."

Luke's image as a mischievous puppy fresh in his mind, Chris couldn't resist. "Take him for a walk, but make sure he doesn't chase the chickens."

Valya jerked a napkin to her lips.

"What?" Luke stopped pestering his victim.

Debra chuckled. "We'll put him on a leash."

Jessie rose halfway from her chair to ruffle Luke's hair. "Or we can lock up our boy, so he won't follow us."

"He loves treats," Peter informed Valya.

"*Et tu?*" Luke jumped from the table, hands pressed to his heart.

Peter snatched Jessie's wide scarf. He tossed one end over his shoulder and propped the other on his hip. Chest forward, chin up, he raised his mug like a chalice, a Roman patrician before the Forum. Eager to express her sentiments about Luke, Jessie gestured madly, her thumbs commanding death for the wounded gladiator.

Unable to speak from laughter, Debra waved them to stop. And Valya—

How strange. The young woman gazed past Luke's chair, her hands gripping her elbows. Her face was passive, except for a slight bend of her eyebrows, but this faint curve transformed her. It erased the image of the easygoing hostess she had been for the past few hours. Her faraway expression belonged to someone very tired. Someone very sad.

Or someone very lost.

As if sensing Chris's attention, Valya blinked and the corners of her mouth stretched upward. The light didn't return to her eyes. The smile was bleak.

Chris averted his stare. The obvious question—"What's wrong?"—didn't leave his mouth. A stranger, he had no right to pry.

His logic scurried to reassure his mind, clinging to a trite assumption: Valya had had a long day.

Debra, always an astute judge of a character, liked their guide. The lunch and dinner, cooked in the cramped kitchen without running water, were excellent.

Chris slowly spread jam on a cookie.

Valya had had a long day.

The cookie crumbled, smearing the sticky substance over his fingers.

As with any one of them, the young woman could have some personal problems. Maybe she had just broken up with a boyfriend. Her momentary pained look didn't mean she'd fail her job. She'd had a long day.

Except, if Chris were to articulate what he saw in Valya's eyes, his unexaggerated choice of words would be "an abysmal hopelessness."

The ease he felt since his return to Vishenky hit a boulder of uncertainty.

* * *

The night rolled up her sleeves, ready for the bash. Darkness alighted on the front yard like an owl on a mouse, thick and final. Chris slowed on the brick-paved path, waiting for his eyes to make out the surroundings. A cacophony of frogs roared by the river. *Clok-krrr, clok-krrr, clok-krrr.*

The cooling air ran riot with an intoxicating scent. Along the concrete foundation, the plants Chris had thought were dying weeds perked up. A moth hovered above mauve petals. They glowed like tiny stars in the trickle of light from the curtained windows where Valya's silhouette stood motionless in the middle of the veranda.

"Dayflowers don't create a fragrance of such potency." The spell of the foreign night gave Jessie's deep voice an ominous quality. "Only those that are not seen."

Chris felt shivers sliding down his shoulders. The shadowy figure hadn't moved in the window.

"No moon," Debra said. "You guys feel something?"

"I feel something," Luke said, his finger jabbing into Debra's ribs. "Right here."

"Quit poking me."

"I do feel it," Jessie said. "Restlessness. The night is like a disturbed anthill."

"What I meant—the air is so fresh," Debra said. She pulled Chris toward the gate. "Sometimes Jessie just drives me nuts."

"Maybe you should go back and help Valya," Chris said.

"Why are we outside in the first place?"

"I thought she was getting tired of us."

"Well, duh. Luke's stupid jokes, Peter bossing everyone around, and Jessie and her feng shui. She moved the bed in her room. Hey, *I'm* tired of us."

Smiling, Chris patted Debra's hand resting on his elbow. Her common sense had brought his runaway imagination back to Earth.

"Valya's overwhelmed," he said. "We should start helping her."

"That's a great idea. I can't wait to see you two team up in the kitchen."

A row of lit windows mapped the metropolis of Vishenky. Chris saw the footpath but not the road that ran twenty yards from the fence line.

"Not a soul on the street," Luke whispered. "What are they afraid of?"

"Hush," Jessie said.

"What are you afraid of, *lovie*?" he asked.

"I said, enough."

Chris sat on the log lying by Valya's fence. "Think about it. When it's ten thirty in the suburbs in Northern Virginia, I walk the dog, and I'm the only person outside."

Luke turned on a flashlight and pointed the beam at the road. "Look at that. You call and they come. Good thing, you said 'the dog,' not 'a bear.'"

A lean big-eared pooch ran by with its nose low to the ground. Gray matter covered its black fur.

"Yuck. It rolled in something," Debra said.

"Cow manure," Peter said. "Dogs love that stuff."

"Or it crawled from a grave. Ah-hoo," Luke howled.

"Shut up." Jessie sounded an octave above her usual contralto.

"Good luck with your hike," Chris said. "I'm sure Luke will make the experience unforgettable."

Debra joined him on the log. "Will you testify in our defense when we come back without him?"

"Another dog." Luke held the mutt, identical to the first one, in the beam of light.

"They look like smaller versions of an Izidian hound, except for the color," Peter said.

Debra giggled nervously. "This is getting creepy."

"Ah-hoo," Chris said.

Above the black contour of a grove on the other side of the river, an orange glow brightened up as if a fire rampaged in a faraway village. The rising moon poked the top of its disk over the tree line, diluting the darkness.

Debra snuggled against Chris. "It sure gets cold here. Should we go inside?"

Valya's troubled look floated through his mind. "Let's give Valya more time alone."

"Look at that," Jessie said. "More dogs."

One pooch trailed another, placing front paws as if testing the ground before each step, the way a blind animal would pass through unfamiliar terrain. Reflecting the beam from Luke's flashlight, their eyes projected a violet shine.

Luke crouched. "Hey, mutts. Who's a good doggy?"

The pooches walked by, showing no reaction. A short trill, like a bird call, sounded from down the street and the animals picked up speed. Chris lost sight of them.

"Is it possible they're a part of Valya's program?" Jessie asked.

"Sounds a bit elaborate for a story-telling tour," Chris said. "Plus, we'd miss them if I hadn't suggested going outside."

Debra dabbed her nose with a tissue. "But Valya did act kind of strange. Maybe she didn't want to be too obvious—'Hey, what could be happening outside right now?'—but at the same time, she worried we'd miss the parade."

"To train four dogs and leave it to chance that we'd see them?" Chris asked. "It doesn't add up."

"It takes only two," Peter said. "She could train two dogs to run by the house, cross the river, and return over the other side."

"Someone called them, and they responded," Jessie said. "Now we know she uses assistants."

"I'll bet Miss Valya can't wait to share some chilling tale about Vishenky's infamous canines." Luke rubbed his hands. "Let's not disappoint her."

CHAPTER TWENTY

I curled up in the chair, grateful to be alone, my thoughts desperate as a hungry mouse gnawing on a forgotten bar of soap in an empty house.

The inescapable images resided inside my head, permanent like scars of a suicide survivor. Dimitry's pale wrists seeping blood onto unpainted floorboards. A shouting pack of my childhood friends blaming me for his death.

That day, I had lost more than my closest companions. Gone was the wealth of our fantastic summers, the treasure of laughter, games, confessions, tears, first loves—everything that bonded our young lives. The memories of good times tormented me as much as the recollection of the hour that ended everything. I carefully avoided reminiscing.

Tonight, my mental safeguards failed. When the darkness blurred the contours of trees and bushes, the yellow glow of the lamp shrank our world to the comfy burrow of the front veranda, filled with smells of cookies and flowers and smoke. I watched my guests, and the wisps of those banned memories began to leak from obscurity.

The numbness flooded me as an emotional deluge crashed into my solar plexus. The voices hummed from faraway. The faces floated in the universe where I had been a moment ago. Only Chris's stare stayed with me, his eyes alarmed. I wanted to flee the table, scurry to the far end of the garden, and crawl under the overgrown cherry trees. I longed to drop the friendly guide's mask and shed some tears.

I didn't. I sat still, and Chris ushered his students from the veranda.

The torturous tsunami had run its course, leaving me empty, weak. I squirmed deeper into the chair, reluctant to return to the reality, but there was a noise flapping against the walls of my solitude. I listened to enthusiastic voices and the tramping of feet on the brick path.

The door opened. Luke ran his hand over the wall, pushed the switch, and gasped. "Why are you sitting in the dark?"

"Imagine if I were standing," I said. "You'd have a heart attack. Did you enjoy the moonrise?"

"Moonrise, shmoonrise. Your dogs rolled in manure."

"What dogs?" I asked.

Luke crossed his arms, staring back at me. His whole look said, "c'mon," as if my question had snubbed his intelligence.

Too much interest flickered in my visitors' eyes. A village mutt, even smeared in cow poop, shouldn't strike them as rarity. My inner alarm unfurled its scaly coils.

"Can you at least tell me what they looked like?" I asked.

"Medium size, black, smooth-coated," Debra said. "Eyes glowing like purple Christmas lights."

"Violet," Jessie corrected her.

My heart battered my rib cage. "How many did you see?"

"Four," Debra said.

I was taking the group to the water possum's habitat in less than an hour. Handling two independent manifestations at once, especially when I had never encountered one of them before, could get dicey. Was there enough time to catch up with the mysterious canines and ensure they didn't interfere with our excursion?

"Where did the dogs go?" I asked.

"Someone whistled for them from down the street," Chris said.

"Ah, Lydia's mutts," I said. "My milk lady's. I'm going to run out and make sure she caught them." I walked to the cupboard, pulled a key out of my pocket, and inserted it into the keyhole in the bottom drawer, my fingers uncooperative.

"I'll come with you," Peter said.

"Just stay here. Those pups get vicious with the strangers."

"They seemed friendly," Luke said.

"Why, did you pet them?" I asked.

"I called, but they ignored us."

"I hate to be a Nazi about this, but let's make another rule." I stared at the drawer, hesitant to unlock it. How was I going to explain the items I needed? "When you run into something unusual, something out of place, an animal or even a person, do not approach. Come and get me first."

"Yes, Valya, that's what we'll do," Peter said.

There was no sarcasm in his voice, but a premonition tightened around my stomach like a boa constrictor. The "do not approach" approach wasn't a part of his plan.

I had to convince my Americans that Vishenky wasn't a petting zoo. I squared my shoulders, the searing determination rising inside me like a whip ready to lash. Time to flip a river card. Time to wreck Peter's game.

Time to play dirty.

CHAPTER TWENTY-ONE

Valya climbed the chair and snatched one of her dried bouquets. "Let me show you a neat magic trick."

A whiff of a scent reminded Chris of garden insecticides.

"Pyrethrum," Jessie said. "I can smell it."

"That, and yarrow, and Quaking Grass—the ingredients aren't important." Valya took matches from the cupboard and offered the box to Peter. "I need a volunteer. Will you light this up for me?"

Peter struck a match and brought it to the mummified flower heads. One by one, they began to smolder, sending thin gray pillars of smoke toward the ceiling.

He stuck his face into the hazy strands. "An interesting smell," he said.

Valya lowered the smoldering arrangement and waved it as if to give it more oxygen. The pleasant scent of burning autumn leaves spread through the room.

The self-proclaimed magician unlocked the bottom drawer in the cupboard. She came up with a pair of pliers and an ampoule containing a milky substance.

"Will you hold this for me?" Valya handed the arrangement to Chris.

He inhaled the smoke. Hints of cinnamon and vanilla blended beautifully with the bitter aroma of fall. The guide knew her incenses.

Valya used the pliers to snap off the neck of the ampoule. She took the bouquet from Chris's hands. "Enough. You'll get giddy."

He reluctantly released the brittle stems. Valya sprinkled the contents of the vial onto the smoking flower heads.

A firecracker-like symphony of hissing and whistles filled the veranda. Inside the bouquet, a small screeching ball of flame flung itself in different directions, like an agitated marmoset made of fire.

Valya scooped a spoonful of wild-strawberry jam and offered the dollop to the darting fireball.

The thing slowed its frenzied swings. It inched toward the treat and sampled the sweet tidbit. Then with a final shriek, it plunged into the teaspoon. The jam began to bubble. The vacated stems turned black.

Valya dropped the scorched arrangement and brought the spoon to her lips. She closed her eyes, put the boiling substance in her mouth, and swallowed.

"Spicy." She ran her middle finger over her bottom lip.

A surf of excited mutters rolled through the veranda. Valya raised her hand, asking for silence.

"No, I won't tell what it was," she said. "Look—your friend needs fresh air."

Peter stood by the dining table, not speaking, not moving, his eyes shut and his fingers pressed to his temples as if he tried to stop a fit of headache.

"Peter?" she called.

At the sound of his name his head snapped back. He opened his eyes. "Yes?"

"Go to the garden. Jessie, Luke, you two keep an eye on him."

"Peter, what's wrong?" his girlfriend asked.

"Nothing's wrong," Valya said. "Fresh air, now. Stay with him and don't leave my property."

Hesitant but out of arguments, the trio walked outside.

"Deb, could you bring me my yellow cardigan?" Valya asked. "It's in the closet by my bed. You must find it."

"Yellow cardigan. In the closet." Debra disappeared inside the house.

Valya dug through the bottom drawer and pulled out a white lace shawl. "Chris, what does Peter know about my tours?" she asked.

A faint smell of burnt leaves hung in the air. "Is this a beak?" Chris asked, his attention glued to a hodgepodge of feathers, faded blossoms, and small bones attached to the shawl.

"From a rooster."

"This piece looks like a claw."

"A wolf's claw." Valya deftly wrapped the shawl over her shoulders. Not a petal fell off. Not a twig caught on her sweater. The tip of the beak touched her neck. "What did your students tell you about Vishenky?"

Chris tore his stare from the shawl. The veranda was too hot. He felt lightheaded. "Peter's half-brother, Kenny, was here last summer. He really liked your stories."

"Peter never told me about Kenny. Why?"

"Where did everybody go?"

"Chris, stay with me. Why did Peter keep Kenny's trip a secret?"

"To throw off your guessing game." Chris rubbed his temples, wrestling to wipe out a pinwheel that popped up between him and Valya. The smoke cast by the pinwheel felt real. He coughed, his throat tickling, and grabbed the corner of the cupboard for support. "It's a part of your act, right? To deduce things about your visitors?"

Valya nodded with the enthusiasm of an alchemist who had just found a golden powder on the bottom of his flask. "That's how they convinced you and Debra to lie." She pried the beak open and positioned it on her shoulder, securing the nasty thing with the folds of the shawl. "I'll show your students something scary tonight. Make their souls hide in their heels, as we say in Russia. You won't mind, will you?"

Chris laughed but ended up in another coughing feat. He waved, "go ahead."

A tumbler filled with ruby-brown liquid appeared in Valya's hand. "Drink this and go to bed."

Like a warrior inserting her sword in its sheath, she tucked a flyswatter under her belt. "Chris, one more thing. When we go to the dam and you're in the house by yourself, don't let anybody in."

"Who would—"

Chris blinked. He was alone.

CHAPTER TWENTY-TWO

Silenced by my spell, Kenny couldn't give his brother sufficient details about what he had witnessed. Peter's tantalized curiosity would be my leverage.

I found my confused commander-in-chief and his adjutants in front of my dad's tool shed. They looked around, evidently unsure of where to go.

"Imagine the irony," I said, "if Chris Waller and Debra Alley stay in Vishenky, and you have to catch tonight's last train to Moscow."

"You can't make us leave," Peter said.

"This is my kingdom. I don't have to give you the keys."

He laughed theatrically.

"You're more than eager to share the wonders of your 'kingdom,'" Jessie said, "or you wouldn't be doing these tours."

Luke bobbed his head.

"But not everyone gets to discover the real Vishenky." I spoke gently. A spider doesn't jerk its web. "Are you sure I want to share the wonders with you?"

Seconds fell like drops of sleet. "Well?" I asked.

"Okay," Peter said. "We'll play it your way."

I exhaled. An unfastened clasp finally snapped shut between us. It wasn't a trust but understanding.

"What do you want from Debra?" Jessie asked.

"To have fun memories of Russia. What else?" I answered quickly.

Neither trust nor understanding germinated in Jessie's pale eyes. All day long, those ash-colored irises soaked up my every gesture, glance, and frown. My tactic of ignoring her had turned into an oversight.

"I have to find the dogs," I said. "Don't follow me. When I come back, I'll take you to see the live water possum."

I hurried toward the front gate, my tennis shoes quiet on the brick path. If the supernatural canines were lethal, the fool who had whistled and gotten their attention was already dead.

CHAPTER TWENTY-THREE

I pressed my back against the fence of the last house. The packed dirt road that circled the village glowed as if made of chalk. A ravine slashed through the field in front of me and flattened out as it reached the river. The moon, bright as a projector, illuminated the placid water surface and somebody's log sauna, *banya*.

No dogs. No dead body.

A nip on my shoulder indicated I had to search harder. Chris had mistaken the serrated jaws of a supernatural fish for a beak. I repositioned my alarm device so the teeth wouldn't puncture my sweater and get to my flesh.

With the flyswatter in my hand primed for a strike, I followed the bottom of the ravine. In spring, melting snow filled it with gushing waters. It dried up by mid-May. I stumbled over the hummocks and undergrowth as I crept along the stream bed.

The ravine widened. Osoka came into the view. At first I didn't understand what exactly crawled through the shallows. I inched forward but kept to the left, closer to the trunks of the willows.

Then I knew what had caused the sandbar under Chris's feet to collapse this morning. The dogs, at least six of them, moved erratically along the beach. They burrowed in and climbed out of the muck with the urgency of rodents bustling about in a cage. Silt covered their sleek coats. Tongues hung out, tails curved up, eyes bulged.

Like a panicky cat clawing its owner, the jaws chomped on my shoulder through the thickness of the sweater. I suppressed a yelp. The warm fluid began to seep into the fabric.

How fast will the smell of blood draw the beasts' attention?

"I led the dogs as far from you as I could," a voice above me said, "but you just wouldn't stay away."

A small form jumped down from a willow branch.

"Andrey," I whispered.

"Be still." He pushed on my uninjured shoulder until I was crouching and yanked out the jaws. "Why are you using this garbage?"

"An old souvenir from your grandma."

"Get rid of it."

"She wouldn't put me in danger." I tried to sound confident for the boy's sake.

"Aha. You're safe. Like a duck with a hawk." A human measuring device of paranormal energy, Andrey took my hand and pressed his fingers into my palm. "You're on zero."

"I'll be fine," I said. "Tomorrow, come over and test my guests."

"You can run a thousand tours, a million-zillion, but you'll never find anybody like you and me."

"We must be sure," I said. "Did you see your grandma today?"

He looked down.

"Your dad might find out," I said.

"Who'd tell him?"

"Lydia. She was upset about the eggs. Why didn't you explain they were for me?"

"So Lydia would eat them, not you," the boy said.

"Why? Do you know what your grandma did to them?"

"Just that the spell is strong."

So was an angry sparkle in his eyes. Andrey couldn't stand not knowing when it came to the supernatural. His drive to learn exceeded mine. Sometimes, the boy made me nervous. Other times, he scared me.

"Next time Dad goes to Kolieno, send the eggs with him," Andrey said.

Away from Vishenky's energy field, the potency of the spell would fade. "I'll ask him," I said. "Now I want you to go home, before

Gregory notices you're gone."

Andrey scrunched his face, for once an offended ten-year-old, a youngster trying to be a hero and sent to bed like a baby.

"Go home," I said more firmly.

"No."

"Sweetie, *solnishko*, please. We don't have time to argue."

"You cannot handle six dogs." Tears glistened in his gray eyes. "You go after them with your flyswatter, and they will pull you under the river."

"How come they ignore you?"

His face lit up. "They're dumb! Here, look." He picked a rock and tossed it low above the ground. The last couple of meters it rolled right past the digging dogs and vanished in the water.

The mutts froze for a moment and then went berserk. Noses down, they ran back and forth along the rock's trajectory. The foam began to drip from their chops.

"They think it was a mouse." Andrey wiped his nose with the sleeve of his sweatshirt. "You'd better hurry. If you don't get your Americans to the dam now, you'll miss the possum. I'll keep the dogs busy till they disappear."

"What if the dogs stay until morning?" I asked.

The boy giggled. "Meeha and Sashok are sleeping over at my house. We locked the door in my room, and I left through the window. Dad thinks I'm home."

I nodded and ruffled his hair, my throat tight. I had friends I trusted like that a million years ago. Then Dimitry died, and the rest of them condemned me forever.

CHAPTER TWENTY-FOUR

Chris expected creaks and rasps. What he hadn't expected was a dead hush. No wind whispers in the chimney. No moths banging on his lit window. Two prehistoric refrigerators, which purred side-by-side while Valya worked her magic in the kitchen, now stood mutely, as if waiting for their owner to return and ignite new life into the comatose house.

"What are you afraid of?" Chris asked Luke's earlier question aloud, not sure if he spoke to himself or the appliances.

Sleep had no power over his jet lag. He should have gone with the group on the hike to the dam, or finished Valya's potion instead of pouring most of the unpleasantly bitter liquid into the sink. He tried to read, but the book couldn't distract him from the gloom of silence.

Just past midnight, Chris finally heard three heavy knocks on the outside door, with a horror-movie pause between each bang.

"It's unlocked," he yelled, wanting to strangle the idiot, namely Luke, for his stupid humor.

No one walked in. The metrical knocking continued.

Okay. Let's play.

Chris pulled the printed-cotton cover from his bed and turned the unembellished side out. Somebody's walking cane of polished light-colored wood rested in the corner between two doors. He pushed the cane's tip into the middle of the cover and carried his creation to the veranda. Leaving the lights off, he hid behind the door, opening it bit by bit and wiggling the "ghost" in the gap.

Good sports like Debra and Luke would shriek, or squeal, or react in some way. Instead, Chris heard nothing but the rustle of cloth brushing against his arm.

He lowered the cane and peeked outside. A tall figure stood at the threshold.

"Hi," Chris said.

Silence.

He flicked on the light switch. Hands clasped under her chest, an elderly woman in black garments swayed slightly from side to side the way a bamboo shoot moves with a breeze.

Oh, boy. Chris set down the cane with the "ghost." "I'm sorry, I don't speak...No *Roosky. Nyet.*"

The woman stared.

"Valya *nyet* here," he tried again.

She squinted, rubbing her hands like a masseuse readying to touch her client. Her eyes opened wide. A cold violet shine blazed in her irises, so intense that it consumed her pupils. She thrust her cupped hands over the threshold and unlocked them. A magician's orb of light flew off her palms, momentarily blinding him.

Do not let anybody in. Valya's words drifted through Chris's mind.

The woman stepped forward. A gasp caught in his throat, Chris shut the door and pressed his back against the curtain-covered glass. He felt for the switch and killed the lights. His heart pounded and he swallowed air in short gulps as if he had just finished a marathon.

But nothing happened. No one tried to open the door. A few drops of rain thumped against the roof, breaking the quiet.

Chris ran his fingers through his hair. A woman with some fancy contact lenses, past midnight, with the big dark house as a setup— Valya's assistant didn't have to use paint over her face, or claws, or fangs to nearly send him hiding in a closet. And that after he had been warned! An interesting business Valya operated here in Vishenky.

His nerve—and heartbeat—recovering a pace behind his common sense, he looked outside. The visitor was gone. Straight above the gate, the clouds unveiled the moon. Chris hesitated on the doorstep, caught in the painting-worthy beauty of the nearly perfect disk floating in the sky on the crests of silvery-black waves.

A cluster of dark figures appeared by the gate. Someone frantically jiggled the latch. "C'mon, c'mon, open up."

Chris never thought the sound of Luke's voice could be so comforting.

While the gang messed with the lock, Chris darted inside, switched on the lamp, and pushed the bedcover and the cane under the couch. He snatched a plastic container with cookies from the cupboard and grabbed a seat at the table. He had no desire to confess how much fright he was given by some old woman. A midnight snack required no embarrassing explanations.

Seconds later, his students scattered around the room like beads from a torn string. Wheezing filled the veranda. Each face glistened with sweat. The color of Luke's cheeks bordered on purple. Debra held her hand pressed to the side of her rib cage.

"What's up with you?" Chris asked.

She made a vague gesture.

The last one to come in, Valya had the appearance of an addict out of funds and luck. Her sunken eyes and parched lips made her face look feverish. Her gaze meandered between the ceiling beams as if she was unable to focus on the surroundings. She didn't shut the door.

"Sit." Peter pushed Valya into a chair. "Start talking. I won't let you leave until I know what you do here."

"What's going on?" Chris asked.

They ignored him.

"Listen," Valya whispered. "I need…Just stay in the house. When I come back, be here." She used the chair armrests to thrust herself upright.

Peter blocked her way.

Jessie wrapped her arms around his shoulders. "Let her go."

"She's not—"

Valya made a short step as if testing herself for steadiness and swiftly slipped past Peter restrained by Jessie's weight.

Jessie released her panting boyfriend. "She'll be back. Then we'll talk."

"Forget about her," Luke said. "Let's get the hell out of here."

"There are no trains until morning," Jessie said.

"We'll wait at the station."

"Could someone please tell me what happened?" Chris asked.

Luke fell into a chair by the table. "Do you believe in monsters?"

CHAPTER TWENTY-FIVE

A greenish circle of an open portal shimmered under the river surface, beckoning me with its otherworldly radiance. Random strikes of violet lightning sparked inside, and the torrent rushed in as if sucked by the mouth of a huge fish. My fingers dug in mud on the bottom to resist the flow while my body devoured gargantuan amounts of energy.

My guests had nowhere to go until tomorrow. Human nature at its best, their minds would scramble to produce a rational account of the evening. Meanwhile, I had the luxury of comprehending what I had witnessed right before I had to dangle my life in front of the monster's snout.

Our expedition had begun as planned. Taught by last summer's incident, I led the group over the dam to the opposite bank. The slope rose above the river like an amphitheater. Ghostly silhouettes of birches clustered behind us. The moon, softened by a passing cloud, painted the world dark pearly gray.

At 11:24, a rectangular hole opened in the river. An aurora of green lights blazed inside. Debra with a camera in her hands tried to stand up for a better shot. I pushed her down on the sheet of plastic. Four minutes later, the long hairless back of the water possum glided along the surface in our direction.

The creature reached the shallows. Jessie, the only one truly spooked and on edge since we had left the house, touched my hand. For the first time I glimpsed her aura. It was cold and white, blinding like fog lights, like diamonds under the brightest display lamps.

As I fought to clear my overloaded senses, she whispered into my ear, "There's something behind us."

CHAPTER TWENTY-SIX

"You don't believe a word I said, do you?" Luke asked.

Chris shrugged. "A gap opened in the river. A monster crawled out, half-possum, half-otter. What's not to believe?"

Fingers spread, Luke shook his hands in a seemingly genuine frustration. "And if it's true? If I saw the friggin' thing with my own eyes?"

"I'd say, 'Bravo, Valya.' Unless, of course, you invented the whole story."

No stealthy glances crossed the room. Luke dropped his head on the table, pressing his eye sockets against his fists. Debra frantically pushed the buttons of her camera. Peter sketched picture after picture on paper napkins.

"You all think the possum was the worst thing out there." Jessie rocked back and forth in the chair by the sofa, cradling something in her palms. "You have no idea—"

"Don't," Peter grumbled over his shoulder. "Not now."

Jessie's swaying switched course to left and right.

Chris felt a seed of worry sprout in his stomach. "Did you get anything recorded?" he asked Debra, hoping to hear "Ha-ha, got you, you believed us."

She turned off her camera. "Everything's out of focus. Imagine the Northern lights, coming from the bottom of the river." She spoke fast, her voice hushed and breaking. "A five-foot-long creature crawled out and charged toward us like a bull moose, and Valya went against it with a flyswatter."

"Did she get hurt?" Chris asked, surprising himself with a quick turn of his concerns.

"I'm not sure," Debra said. "The attack happened fast and in the dark. Valya could have been injured."

"Maybe that will teach her," Peter spewed out with a spiteful laughter. He wiped his mouth. "That thing, it could kill us. Valya has no clue. Not the slightest idea of what she's doing."

Jessie lunged from her chair. "Yes, she does. Look." She tossed on the table an oval metal locket on a torn red thread. "Open it."

Peter recoiled as though a poisonous frog had landed next to his pencil.

Chris pulled the locket by the ends of the thread. Smooth and silvery on both sides, the adornment had an intricate hinge. Some tarnish covered the delicate flower vines that served as a spring to keep the piece closed.

"Where did you find this?" Chris asked.

"Valya's lucky charm," Jessie said. "Open it."

Careful not to damage the filigree work, Chris pried the locket with his fingernail. A tuft of algae-colored hair twisted in a tight roll rested inside. The light from the lamp gave it a golden sheen.

"Is it human?" Chris asked.

"'Larger than a cat,'" Jessie said, "'has green fur with a golden shimmer, and it will kill you if you pass the bridge when it hunts.' Does this sound familiar?"

"Chupacabra?" Luke asked without a trace of humor.

"Don't you remember what she told us by the bridge?" Her hands on the back of Luke's chair, Jessie made a serious effort to deep-freeze Chris with her strangely pale eyes. "You're looking at *volkanok's* fur."

CHAPTER TWENTY-SEVEN

"Let's not get into paranormal baloney." Peter tapped his finger on the napkin with his drawings. "Brazilian river otters reach six feet in length. This one has escaped from a zoo. The locals have an underwater tunnel with a mobile platform on top. The otter kicked it open."

"We'd see a whirlpool." Debra perked up, given a prospect to find an explanation. "The opening was rectangular."

"Not if the platform is right under the surface," Peter said.

"Such a structure would be full of water."

Peter pulled a fresh napkin for another sketch.

Chris glanced at the clock. Valya had been gone for twenty minutes.

"Here," Peter said. "The top of the tunnel is usually exposed above the surface. It extends under the dam and comes out on either bank. Then the tunnel's empty. But because it rained, the water level is higher and just above the platform."

"Did Valya tell you where she was going?" Chris asked Jessie, who hadn't moved from her spot behind Luke's chair.

"No."

"Why do you have her locket?"

Jessie studied Chris as if deciding whether to grant him access to a secret society's archive.

"Oh, c'mon, it's your chance to make a believer out of Mr. Waller," Luke prompted.

Jessie's cheeks turned two shades darker. "It's much easier to ridicule than try to understand. You think you have a right to judge me, Luke?" She grabbed a handful of his hair and shook it lightly. "You don't feel a presence when no one is there. You don't wake up from weird sounds in your room. You don't see things floating above your bed. You've never experienced anything beyond belief to judge me."

The girl was more messed up than Chris imagined. He put up his hands. "Jessie, no one is judging you. I just need a clue as to what happened to our guide. Somehow you ended up with Valya's locket."

"You won't believe me."

"Just tell us already," Debra said.

Jessie's shoulders rose defensively. "When the otter came to the bank, I...I heard something. I heard something moving behind us."

She "heard." Jessie had emphasized the word as if the group accused her of using psychic powers. *What a nut,* Chris thought.

"I told Valya," she continued. "She tore the locket off her neck and said, 'Don't let him come close.' She went down to the river, and I climbed up the hill, almost to the top."

Jessie swallowed. Her fear infected Debra, who was twisting the strap of her camera into a knot.

"I saw a human-like shape against the sky, moving through the field, in my direction. It had two violet dots where its eyes should be."

Debra covered her mouth.

"You'd probably run," Jessie said, "but I didn't want a monster to attack me from behind. When the figure reached the tree line, I turned on my flashlight. It was a guy, about thirty, long brown hair, deathly pale. His eyes looked normal when I shone the light on his face. He kept coming. I put Valya's locket in front of me. That stopped him. He said something in Russian and leaned against a tree. I thought he was raising a gun, but he held his wrist in his right hand. His left hand was missing. Something ripped it off. I saw the bone, tendons, and shreds of flesh, but no blood. The guy was dead. He was a walking cadaver."

Observing two females on the verge of tears, Chris coughed to break their spell of terror. "Ladies, please. I had a visitor while you were gone. An old woman shining violet light bulbs at me just like your guy and the dogs." He felt an unpleasant aftertaste from the memory. "'*Legends and Supernatural Phenomena*: Are you brave enough to experience them?' Valya and her assistants have one objective, and that's to scare you silly. That's what you've signed up for."

Peter laughed quietly. "Very good. Very fucking good."

"Obviously, this circus is too much for you," Chris said. "We'll leave tomorrow, but right now I'm worried about Valya. If they're using an exotic animal, something might have gone wrong. Did anybody see how she got hurt? Was she bitten?"

"The otter tried to get past her," Debra said. "Valya kept running sideways, and she tripped and fell once. It could be her head or her shoulder."

Luke shoved his elbow into Peter's ribs. "She did turn green when you pushed her into the chair."

"Like she wasn't green already," Peter grumbled.

"What happened to the otter?" Chris asked.

"After they chased each other for…oh…probably two minutes," Debra said, "the otter stopped, sniffed the air, and took off along the bank, jumping like a giant rat. It must have smelled an easier prey. Valya came back looking like another five seconds would kill her."

Chris got up. "I'd better find her."

"How?"

"It's past midnight. The village is asleep. The house she's in will have the lights on."

* * *

I opened the door just as Chris was about to step out. He wore jeans and a windbreaker—no shirt beneath it. He must have jumped out of bed in a hurry when his students had shown up with a load of amazing tales.

Mercy. For a woman charged with otherworldly energy, the man was too darn handsome to ignore. At once, his presence affected me like a balmy afternoon, made me feel too cozy to get straight to my agenda. How was I supposed to keep my focus?

I glanced in the mirror above the chair. Water dripped from my curls, leaving spots on my crimson sweater. Good, because the punctures inflicted by the fish jaws had started to bleed. The therapeutic session at the portal had erased gray circles under my eyes and left my cheeks rosy. My lips matched the color of my sweater. I liked my look, and so should Chris.

"Thank you for coming back," he said. "I had a brilliant plan how to find and rescue you, but then I heard the place is infested with Komodo dragons."

"You can handle this gang but you're scared of dragons?" I asked.

Chris grinned. "Or the dragons' handler."

He joked with me, practically flirted. I wanted to kiss him for being so happy that I was home and unharmed, but I settled on a cheeky smile.

I turned to Jessie, who had jumped back from Luke's chair and plastered herself against the cupboard when I had walked in. "You did well. Glad you're on my team." I pointed my finger at Debra. "And you, my dear. You almost stepped off the plastic. I cannot guarantee your safety if you break my rules."

"Cut it out." Peter didn't even turn to look at me. "You're out of your mind to run these tours."

I wasn't going to talk to his back.

I plugged in the electric kettle. The water level was low, but it would do. I put five espresso cups on a tray. Jessie moved aside to give me some room.

"What is this place?" she asked. Fear veiled her like black smoke.

"Tomorrow," I said. "We'll talk about everything tomorrow. Whatever happened tonight, in the daylight it won't seem so scary."

"I saw a dead man with a torn hand, walking and trying to communicate. Tell me who he was. Right now."

"Probably Mahkar." I pulled out a glass jar with a blend of dried and crushed plants. "*Volkanoks* killed him over a hundred years ago. Or Yurka, who died a decade ago. Was the guy heavy? Gray beard, white shirt? Mahkar perished on a holiday. Or did you see a skinny redhead in a t-shirt with some rock band?"

"No beard, long brown hair." Jessie said. "In a parka."

A few words, a tome of implications. I set down the jar. "Terentey. Slaughtered last February. The official report named an attack of stray dogs as the cause of death." I paused, thinking, my fingernails pounding an unhurried rhythm against the wood. "I've seen *volkanoks* at night and watched them play with their pups. They hunt mice and steal chickens. No matter what the stories about them say, it's extremely rare for a *volkanok* to maul a human. But only people killed by *volkanoks* show up as 'undead.' This makes Terentey their third known victim."

I went quiet, wondering if I had said too much.

The kettle whistled.

I poured the herbal mix into a teapot and added hot water. While all the stares burned holes in my back, I splashed the brew on the bottom of each cup then filled them to the rim with the potion I had given earlier to Chris.

Now came the hardest part of my act.

I carried the tray to the table and placed it on the corner between Debra and Peter. The latter did a fantastic job depicting on my napkins tiny people trapping a giant chipmunk in some kind of a tunnel.

I pushed his drawings around. "Interesting hypotheses, but they are flawed."

"I agree. For example, you charge pennies for your tours," he said, surprising me with his conversational tone. "Maybe you're not ready to open for business. Maybe this tour is another trial run. Maybe you hosted groups before and every time something went wrong."

"Or maybe, things are much more interesting than you imagine," I said. "Did the water possum look like anything you're familiar with?"

"You stole a giant otter from a zoo and shaved it," Luke said.

I nudged Debra's shoulder. She scooted over to a chair across from Peter. I took her seat at the head of the table. "Every July, here in Vishenky, portals from another world release otherworldly energies. They manifest themselves as visions and entities, or materialize as fantastic creatures."

"And you're the only one who knows about this?" Jessie asked.

"Of course not," I said.

"Then who are you? What do you want from us?"

"Jess, drop it," Peter barked.

"What's funny, I don't have to tell you anything, do I?" I asked. "You're not going anywhere, because all you want is to solve the mystery."

Jessie's wordless anger surpassed her terror.

Peter took off his glasses and rubbed his eyes with a deliberate slowness. He looked exhausted, overwhelmed by the buildup of mystifying facts. This proud man struggled to get a step ahead of me while his teammates watched their leader. A futile effort, considering the circumstances, but I respected his fortitude. Peter wasn't going to fall apart when presented with irrefutable evidence of supernatural occurrences. I regretted that tonight I couldn't offer him another manifestation.

He pointed at the steaming cups. "You can't possibly expect that we'll drink your brew."

"Uh-huh," I said uncertainly, as though he had just explained to me the famous Schrödinger equation. I looked around, searching for a weaker opponent.

Chris took the chair by the sofa, his amiable grin now replaced by a frown of disapproval. Jessie clung to her new best friend, the cupboard. Luke viewed me as if I'd turn into an angry bear as soon as he dared to take his eyes off me.

But Debra seemed okay, her cheeks healthy pink and her face with the halo of black curls doll-pretty against the curtained window. Waves of her friendliness continued to stroke the shores of my paranormal senses. Could her exposure to the energy have sparked off that lively look and her irrational trust in me? Or did she simply enjoy my toying with her nemesis, Jessie?

"I buried plastic food wrapping along the house walls and the fence," I said. "That prevents the creatures from invading my home and property." No need to disclose what had accidentally been trapped inside in the process. "They don't like modern synthetic materials. I conducted a little experiment a long time ago: I pushed the tip of a flyswatter through a portal. The plastic turned into a black film and came after me. I intercepted it with my free hand before it reached my face, and the skin burnt like I stuck my arm into an anthill."

My eyes caught Jessie's. "In other words, I worked hard on planning a safe tour, but this is a complex system. You got to witness way more than I intended for you on the first evening. What will happen when we turn off the lights? Will you fall asleep? Or will you lie in bed listening to every rustle in the house?"

Her lips trembled. "If I drink this, I will just sleep, right? No dreams? No voices?"

"Correct." *She hears voices?* The girl was nuts. On the other hand, that's what my uncle, a behavioral scientist, said about me.

Jessie unglued herself from the cupboard and picked up a cup but didn't taste the potion.

I offered another cup to Debra. "This will let you sleep without nightmares."

"Wait a minute." Chris was on his feet. "What's in the brew?"

"Herbs," I said, "to ward off bad dreams."

"Perfect." Debra put her slim fingers around the delicate porcelain.

"Deb, no," Chris said. "You don't know what's in it."

"Cheers," Debra said.

I thought she sipped the liquid by a drop. It took her at least ten swallows to finish the potion, while I fumed because of Chris's attempt to interfere.

Jessie emptied her cup. "There."

I nodded in the direction of Luke and Peter. "This has to be done."

Jessie put her arms around the guys' shoulders. She whispered into Peter's ear for a long time.

"Goddammit, Jess, why can't you keep it real?" He downed the drink in one gulp and exited the veranda.

To convince Luke, Jessie simply kissed him on a cheek.

Luke smelled the liquid, put the cup against the light, dipped in and licked his finger, drank, and made a show of grasping his throat and coughing as though he had swallowed poison.

I turned to Chris.

"Could you please make coffee?" he asked.

"Why would you want to stay awake?"

"You just drugged four people. I'm not sure how much I trust you."

"Chris," Debra said.

I hadn't heard her calling him by his first name before.

He didn't correct her.

The professor and his lovely student were closer than I thought.

I put my hand on my wounded shoulder and pressed hard, focusing on pain, not letting my jealousy ignite the torch of anger. "Is decaf okay?" I asked Chris, my voice sweeter than caramel.

His face darkened. "I'm a guest in your house. I won't search your cupboard. Could I please have regular coffee?" Dreadful anger pulsated in him, as unpleasant to my senses as a splinter under a nail.

"Fine. Be our night watch." I got up to get water for the coffeemaker.

While I puttered about in the kitchen, I heard Luke, relaxed by the potion, advise Chris to check his cup for rat poison and not to mess with Russian witches.

I pondered if I ought to change Chris's mood, but I was too annoyed to waste my precious energy. Mr. Waller had set himself up for an interesting night.

CHAPTER TWENTY-EIGHT

From my bed, I watched the window where the moon crept into full view. Not the bad dreams but troubling thoughts kept my mind awake.

Mahkar's death, followed by Leontina's disappearance. Yurka's death, followed by Anna's disappearance. Terentey's death....

If only I hadn't lost Leontina's diary. My guru, my audacious great-great-grandmother. What did you know just before your untimely end?

Leontina Gretishnikoff had desperately searched for her slot in the universe. She had risked her life confronting the monsters and the villagers she had been trying to protect. She had left the manuscript that had given me the insight into my life deeper than any living soul could ever offer.

Prolific in her experiments, Leontina left such pearls as how to keep wasps from building their nests under awnings, but most of her entries described the manifestations. Creatures, locations, safety precautions—the incredible collection of data had become a foundation stone in my affair with Vishenky. Reading it took me years. She had written her chronicles in scrambled sequences of words and sentences, the way Andrey often spoke when he was a toddler. Sometimes I needed days to grasp the meaning of a single page.

Last year, I finally approached the manuscript's final chapters. The tone of her notes had changed. She grieved about the gruesome death of a local man, Mahkar. She complained that so many harmless creatures—including *volkanoks*—were turning aggressive. And then I read something that made me drop everything and run to Prascovia. Leontina was pregnant, and she lamented her beloved sister's absence. Only Alexandra could bring her from "the other side." But if Leontina didn't step through a portal after the birth of her child, *"everything alive would soon be dead."*

"What happened to her?" I asked Prascovia. "Did she have to stop an attack of the Violet Lights?"

I'd never forget the witch's reaction.

It wasn't dread, or resentment. If the stench of a rotting corpse could be conveyed in an emotion, that's what passed through the chasm of Prascovia's heart.

Mortified, I turned and walked away. That night Leontina's manuscript vanished from under my pillow.

Frankly, no matter how spooked I was by Prascovia's dead aura, I had more reasons to suspect my parents than the witch. A splinter-thin line separated my sane reality and the absurdity of Vishenky's ethereal world. I had to be judicious in my beliefs if I wished to venture out into the paranormal world and not succumb to madness. Out of all the possibilities, I deliberately opted to choose the most rational one. My mother, often with her twin brother's encouragement, tried many cruel things to keep me from "all that mystic nonsense." After I found the spot under my pillow empty, I gathered my nerve and asked her how she dared to touch my stuff.

And in the combustion of our argument, I had learned that I was a stillborn miraculously resurrected under Vishenky's full moon while my parents tried to bury my body illegally in their garden.

My mother yelled that I had sustained brain damage while being dead. I was petrified to contemplate how I had ended up living. Her admission turned the corner stone of my existence into dust. I didn't read human emotions or handle paranormal manifestations because I possessed some miracle DNA. No, my abilities were generated by the otherworldly energy residing in my body.

I was a monster, brought back from death by some damn entity that dictated my every crave and mood swing.

The Legend of an Unborn. A splinter-thin line.

I panicked then, the fragments of facts spinning in my head like a freakish kaleidoscope. The grim statistics reflected in my family tree took a new meaning. Antonina's daughter and several females in the subsequent fourth generations disappeared soon after childbirth. Not all of them, but some. *Propala*, the comment said. *Gone.* Was this the cycle, the Violet Lights emerging every four generations?

Those who lived to old age were cousins.

Leontina belonged to one of the fourth generations—and so did I. She needed her sister to pull her from "the other side." If family ties meant something after all, who did I have to bring me back if one day I had to stop an invasion of the Violet Lights?

Anna's son, Andrey? She thought so, but I wasn't so sure. He was Prascovia's progeny. Genetically, emotionally, we were too far apart. If I wanted to survive, I needed to locate another descendant of Antonina. The Gretishnikoff bloodline. My distant cousin would be a normal human being living a normal human life, but I hoped it wouldn't matter. The genes we shared, that's what counted. I believed I could ignite a bond that would ultimately save my life.

So I found Debra.

I pulled the comforter to my chin, the chill inside me unyielding to the warmth of the room. Irrationally, inexplicably, I hoped for something else. Debra couldn't be a stillborn resurrected by an entity. If I exposed her to an open portal and she exhibited paranormal powers, I would know that our supernatural talents were the result of our magnificent DNA. Even if an otherworldly entity resided in my body, it did nothing to affect my mind, my emotions, my choices.

Please, Debra, please. Show me, you and I are alike. The Gretishnikoff bloodline, the newest fourth generation, the heirs of paranormal abilities. Prove that you could bring me back from the alien world if one day I had to cross the threshold.

She slept, my delicate hope, my beautiful chance.

The door from the kitchen squeaked and the sounds of footsteps drifted toward my bed. The timing was right. The beginning of the manifestation that happened annually on the second floor must have spooked Chris. I feigned the deep breathing of a healthy slumber.

The mattress took his weight as he sat by my side. After a few seconds of hesitation, he touched my arm. "Valya?"

I recoiled in a calculated motion and backed against the wall. "What is it?"

"I heard footsteps upstairs."

"Neighbors' cats. They sneak in."

"Too heavy for a cat."

"I told you to drink my potion. You'd be sleeping." I turned toward the wall.

He squeezed my shoulder and pulled me to face him. "I'm telling you, there's someone on the second floor. Is this a part of your theater? It's pretty stupid if you think I believe in poltergeists."

The grip of his fingers hurt my flesh. What happened to the nice, amiable man?

I brushed off his merciless hand and rose to lean against my elbows. "You are my guest, but you're welcome to search the house. Nobody's upstairs."

"How do you know? What if someone broke in?"

"The second floor is empty," I said. "Absolutely nothing there to steal. Go and check for yourself." Good luck with rationalizing and explaining the vision he'd have to his students tomorrow. Even though the image never lasted longer than three-four seconds, it would shock him to discover his own replica gazing out of a window at a supernaturally huge moon.

The distinctive astringent taste of sea-buckthorn berries in my mouth made me skip a breath.

Impossible. Too chilling to admit. Why now? The whole universe was turning into a category-five cyclone in the course of an evening.

Pulled into the whirlpool of panic, I bit my lip. Chris's flared temper was only a symptom. I pushed away the comforter and sat up. Afraid to touch him, I kept my face inches from his while I spoke quietly about the banging pipes, the creaking floorboards, a raven walking on the roof. The words meant little, a mere distraction to keep the man engaged.

The hum of throbbing blood vessels filled my ears. If rage resided in a vibrating metal flagpole, I was sending my energy, my whole being into that pole to stop the tremors.

"Well, if you're sure…." The uncertainty crept into Chris's voice. The shudders of his anger started to subside. The oily tang of sea-buckthorn left my taste buds.

Taking it as a sign that my energy was working, I collapsed on the pillows.

Chris rubbed his right temple. "Shoot, I…So sorry I was rude to you. It must be a lack of sleep. I wasn't myself."

"I have a busy day tomorrow." I turned away, trying not to break into sobbing.

"You're right," he whispered. "Apologies don't amend the past."

I realized his words weren't meant for me. He spoke to himself.

I longed to pull him down next to me and hold him, make sure that nothing, nothing malevolent and sinister and wicked would ever touch him.

Chris sat in silence for a few more seconds, gave me a peck on the cheek, froze in brief confusion, and then beat a hasty retreat. I exhaled. I knew kindness when I encountered it. I accepted compassion when it was offered.

"Don't go upstairs," I thought I whispered, but drowsiness wrapped around me like a warm blanket, the leaden thoughts let go of my brain, and I glided through a meadow of harebells and daisies and maiden pinks. Above me, an ominous shadow soared like a hungry bird of prey. The lethal entity that had killed Dimitry was back, and it had found Chris.

CHAPTER TWENTY-NINE

A loud knocking awoke Chris. He opened his eyes. Debra pounded her knuckles on the table.

"Ten thirty," she said. "You can't sleep the whole day. We're about to have breakfast."

The smell of pancakes enhanced the syrupy ambience of the country-styled bedroom. The morning tranquility percolated through the lace curtain with the sounds of chirping birds and the distant bleating. A pink petal separated from the bouquet in the vase and spiraled down on the ochre tablecloth.

"Is everyone else up?" Chris asked.

"Luke's still in bed," Debra said. "I told him to hurry. Valya wants to show us the cemetery before it gets too hot."

"And you all want to see it?"

"Of course we do, *dahling*."

"Is there any point of reminding you how frazzled you were last night?" Chris asked.

"Do I look frazzled to you now?"

She didn't, and that was the problem. Her friends would be just as enthusiastic to continue the tour.

"I'll be out in a few," Chris said.

Instead of joining the guide and her groupies, he walked through the kitchen and the girls' quarters. The back veranda's door was open. Luke sat on his bed, rubbing his eyes.

"Care to go for a swim?" Chris asked.

"Not really."

"We need to talk."

Luke scratched his chest. "Can't we talk—"

"Not here. See you at the beach."

* * *

About forty feet wide, the river mirrored swaying willows and the rising sun in the milky-blue sky. A feather, pushed by the breeze, sailed against the flow. Beneath tall weeds on the opposite bank, five snow-white geese rested, beaks tucked under their wings.

Luke clapped, bringing the flock alert. The leader flapped his wings and screeched a warning. The birds wobbled off the bank and glided down the river.

Chris made his way through the tangles of sedge and forget-me-nots to the sandy shallows. He let his back soak up the warmth of the sunshine and plunged into the cool, gentle current. Luke took a dip, leaped out, and settled on the bank, hugging his knees and shivering.

His flesh and bones saturated with chill, Chris joined his student on the grassy beach.

"After our little shindig with the water possum, I thought I'd never go anywhere near the river," Luke said.

"You agree that Valya's business is far from normal?" Chris asked.

"Totally."

"Last night you were anxious to get out of here."

"I still am," Luke said.

"But...?"

"But there's no force in the universe to make Jessie leave." Luke unclenched his hands, stretched, and lay down. "She and Valya together, man, that's lethal. Somebody has to watch Peter's back."

"I'll talk to Jessie."

"Nah." Luke drew circles in the air around his temple. "She's totally into Valya's paranormal crap."

"If you don't mind my asking, what's Jessie's story?"

"You never heard it from me, okay? Four years ago, Jess was carrying groceries from the car and a lightning bolt hit right in front of her. All she remembers is a super-bright light and falling to her knees."

"And she started having visions?"

"Don't jump to conclusions," Luke said. "Jessie's no fool. She had her head examined, MRI, CAT scan, all the good stuff. Everything's fine. Except, she wakes up several times a night, and when she does, she sees things."

"She needs a psychiatrist."

Luke sat upright. "You know what Jessie told me once? 'Something found me that day.'"

"More reason to get her out of here. I'd feel much better if we all got on a train."

"Understood. Is your cell phone working?"

"Not a single bar," Chris said.

"How about this. You and Deb leave. If we don't show up at the hotel tomorrow night, in the morning you start search-and-rescue."

CHAPTER THIRTY

Nothing in life is quite like a meal with friends.

Peter chatted about his time under Arizona's baking sun during the dig Jessie dragged the gang to the previous summer. Luke returned from his short swimming session and teased Debra about the incompatibility of her waistline with my rich Russian cuisine.

The brightness of the day—and my potion—had driven the water possum out of their flexible minds. My guests enjoyed breakfast and each other's company. I basked in the campfire kind of camaraderie, a long-lost part of my existence. Only Chris's absence was the proverbial spoon of tar in a barrel of honey. No matter how much I trusted my powers, I needed to be certain he was okay, that the energy I had given him was doing its job and holding the entity at bay.

Just when I thought he had decided to skip breakfast, Chris made his appearance. His hair was wet and pushed back. He sported a fresh tan on his forearms and deep lines on his high forehead. Evidently, his rendezvous with Luke hadn't generated a blast of good morale.

"How was the water?" Jessie asked.

"Great," Chris said. "You all should try it."

"Your lips are blue." Debra pulled out a chair for her professor. "Russian pancakes. What would you like on yours, caviar or sour cream?"

"The best is to mix jelly and marinated herring," Luke shared his teeth-on experience.

"Out of the mouths of babes," Debra said.

Chris poured himself some coffee. "I asked you to wake me up at nine. The whole morning is gone."

I pushed the milk pitcher toward him. "I told Debra to let you sleep since you stayed up all night."

"What are you talking about? I was dead to the world before my head hit the pillow."

I sat too close to miss the tickling waves a lie would emit. Chris believed in what he was saying.

Luke shook his finger at me. "Tell me if I got it straight. Last night Mr. Waller consumed a pot of caffeine but had no problem hibernating. Why did I have to guzzle that yucky, nasty, disgusting potion?"

"So you wouldn't jump out of bed to check the house for neighbors' cats and burglars," I said.

Chris frowned. My words stirred some memories.

"Neighbors' cats?" Debra asked.

"They sneak in sometimes," I said.

Chris put down his mug. "Last night—did you drug my coffee?"

"I did not." I dumped every bit of my rightful annoyance into my glare.

Chris didn't resume his breakfast. He crossed his arms and sat back in his chair, his stare frozen on me, an eyebrow arched in the condescending greatness of his indisputable superiority. Every year of our age difference was embossed on his handsome face.

"I never remember my dreams," he said, "but this time everything felt realistic. Vivid."

My God. He thought his escapade was a fruit of imagination. But what I found sobering was his haste to lay a distance between us. A vast, formidable wasteland.

"And after all that buzz, you're upset we let you sleep in?" I asked.

Chris tried to stare me down a bit longer. Then he picked up his fork. "Forget it."

"No, Chris, be reasonable. Jet lag, new surroundings, plenty of stimuli to stir up your brain. It's offensive to suggest I spiked your coffee."

"Okay, I'm sorry."

"I hope you mean it." Debra's pout looked childish but cute.

"Sir, if you try herring on a pancake, they might forgive your outrageous accusations," Luke advised.

"No, we won't," Debra said.

"Mr. Waller, your dream, the strange part," Jessie spoke as if her words had complicated phonetics. "How strange was it?"

Chris hesitated. His eyes twinkled with the returning good humor. "At a wretched hour of the night, while evil skulked in the shadows, I heard footsteps."

I couldn't resist a smile.

His students were quiet. Jessie leaned forward, her eyes wide open, unblinking. Funny how she expected the house to be haunted.

"To protect you all from a wicked intruder, I climbed up the ladder and opened the panel. I saw no one, but the sound of the steps lured me into the next room. A lonely candle burned in the window. Its minuscule blaze quivered like an orange tear on the unblemished face of the moon."

The smile froze on my lips. *A burning candle*. A random vision? Or was it a real poltergeist, a reenactment of Dimitry's death?

A coincidence. *An orange tear on the unblemished face of the moon?* Chris's romantic imagination.

"I blew out the candle and climbed down." His tone changed from hushed to normal. "That's all I remember."

Jessie's oddly pale eyes stopped on me. "What's on the second floor?"

"Are you brave enough to find out?" I asked.

"I am." Luke jumped from his chair and ran to the kitchen.

The rungs of the ladder squeaked. I toyed with the handle of the porcelain milk pitcher, my fingers dancing centimeters away from Chris's hand. I had a clear reading of his abrupt discomfort.

"Found it," Luke yelled. The ladder protested his passage louder. Seconds later, he barged to the veranda holding his arm behind his back. "Three windows. Where was the candle?"

"In the middle one," Chris said.

"Good answer. Ta-dah!" Luke produced his trophy.

"Old and dusty," Debra said.

"A neat coincidence." Peter ran his fingers through Jessie's blond strands. "If someone burned this candle recently, my friend here would be intrigued."

I had burned a lot of candles under my friend Tamara Karpova's watchful eye. We had tried to recreate the circumstances of Dimitry's death to understand what happened. It had been a while since our last experiment.

I felt Chris relax. He still couldn't distinguish his second-floor adventure from a dream.

He refilled his coffee mug. "So, when is the next train?"

I knocked the pitcher, spilling the milk onto the oilcloth.

"But Chris—" Debra said.

"No arguments." He blotted my mess with a napkin.

The same icy tone that failed to intimidate me silenced his student. Avoiding eye contact, Debra rose from her chair, ready to follow her professor back to the hotel.

I got up, too. A wicked, insane plot was forming in my head. I'd make the rest of the morning so entertaining that my two favorite guests couldn't resist giving Vishenky another afternoon.

CHAPTER THIRTY-ONE

Chris sent Debra to pack her bag. She sulked but obeyed. He asked Luke for the final time if he was coming with them. The boy swiped the last pancake from the plate and shook his head.

Valya laid the train schedule in front of Chris. "You can make the twelve fifteen or the twelve forty." Her finger on departure times, she leaned closer to his shoulder. "May I talk to you in private?"

"I won't change my mind."

"What makes you think I want you to?" Valya asked.

"Then we have nothing to talk about," Chris said.

"It's about Debra. Something you need to hear."

What would his cousin choose to share with a friendly stranger, a female of her age, but not to tell her family? Valya's somber tone left Chris worried that the guide wasn't concerned about some silly crisis in Deb's love life.

Valya led him around the corner of the house. They stopped just past Jessie's window.

Undisturbed by the foot traffic, emerald-green moss spread freely on the ground. The maple hid them from anyone walking along the path to the gate. A row of chokeberry bushes by the fence provided a screen blocking the street.

Chris put his hand against the wall. The bricks felt warm under his palm. "What is this about?" he asked.

"Not to question your pedagogic approach," Valya said, "but I know that Debra would like to stay."

"Is this why you dragged me here?"

"I think it's better for everyone if you go to Moscow alone."

"Well. Not to question your creepy operation here, but Debra's not into phony mediums or fake folklore."

"I'm sorry, Chris. I won't let you take her away."

"Excuse me?"

"Why did you tell your students the candle and the steps were a dream?"

"What was I supposed to tell them?"

"The truth."

"Do you ever take breaks?" Chris asked. "It's a nice morning. I'm about to leave. Let's not waste each other's time. Your show doesn't have to go on every waking moment."

"Am I the one who is acting?"

Arguing with Valya was like telling his dog, Jack, not to chase the ball. "I need to pay you," Chris said. "And I have a word of advice. If you want to run this circus, you should learn to adjust your program and accommodate the wishes of all your guests. If someone tells you to drop your theater, do it."

A pained smile curved her lips.

Chris wasn't going to apologize.

"Let's cut through the charades," Valya said. "You know what happened last night."

"What exactly?"

"Debra's relationship with you is her business, but I don't trust you with her well-being."

"Let me remind you. I'm in charge of Debra's well-being. Whatever your problem is, you have no right to tell me what to do."

"I will if this liaison is harmful to her."

Liaison? She doesn't know we're cousins!

"Hold on," Chris said. "This is not what you think. Debra and I—"

"I can't keep Debra safe from you forever, but as long as she stays with me, she's under my protection."

Chris stared into her angry hazel eyes. Valya's reaction to his hypothetical fling with a student seemed overblown. Was the young

Russian that prudish?

"What exactly bothers you?" he asked, careful to keep challenge out of his voice.

"You're capable of hurting a woman and joking about it."

"Please, Valya, we're not sixteen. I don't know what I said, or whose little girl's feelings I hurt, but—"

"'Feelings'?"

Her voice was a breath of arctic winter, cold, monochrome, and penetrating to the bone.

"What are you trying to tell me?" Chris asked.

"You left out a part of your 'dream.' The one where you came into my room and said you heard footsteps upstairs."

"Wait a minute…."

"I told you to go to sleep because I had a busy day ahead of me."

"Valya, wait. This can't be—"

"Recognize your hand?" She pulled at the neckline of her blouse, exposing her shoulder where four bluish spots marked her tanned skin. "Dreadful dreams you're having, Mr. Waller. Excuse me."

Valya moved straight at him, forcing him to step out of her path, and strode by, her back straight and her chin high.

CHAPTER THIRTY-TWO

Overcome with embarrassment, Chris unpacked his bag.

Debra walked into the room. "What are you doing? The train leaves in forty minutes."

"We can't leave."

"What do you mean?"

Chris smoothed the bed blanket. "Deb, I...screwed up."

"You scare me."

"I was angry last night. I got into an argument with Valya."

Debra pulled out a chair. "'Last night' when?"

"You were already asleep. I grabbed Valya by the shoulder and apparently I bruised her."

"You did what?"

"My fingers left bruises on her skin."

Debra shook her head. "Valya fell on her shoulder when she chased the otter."

"I saw fingerprints," Chris said. "Deb, I swear I don't know how it happened. I didn't realize I was squeezing so hard."

"What made you so angry? Is she the first one to refuse your advances?"

"Stop it."

"Then why?"

"The footsteps upstairs, it wasn't a dream."

"Why did you say it was?" Debra asked.

"That's what I believed. Now I think Valya drugged me last night."

"Sure, blame the victim."

"Deb, I saw a burning candle. I heard the steps. By morning I couldn't tell if it was real."

"Don't say anything to Jessie."

"This is just a small village without plumbing. Why is everything so elaborate? An exotic animal, zombie makeup, special effects?"

"I'd love to find out," Debra said, "but you tried to strangle our guide. Repack your bag. I'm sure she'll kick us out."

"About 'us,' did you tell her we're cousins?"

"No. The plan was not to disclose any personal facts. She's supposed to guess these things."

"She guessed all right. She believes you and I are having an affair."

"*Dahling*, that's embarrassing. Did you explain to her our profound family ties?"

"She didn't give me a chance. She just wanted me out of here."

"Did you at least apologize?"

"After saying in front of everyone it was a dream? Her logic is impeccable: Why would I fake memory loss if I wasn't guilty?" Chris looked out the window, at the carefree swallows slicing the cerulean expanse. "Deb, how do I get myself out of this mess?"

"Oh, brother." She played with the fringes on the tablecloth. "What if we just leave? We'll never see Valya again. I swear I won't think less of you."

The suggestion was tempting.

"Then what?" Chris asked. "I have a bad taste in my mouth whenever I think of Russia? And Valya? She doesn't deserve ugly memories."

Debra touched her bottom lip with her index finger, a telltale sign she had little faith in the plan she was about to propose. "Let's stay for another day. I'll talk to Valya. Maybe she won't throw you out."

CHAPTER THIRTY-THREE

My skin, just like my feelings, didn't bruise easily. I had smeared charcoal dust on my shoulder, a purple-gray imitation of four fingerprints.

I had tossed the dice. Chris could say, "Sorry," get on a train, and forget Vishenky like an unsavory meal, but I had a hunch. A man with such a powerful sense of responsibility wouldn't run if he thought he had hurt someone, especially if he believed he had done harm in anger.

Guilt sandpapered my conscience. Was I out of my mind to compel Chris to stay in the house where a lethal entity so easily dominated his will? If I were a mere human and the paranormal energy bore no impact on the firing rate of my neurons, would I put his life at risk? Or would I be more merciful and let him and Debra go?

I paced. The bedroom's gray walls nurtured my gloom. I wanted greenery and sunshine, breeze worrying the willows, and the river snaking through the pastures. I craved Luke's jokes. Chris's smile. I was a human being. I wasn't—

"I know you're angry," Debra's voice said.

I spun around. She stood in the hallway between the kitchen and the bedrooms. Her travel bag lay at her feet.

She stepped over it. "After what Chris has done, it was very decent of you to talk to him in private."

"No reason to set a precedent to Luke and Peter."

Debra bit her lip and looked around the room. Then she held her gaze on me. "It's hard to find arguments why you should change your mind about Chris. If I tell you it was an accident, you won't believe me. If I tell you it will never happen again, you won't believe me. If I tell you Chris is one of the most decent, nicest people I've known in my whole life, you won't believe me. But the fact is it's killing him that he hurt you."

"How touching. Who will he send next to apologize on his behalf? Jessie? Luke?"

Debra's mouth hardened. Her fingers gripped the doorpost with power that whitened the flesh under her unpainted nails. "Valya, these twenty-four hours I trusted you. Things got weird. Things got out of hand. I had no idea who you were or what you wanted, yet I trusted you. Is it too much to ask you for a favor?"

"That I forgive Chris Waller? I don't know why you care. You two are leaving. We're done."

"Actually, I'm asking for your permission to stay."

My heart flopped like a carp out of water. I tried my finest bitter smile on her, hoping it didn't come out too jolly.

"Please," Debra said.

I held the pause to show her my terrible emotional struggle, and during those seconds of static electricity between us, I received a puzzling vibe:

Her smugness.

My crafty girl was leaving something out, an ace of trump, her last resort to make me change my mind.

Let her keep it. Let her hold on to her winning hand and feel invincible in my enthralling company.

"Have faith in me a little longer," I said. "Until sunset. Then I'll tell you who I am and what I want."

"But Chris can stay?"

"If you keep an eye on him. Vishenky affects him in a strange way, and I don't like how his behavior fluctuates. If you notice something atypical, the sooner I know the better."

She beamed. "I'm telling you, last night was completely out of character. Chris is a wonderful person."

So was Dimitry.

CHAPTER THIRTY-FOUR

Chris pulled at the chain, double-wrapped around the posts of the front gate. Valya had deducted his intentions correctly, but the five-foot-tall fence wasn't going to stop him.

The strangeness mushroomed like a radioactive cloud, and he meant to regain at least some level of control over the situation. No more tall tales. He wanted a real explanation for this mid-summer Halloween.

Valya had been adamant about not allowing him to stay in the house by himself. She offered a barrage of excuses. Vishenky's cemetery, where she was taking the group, had begun to sound like the eighth wonder of the world.

She'd probably have canceled the hike if Chris hadn't assured her he wished to see the neighboring villages.

"I'll be back in three hours," he had promised.

Valya couldn't say no, but she had waited for him to mount the bicycle and head off.

The ride around Vishenky took him ten minutes. By the time Chris got back to the house, the front gate was secured with a padlock.

Not a problem. He propped the bicycle against the fence and used maple branches to climb over.

Neither door would budge. Chris checked under the welcome mat and turned a couple of rocks. No key, but he anticipated such a predicament. He had left the window in his room unlocked.

As he scrambled over the ledge, he caught an eye of Valya's neighbor, a fair-haired gaunt guy in a stained beige jumpsuit, watching from his backyard.

Chris waved. "I forgot my hat," he yelled.

He got no response. The grim-faced dude was probably just leery about Chris's activities. Or he could be Valya's assistant waiting to get in and set up new hoaxes. Would he choose to report Chris's raid immediately to Valya?

Good luck chasing her around the cemetery. Hoping for at least an hour at his disposal, Chris crossed his room and walked into the kitchen. The place still smelled of pancakes.

He climbed the ladder and moved the panel blocking the entrance to the second floor. A wave of hot air poured out. Chris pulled himself in.

The overheated room reminded him of an attic on a summer day. He tried to open one-half of the folding window, but the rusted nails gave out and the whole frame fell into his arms. Chris placed it on the unpainted floorboards, thankful he didn't break the glass. He wiped the sweat off his forehead. The breeze felt nice.

A worn-out couch with a red plaid throw tossed across an armrest looked familiar. He had definitely been here before. A curious assortment of collectibles was piled up in a plastic crate by a coffee table in need of fresh polish. A Chihuahua-sized bronze moose with a missing antler peeked from the top. From underneath, Chris extracted a plaster figurine of a shepherd boy with his face delicately sculptured and his feet broken off. Chris debated whether he had found a Russian version of a voodoo doll. The idea of Valya casting spells over a symbol of an unfaithful boyfriend didn't seem farfetched.

In the second room, Chris recognized the supporting beams for the downstairs ceiling and dry clay spread on the metal mesh between them. Thin boards, heaped without order across the beams, led to the wall of windows. Chris found a round dust-free print on the windowsill.

A thick candle, the right acoustics, a CD with the sound of footsteps could have furnished Valya's theater of poltergeist. She had hours before dawn to replace the candle with the one Luke had found later.

The whole matter was nuts, but at least a few things now made sense.

Except for his performance at breakfast. Why had his brain twisted the truth? And even taking into account his jet lag and first day in Vishenky, which had lasted an eternity, how could he have so badly miscalculated the force of his grip?

Chris had one plausible explanation: Valya had lied about his coffee. She had drugged him, just as she had drugged his students.

Very well then. He didn't have to apologize, because she knew he hadn't meant to hurt her. Chris had no power over Jessie's or the boys' decisions, but Debra was coming with him to Moscow this afternoon.

As he walked back to the ladder, the draft pushed a crumpled piece of paper across the floor by the couch. One of the cushions appeared disturbed, as if it wouldn't fit all the way in its place. Chris looked at a plastic pen and a pencil resting on the coffee table. Struck by a brilliant deduction, he lifted the cushion.

A tattered notebook lay buried beneath. Chris opened a random page, and whistled.

CHAPTER THIRTY-FIVE

Valya's salads tasted fine, but Chris didn't savor his meal. The front veranda felt excessively hot, stuffy, or maybe it was his mood that kept him out of his comfort zone. He had been focused on the wrong problem. The mechanics of Valya's illusions didn't matter. He should have asked the correct question twenty-four hours ago: Who was Valya Svetlova?

The guide sat in her usual chair at the head of the table, for the moment the most exuberant woman Chris had ever met. Some inner torch lit her eyes and smile, brought color to her cheeks. She spoke, laughed, and enjoyed lunch as if a doctor just reversed a grave prognosis. The body language of Chris's companions corroborated the power she held over her audience. Everyone was leaning in her direction.

Would a bipolar disorder explain her spells of utter exhaustion and sudden surges of energy? Or was it substance abuse? Chris wished he had Internet access.

"I could describe tonight's manifestation in detail," Valya said, "but it won't make any difference. When the phenomenon starts, you'll be absolutely unprepared."

"It depends," Debra said. "A UFO landing in your backyard—I could tell myself I'm on a movie set. Bigfoot—a guy in a bear suit. Give me something."

"A herd of dinosaurs?" Valya asked.

Debra wrinkled her nose. "A bad dream?"

"Sounds about right. They're moving toward you, and you can't wake up."

"Does this mean it's dangerous?" Jessie asked.

"Of course it's dangerous. Everything here is dangerous." Valya propped her chin with her palm, her grin sly, mischievous. "So what? Not a chance you're going to back out. You're dying to witness another occurrence."

Chris felt a chill slinking up his spine. She had them and she knew it. Suddenly it was clear that unlike whitewater rafting or skydiving or safari, Vishenky delivered its adrenaline rushes without any safeguards. A controlled environment? Legal implications? Uh-uh. His students had chosen to become the participants in something completely unpredictable, unregulated, and handled by a capricious woman who didn't give a roadkill about their safety.

Valya put her fingers on the edge of the table, a wild blaze dancing in her gaze. "But I give you all my word. I won't hesitate to step between you and any threat." Her fervent stare fell on Chris. "No reason to panic."

He touched his forehead. It was coated with a film of sweat.

"Someone's at the gate," Luke said, his voice uncharacteristically quiet.

Chris recognized the next-door witness of his unauthorized entry, Valya's sullen neighbor.

She slid from her seat and pulled a piece of paper from her jeans' pocket. "It's Gregory. He's driving to town tomorrow. I just need to give him my grocery list."

Watching Valya trot past the windows, Chris pushed away his barely touched plate.

"No appetite?" Jessie asked.

"It's hard to swallow. I'm absolutely certain Valya uses hallucinogens."

"Is that why you played a health inspector while she made lunch?" Debra asked.

Chris raised his glass. "And why I'm drinking water. I don't know what she used for your iced tea."

"What makes you so sure?" Peter asked.

"While you toured the cemetery, I snooped around the upper floor."

"Unbelievable," Debra said.

"I don't understand why both of you are still here," Jessie said.

Chris felt heat rising to his face. "Because I can't have a peaceful vacation while you—"

"Something's up." Luke pointed at the row of windows facing the street.

Her fingertips pressed to her mouth, Valya stared at her house the way someone would watch a burning building. Gregory reached over the fence and patted her shoulder.

Peter twisted his neck to see what she was looking at. "Hey, what happened to the upstairs window?"

"Oops," Chris said.

"You had something to do with it?" Jessie asked.

"How I wish you'd pack your bags and leave," Chris said. "Yes, I had something to do with it. It was hot, the window wouldn't open, and I yanked on it too hard."

"Then brace yourself," Debra said, "because here comes wrath and fury."

Valya walked past the veranda's door.

"She's heading to the tool shed," Luke reported. "I'd worry if I were you, sir. I heard Russians are proficient with pitchforks."

"Was it worth it?" Peter asked. "The search?"

"Oh, yes," Chris said. "I found what I believe is Valya's recipe book. Before I show it to you, I want Debra—"

Valya marched in. She dropped a handful of nails in front of Chris. She put down a hammer with a force that made circular waves in the pitcher of iced tea.

"You know how to use these?" she asked him.

A number of answers tickled the tip of Chris's tongue, but he kept his mouth shut.

"Fix it," she said.

Chris lifted a few nails and let them fall. "They won't rust, will they?"

"What do you mean?" Valya asked.

"The old ones corroded all the way through. That's why the frame came down."

Drama being a permanent feature of the tour, Valya's breathing, suddenly labored, changed into gasps. She put her hand at the base of her throat. "It takes two men to hold the frame. Chris, don't go upstairs alone." Grasping the cupboard, the wall, the doorway, she staggered into the kitchen.

A creature of compassion, Debra moved to get up. Chris held her shoulder to keep his cousin in her seat. "Leave her alone."

Peter rubbed his upper lip. "What kind of thoughts do you play in your head to give such an award-winning performance?"

"To Valya, this is not a show," Chris said. "Deb, I need you to take a look at her recipes."

She pushed off his hand. "I think you just *bruised* me."

"I did not!"

"You stayed here to apologize," Debra said. "Instead, you violated Valya's privacy. Don't kid yourself. I won't join this witch hunt."

CHAPTER THIRTY-SIX

Debra shut her paperback, her irritation stronger than her concern about the characters' doomed love affair.

The world succumbed to paranoia. Jessie, Peter succumbed to paranoia. Even Chris succumbed to paranoia.

Lying on her stomach, Debra studied the delicate profile of the woman who just put a plate of warm cookies in front of her nose, plopped her denim-clad skinny Russian butt on the beach towel, and stretched her long legs. If anyone suspected Valya in sinister endeavors, the universe had gone insane.

Branches of an apple tree sheltered their divine garden retreat. Palms against the ground, Valya leaned back and turned her face toward the dappled sun. The tip of her braid almost brushed the ground. A tight coral-colored top accentuated her curves.

Attractive and mysterious. Outgoing, witty, running an intriguing business. A perfect woman to remind Chris the opposite sex didn't entirely consist of the cold-hearted bitches with whom he tended to get involved. Debra inhaled the delicious aroma of cookies. She came to Vishenky to enjoy herself, but it was impossible, given that Jessie, her entourage, and Chris opted to seethe, conspire, and trespass.

Would it be possible to reignite her cousin's interest in Valya? A distracted Chris would be an easier-to-deal-with Chris.

Alas, even his basic civil rapport with the guide required some serious mending.

"Did you lock Mr. Waller in the tool shed?" Debra asked.

An uncharacteristically shy smile appeared on Valya's lips. "Your friends invited him to go on a bicycle ride, but he said, 'No.' Chris hasn't left his room since lunch."

"Hiding, huh? I can't believe he broke into your house. You must be livid."

"Technically, Chris had my permission. Last night I challenged him to search and find something incriminating."

"You're a saint," Debra said.

"Not at all. Chris is your problem, not mine."

Oh, yeah, the guide's wrongful notion of their relationship. This was the time to enlighten Valya about Chris's big-brother part in Debra's life.

"You're so good at reading everyone," Debra said. "Have you ever been wrong?"

"Nope. Haven't I given each of you what you came for?"

"Like what?"

"The obvious," Valya said. "Jessie's obsessed with everything paranormal. Peter feeds off puzzles. Luke's like a puppy. He gets excited whenever others around him are wound up."

"And me?"

"Are you unhappy here?" Valya leaned over and brushed something off Debra's shoulder. "You had an ant crawling on your arm."

"Thanks."

A curious feeling was building inside Debra. The ease. The warmth. The same lenience toward their imperfect world that her psyche would generate whenever suffused with a glass of champagne.

She picked a cookie and bit into its flaky, buttery sweetness. "I have to admit, I'm having fun."

Valya watched her with gentle attentiveness. "Then I'm doing my job."

"But what about Chris?"

"Mr. Waller has a strong protective instinct. He needs to guard you. I have a hunch I provide for him plenty to worry about."

Debra laughed. "You're brilliant."

Valya pulled her knees and rolled to sit sideways. "There's another interesting thing about Chris. He says he wants to be in Moscow, but in fact, he likes being here with the group. I wonder if something spoiled his own student years."

Legs of a thousand centipedes ran over Debra's skin. "What makes you think so?"

"You said it yourself. I'm good at reading people," Valya said.

"That's far from a casual observation."

"Do you ever get a feeling that you sense someone's emotions as clearly as your own?"

Valya seemed to hold her breath while waiting for an answer. Debra saw through the guide's sneaky strategy. A speck of data here, a tad of info there, and the smart Russian put together a whole profile. Perhaps their hour of candor and revelations hadn't yet come. Debra would gladly share many things, but not her cousin's past.

"The sixth sense is really Jessie's department. As for Chris...." Debra swept the imaginary cookie crumbs from the cover of her paperback. "Maybe he misses his time in college because he had a lot of fun back then?"

Valya looked at her for several long seconds before her eyes shifted and focused on something in the distance. The posture of a chastised Golden Retriever about him, Chris stopped on the garden path as if uncertain whether his company would be welcome.

"Here comes Mr. Waller," the guide said. "Let's ask him about his college years."

"Let's not!"

"That bad?" Valya asked softly.

A heat wave of guilt brushed Debra's neck. How could she doubt even for a moment Valya's genuine compassion?

"Sometimes the past is a dangerous animal," Debra said. "Why wake it?"

"Indeed." Valya loaded the brief word with rock-heavy burden.

Sending Chris away and prying about the guide's own past was tempting, but if he was ready for peace talks, Debra wouldn't want to interfere. She waved at her cousin to join them.

Chris acknowledged Valya with a reproachful scowl. "Your cookies are burning."

"Did you turn off the oven?"

"Sure…and peeled potatoes, washed the dishes, and swept the chimney. Go and do your job." He had the audacity to point his finger in the direction of the house.

"Chris!" Debra choked on her own sizzling words.

"Just like you told me, the nicest person you've ever known." Her eyes hard, Valya got up on her feet. "All yours."

"Valya, wait!"

The guide didn't look back as she cut through the vegetable beds and walked down the path.

"So glad you two are getting along," Chris said.

"Have you lost your mind?" Debra asked. "Valya works her butt off for us."

Her cousin unbuttoned his shirt and extracted a dog-eared notebook. "Curb your admiration until you see this."

CHAPTER THIRTY-SEVEN

"Look how the handwriting changes," Chris said. "Valya started this thing as a child."

Debra turned a few more pages. Superb drawings of wildlife, some in ballpoint, some in ink, filled the lined sheets. Reptile-like species crept, fought, and hunted in the meadows and brush. Detailed sketches depicted webbed paws, spiny tails, and claw-armored leathery wings.

The planet Earth never produced such fauna. Someone's rich imagination—or nightmares—did.

Chris picked a spot to sit on the grass. "Can you translate it?" he asked.

Debra returned to the first page. "A tablespoon of acorns soaked in the Newt Spring, a handful of sea-buckthorn berries, two cups of milk from a four-year-old cow, six petals of a pond lily...." She skimmed the column. "Basically, each chapter describes a local plant, harvested in a specific area at the precise time, how to process it, and which creature the extract will repel."

"Look at the drawings. A very disturbed mind created these mutants."

"That's not what bothers me. The last few pages show only the monsters, not recipes for how to deter them." Debra lowered her voice to a whisper. "Chris, what does this mean?"

"Valya's mental state is not a joke. Don't tell me this is another prop."

Debra closed the notebook. "Do you want to know what happened on our walk, while you shamelessly rummaged around Valya's digs?"

"She left me with no choice."

Debra grimaced at his stubbornness. "Vishenky's cemetery. Talk about creepy. No order to the layout, fences on top of each other, and dead people staring from every headstone. Tables 'to sit, remember, and drink vodka for the peace of the soul.' Valya's words. I think she dragged us in circles, just to put everyone in the right mood."

"Lovely."

"Shut up. She brought us to a steel obelisk. Some guy, only twenty-nine, died last February. Jessie grabbed Valya's arm. 'It's him.' Imagine Valya's best performance: widened eyes, the-apocalypse-is-near voice. 'What's left of Terentey is buried here.' She brushed the dirt in front of the obelisk. Guess what was conveniently buried under a wilted peony?"

"A rotting corpse?"

"A locket with a silver filigreed hinge, just like Valya's. This one was empty. She divided the dog fur from her locket—pardon me, *volkanok's* fur—and filled up the one at the grave. 'This will keep him from wandering around.' By then, Jessie was whiter than milk."

"What a friend you found in Valya."

"'I thought you didn't know he was killed by *volkanoks*.'" Debra did her best impersonation of Peter's girlfriend. "And Valya said, 'I didn't. It's not my locket. Some stranger adds them to the graves, but I haven't seen him since I was a child.' Now Jessie's all wound up, looking around like someone might be hiding behind the gravestones. Next, we went to *Bezdonny prood,* the Bottomless Pond. It's fed by a nearby spring. The birch grove serves as the backdrop. Sunny, dragonflies, cattails, the river below. It's just beautiful. Serene. I mean, in a setting like that, how can you scare someone with silly stories?"

"But Valya managed?" Chris asked.

"She didn't even try. She brought a spool of fishing line with her, with a big bolt tied at the end, and dropped it into the pond. Two, maybe three hundred feet of the line, all went in. Guess who got excited?"

"Peter?"

"Of course. He prowled the banks, tossed twigs into the water looking for the underground flow, and asked Valya where he could get a bucket of dye. He wants to dump it in and see where it will show up in the river."

"I can see our boy," Chris said.

"Meanwhile, Jessie's color returned and she asked what made the pond bottomless. Valya earnestly explained how a portal into a different dimension was open right at that moment. 'See that spot of light?' The power of suggestion—the water was green and murky, but I swear I could see a pale circle."

"I'm not worried about you."

"Thanks. Valya let them play for ten minutes. Then she asked Luke, 'How about lunch?'"

"And Luke was hers." Snapping his fingers, Chris looked at the house, then at Debra. "What's in all this for you?"

"I watched."

"How Valya manipulated your friends?"

"Exactly what they're paying her for. Chris, this is so uncomplicated. Valya gives us what we want, which is supernatural for Jessie, mystery for Peter, yummy chow for Luke, and amusing company for me. She tagged you precisely. You can't resist taking on responsibility. If you're looking for a nutcase, go to Jessie, but Valya is the smartest gal I've ever met. This recipe book? It wasn't hard to find, was it?"

"I guess not," Chris said.

"Because it was meant to be discovered. Probably not by you but by Jessie. Why else would Valya dare her to go upstairs this morning?"

Chris shrugged.

"By the way, how did you get inside?" Debra asked. "The gate and the house were locked when we came back."

"Climbed over the fence and used my window to get in."

"If you didn't storm off on your bicycle, you'd know, like the rest of us, where Valya keeps her spare keys for the gate and the front door. I'll show you, just to prove there's no international conspiracy to keep us out." Debra paused before going in for the kill. "Let me ask you something else. Remember when you were married?"

"Yes?"

"How every instance when you had a crisis you ran to your sister instead of talking to your wife?"

"Debra!"

"You have a problem with Valya. Laurie is not here, so you run to me." Debra pushed the notebook into her cousin's hands. "No more of this nonsense. The villain's not the guide, but the man who hurt her, searched her home, and just insulted her. You have issues with what Valya does? She's the one to talk to."

"I can't believe you threw my marriage at me."

"I threw your divorce at you. Chris, listen to me. Luke, Peter, and Jessie are on a bike ride. Valya's baking. Go and ask her every question you have, and don't come back until you've sorted things out."

CHAPTER THIRTY-EIGHT

The afternoon shade wrapped around the front veranda. With Chris in Debra's capable hands, I had a moment to myself. My portable electric oven, the size of a small microwave, was heated up and ready for another batch of sweet treats. Cooking soothed me. I sprinkled nuts, rolled and cut the dough, enjoyed the aroma of cinnamon.

That's good, that's good. Keep your empty smile on and maybe the tears won't come.

I vigorously kneaded the cookie dough, as if the action would mend the stinging hollow in my stomach. Chris had ripped my emotions out, torn them to pieces, and scattered the shreds all over the garden where they lay twitching like lizards' lost tails.

A shadow moved past the window. The man who took me for a paradigm of evil walked in. Chris sat in a chair and tossed a notebook across the table, barely missing a cup of sugar. Tension erupted through his aura like solar flares.

My parents thought that after Dimitry's death I'd never dare to visit the second floor. Who would? But for once, their one-dimensional logic worked for me. As soon as the floorboards soaked in Dimitry's blood had been removed, I had a perfect place to hide my diary.

Until I invited a bunch of ignorant strangers under my roof...Bravo, Mr. Waller. How many moral barriers have you overstepped when you searched my house and stole my records?

Nails rusted. My goosebumps gamely perked up. Since Chris had uttered the troubling words, I couldn't shake off the picture of the missed blood spatter.

I pushed the journal around with my fingernail. "You found it! Andrey, my neighbor's son, has nightmares. We invent magical recipes, remedies to fend off his monsters."

Chris's shock hit me so strongly that I stepped back to catch my balance. "You mean you two are just playing a game?"

Then came the flood of his relief, contentment akin to the pleasure of walking in a bakery on a crispy winter morning.

"More like drawing our own comics," I said. "Thanks for bringing it over. Andrey would be upset if I misplaced his recipes. Where did we lose it?"

Chris turned sideways toward the table and crossed his legs. "It was…just lying there."

"Glad you picked it up." I began to grease a cookie sheet with butter.

The mere presence of this man pacified my emotional mayhem. Chris wasn't asking me any questions, as if simply sitting across the table and watching me roll cookies would give him peace of mind. I had the strangest feeling that he *wanted* to like me.

"How can I reinforce your tentative hope that nothing out-of-the-ordinary goes on under my roof?" I asked.

His eyebrow rose slightly. "What's your training? Acting, psychology? Circus?"

"Research. A postgraduate student. My field is biology. I lead an ordinary life in Moscow, but let's not talk about it. You might accidentally mention something to your students."

"So what?"

"So that mundane image will compromise the character I strive to create for them." I leaned across the table and turned toward him *Mukah* and *Sahar* inscriptions written on two yellow plastic jars. "Which one is flour, and which one is sugar?"

"Do you want me to open the containers?"

"No. You don't understand Russian, do you?"

"I'd tell you if I did," he said.

"Would you tell me if Debra read Cyrillic?" I asked.

"And get myself in trouble?"

I liked how humor changed his eyes. "When I was making pancakes, I asked Debra to bring me sugar. She picked the right jar, and she didn't look inside."

"I'll tell her she can stop pretending."

"Thank you. Anything else I can clarify for you?"

Chris gazed in the direction of the garden for a few moments. He straightened in his chair, losing his casual pose, and licked his bottom lip. "If I promise to keep it between us, will you answer one question for me?"

He most certainly meant, *will you answer it honestly?*

And I most likely couldn't and wouldn't.

I put down the rolling pin, wiped my hands, unplugged the oven, and took a seat. "I'll try."

"About last night. What did you put in my coffee?"

"Do you prefer a different brand?"

Chris shook his head, looking at me as if I were a troubled teenager without prospects of rehabilitation. "Valya, please." He pointed at the dried flower bunches hanging from the ceiling. "Was it your herbal stuff?"

"You're looking for an excuse because you hurt me," I said in a flash of insight.

"Not for an excuse." His voice was quiet, but his determination came through. "For an explanation."

I reached up, broke off a twig, and handed it to Chris. "Rub it between your fingers and tell me what you smell."

He touched a brittle leaf and pulled back. "Whew. Stinks like some seasoning I can't stand. Cloves? Cardamom?"

"You're allergic to a species of *Primula*," I said. "No wonder you got so agitated last night. I'm sorry. I just wanted you to get some sleep."

His need to believe in his innocence was so great that Chris didn't question my explanation. He simply nodded. I waited for his next inquiry into my shady deeds, but rigid in his chair, he wouldn't look at me. He wouldn't smile. He wouldn't speak. Just as I thought my frosty professor was thawing out, another balloon of doubt began to swell between us.

"Something still bothers you," I said in my push for a truce.

"The girls returned scared out of their minds after supposedly seeing your water possum." Chris pinched off a bit of the cookie dough, rolled it between his thumb and index finger, and smelled it. He wiped his fingers with a napkin. "You had given them some mild hallucinogen *before* you took the gang to the dam."

It's all real, I wanted to yell. *Vishenky is real. The monsters are real. I'm real.*

I masked my frustration with a coy smile. "A slice of a mushroom in the soup you had for dinner." *If I can't win your good graces, I'll boost the thrill, fuel your worries.*

His grip tightened on the table's edge. "You'll pull the same thing tonight."

How far could I push him? "I already did," I said. "The salad dressing everybody liked so much at lunch?"

"You ate it, too."

I glanced at the clock. "This reminds me. Time for my antidote. But I'll share it with you. Wait here."

I went to the kitchen, rummaged through one of our overstuffed refrigerators, and returned with a chilled decanter. The liquid the color of muddy milk looked unappetizing. I swirled the concoction and filled a couple of tumblers.

"If you don't mind the taste," I said, offering one to Chris.

"You first," he said.

I took a sip. Bitterness pinched my mouth. "I was going to trick Luke into drinking this stuff. He's lucky you decided to do this."

"Why Luke?"

"Peter would be much harder to convince, and I never imagined you'd be willing to participate."

Chris set his untouched drink on the table. "Participate in what? This is supposed to be the antidote."

"But that's not what I'd tell Luke. I'd say I need two volunteers, male and female. We'll see a herd of supernatural animals. If we drink the mixture, our skins will acquire a distinctive scent, the same as the creatures'. And because we also smell human, they will accept everyone in our group as their kind."

"Who writes your scripts?" Chris asked.

I braved another quick sip. "I'm glad my backup will be you. Luke has a tendency to panic."

"Are you worried someone will freak out, like what happened yesterday, because you keep drugging us? Is that why you need another clear-headed person?"

I saluted his deduction with my cocktail.

"God...I can't let you do this. Give the antidote to everyone."

"I used up the last ingredients." I finished the beverage and wiped my lips. "Sorry, Chris. For my business, a lot is on the line."

"Are you insane?"

"Did anyone get sick last night? Your group is not my first. I do what I do. Would you like to report me to the authorities? Oops. No one will believe you." I pushed the second tumbler toward him. "Drink it. Your mind will stay clear and you'll see what's really going on. Take pictures, gather proof my business is dangerous."

"You are...." Chris held my stare, his green eyes bright with the scorching fury.

Green eyes, green eyes, green eyes, my brain sang. Then a giant piece of the puzzle fell into place like a stone trapdoor sealing a pharaoh's tomb.

Blood ties, not a student-professor fling, connected him to Debra.

"Drink," I said, "if you want to learn how my shows are put together."

Chris snatched the tumbler from the table and swallowed its contents hurriedly, as if afraid to change his mind.

"What the hell was it?" he mumbled, covering his mouth.

"Sea-buckthorn berries, pond-lily petals. Milk-based, with an extract from the last year's acorns."

His eyes widened. Chris grabbed my journal. He stopped on the first page, where a hideous cross between a bird and an elephant glared with a single eyeball bulging in the wrinkles under its scaly trunk.

Chris poked his finger into the picture. "Debra translated this recipe. These are your nightmares."

CHAPTER THIRTY-NINE

"Finally," I said.

"'Finally' what? I've finally proved that you're a certified nutcase?" Chris asked.

"You've finally arrived to the point where your accusations can't get any more ridiculous. Yesterday, Debra didn't eat the soup and Peter warned me he's allergic to mushrooms. I'd never harm my visitors."

"Yeah, you're a real sweetheart, aren't you?"

I didn't mind his rage, as long as my conduct and not the sights of Moscow remained the center of his attention. "If I drugged and poisoned my guests, would I confess?"

Chris frowned. I watched him trying to rewind our conversation, to remember where the things I had told him had gotten spooky.

"If I didn't need the antidote, then what on Earth have you made me drink?" he asked.

I plugged in my little oven. "Four squirts of some condiment, whatever I grabbed in a hurry from the fridge, mixed with water. Could be my dad's seafood sauce."

The spots just below his cheekbones were beet-red. "What happened last night at the dam?" he asked.

"Everyone in your group wants to know, but I have no reason to give up my professional secrets." I picked up and kneaded a chunk of dough to show Chris the entertainment hour was over.

"Here's the reason: I have no interest in playing your stupid game."

"You're not much fun to play with."

"And you're a pathological liar, maybe even a criminal."

"It's all in your head," I said.

"Or simply a mediocrity with a load of ego."

Blood heated my face. I threw the dough back into the bowl. "That's interesting. You're not just angry. You're heartbroken I'm such a disappointment."

"Bullshit."

"No, I know what I'm getting. You're easy to read."

"Ah, so now you're a mind reader. Lie away."

"Not the mind. I perceive and evaluate the energy of emotions. You have something terrible buried in the vaults of your consciousness. Painful, raw, so unbearable you don't dare to exhume it. Even if that would help you heal."

His eyes glistened as if his indignation drove him to the verge of tears. "Phony. Fake. Fraud."

"Chris, that's enough. You know I'm right."

"You should be committed."

My composure imploded. I tossed a fistful of flour on the thick wooden cutting board and divided the coated surface in half with a straight horizontal line. I drew another line over the first. This one flowed slightly up and down.

"An average existence. Good and bad stuff, more or less evened out." I added a sharp "V" on the bottom half of the board. "You weren't so lucky."

I had never had such a heavy gaze land on my face. I boldly continued. "You cling to normality, desperately trying to avoid any fluctuations, even good ones, because you fear something horrible might happen again."

In the air around Chris, flickers of his emotions began to fade like sparks of a dying campfire. His face became a gray, expressionless mask. He was shutting me out.

What had I done?

"Chris."

"We have nothing to talk about."

"Chris." I waited for him to look at me. "You can go to Gorky Park and stare at Moskva River until you drown in your melancholy. Or you can stay here and let me jolt you out of your routine."

"How long did it take you to get Debra to gossip?"

"I tried, but she protects you. And there's a degree of familiarity between you two, which I misread at first. I don't see much of a family resemblance, except for your green eyes. Is Debra your favorite niece?"

"Why don't you drop all this bogus insightfulness?"

"Am I right? Are you related?"

"You really don't know?"

I shook my head.

"She's my cousin."

"On whose side?" I asked.

"Deb is the daughter of my mother's brother, not that it matters."

Chris wasn't Gretishnikoff.

He got up. "Your company is like high altitude. I need to get to a safer elevation."

"I imagine you've never thought less of any other woman in your life," I said. "But as long as your students—"

"You're not a woman in my life."

He walked out and slammed the door, then strode down the path and off the property.

I wiped away a hot tear. "I'm not, but if I wanted, I could fix that little glitch by midnight," I told the empty veranda.

CHAPTER FORTY

Chris closed the gate. Ignoring him, a huge goat planted his front legs on the fence and munched on the maple branches. Teenagers played volleyball in the meadow a few houses down the road, their excited shrieks and the *tonks* of their punches generating an atmosphere of happy commotion.

The world sent out carefree vibes. Behind him, within the brick walls, a young woman was mired in a disturbing maze of fantasies and lies.

He walked to the two wooden platforms of different height, jutting out over the water. Each household had at least one, the river serving many domestic needs. Chris sat on a step. The sunrays broke through the ragged edge of a slow-moving downy cloud and touched the algae-covered rocks on the bottom. Mosquito-looking insects merrily skimmed the surface. A shiny black bug frolicked among them, smooth and fluid like a drop of mercury.

Chris was being watched.

An elderly man in a faded brown t-shirt, camouflage pants, and a fishing hat stood among the willow trunks on the opposite bank. His face consisted mostly of the bushy beard and eyebrows, with a thin hooked nose poking out in between. Chris raised his hand in a greeting. Seeing that he was spotted, the man turned around and walked unhurriedly uphill, toward the cemetery, a shotgun slung over his shoulder.

What do they hunt here? Chris wondered.

A female turkey, gray and slim, sauntered within his reach, her mouth open. Domesticated, she couldn't be the hunter's game. The bird regarded Chris with her round eye, expecting handouts.

He spread his arms. "I don't have anything for you."

Cuoh, cuoh, cuoh, she scolded and took off after a white butterfly.

Ripples scurried over the water, silvery like flickers of ice in the streetlights after frozen rain. An idyllic afternoon, if only the silt of memories that Valya had managed to stir in him would ever settle. What on Earth would compel his thoughtful, compassionate Debra to share his past with a stranger?

Chris had been eighteen when frozen rain on Christmas Eve caused a pileup on I-95. Home from college for the holidays, he had been in the backyard, taking pictures of the ice-glazed bamboo arching in whimsical formations over frozen azaleas. Chris didn't know that his parents' bodies had just been extricated from a pile of contorted metal.

To cope with the loss, Laurie, his twenty-four-year-old sister, had signed up for an appointment with a psychiatrist. Instead of becoming his patient, she had become his wife. The wedding had taken place less than three months after the crash. Chris tried not to judge his sister for her haste.

He kept away from his parents' empty house during the spring break, but when summer loomed, he realized he couldn't travel forever. Aunt Rita, Debra's mom, had opened her home for him for as long as he wanted to stay.

During the weeks when Chris accepted her much-appreciated hospitality, he received the full cushion of Aunt Rita's motherly love. Chris didn't mind. He needed Aunt Rita's "Where's your jacket?" and "Be home by nine." He needed her "Because I said so" and "Eat your vegetables." He needed her stable routine to push him past the shattered normality of his former life.

She executed the estate sale of his old home, so Chris and Laurie never had to go through their parents' belongings. She welcomed Chris's wife, Sheryl, into the family. Then she supported him through his divorce. She trusted Chris to take her treasure, Debra, to a foreign country.

The trust he was failing, but he couldn't grab Debra, run, and leave the rest of the group at Valya's mercy.

The turkey brought over a crumbled piece of cellophane, dropped it in the grass, and gave it a few pecks. Then she looked up. Chris turned. The woman who managed to create hype and mystery and a false sense of adventure was walking toward them.

"Hey, give it to me," Valya said to the bird. "Look what I brought you." She tossed a few bread crusts away from the path. As the turkey charged after the treat, Valya picked up the abandoned food wrapping and stuffed it into her pocket.

"Chris, dinner is ready."

"I'm not hungry."

"Come inside and take your poison like a man."

Her taunting raised him to his feet. "You're ignorant, reckless…."

He stopped.

Little imps of amusement danced in Valya's intelligent eyes, smashing the dry ice of his anger. "I told Peter I use hypnosis."

"And he believed you?"

"He seemed immensely in awe of my talents. Looks like your mentoring skills cede to my influence over your pupils."

"I guess they find evil intriguing," Chris said.

"What will you do about it, Mr. Waller? It's your move."

"What can I do? The game is rigged."

"Don't you wish we were on the same team?"

"Who else is on yours? Jack the Ripper? Vlad the Impaler? Lucifer?" Chris walked past her.

In the middle of the muted dinner, a boy of nine or ten ran past the windows and burst through the door. He squeezed Valya in an affectionate embrace, which she didn't return. He whispered into her ear then pulled from his pocket a macramé piece woven out of rough yarn.

The boy placed the ornament on Valya's naked upper arm and tied the strings. White curly tips of what appeared to be birch bark worked into the yarn protruded throughout in a geometrical pattern.

Grimacing, Valya wiggled her shoulder and rubbed the armlet as if the papery strands tickled her skin.

"Pretty," Jessie said. "Can I have one?"

Valya's quiet translation to Andrey lasted longer than Jessie's question required. The kid froze like a startled squirrel. His gray eyes darted from face to face.

"Andrey?" Valya called.

The boy walked along the table, moving in a jerky manner of an inquisitive rodent. He pointed his finger at Chris.

"*Ti uveren?*" Valya asked.

Andrey treated her to another round of whispering and ran out the door. Valya looked like he had asked her to drown a bunny.

"Is something wrong?" Jessie asked.

Her eyebrows drawn together in furious thinking, Valya exhaled sharply and straightened in her chair. "Last night, just before we came back from the dam, Andrey saw his grandmother leaving my property. Chris, did you see her?"

"That's right, you did have a visitor," Jessie reminded. "An old woman with violet eyes?"

Who had managed to terrify him just by standing on the front step. Chris felt his face redden. "So what? She's a part of Valya's circus. Do we have to discuss this?"

Valya dipped her head sideways, as if imploring him to take her concerns seriously. "Did she…do anything strange? Did she give you something?"

"Her ATM pin number. Just leave me alone, both of you, okay?"

CHAPTER FORTY-ONE

If only this were a conventional tour with a group of rational people. Chris gazed out over the landscape. Majestic in their serenity, olive-green swells glided over the rye fields, slowly turning golden under the brush of the approaching sunset. Above his head, a single pink contrail cut through the clear sky. The sun slid behind a strip of low clouds, and a fan of rays sprouted above the horizon.

So beautiful. So pastoral. So normal.

"If I could paint, I'd never leave this place," Debra said.

Several mature oaks grew on both slopes of the ravine. Peter studied the valley below. "This must be the bed of a prehistoric river. I want to see what else is out there."

Luke chased Jessie down the incline, to the pond overgrown with cattails. When she tried to snatch one of the chocolate-brown heads, the squishy ground swallowed her foot to Luke's wild delight. The rescue operation involved lots of laughter and poking Jessie with a gnarly limb that kept breaking whenever she seized its brittle branches.

"She'll lose her shoe," Debra said.

"Ten more minutes and the shoe will be the least of Jessie's problems," Valya said. "C'mon, find some sticks for her to step on."

Clumps of shrubbery marked the stream that fed the pond. The water cut a three-foot-deep channel meandering through the valley floor. The banks felt spongy. Peter, Debra, and the guide attacked a bush, harvesting the branches. Chris kept his hands clean.

Once Jessie and her shoe were extracted from the marsh, Valya rushed her to the stream to clean up.

"Wait." Jessie pulled her muddy wrist from the guide's hand. "Hey, guys, look at this."

The candles of mauve flowers rose in clusters over the mottled leaves.

"A swamp violet," Valya said. "Please, hurry."

"An orchid." Kneeling, Jessie lovingly rubbed a leaf between her fingers. "*Dactylorhiza.*"

"Ladies, watch your language," Luke advised. "Hey, look, nature's crawling all over you!" He plucked a green caterpillar from Debra's hair.

"We must get out of the valley," Valya insisted.

Chris hiked uphill, leaving the guide to plead with the students. He picked a spot to sit under the biggest oak, the slope dry, the bark coarse against his back, and the warm breeze pleasant on his face. Benign to the naked eye, the copper-colored sun was sinking into the fields. The grasshoppers chirped. The fragrance of the blooming meadow lush around the water floated in the clean air.

Valya herded the group toward his haven.

"If we climb up the tree," Peter said, "we'll have a better view."

"Go for it," Valya said. "Chris, you stay where you are."

He didn't acknowledge her instruction.

"When does the show start?" Luke asked.

"It has started," Valya said. "The portal's open. You just can't see anything yet."

A light wind rippled the pond's jade-colored surface and made the cattails move, creating the illusion of silhouettes prowling through the shallows. Valya sat next to Chris between the oak roots, hugged her knees, and pointed to the pond. He saw nothing different, only the same play of shadows.

Then he held his breath. In the bright, ordinary summer twilight, the shifting dark forms were morphing into creatures. Dozens of them moved among cattails, crushing the clumps of vegetation and snatching something out of the water. Emu-like legs carried the egg-shaped upright bodies, headless and covered with elephant-gray skin. Meaty trunks, wormy appendages outfitted with sucking tips, protruded from the bald scalps.

"Have a lot of these in Virginia?" Valya inquired politely.

Chris exhaled. Massaging his temples, he squeezed his eyes shut, then opened them. The yellow color of Valya's sweater, a wisp of her hair fluttering in the breeze, her amused face—every little detail looked vibrant, life-like. Chris grabbed a handful of dirt. The pieces of debris poked his palm. The pain felt real. The creatures didn't vanish.

"You drugged me," he said. "I saw the pictures in your journal. My brain filled in the gaps."

"Has everyone seen my notes?" Valya asked.

"Just Debra and I, but—"

"Good." Valya leaned away from the tree trunk, trying to peek through the branches. "Jess, the Gray Sniffers, can you describe them?"

"The frigging ugly giant walking eggs? What are they eating, the tadpoles? There can't be that many fish in the pond."

"The muck is loaded with last season's acorns," Valya said. "Peter, what do you think? Is this an illusion?"

"A mass hallucination," he said. "Swamp gas explains everything."

"Aren't you filming them?"

"I hope I am, unless I'm imagining that, too. Actually, maybe we *are* looking at the physical objects." Peter's speech streamed rapid and hushed. "If you're using puppets, we'd see them as something real because of the gas. They're far enough to appear authentic later on film."

"Puppets would need puppeteers," Debra said. "How about a few village kids in costumes?"

"O-o-kay." Valya wiggled the flyswatter from under her belt and laid her silly weapon across her lap. "Let's bring them closer." She picked up a rock and sent it rolling downhill.

The feeding frenzy slowed. Instead of sucking mud, the flat tips of the trunks probed the air. One of the creatures waddled out of the water, stamped its feet, and took off running toward the oak. The four-foot-tall wrinkly blob stopped in front of Valya.

"The Gray Sniffers react to smell and motion," she said. "Talk, take pictures, but move very slowly."

Inch-long raptorial claws stuck out from brown toes, two facing forward and one backward. The movements of the trunk dancing in front of Valya's face reminded Chris of a snake exploring its surroundings. The only thing missing was a forked tongue.

Chris caught himself feeling around for a stick. *Get a grip. You're delirious because she poisoned you.*

"This is what the potion was for," Valya said, calmly letting the thing become acquainted with her. "I smell of acorns and I smell human. The Sniffer will recognize all of us as a pack."

"Do you know much about the drug you're using on us?" Chris asked. "Any side effects?"

"Yes. Everlasting bewilderment."

He curbed a string of angry promises—to go to the police, to get the madwoman endangering human lives detained.

The phantasmagoria continued to unfold, the details astonishing. Valya passed the creature's inspection. Its trunk stretched and wound around the lowest oak branch. The Sniffer pulled itself up.

"This thing is horrid," Luke whispered through the branches.

"Sit still," Valya said. "They will start fading soon."

Another creature had separated from the herd and sprinted to the oak. It stopped a few yards away. The Sniffer bent the top of its plump elliptical body right and left, as if deciding who was more interesting, Chris or Valya.

It chose Chris. The thing lumbered toward him sideways, sticking one leg forward and dragging the other in a comical fashion of a timid cartoon character. Chris shrank back, pressing hard against the unyielding oak. The muck-covered tip of the trunk appeared in front of his face.

"Don't push it away," Valya warned.

With no place to retreat, Chris shut his eyes. Even without the visual stimuli, his brain continued to fool him. He heard the snorts of the single nostril, felt its soft puffs on his forehead, and smelled the odors of the pond's silt and the freshly chopped vegetation.

Valya gasped.

Suppressing his reflex to shove the creature, Chris opened his eyes. A single unblinking orb peered at him from under the raised trunk.

"Attack mode," Valya muttered. Her fingers locked around the handle of her flyswatter.

The Sniffer shifted its weight and raised its right foot, positioning the claws in front of Chris's face.

"Chris, don't move." Valya slowly rose up off the ground.

Instead, Chris leapt to his feet. Debra screamed. Valya rammed the aggressor.

The moaning lump of the Sniffer tumbled down the slope and bumped into another creature. The offender and his victim jumped back and froze in the position for a strike. The rest of the herd circled the contenders, cheering them like a disharmonious band of oboes.

Valya examined her arm. The sleeve was sliced above her elbow, exactly where the neighbor's kid had attached the macramé ornament. "Good, no blood. The Sniffers can be so fast." She ripped off the remains of the armlet. "I wonder what happened. They don't attack unless provoked."

Suddenly too lightheaded to stand or talk or think, Chris slid back into his seat between the oak roots. His heart thundered like a speeding locomotive. Barely perceiving his surroundings, he focused on breathing, but even that uncomplicated act was depleting his remaining strength.

Valya knelt and pressed the backside of her fingers to his neck. "If you think all of this is an illusion, why are you so frightened?" she asked.

"Because I can't shake it off. You locked us in a cage and it's sinking."

The circles of her pupils expanded, swallowing her irises like black sinkholes. "I *should* have drugged you. You're not processing what you're seeing, and I can't help you." She dropped her hand. "Can you get up? I'll get you out of here."

Chris nodded at the oak's canopy. "You know damn well I won't leave them."

Valya responded with a solemn nod. She moved a few yards up the slope, as if her disappearance from his field of vision would diffuse his anger.

Night was taking over the sky, forcing the creatures to return to their shadowy forms. The friendlier Gray Sniffer climbed down the oak trunk. The two fighters at the pond hopped and trumpeted their threats but never resorted to an actual attack. Soon Chris couldn't tell if the bouncing shadows were the creatures or if the breeze tickled the cattails.

He heard mumbling in the branches, voices interrupting each other, growing louder.

"I hit 'play' and I still see them." Debra—the cool, levelheaded Debra—sounded panic-stricken. "How could the camera record the same thing?"

"I don't know," Peter said. "I *don't know.*"

"What if something is poisoning the local wells?" Luke asked. "Bacteria? Dissolved gases? Dead rats?"

"The whole village would be delirious," Peter said. "It wouldn't get past the authorities."

"Guys, this is not your fired-up imagination," Jessie said.

"Never was," Valya echoed.

CHAPTER FORTY-TWO

Impartial witnesses of the devious spectacle, the displays of both cameras glowed faintly, their battery indicators flashing on "low." Chris had done his share of pushing the buttons. By now, the shocking truth—what Valya had done to them precisely—saturated his mind.

He and his students stood on the edge of a rye field. Their reasonable explanations sounded pathetic and the alternative ideas were exhausted. The facts just seemed too wild, too quirky, too much. Valya sat a few yards away, the black void of the ravine formidable at her feet. Luke's flashlight brushed her back as if the boy was afraid something would pull her down into the lightless chasm; or maybe he was checking to see if she would turn into a specter forlorn in the starry vastness of the Russian night.

Chris experienced a strange detachment. His common sense fought to hold onto reality, but something about the young woman sitting boldly before the eerie dark abyss like a mythical maiden with a giant ogre sleeping at her feet was affecting him deeply in his core, waking up a peculiar emotion, a sentiment he had trouble naming. Half-premonition, half-certainty.

Nostalgia? Chris sensed his life could never be the same.

He felt no panic, no real fear. Mostly numbness. And deep down, a dull desire to murder the woman who had ruined his world.

"What do we do now?" Luke asked.

"Talk to the gatekeeper," Jessie said. "Are you ready to enter the maze?"

* * *

My guests' reality had finally caught on fire, and I'd feed the flame until their concept of the universe burned to ashes. A new world awaited them. Welcome to my kingdom, dear friends.

"Valya," Jessie called.

I waved for them to join me.

Their footsteps halted behind my back. No one broke the silence.

"Well, sit." I waved my hand over the ravine. "The stage is empty, but the night is beautiful. Enjoy it."

"Go ahead," Jessie said, as if encouraging her companions to touch a pet cougar. "It's okay."

Chris chose a spot to my right. For an instant, our shoulders touched. I froze, imagining what it would be like to snuggle against his chest, to have his arms around me. For once to feel protected, sheltered, cocooned in someone else's courage and insight. I was so sick of marinating in my aloneness.

Futile hopes. Separated from Chris by only inches of darkness, I couldn't avoid perceiving his unequivocal emotions toward me. At this moment, an iceberg would be cuddlier than Chris. His world had flipped, and I had pulled the lever.

"The ugly structure past the tool shed in my backyard," I began without a preamble, "is an ancient cellar. Gets flooded every spring when the fields thaw. When I was little, my parents told me it was full of monsters, but one day I broke the lock. A few things on the shelves had survived the water damage, a sealed wooden box among them. It stored a manuscript, handwritten in the pre-Revolutionary Russian and filled with drawings. The writing didn't make sense because the author scrambled the words. The plants in the pictures were local. The animals looked like somebody's nightmares.

"I was fascinated with the archaic alphabet. I read a page, and in a few hours, I suddenly knew the meaning. The entry described a vine growing by the old ford, its harvest time, and how to use it. Debra might have read that recipe in my notebook, the one Chris found. Let's say Luke's vindictive ex-girlfriend added its powdered form to *rassolnik*, soup with pickles, and Luke ate it. He'd see that girl every time he looked in a mirror. Only for two seconds, but for the rest of his life."

"God," Debra said. "That's dreadful."

"When you're ten, it's magic," I said. "Accepting the supernatural is easier for a child. I didn't have to come to terms with the new reality, like you do tonight. It was my world from the beginning."

"When Deb mumbled 'dreadful,' she meant the soup with pickles," Luke clarified.

Good boy. His teeth chattered, but at least he put up a struggle trying to tune in to the situation. He didn't generate any antipathy toward me as Chris did.

"I want to know how you managed to keep something this big from the rest of the world," Peter said.

He and Luke had chosen to sit in front of us, our valiant first line of defense. The relentless beams of their flashlights scanned the slopes. I leaned forward and touched the guys' shoulders. "Turn off your lights. You'll see more."

They obeyed. The blue velvet of the night fell around us. The rising moon produced weak shadows. I squinted as I studied the bottom of the ravine. Two fluorescent pools sprawled not far from the black crater of the pond. Portals. That's where I needed to take Debra.

"You probably want to shout about your discovery from the top of the Empire State Building," I said. "I promise you, before long Vishenky will change your mind."

"But h-how…how many tours have you hosted?" Chris asked.

I realized he was trembling. The evening air wrapped us in its calming blanket, fresh but not that cold. It was the shock that sent shakes through Chris's body. To him, life was what he read on the front page of a newspaper. Older than the rest of us and closed to anything deviant by his nature, he barely held onto the safety line of his common sense. I wished I could lessen the blow, but his terror was too intense for me to overrun it.

"You're a member of a very exclusive club," I said.

"Care to explain what's so special about us?" Jessie hovered somewhere behind me, out of my paranormal reach. She spat the words as if they were bad grapes.

I clasped my icy hands and blew a breath on them. The rust of disappointment corroded my confidence. Why had I imagined that the revelation of another universe would instantly make these people my best friends?

"I reached the emotional limit of my isolation," I said. "I searched for someone who would offer an opinion but have no means to impinge on Vishenky's existence. Your group seemed smart, inquisitive, and daring."

"You can't convince me you're the only one here who knows about the manifestations," Peter said. "The whole village must be in on it. Surprising that the authorities never caught up with the occurrences."

"It's not as obvious as you think," I said. "With our abundance of folktales and superstitions, would you take the accounts of sightings seriously?"

"What about your family?" Chris asked.

"Clueless," I said. "If you were a parent and your ten-year-old persistently described to you the Gray Sniffers, what would be your reaction?"

"They ignored you." Some pity nibbled at Chris's coldness but not enough to change his feelings about me.

My parents had done something worse. They had allowed Anatoly, my mother's cold-blooded twin-brother, to medicate me. That summer Prascovia had taken me under her wing. Her mentoring had nothing to do with the supernatural occurrences. She had taught me how to deceive my uncle and not to swallow the psychotropic pills.

"Technically," Peter said, "the manuscript was in your family's possession. Who wrote it? How did it end up in the cellar?"

A string of lights dotted the skyline, a long-distance passenger train crawling along the railroad embankment, so far away that I couldn't hear its clanking. All of a sudden, I wanted to be on board—an anonymous passenger granted a short but absolute reprieve from all the duties and ado.

"Who cares how I kept Vishenky a secret or who wrote the manuscript?" I asked. "You haven't asked me a single meaningful question. You're stuck on the human aspect and avoiding the subject of the phenomenon itself. I'll take you home. You need time to process what you saw."

As I leaned forward intending to get up, Jessie's strong hands landed on my shoulders and pushed me down. "Who says you can leave?" Her already-low voice dropped to the rumble of a volcano before an eruption. "We're discussing the human aspect because you're an arrogant, egotistic, selfish lunatic. Everyone's beneath you. You see yourself as a queen who grants her subjects an access to her whimsical gardens. I see you as a sociopath experimenting on your captives for your own amusement. You don't care if you ruin lives."

I exhaled, struggling to hold back the choking emotions. She couldn't be possibly talking about Dimitry's death, but that's where her wrath pushed my mind. Wrapped in the steel-wool shroud of my darkest memories, I couldn't argue with her, or ask her why she was so angry, or defend myself.

"Jess, not now." Peter looked back, trying to see her in the dark.

"Why not?" Jessie asked. "You know better than anyone what happens here." She bent over me, her abhorrence pulsing like contractions of a feeding snake. "Let me tell you something. We're not your pawns. We won't follow your orders."

Pitted against her charge, the sea of Debra's compassion toward me evaporated down to a puny puddle.

Self-pity stung like alcohol splashed on a wound. I'd been through this anguish after Dimitry's death, when the people whose empathy I craved had cast me off. I brushed away a worthless tear that wandered down my cheek and cleared my throat. "You think you know enough about me to defy me?"

"Did you crawl out of a swamp and take on a human form?" Jessie asked.

My chest stiffened. I wrapped my arms around my body and squeezed tightly, keeping my lungs deflated and the sobs shut in my throat. Then something unexpected happened between my five opponents and me. Our inflamed emotions collided, merged into a spinning sphere inside me. Fueled by my despair and their terror, shock, aversion, it burst. A dying star became a supernova.

I gasped. The cooling air filled my lungs. A euphoric sensation of being unstoppable sent an electrical charge through my skin. I spread my imaginary wings. Barriers and ethics of the human species no longer mattered. I'd break into Debra's psyche. Her unconditional friendship, her loyalty, an everlasting bond between us—I'd elicit it all. I got that kind of power.

Chris.

The thought of him hit me like a bear trap.

Some painful drama in his past affected his existence. If I superimposed my emotional aura on his, my energy would fuse the wound, instigate his healing—not to mention that the entity issue would be resolved for the duration of his stay in Vishenky.

My nails dug into my palms. I didn't have the power to handle two people.

Chris or Debra?

Debra or Chris?

My internal timer had already started the countdown of the minutes at my disposal.

Oh, hell.

CHAPTER FORTY-THREE

"What are you punishing me for, Jessie?" I asked. "For what you'd like to be but can't?"

"Don't pretend you understand me."

"No, really. Imagine you had my powers. What would you do? Talk to the dead? Predict the future? Use telepathy to communicate with your hamster?"

Debra laughed softly.

"What powers?" Jessie asked. "You showed us a natural phenomenon."

"Unnatural," Luke corrected her.

"Right," Jessie said. "So, you've learned the locations of the occurrences. It doesn't make *you* anything special."

"You want a little demonstration?" I asked.

"Can you turn into a werewolf?"

"Not easy, but since you asked…." I switched my pose to sit on my knees, to advance my body's stability. "Ready?"

She huffed. "Bite me."

I closed my eyes. The sounds of the night trickled into my ears. A dog barked somewhere in the village. A single *ploomp* disturbed the pond when a frog jumped into the water.

I am a nerve. A thought. An instinct.

I slowly exhaled, willing my human body to shrink the boundaries that restrained my spirit.

I want to roam through time and matter.

The energy within me swirled, expanded like a storm cloud.

I morph. I mimic. I blend in.

The lightning-spitting cyclone filled my chest. My skin began to tingle as if electrical sparks bombarded my skin. I hoped I hadn't turned into a mast wrapped in St. Elmo's fires.

A rustle of wings intensified above my head. Nocturnal hunters, tiny bats, patrolled the air. Crunching and ripping noises came from the ground. A cricket chewed on a blade of grass, and a worm pulled a dry leaf into its hole. I reached the needed level of immersion.

My voice silk and satin and lace, I spoke about the eternal sky above our heads and the sighing fields of rye. I spoke about the pond, a mischievous life form scheming against its human targets under the thick blanket of duckweed. I spoke about us absorbing the night with our eyes and hearts, and being absorbed into its misty depths and whispers; about the fairyland of Vishenky, the place where my guests might never be again; about a fleeting treasure of time when we shared this incredible adventure.

I stopped to catch my breath.

Their trances profound albeit short-term, my subjects sat slumped around me, engrossed in a fabulous fantasy—traveling in time, fighting dragons, solving cosmic mysteries—whatever these kids' minds came up with, in the most vivid and heroic scenario.

Enjoy your enchanted forests.

"Chris, give me your hand," I said.

I used my softest tone, a whisper of a tiny waterfall, a promise of a rainbow, but his body jerked as if I poked him.

"Why?" he asked.

I read him clearly. With every protective shield and filter in his psyche demolished, he couldn't take another bit of strangeness. Whether his present company was an ordinary woman, a sorceress, or a swamp thing, getting far, far, far away from me was his greatest urge.

Not that I would let him. "What's the capital of Portugal?" I asked.

As his attention turned to the unexpected question, my fingers closed on his left hand and pinned it against the ground. Focused more intensely than a sharpshooter, I imagined driving a car with broken wipers. A passing truck spattered the windshield with muddy slosh.

An array of feelings rushed through my system. I amplified confusion and helplessness and propelled them like two poisoned darts into Chris's mind.

"What are you doing?" He weakly stirred to pull away.

I pushed my fingers through his and curled them, locking his hand in mine. "Your coping mechanisms are broken. I can fix them."

"Prove that Jessie's wrong about you. Let us go." Vestiges of his will fluttered against my emotional grip like the wings of an injured moth.

"Your subconscious is an underground river. The whirlpools of unresolved sorrows will pull you into perilous depths. Allow my words to be your flare. Make my emotions your life buoy. Take what you need to survive."

Before my shut eyelids, Chris's inner aura shone steady tans and yellows, the colors of anticipation. I reduced the pressure on his hand but kept a tight contact.

"An injured puppy in a blind woman's lap," I said.

Peacock-greens and blues and violets burst in my mind, the spectrum corresponding with a man's compassion. The vivid colors blended in a fluid pattern, like oil on water with someone running a fingertip over the surface.

"A fender bender. Coffee spilled on a white carpet. Slipping on ice. A narrow escape from an approaching train." I hurriedly prompted Chris's reactions, searching for the wrong hues, but I saw nothing out of place.

I moved toward the positives. Affection, joy, fulfillment could harbor acrid smoke of regrets and bitterness.

"An old-world street café on a summer day."

I anticipated a cheery polychrome palette from someone who carried in his wallet a collection of European metro tokens. Instead, a quivering mosaic of black rhombs spilled on muddy mauve.

What happened to a proper delight with cobbled streets and delectable pastries? Where were the garnets and turquoises of a person blissfully lost in his surroundings on a marvelous afternoon? And this dreary mauve—who'd fly overseas for a bout of loneliness?

I patched the palette, treading cautiously on the unstable terrain. The lifeless rhombs siphoned my energy the way vacuum sucks the air.

"Walking into your hotel room after a long, long trip," I said to assess my progress.

Pastel-blues, soft-yellows, and eggshell-whites created a two-dimensional landscape like layers of colored sand poured between glass panes, a pattern living but barely, too muted to qualify for a heartfelt relief. Somewhere in Chris's psyche, more blackouts cast shadows on his ability to welcome life's pleasures. Knowing so little about him, I didn't know where to look, which scenario to suggest. Or was it an issue solely with his travels? Just getting on a plane could dampen a person's experience—fear of flying, motion sickness, claustrophobia.

"Booking a flight?" I asked.

Two shades of red jumped into the picture. Not fright, not panic...liberation. What did Chris run from? Why couldn't he savor his escapes?

He had to relish something in life. "An evening with good friends," I said.

Dust bunnies crawled over lavender and sage-green, a pretty combination, but it stood for sadness and a desire for solitude. Chris dragged his melancholy around as if it were his most prized possession. I threw in tangerines, azures, and rubies, my brightest blend of happiness, and watched in astonishment the colors dissipate, fade into a palest opal. *Embarrassment?* For what, for being carefree and joyful momentarily?

I had never seen such an anomaly. I knew by now I was applying superficial bandages to a third-degree burn. By morning, Chris would be back to where we had started, in his well-concealed misery.

But he was capable of being happy. I detected his contentment every time he was around Debra.

And Debra is his cousin.

"Christmas morning with your family," I nailed.

If there were colors, I didn't see them. A sword of pain cut through my torso. I gasped for air, only to hear a peep squeezed out by my constricted throat.

My battle-hardened self-control switched me to autopilot, and through the haze stifling my consciousness I held on to Chris's hand. The same reflexive shield blasted my brain with images of glaciers and foggy lakes. It took a Niagara Falls of my energy to extinguish Chris's inferno.

I could finally breathe. What happened? Which emotion had my psyche converted into a physical agony rather than allowing me to experience it?

The answer came instantly. A ball of barbed wire had lodged in my heart after Dimitry's death, twitching with every beat. *Survivor's guilt.* But I had turned to Vishenky, and its inscrutable forces had healed me. Chris, on the other hand, had never gotten over an awful loss. He wandered through the chambers of an endless dungeon crawling with silverfish of memories, a prison his conscience readily created when he failed to forgive himself. Poor sweet man. Did I have the power to find him there and bring him back?

The task would be more formidable than a bungee-cord jump to a person who in a high-speed elevator skipped a breath at a split second of free fall. If I sank deeper in the realm of his emotions, if I abandoned my own consciousness to pervade the energy that formed his essence, immersed myself in someone's spirit on such unfathomable levels, would I be able to return?

Something about Chris was pushing me to take that risk.

Using both hands as so not to break the contact between us, I moved his arm over my shoulders and pressed his palm to the side of my neck where my carotid artery quivered with my heartbeat.

"Let me in, Chris," I whispered. "Let me in."

No wonder he occupied my mind my every waking moment since we had met. Characters can clash, and so can human energies, but the one flowing from Chris's warm fingers into my bloodstream felt comforting, incredible, and craved by my body like chocolate, sleep, sex.

We seemed so close, yet he granted me no passage to his subconscious. An elusive phenomenon of soul mates, two people in perfect unison, sensing each other's thoughts—I needed that kind of intimacy to get me past his natural defenses, his instinctive resistance. The essence of his individuality had to crystallize in my psyche until he recognized himself in my interpretation of his persona.

With a close friend it would take me seconds, but in this case, I would be focusing each of my five senses on the man I barely knew. How strong was my subliminal awareness of Chris?

The students' trances wouldn't last much longer. I adjusted my shallow, nervous breathing, making each intake of air expand my lungs and last.

I'm your soul mate. I'm aligned with all your planets and tuned to all your moods. I'm closer to you than any woman you have ever loved.

First, the eyesight. To see—and think of Chris at once. To see and think....

His face. His lips.

Too nonspecific. I needed something keenly personal, over-the-top poignant. Sadness in his eyes? His boyish grin?

Nope, those were my rational ideas.

A string of snapshots flashed through my brain. Chris chatting with Debra. Riding a bike. Reading. On the front veranda, in the garden, by the river....

The last image stayed. This morning I saw him standing in the shallows, his face turned upward. A rare instance when Chris didn't dread his visit; would this be my most profound recollection of my guest?

Anyone would see that he enjoyed the sunlight and the water. What I needed was a gesture or a smile, a raise of his eyebrow that only I would understand.

Time was running out. I pulled a flask the size of a bottle they give you on an airplane from the back pocket of my jeans. Another odd but handy relic from the old cellar, the silver vessel traveled with me in case I needed to disinfect a nasty bite or scratch. A thick phosphorescent disk clanked on the bottom, too wide to be removed. It slowly got bigger, like a live seashell.

I usually avoided intake of alcohol while dealing with the supernatural. It turned me into a frenzied mercenary in a jungle, pulling the trigger at every sound, movement, and shadow. But this time my brain got in the way of good instincts. I scrutinized too much. I had to let my intuition reign.

I unscrewed the cap.

Cheers.

Sip by sip, I slogged to finish the bitter herb-infused concoction, its potency amplified tenfold by the mysterious disk. The fiery liquid still burned my throat when the clamps keeping my sound judgment snapped.

My thoughts flitted in all directions like happy-go-lucky butterflies. What the hell was I trying to find in Chris?

Oh yeah. Poignance. Intimacy.

The picture of him in the river clung to my mind's eye, but this time my imagination put me a few steps behind Chris, staring at his naked shoulder. *Personal.* I craved to cut the distance between us and press my forehead against that shoulder.

Perfect. Next, the taste. Not citrus. Not coffee or liqueur. Bread? Dairy? Fruit? Spices? Not mint, not saffron. Definitely not curry—that would be Peter. Chris—sweet, light in color. Vanilla ice cream? Meringue? Lemon soufflé?

Coconut cream pie.

Good; move on. The hearing.

A chanson from the 1960s played softly in my head, the gentle voice singing in French about happiness and solitude. From this night on, I'd think of Chris whenever I listened to the song.

Now the touch.

Glass. Velvet. Marble. Warm sand sifting through my fingers. Sensations washed over my skin, but nothing clicked.

Don't get stuck. I switched to the sense of smell.

Which one would make me miss him? My wild-strawberry jam? Too intense. I needed something softer, tamer. A flower with a slight scent, not your jasmine or edelweiss. Tulip? Iris? Oh, oh, I had it: dianthus. My nose in a cluster of carnations, the cool, silken petals caressing my face. The smell, and I also had the touch.

The alcohol romanticized the hell out of Chris. I smiled, but my train of thought was fading like cranes' calls in the autumn sky. With my five senses tuned to Chris's personality, I gained the right of entry and I was sliding, falling, dissolving into an unfamiliar dimension, his emotional world.

Rational thinking didn't exist where I roamed. Words and images couldn't describe hope, surprise, irony, trust experienced by someone else and then registered as interferences in my energy field. A ghost in a never-never land, barely perceiving myself, I glided through the frames of Chris's feelings, searching for the roadkill of his happiness.

The attack came quick and brutal. A deafening and blinding presence encompassed me. Then it was tearing me apart.

A life-threatening fever would inflict such an agony of being extinguished cell by cell. The force was mindless. I couldn't plead with it or reason. If I tried to break free, my energy would only feed the monster.

The truth detonated in my freaked-out brain. Chris didn't just suppress his happiness. His subconscious generated a crusher to destroy it. I had dared to turn myself into perhaps the greatest thing that ever happened to him—a model best friend. For that, I was a subject to annihilation.

An invisible paw clawed at my stomach. Another squeezed my lungs.

"Chris, let me go," I whispered, or thought I did.

But I knew that even if I reached him on some level, Chris couldn't abolish his demons at will. What would happen to him when my super energy fueled his suffering? Anything positive he had in his life, his fondness of Debra, his love for travel, would be erased. Another casualty of my unbridled self-confidence, how would he survive?

The tension ripping my essence to bits crept toward my heart. I wouldn't last much longer.

Curry. The thought came out of nowhere. The blackness jumped back.

And I was throwing lightning bolts, a tornado of exuberance, a hurricane of passion, a crazy fusion of rage and thrill, wiping out the murderous blob of the shadows. Defibrillating the rusty carcass of Chris's happiness it left in its wake.

Ignite.

Live, dammit.

Then it was over. The taste-key broken, Chris's subconscious kicked me out.

My body welcomed me with pain sinking a hundred fangs behind my eyebrows. Shiny specks filled my vision and whirled around me like a blinding swarm of fruit flies.

I summoned the last iota of my paranormal senses to read Chris.

Heavens, I did it. I bludgeoned the barracuda of his guilt. The Antikythera mechanism of his positive emotions began to turn its gears.

"Who are you?" Chris whispered into my ear.

My otherworldly fuel depleted, I sagged in his arms. I could no longer identify his feelings, but something warm and good blazed in him so brightly it decelerated my spinning landscape.

His energy of living, just what I desperately needed. A cozy blanket of serenity settled on my chest and eyelids.

"She almost killed herself," Peter's voice announced, his tone all business.

CHAPTER FORTY-FOUR

Jolted by the rude intrusion into my precious moment of peace and quiet, I pulled away from Chris and peered at the silhouette before me. The lens of Peter's camera stared back wide-eyed, like an importunate kid spying on his adult sibling.

"When did you wake up?" I asked.

"A minute ago," Peter said. "You weren't breathing. I checked your pulse, and it took, like, ten seconds before I got the first heartbeat."

Curry. By touching my wrist, Peter had broken the link and saved my life. "Putting all of you in trance at once exhausted my powers," I said.

Chris stared at me with an odd expression.

"Gosh, this is so…." Peter spoke with all the enthusiasm of a child overstimulated by his first magic show. He swept the camera to catch the three motionless forms, his buddies, slouched on the grass. "I always thought only a compliant subject can be hypnotized. I resisted you as long as I could, but—"

"You all did." I stifled a hiccup. "Resisted me as long as you could." I patted the ground and discretely slid the empty flask into my jeans' pocket. "I need a few minutes to recover. You two stay here and see if you can wake up the rest. I'll be back."

I struggled to my feet before either man worked up an inclination to argue. The scenery resumed its nauseating rotation. I stepped around the heap of Luke's body, careful not to crush Debra's skinny outspread limbs, and plodded downhill.

Strong portals sprouted without order in the three springs that fed the pond. Two currently glowed in the dark. I walked to the brightest. A wide flat board was thrown over the runoff, and a dainty path scratched the meadow—some of the locals found the water irresistible for drinking. I dipped my fingers into the clear reservoir.

In the eyes of a chance observer, I'd appear composed, even serene. Inside, I was a shipwreck caught in the surf, banging dully against a rocky shore. The decision I faced was more of a verdict than a choice, yet I prayed for an excuse to prevent the unavoidable.

When I planned this international assembly, everything seemed straightforward. They'd arrive. I'd expose them to a few occurrences and explain to Debra the whole hullabaloo about Vishenky. I desperately needed another rational, educated member of the Gretishnikoff clan to dissect the Legend of an Unborn. My future, my survival depended on Debra's insight, friendship, and help.

I had thought that nothing could have sidetracked me from my goal.

Where was I instead?

Drifting beyond the horizon of my rationality, with a defective compass and broken helm. I had met Chris, and the tower of my priorities collapsed like a decayed willow. My way of life dangled over a gorge on a thread of a spider web, yet I allowed myself to get distracted, sinking deeper and deeper into the quicksand of his issues.

Willingly.

Every step, every effort of investing myself into his well-being made me care more about Chris. A beautiful sentiment, but it steered me toward a disheartening outcome. Unfit for each other's worlds like a pike and a hedgehog, we had no chance for a shared future.

Don't prolong this sweet agony, I thought. Put him on the first morning train, then deal with everything else. Farewell. Adieu. Nice knowing you. *Proschaite.*

I could do that. I had to. With my emotions running on paranormal fuel, saying goodbye to Chris already felt like facing a cherished friend's betrayal. Irrevocable. Senseless.

Let him go.

CHAPTER FORTY-FIVE

Debra hurried down the slope. "Valya?"

"Over here." The guide's silhouette darkened against a fluorescent circle that lay half-hidden in tall grass.

"We can't wake up Jessie," Debra yelled.

"Her vision has to run its course."

"Are you sure? She's unresponsive."

"I'm sure. Deb, come here."

"I have to tell the guys she's okay."

"Come here," Valya repeated.

The grass felt taller and the ground squishier as Debra anxiously made her way to the black shadow in the glowing circle.

The puddle of light turned out to be a spring. Visible as clearly as if the bottom was covered with underwater lamps, the tiny jets stirred the grains of sand. Translucent newts scurried on the mud-covered banks, each shining brightly enough to illuminate the wet logs and vegetation. In constant motion, some climbed out of the rocky basin while others slid in, dissolving from sight and making the spring glow.

On her knees, Valya stared into the pit. Her left hand, submerged just under the surface, acquired a slight sheen as if the water was heavily ionized. The guide seemed to forget she had requested Debra's company.

"Very pretty," Debra said. "I'll just tell the guys—"

"Touch one."

"Huh?"

"Pick a newt and touch it."

It couldn't get any more insane. Well, maybe, if Debra took an afternoon nap and awoke on Jupiter. But to Valya, this was probably another pleasant summer evening.

Rather than arguing, Debra reached for the nearest amphibian. Her finger pierced the luminous body. She gasped and jerked back her hand. A disturbed but unharmed critter changed its position.

Debra tried to grab another newt's tail. The tips of her fingers met every time.

"There," Debra said coolly. "I can't even feel it. Now, let's go."

"I want you to catch a newt," Valya said in the same quiet, impassive voice.

"I can't. They have no substance."

"Pick one and place your hand in front of it. See if it comes to you."

"Why?" Debra asked.

Valya wiggled her fingers, creating colorful swirls. "The water is so cold."

Chills ran through Debra's arms and chest, chewing her skin like hungry larvae. "Valya, can we go? Please."

The guide finally tore her eyes from the pool. "I have to know if I can trust you."

"You need a reptile from another dimension to test my honesty?"

"Does anything look simple to you here?"

"Okay." Debra got on one knee and put her scooped palms in front of a critter. It crawled into her hands. The lithe body was weightless, the touch of the minuscule toes imperceptible. "Well?" she asked.

"Release it into the spring," Valya said.

Debra lowered her hands to the surface but hesitated.

Above her, the stars jostled one another like simpleminded spectators at a crime scene. The sky, the black dome pierced by myriads of suns, made her lightheaded. At her feet, an alien glow rose from the pit crawling with otherworldly amphibians. Not a dream. Not a vision. The slightest push from the strange woman who entered her life less than forty-eight hours ago, and maybe Debra herself would vanish into some unimaginable dimension.

The sudden insight was brighter than a laser. "You're testing *my* trust," Debra said.

"Do it." The guide's voice snapped like a whip, unfamiliar, pitiless. Desperate.

Debra plunged her hands into the luminous pool.

The newt dissipated from her sight. Violet underwater tornadoes formed on the bottom, snaking out of crevices like angered morays. Debra recoiled and landed on her butt. Transfixed by the twisters' synchronized movements, she couldn't look away from the tips inching, stretching toward the surface. The fastest one licked Valya's palm.

"Watch out," Debra screamed.

The guide stared back at Debra, her irises two violet circles of unearthly radiance.

The sky rushed down, pushing, pushing on Debra's chest. She wheezed. She scrambled to her feet, barely saving her balance on the bouncing board. The multitude of spooked amphibians leaped down the banks. The pool grew dark as the wiggling streaks of light flowed into the cracks.

"Bloodline," Valya said.

Debra ran.

CHAPTER FORTY-SIX

Chris feared one thing. It wasn't hiking through the monster-infested landscape or losing his sanity because the world imploded in a spectacular display of absurd creations. He feared the universe could revert to normality.

The sounds rasping over the steaming river, the scents billowing in the breeze like residues of ghostly presences, the brilliance of the moon—everything appeared more conspicuous, more flamboyant, and more complex. This new magnificent reality included their guide. Just an hour ago, Chris was cursing Providence for bringing Valya into his life. Now—

"You're not listening to me," Debra said.

"I am," Chris assured. "Kenny, Peter's half-brother, refused to leave his room for weeks after his brush with Vishenky. You saw a spring, the transparent newts, and a demonic gleam in Valya's eyes."

"We need to get out of here."

Chris laughed.

A few yards ahead, Valya walked next to Peter, with Luke and Jessie trudging behind them. The guide answered Peter's questions in a conversational fashion, her words too quiet to sound clear over Debra's fervent whispers, but her tone the one of a student who didn't skip her homework, confident, eager. At the same time, she moved like a primeval scout expecting an ambush, pausing to listen, and checking on those behind her. Chris sensed her utter focus.

"Do you hear me?" Debra asked. "We must run while we still can. We won't even go into the house. Straight to the train station—the hell with our bags."

"Would be crazy to bolt now," Chris said.

"What?"

"Do you realize the magnitude of what's happening?"

"Do I?" Debra asked. "We're ears-deep in some seriously horrific shit."

"Deb, calm down."

"You were supposed to keep us out of trouble."

As though he hadn't tried. "This is the most incredible place on Earth. We're damn lucky to be here. I can't believe you have no appreciation whatsoever."

"We're as lucky as lobsters in a trap—done for, but the bait is so tasty. Wake up, cousin. The place is Dracula's castle. We're guarded by a woman who fantasizes she can control supernatural forces. *If* Valya's a woman."

"She is, and she's in control," Chris said. "Look at her."

"I already looked at her," Debra said. "I'll be on sleeping pills for the rest of my life."

"You've imagined the whole thing. What's '*durashka*?"

"'Little fool' in Russian. Why?"

"When Peter tried to wake you up, you called him a *durashka* and demanded some magic claw and feathers. Then you announced you'd run down to the pond to fetch Valya so she'd rouse Jessie from her trance. Except, Jessie had already been up and working on Luke."

"No way."

"Your head wasn't clear. Why would Valya want to scare you?"

"I don't know." Debra was silent for a few moments. "What was your vision?"

A coconut cream pie, a bunch of carnations, and his overpowering closeness to Valya.

"I don't remember," Chris said. "Something odd, something good. Deb, look, if you're afraid, go. I can't. I have to know who she is."

Debra grabbed his elbow, making him stop. "She used hypnosis to elicit your trust."

"If you were abducted by aliens," Chris said, "would you tell me?"

"Yes."

"Would I believe you?"

"No," Debra said.

"Think of Valya's isolation—from her family, from everybody. She desperately wants to share her secrets. She chose us because we wouldn't destroy her precarious reality. I believe that."

"You don't think we're in danger?"

"With the guide who has studied Vishenky since her childhood? Here's a more essential question. An hour ago, Valya was your best friend. Then she showed you what her life really looks like. What do you choose to do? To run? Or to stay?"

Debra stopped. "Oh my God."

"What?"

"On the way from the train station yesterday morning, Valya asked me, 'Who will stand by you at the end of the day?' What she meant was would I stand by her?"

Jessie looked back, and Chris thought he saw his student shake her head in disbelief.

CHAPTER FORTY-SEVEN

In the chair by the front door, Debra entwined her arms with neurotic exertion. Valya reached behind her to pull the last curtain. Chris liked it better now, the blue flat face of the night no longer staring in the windows.

He had given the students plenty of time to grill Valya about her extraordinary experiences. Now it should be his turn, his chance to....

Question her? No. The words would be an intrusion. Just one look into her eyes would tell him what he wanted to know.

But no one was leaving the veranda.

"We need more equipment." Peter stood leaning against the back of a seat at the dining table. "Cameras, tripods, brighter flashlights."

He kept his composure, the spark of curiosity intense in his black eyes. Luke fidgeted with the sliding plastic tips on the ties that fastened his windbreaker's collar. Jessie perched on the sofa, her face the mask of apprehension, her lips tight, nostrils flaring, and her gaze attached to Valya like a remora to a shark.

"Why don't you try to get some sleep?" Valya suggested. "As we say in Russia, the morning is wiser than the evening."

"How do we know the house is safe?" Jessie asked.

"Manifestations inside the house are rare, and tonight's not the night."

Defying Valya's statement about tonight not being the night, a crash somewhere upstairs shook the ceiling lamp.

"C'mon." With camera in hand, Peter slapped Luke's back and darted to the kitchen.

"Luke, don't go," Jessie called.

He threw her the glance of a man on his way to a guillotine but switched his flashlight on and went after his friend.

"Stop them," Jessie told the guide.

Valya made a move as if to join the investigation, but instead of climbing the ladder, she froze at the threshold between the veranda and the kitchen, her spine pressed against the door frame.

"There is blood everywhere!" Luke's high-pitched voice squealed from upstairs.

Like a marionette with her strings snapping one by one, Valya began to slide down.

An adrenaline kick carried Chris across the floorboards to catch her before she fell. Then he stopped, confused by what he felt, what he was seeing.

His brain registered the commotion. Debra dashed past him into the kitchen, calling the boys. Jessie threw the door open to let in some air. Their steps and the staccatos of their voices were muffled, as if he watched the girls through thick glass. He should be moving, too, doing something to revive the woman in his arms. Chris couldn't. He stood still, blasted with the feeling of utter isolation, certain that even if he tried to speak, no one would know he was there. Even Valya, though present in the flesh, had abandoned him, a shell vacated by its lively owner.

"On the sofa," Jessie barked into his ear. Her angry voice broke his stupor.

Chris laid the lifeless body on the compliant cushions. Jessie held a pillow over Valya's ashen face as if contemplating suffocation before sliding it under the guide's head.

Debra appeared by his side with a shallow aluminum pan used as a water scoop, and a towel. "It's okay. I got it."

Chris pulled a chair from the table, his eyes on Valya. *It's nothing major, nothing life-threatening.* The young woman was so hypersensitive to the sight of blood that even Luke's mentioning of it made her faint.

As for his ridiculous freaking out, it was predictable. A grueling day of fears and suspicions, then the euphoria caused by Valya's strange hypnotic session, and he crashed.

Jessie crouched by the sofa, her index finger on Valya's neck. "I can feel a pulse."

"Jess, you're in my way." Debra pressed the wet towel against Valya's temple and cheek.

Luke emerged from the kitchen, his face gray. "It's like a massacre scene upstairs, after the bodies have been removed." His mouth quivered as if he was about to cry. "There are dark-red splotches, trickles, small puddles all over the floor, stains on the walls, and a larger pool by the couch."

"If this is one of your inane jokes—" Debra hissed without turning her head.

"Go look for yourself! Moss is filming every drop. Hurry up, because it started to fade."

"So it's not real," Debra said.

"Yeah, like the fact that it's supernatural makes everything so much better." Luke walked around the dining table and moved a chair into the corner between two curtained windows, as if trying to put the maximum of veranda space and furniture between him and the group. His bulky form shrank on the seat, shoulders slumped, big arms wrapped tightly around his body.

"Blood fits," Jessie said.

"Fits what?" Chris asked.

"Why are you so eager to trust her, Mr. Waller? I heard you telling Debra Valya's in control, but don't you understand your friendly guide is not in it alone? Who was that boy? Or the woman with the violet eyes?"

"All you have to do is ask her."

"Oh, I will. But why are you so inclined to take her side?"

Chris wished he had a rational answer.

Debra dumped the towel into the scoop. "She's not waking up. Has anybody seen a medicine cabinet in the house? Maybe Russians have smelling salts."

The powerful fragrance of the night flowers in bloom filled the room through the open door, giving Chris an idea. He stood on the chair and pulled a couple of Valya's dry bouquets from the ceiling. He crushed a few leaves to find the right plant, the pungent specimen that Valya had made him smell earlier.

He rubbed a few stems and brought them to Valya's nose.

She pushed his hand away. "Nails rusted. I should have known," she muttered. Her eyes remained closed.

Jessie put her hand on Debra's shoulder. "I'd like to talk to Valya without all of you hovering around."

A metallic edge in her voice guaranteed trouble.

"No," Chris said.

"All right." Jessie leaned over Valya. "How old is your cult?"

CHAPTER FORTY-EIGHT

I wanted to be alone, floating in the cool opaque mist. Carefree, like a leaf in the autumn wind. Memory-free, like a puffy cloud. Guilt-free, like falling drops of rain.

"I said, how old is your cult?" Jessie's seething voice ruptured my quiet space.

I fished myself out of the fog and propped my body with my elbows.

Somebody had put me on the sofa after my mind had given up on dealing with my problems. The black mouth of the night sucked out the room's warmth through the open front door. Jessie towered above me. Behind her, Chris and Debra exchanged troubled looks. Luke stooped in a chair on the other side of the veranda.

"Where's Peter?" I asked.

"Filming your bloodied floorboards upstairs," Jessie said.

The aftermath of Dimitry's death. The air quivered, golden dots bursting like bubbles in boiling water. Suddenly I tasted sea-buckthorn juice on my tongue.

The lasers of Jessie's eyes beamed into my pupils. "What do you worship? Which creature wants a human sacrifice?"

"Don't be ridiculous." My parched throat produced the sounds much harsher than I intended. "There's no cult."

"Oh yeah? Only a handful of people are in on the secret. You find your guests without attracting much attention. Your house is haunted.

The blood pattern Luke saw screams murders."

"You watch too many horror movies," Chris told her.

"Sir, do you seriously believe she'd risk bringing random visitors off the Internet to a place like this?" Jessie asked. "No. We're here for a reason."

Her agitation bordered on terror. My heart beat faster as the Frankenstein of a hypothesis began to grow muscle tissue and skin. Every portal served as the gateway to a specific manifestation. Twenty-four hours ago, Jessie returned from our late-night excursion petrified after her encounter with the dead Terentey, and the entity reappeared out of nowhere after ten years of dormancy. The girl was just as frightened right now, and once again, I sensed the entity's subtle presence. What if my visitors and I, twisted into knots by our emotions, generated the energy field of such potency it could sustain a passageway between the two worlds?

My priorities lined up like shish kebab on a skewer. I scrambled to the corner of the sofa and pulled my feet beneath me, pressing my back against the cushions to appear small, unthreatening.

"Jess, you need to calm down," I said. "Your fear is a putrid fish on a beach and the manifestations are crabs. If the feeding frenzy starts, I will have no power to control them. Think of something simple, mundane, something you like. Think of lobster, heather, mother-of-pearl buttons."

Her jaw dropped. The white fire in her eyes went out, replaced by the smoke of confusion.

Poor Jessie. I compared her fear to a dead fish, but it was more like a cherry pit in her windpipe and I performed the Heimlich maneuver. She didn't know I had read her blog. She traveled once across New England, enjoying seafood and collecting heather seedlings at the nurseries along the highway. She spent an hour picking unfinished mother-of-pearl buttons out of the mud by the wall of an abandoned button plant where her friends were having a picnic.

Jessie's hand froze in midair, her thinking process laborious on her face. "You wanted *me* in Vishenky."

"I came across your blog. You perceive the places you visit so differently. The German who left the comment about Vishenky—that was I. I thought I used a perfect bait to lure you in."

"Why didn't you contact me directly?" Jessie asked.

"What would I say? 'I have issues with the portals into another dimension'?"

"Yes! I'd be here in a heartbeat."

I suppressed a smile. Jessie Hunt was from a fading West Virginian town. Like most of us, she yearned for acceptance. I was giving it to her, and right now the enthusiasm on her face outshone a diamond necklace.

She wasn't going to become my BFF. Her next attack would come, as inevitable as Luke's food cravings, once she had time to think and find weak spots in my story.

"The blood was a manifestation caused by your fear," I said. "I fainted when I tried to help you—I spent too much energy when I put you in a trance. If I don't get some rest, I'll be useless as a guide." I nodded at Luke huddling in the corner. "He might be in shock."

"I'll take care of him," Jessie assured me.

"And tell Peter to come down. No reason for him to keep watch all night when I have so much to show you tomorrow."

I stepped off the sofa into Chris's supporting arms.

Instead of just saying goodnight, he followed me through the kitchen and the hallway, into the room I shared with Debra. He closed every door behind us. Surprised and pleased, and wondering if Chris experienced at least a trace of the overwhelming, blinding affection that in the past two hours I felt for him, I crossed the moonlit space and hit the light switch. We stood staring at each other from the opposite sides of the room, but I wished I were still in his arms. I'd babble about wonders of Vishenky and mysteries of life, or just kiss him to keep him with me, to stay immersed in his sweet aura. He seemed unaffected by the entity's presence, but I wanted to be sure.

"Valya...." He looked at the ceiling lamp. "I can't explain why, but I need a piece of green glass."

Gray moths hammered the dark windows. I should have closed the curtains. Then it dawned on me that the pounding was in my ears.

"Oh, Chris." I walked to him.

I wrapped my arms around his waist. His hands tentatively slid across my back until I was in his embrace.

"The old woman who visited you last night, what did she do?" I asked.

I hoped he'd say "nothing." I didn't want to discover that Prascovia was somehow responsible for making Chris the focus of the entity's attention.

"She freaked me out." Chris chuckled. "Her eyes were purple, and she tossed something into the air. Like a ball of light."

My heart so heavy it barely had strength to beat, I asked, "What did you feel?"

Chris pulled me closer. "I was mad at you for staging all that absurdity. So strange," he whispered into my hair. "What would I do with the green glass?"

I didn't answer, thinking how at this moment of tenderness, no power in our whole galaxy could force me to step away from this man.

What could I possibly tell him anyway? That the glass would break if held over a candle flame? That the shards sliced human skin as smoothly and swiftly as a blade? That only a thin layer of wooden boards and ten meters of space had separated me from Dimitry, but he never called out for me? That twenty minutes passed from the moment it started to the instant he fell, but despite all my supernatural senses, I never felt that my beloved friend was dying?

Chris held me tight. I melted into our silence. I read his puzzlement and his nascent affection for the woman in his embrace. Nothing indicated the entity had a hold of him. Just his dangerous request. And the astringent tang of sea-buckthorn in my mouth.

CHAPTER FORTY-NINE

Prascovia had brought the entity into my home.

Another sleepless night hung above me like a scorching cloud of volcanic ashes. Prascovia's involvement had changed the situation. The threat of the Violet Lights sounded far-fetched and unimportant compared to the chilling possibility of losing Chris. My energy was no longer protecting him, but sending him away while he was affected by an unknown spell wouldn't ensure his safety either.

The quivering candle kept the front veranda in the dark, exposing only the flowery pattern of the oilcloth disrupted by a single white rectangle, the piece of paper with my list of facts. I couldn't figure out Prascovia's motives.

She sent the lethal entity to exterminate the men whose presence in my life had made it matter from an entirely different perspective. Dimitry Remizov was my first love—that balmy, intoxicating, euphoric feeling when my every waking minute was about him, an overwhelming longing to be together, to see his smile, to hear his voice.

But when he died, I survived.

I was ten years older now. Sometimes my sentiments were so excruciatingly profound, I had to wonder if my overindulgence in Vishenky's energy turned my emotions into a giant mycelium-like formation, its filaments reaching and stirring up my every cell. If I lost Chris, the grief-and-guilt grinder would be an inescapable hell. I might just leap into a portal.

Was that what Prascovia wanted?

The tip of my pen touched the paper but didn't go anywhere. That theory was just too contrived.

Minus a rock-hard motive, I couldn't see Prascovia as a villain. My whole life, Vishenky's most-feared old woman watched me from a distance, letting me test the supernatural waters as deep as I would dare, but she never tried to harm me. Never.

Old woman?

The comprehension rammed me like a falling tree. Prascovia was so ancient she had probably lived through Genghis Khan's invasion. What if she had been raising her replacement?

Another hunch flashed through my mind, some vital element that I was forgetting to take into account, a detail about my lineage, but the ghost of the idea dissipated before I could fully grasp it. Unable to flesh it out, I wrote down and circled frantically the word "replacement."

Prascovia's own brood, Andrey, was too young. My connection to Prascovia was thicker than water. Aware she had lost my trust, the cautious witch might be hesitant to declare me her successor, just as I didn't have the nerve to tell Debra the whole truth.

I put down my pen. My hands felt clammy. A knot of anger and frustration thundered in my chest. Only twice in my twenty-three demanding years had I deemed someone so wonderful that my attraction prompted me to doubt my Vishenky dependence. Prascovia would rather slay another innocent man than allow me to be diverted from my paranormal quest.

Hot tears welled in my eyes. Sniffling, I crumpled the piece of paper with my notes. Then I smoothed it down. I stuck a corner in the candle flame, pushed the salt and pepper shakers from their fancy nickel-silver tray, and dropped the blazing page on the polished surface. The paper withered and turned black.

Watching it, I summoned my courage. Before the light of dawn dispersed the night and changed my mind, I'd engage the most loathsome resource in my arsenal. My blackest secret. My profound fear. A grim souvenir from the Medieval Ages.

A manual on how to defeat Prascovia.

CHAPTER FIFTY

Six half-rotted, half-charred sheets of parchment had come into my possession with Anna's letter without an explanation of where she'd found it. The unknown illiterate author invented his or her own symbols. Despite the deteriorated condition and the missing portions of the script, I had understood it instantly, as if I were tuned in to the ancestral memory, to the data etched for generations in Gretishnikoffs' genes.

How to ward off Prascovia's spells and curses.

Sealed in a plastic bag, the brittle masterpiece lay buried in the crawlspace under Jessie's bedroom. I dreaded the idea of opening the access hatch in the hallway's floor and going into the mosquito-infested darkness. The noise could wake up Jessie. I had to trust my memory and recreate the elixir without help from the written source.

I picked a hand shovel and spent the next few minutes fighting the roots of a chokeberry bush. The blade finally scraped the glass side of the jar. I carried it inside.

The seeds of lady's mantle, crushed and boiled in Dirge Birch's juices collected on a month of a bad drought and kept for seven years underground, looked like a corpse of a frog rotting in a test tube. I pried open the metal lid, keeping my face away from the jar, filled a pitcher with water from the Newt Spring, and added four drops of the stinking brew.

The mixture hissed and released putrid vapors. A greenish puff darted in my direction. I jerked back. Inside the pitcher, luminescent forms rushed about like a school of frightened minnows.

I struck a match and brought it to the surface. The potion caught on fire like an extravagant cocktail.

The recipe required pouring the blazing concoction on Chris's chest and stomach. Supposedly, the flame would cleanse him, burning Prascovia's spell.

Whatever I had created looked, smelled, behaved, and *felt* wrong. As I stood spellbound by the ensued carnival of iridescent colors, a web of fractures crisscrossed the glass. With a quiet pop, the pitcher fell in two. Olive-colored ribbons of fire snaked across the gooey mass crawling over the oilcloth.

Feeling absurdly relieved, I opened the door to rid the veranda of smoke and spilled some ash over the burning substance to exterminate the twisting flames. I must have sabotaged the experiment subconsciously, not wishing to put Chris in more danger than he already was. I slipped on a pair of rubber gloves and swept the fetid mess into a plastic trash bag. Coughing and gagging, I tossed it under the white rugosa rose puffed up in front of the doorway like a giant angry turkey.

I felt into a chair, out of inspirations and bravado. I wanted a drink, but my flask was empty and exhaustion held me down with centrifugal force.

A sudden desire engulfed me. I wished to wake up Chris, explain to him at least a fraction of my doings. *I only sought to meet Debra, but inadvertently I put your life at risk.* Would he understand?

Too much deceit, too much self-interest to hope for his forgiveness. The spikes of disillusionment prickled my heart. I squeezed the polished armrests. I couldn't loiter here waiting for the sunrise. Inaction led to thinking, and thinking hurt.

I replenished my flask with chokeberry wine, a bit concerned what the phosphorescent disk would do to the already potent beverage of my grandmother's making. *Just a few sips.* The spicy fragrance of the blooming night stock lured me out. Tasting the thick, sweet liquid, I walked through the backyard, past the tool shed and the ancient cellar. I wandered into the misty garden, whisperless in the predawn hour.

The stars had faded, and the night had lost its charm. Hushed gloom still wrapped the apple trees, but soon the skylark would announce the birth of a new day. I was so fatigued I felt lightheaded. I closed my eyes and inhaled the silence.

There was another way to repeal Prascovia's spell. It was uncharted, risky, but if done correctly, the procedure would free me from my worries about Chris's safety.

Would I dare?

Damn you, my nameless predecessor who wrote the parchment. I swallowed more wine, strolling through the patch of gooseberries and currants.

Prascovia was convinced I needed her help and patronage. I wanted her to choke on her amulets. I couldn't change the past, but I would fix the future. The rules, the fate existed for the weaklings. I had the power to take a stand against the deviant forces.

I shook the flask. The disk banged noisily against the empty bottom. I hadn't noticed that I had left the garden. The tool shed loomed before me—walls of charred logs, survivors of the village fire. *So be it*, I thought.

The door stood ajar and the entrance gaped expectantly. My imagination stirred. A monster's lair, ghosts' nest, the first threshold to cross, first lock to pick, first obstacle to overcome.

The shivers came in tidal waves. I held my breath to stop the hiccups. The chilly dampness of the air crept along my body like tentacles of something soft, slimy, and deep-sea. I stuck my icy hands into my jeans' pockets. Heels to toes, heels to toes, I rocked myself.

I managed a tiny step. I felt like crawling, pinning every cell of me against the ground. Or changing into quicksilver and rolling in a string of swift droplets.

Now or never.

I took another step and struck a match. The shadows danced like drunken demons. I realized that when the match went out and before I lit another, I'd panic, I'd go mad.

It's just the tool shed, for goodness' sake.

Furious at my display of weakness, I killed the flame before its time was over. *My way. My terms.* The darkness fell on me like smothering miasma.

I willed myself to breathe.

I searched the shelves by touch. I stuck my dad's jackknife into my pocket. I lit a candle—the hell with demons writhing on the walls—and picked up a heavy-duty shovel. By the water pump, the well-packed dirt floor was hard to dig, but I unearthed an iron pot in minutes.

The lid resisted my fingers. I couldn't tell if it was just stuck or welded to the container. To get the prize preserved inside, I had to break its sealed sarcophagus.

I tossed the shovel and grabbed a sledgehammer.

The noise would wake up the whole neighborhood. I carried the pot to the back gate where old cherry trees lost the decency to grow like ordinary garden vegetation. Under dense, tangled canopies I secured the pot between two roots, brushed dirt and cobwebs off my fingers, and swung the sledgehammer sideways.

Rusty cast iron was no match for a determined woman. Among the fragments lay the object of my efforts.

A mummified finger.

Ostov's, I guessed. Rumors claimed that Prascovia had a strange pet. Its name, Ostov, meant skeleton. The creature had never fully materialized in our world. The only sketch in my possession, charcoal-drawn and smudged, reminded me of a mummified polydactyl Great Dane, eye sockets enlarged, tufts of hair attached to parched skin.

I didn't know what I would find; just that once freed, it would be living. Its tip ended with a single claw, thin, colorless, and cat-like. I poked the piece, my ears still ringing from the metal boom. The artifact felt dead.

And hollow.

Trying to suppress repulsion and praying my instincts didn't lie, I pulled the thing onto my right index finger.

The leather came to life. Suddenly all muscles, the relic constricted around my flesh. Needles poked my skin like a leech that had once found my shin in the river. A pungent odor filled my nostrils as if I put my nose to the entry of a beast's den.

My finger throbbed. The stinging made me nauseated, red circles swam before my eyes, my legs felt shaky. My heart skipped, leaped, and quivered without rhythm. I wasn't sure if the monstrosity was taking something away from me or giving me its poison. Wheezing, and swallowing saliva to keep myself from getting sick, I staggered along the garden path.

I made it to the front veranda before collapsing. Contorted by the mind-deadening cramps crushing my whole body, I thrashed on the floorboards. Then I couldn't move at all. My fingers gripped Dad's jackknife involuntarily, the way a person clutches a live electric wire.

Who'll find me? I thought, feeling the approaching darkness. Then my mind gave way to the pain.

CHAPTER FIFTY-ONE

The milky murkiness of the dawn seeped through cracks in the blinds. *Alive!* I assessed the damage, barely believing in the successful outcome. The pain subsided. I wanted food and coffee so badly everything below my diaphragm was trembling.

The thing violating my finger seemed to breathe. I tugged at a tuft of fur and was the one to feel the twinges. Hoping I had my human skin beneath the beastly leather, I pressed the blade to where *I* ended and *it* began.

I hesitated.

Where did I stand? The day would start, and I'd meet it plagued by the same disastrous problems and flaunting a finger of an orangutan. To go through all the agony and relinquish my hold on the relic while it was alive would be inexcusable.

The clock showed a quarter after five. Not one of my visitors was an early bird. I rummaged through the cupboard, stuffed a cube of sugar into my mouth and a tester-sized vial into my pocket—not eau de parfum—and carefully pushed open the heavy pine door between the front veranda and the kitchen. It knew better than to squeak.

I tiptoed into Chris's bedroom. While my eyes adjusted to the darkness, I listened to his calm breathing. He hadn't had any nightmares during the night, but one was leaning over him right now.

Bent at the elbow, his left arm was thrown over his head.

I closed my fingers around his wrist. "Chris."

He opened his eyes. I laid his arm along his body and plunged the claw where a needle would go to draw blood.

The supernatural venom spread faster than any bloodstream could possibly carry it. Chris exhaled and his chest didn't rise again, but his right hand flew to the brick wall, contorted fingers scraping the coarse surface. While his diaphragm and rib cage muscles failed to contract, the others cramped and paralyzed his body, undoubtedly causing excruciating pain.

I wished I could do this without waking Chris up. No longer able to inhale, he knew the life was draining from his body and that his murderer was I. But if he didn't stay awake, I'd miss the right moment to stop the deadly injection.

The sharpness of his stare began to fade. I held my own breath, ready to pull out the claw. Something small and bright darted past me and hit the mirror hanging on the wall by the head of the bed.

The entity, a bluish-purple sphere the size of a grapefruit, bounced back. Growing painfully bright, it hovered above Chris as if considering the possibility of returning to its dying host, then jumped to my face. My hand jerked instinctively, yanking the claw from Chris's arm. I swatted the glowing ball, suspended in the air right before my nose. It shrieked like a frightened bird and zoomed away.

I swallowed, my heart and thoughts racing. The entity didn't attack Chris sporadically, as I assumed before. I had ignored Andrey's conclusion when he searched for paranormal force in Debra but pointed at Chris instead. The boy's senses were correct. The alien energy had been with Chris all along.

Would it survive once driven out?

I hoped it was already dead. I took a long breath, counting to six. I imagined molecules of gases moving in my lungs, propelled by the supernatural force that nourished me, entropy rising, alveoli snatching oxygen, then releasing something else along with carbon dioxide—a chemical, a molecule that came into existence during my exposures to portals.

Chris was still. I pressed my lips to his, exhaled through my mouth, and stepped away.

Convulsion shook him while the torrent of particles rushed through his larynx and trachea, made its way past bronchi and flooded his lungs. Absorbed, it traveled through the bloodstream, soothing his every muscle. It poured into his brain cells, mixing his will, his fortitude with mine, erasing Prascovia's bidding.

Chris gained enough strength to prop himself with his elbows and look at me before collapsing back on the pillows. I opened the vial and let a few aromatic drops of a mild sedative roll down and wet his lips. He licked them reflexively.

"Sleep," I said. Chris closed his eyes. A frown engraved his forehead, but his ordeal was over.

Not mine. I waited for his breathing to resume its even rhythm. Then I rushed into the kitchen. Over the sink, with my dad's knife I made four cuts along my finger, slashing the relic's leather and slicing my own skin in the process. Grinding my teeth, I peeled off the alien pelt clinging to my flesh as if glued with epoxy. Splotches of blood blackened the white ceramic. I tossed the ruined artifact into the furnace to burn it later.

Ten minutes later, sheer willpower carried me to check on Chris, not that I could aid him if he needed me. He slept peacefully. I dragged myself to my room, praying for the salve on my finger to work and for the blood not to soak my sheets through the bandage.

Slumped under the comforter, I hid my face in the pillow and wept. Not from pain and not for Chris or the kids whose lives I risked. I wept for myself, ashamed of my eagerness to brush off any humanity and become something I fought so frantically to prove I wasn't.

A monster.

CHAPTER FIFTY-TWO

Chris awoke to a misty morning.

A drizzle palpated the front veranda's roof. The lilac shrub by the tool shed looked like a staggered fountain, droplets rolling down from one glossy leaf to another.

A sheet of plastic thrown over the picnic table and benches sagged under the weight of water. An ecstatic sparrow splashed and frolicked in the puddle. Chris smiled. It was too cold for a swim in the river, but he felt invigorated by the freshness of the air, the company of his terrific students, and the promise of a new adventure. It was good to be alive.

Valya's chair was empty, and the girls took over serving breakfast. A heap of the overly browned French toast bulged on a platter. Judging by the smell and frantic sizzling, there was more burning in the kitchen.

"Dreams? Nightmares?" Debra asked, filling his coffee mug. "I managed to fall asleep, but I wish I didn't."

A faint memory, Valya's lips on his. "Just dreams, I guess," Chris said. The urgency to see the young woman swept over him like a blast of hot steam. "Where's Valya?"

"She didn't come to bed till morning," Debra said. "We decided to let her sleep."

Luke lifted a piece of toast with a fork and dropped it back onto his plate. "Which was a horrible mistake."

As if nothing had happened, Chris thought. Had he imagined the glorious manifestation of the feisty walking blobs? "Listen, last night at the pond...."

"Creatures, portal." Peter sipped his coffee. "You're not crazy."

"Then what's the plan?"

"We're going to Kolieno," Debra said. "It's something of a local metropolis. Thanks to you, I came to Vishenky just for one night. I need fresh clothes—"

"Do your laundry in the river," Luke suggested. "I'll take pictures."

"—but I don't want to go all the way to Moscow."

Chris glanced at the raindrops covering the windows. "You can take my umbrella. What time is your train?"

"I asked Valya's neighbor if we could join him on his shopping trip," Debra said. "We have one more seat for you."

"I'd rather stay here and keep Valya company when she wakes up," Chris said.

"I have a feeling I made Mr. Gregory nervous," Debra said. "He'd probably appreciate it if you came along. You know, another responsible adult, not just a bunch of us foolish kids. Jess will stay with Valya, which is a good idea because I think I heard her cry when she came to bed."

Valya was crying?

Would it be inappropriate if he went to see her right away? Just for a second, just to know that she was okay?

No. Barging into her bedroom was not cool.

A Russian-made boxy SUV carved a sharp U-turn in the river meadow and halted by the front gate. The driver honked.

"Your ride is here," Chris said. "I want to eat my breakfast without a rush."

"Sir, they have fast-food joints in Kolieno," Luke said.

"And you can help pump Gregory for information." Peter exercised his long fingers, making popping noises in his knuckles.

"No, thanks," Chris said.

"I'd like to talk to Valya alone," Jessie said.

"Sorry."

"Mr. Waller." A sour smirk distorted the girl's mouth. "A little privacy, that's all I ask. You're not leaving Vishenky forever."

"Yeah, just a chance to visit civilization," Luke said.

Civilization. To walk on asphalt, read a newspaper, find a burger and ice cream. Crowds, traffic, the stench of gasoline.

Debra tapped her spoon against her teacup. "Well?"

Chris looked at the branches of a white rose, its blossoms heavy with moisture, leaning over the path. "How quickly can we get back?"

* * *

I unlocked my eyes and assessed the situation. A throbbing finger, a ghastly taste coating my tongue, the curtains closed, and the house silent. Debra's makeup kit was sitting on the end table—she hadn't left the village for good. It was eleven thirty on the clock. I threw off the comforter.

The walls seemed intent on getting in my way as I headed to Chris's room.

His bed was made and Jessie lounged in a chair with his book.

She wore a white tank with some golden logo, half-covered by a crocheted cardigan the color of pistachios, and a camouflage-green skirt flowing to the floor in layers of frills. While Debra exuded natural, graceful femininity, in Jessie it was choreographed and practiced—the way she sprawled diagonally across the chair, the way the tips of her taupe flats peeked from under the edging of her skirt.

"Looking for someone?" she asked me sweetly.

"You the only one left alive?"

"Sorry to disappoint you."

"I won't be if you can brew good coffee," I said.

"Say 'please,' and I'll make you breakfast."

I sniffed the air. "Is there any food left that isn't burnt?"

Jessie laughed in her beautiful contralto. "In case you want to know, Gregory drove everyone to Kolieno."

"Now I really wonder."

"Debra craved to check out the local fashion."

"Do I dare ask why?"

"It was that or connecting with the nature by doing her laundry in the river. Luke couldn't wait to stuff his face with hotdogs, and Peter thought the best way to deal with monsters was to stock up on booze."

"And Chris?" I asked.

"Well, Mr. Waller...."

"Yeah?"

"It took us a while to persuade him to get out of the house," Jessie said.

Chris needed me.

It didn't matter. I had made up my mind.

Jessie broke a couple of eggs over the skillet. As I watched her, I realized that the hexed eggs still sat on the floor in the tool shed. I had overslept and missed my chance to ask Gregory to dispose of them in Kolieno.

Whatever. Prascovia won. I was naïve to think that I controlled my life.

I rinsed my mouth and gingerly unwrapped my sore finger. Jessie glanced at the bloody scabs and mumbled something about Luke's experience with the garbage disposal under his sink. "Do you need help with that?"

"Please." I raised my hand, and the ties of the cotton dressing dangled under my knuckle.

"What happened?" she asked as she secured the strap.

I nodded toward the stove. "My breakfast is burning."

Jessie dashed to turn off the gas.

She let me drink my coffee before she shot her opening question. "What do you fear most?"

Really, what on this lovely, wet morning did I fear the most?

Not what but who.

Myself.

"Last night, you accused me of ruining lives," I said. "What have I done to deserve such a charge?"

Her pale eyes narrowed. "A year ago, you hosted another group. Kenny Ogden? He's Peter's half-brother. He read the flier you had sent to their home address. You didn't know, did you?"

"Not back then. Kenny told me they found me on the Internet."

"You turned a healthy guy into a wreck. He spent weeks refusing to leave his room. Months of therapy, and he still freaks out when he hears the word 'Vishenky.'"

"That wasn't supposed to happen. What about the rest of his

group? Ron? Amanda?"

"They seem fine."

"Did they tell you anything about me?"

"We got blank stares when we asked them about the trip."

Something wasn't right. Ron and Amanda behaved the way I intended them to, so the spell was done correctly. What combination of factors could have caused Kenny's extreme reaction?

"I need to think about this," I said. "Maybe because you keep prying, your questions short-circuit Kenny's brain. That's another argument why you must do what I tell you to. I'm afraid you're not going to like what I'll ask you to do next."

"What's that?"

"When your friends return from Kolieno, I want you to pack your bags and go to the hotel."

"You're kidding me, right?"

"Jess, not everything went as planned. Your presence stirred the forces beyond my control. If I don't send you away, someone might get hurt."

"You risked our lives all along and it didn't seem to bother you," she said. "Are you saying all this just to pique my interest?"

"Oh, yeah, like your interest is low. Things started to happen since you arrived. It's too dangerous to expose you to manifestations that I'm not equipped to handle."

"Like what?"

"Like the dogs the other night or the blood upstairs," I said. "I have no clue what these paranormal novelties can do."

"If you don't know, then the dangers are purely hypothetical."

"There's something else. Prascovia, the woman who showed up when Chris was in the house alone."

"What about her?" Jessie encouraged me.

"She brought with her an entity which can jumble your emotions and take over your will, and she sicced it on Chris." I raised my bandaged finger. "I was able to stop it from harassing him, but for a price. My relationship with Prascovia is complicated. Her ties with Vishenky are much stronger than mine. I don't know her reasons. If she uses another spell, any one of you can be next."

"Do you want us to sign a waiver?"

"I want you to leave."

"Look, no matter what you tell me, it won't work," Jessie said. "You read my blog, but there's more. Four years ago, I was carrying groceries from my car, and a super-bright white flash went off right in front of me. It was like a lightning bolt. I didn't hear a sound, not even a pop, but my knees buckled as if the blast wave punched me in the stomach."

"Were you hurt?" I asked, thinking about her blinding-white aura that I saw on the night we watched the water possum.

"Not physically, no. But ever since, something plucks me from my sleep. I open my eyes and I see things that are seemingly tangible, very detailed, but at the same time very unreal. Things like a giant Chinese lantern hovering above me like a blimp, or a row of silver threads with water trickling down each strand."

"What happens if you grab it?" I asked. "Has anything ever materialized in our world?"

"No. The object immediately floats out of my reach and vanishes. The occurrence lasts about three seconds. Then my whole body starts to vibrate and I feel awful, as if my heart is about to stop, but my mind shuts itself down and I drift off."

"And how often does this happen?"

"At home, about twice a week. When I travel, sometimes nothing gets to me for the whole trip. Other times, it finds me right away."

"What's your theory?" I asked.

Her fingers were tearing a paper napkin to pieces. "I believe I have become a key to another dimension."

Jessie stared at me with poignant hope that I'd recognize her visions as paranormal encounters. But in my experience, the manifestations were anything but subtle. A real otherworldly apparition would interact with her in very physical ways. *Three seconds?* Rubbish.

"You don't believe me." Her shoulders slumped. "Not even you."

"Oh, I believe that something bothers you. Your mistake is that you wait for someone to save you. Start looking for a way out. Find what triggers your visions."

"But I don't want them to stop. I want to understand them. I want to control them like you control the creatures here."

A bitter smile seized my lips. Boy, did I have an answer for this one.

"My dear Jessie, and what price are you willing to pay for the privilege? How much can you take when something goes wrong? And it will. Your best friends betraying you—how does that sound? Never-ending isolation? How about the moment when you realize that your parents slip psychotropic pills into your food? Or can you picture even for a second the death of someone you love caused by the choices you made?"

Her nostrils flared ever so slightly. Her eyes were two gray pools of melting ice.

"Do the right thing," I said. "End your visions before they take over your life."

"Then why do you—?" She stopped. Her hands, clasped in front of her on the table, trembled despite their white-knuckled grip.

"Keep coming back to Vishenky in spite of everything? Because I was a child when it took hold of me. I'm an addict. I need its thrills. I crave its energy. But you're free. Get out while you can."

"You think I haven't tried?" Another decibel lower and her voice would be inaudible.

"Have you really? Four years and Chinese lanterns hover over your bed?"

"What would you search for?"

"For something absurdly simple. Quit drinking coffee after three o'clock, make a circle out of paperclips around your bed, put a mirror under your pillow, get a cat."

"Endless tries that may never work."

"Jess, whatever activates you, it's a real thing in our dimension. If you're the key, the door can be locked. Find what puts you into the keyhole. Before you go to bed, look around. Something will feel wrong to you. You might discover an irritating light reflection from a picture on the wall. Get rid of it, and your visions will go away."

If she convinced herself she found something off and fixed it, I'd bet her brain would stop tormenting her.

"I wish I shared your confidence," Jessie said, but by her pensive squint I knew she'd try.

"Have you had any visions here?"

"Not yet."

"Good. Let's keep it this way, because who knows what will happen to Vishenky if you open a portal into some crazy new dimension."

"You don't even believe I can do that."

"But if *you* believe it, do you want to take that risk? Be an example, start packing your bag."

"Just one more night," Jessie said. "Please. Let me get closer to a portal."

I heard three honks outside. Gregory's SUV pulled in front of the gate. The doors opened. Chris, Debra, and the guys slid from their seats. Eyes on the ground, Gregory marched past them to open the hatch.

"The entity might be still on the loose in the house," I said. "I have no right to expose you to anything truly hazardous."

"What's the risk?" Jessie asked.

"It killed my best friend."

Her face fell.

Loaded with the linen grocery bags, the men walked through the gate. Debra lingered by the driver's window, probably thanking Gregory for the ride.

Jessie got up and put her hand on the doorknob. "So, this isn't Shangri-La. You think we'll choose to run?"

"Your lives are at stake."

"So is yours." She threw the door open. "Valya wants us to leave," her powerful vocal cords announced to the world.

"Does she?" Chris stepped inside.

The sound of his voice stirred up an animal in me, a helpless, needy kitten.

"Some ghost wreaks havoc on the house," Jessie said. "Valya worries it will ruin our sleep."

Tell him she's lying, my conscience screamed.

You don't have to, the kitten murmured. *Not your fault if Jessie makes them stay.*

Chris dropped off his load in Jessie's hands and crouched before my chair. "Won't you miss us?"

His boyish smile sent my jangled psyche into overdrive. A feisty drummer with the taste for heavy metal replaced my heart. I opened my mouth, but speaking seemed pointless. The objects and the human silhouettes dissolved into a tawny blur. All I could see was Chris's elated face glowing with a peculiar emotion.

I wanted to feel it, too. I looked past him, through the hazy figures, through the windows and the rain, tuning to his mood, letting the emotion bounce between us like the innumerable images of an object put between two opposing mirrors. I recognized the sentiment. My memory played back the setting where I had experienced it.

Late evening sprawls over a city that is older than Moscow. A formidable cathedral rises over staggered red roofs. In the crisscrossing beams of light, seagulls flash like pallid spirits, their calls akin the doleful warnings in the moonless blackened sky.

I tore myself away from Vishenky once in a while. On those rare journeys I found locations with so much character, such high voltages of aura, I felt like those places had souls.

I read the same response in Chris. I sensed his boundless wonderment, his awe of the most incredible place on the planet, Vishenky. And in his eyes, I was its heart and spirit.

"Chris—"

"Do you really want us to leave?"

What woman could resist a man who looked at her like that? I shook my head, my honorable intentions out the window.

CHAPTER FIFTY-THREE

The overcast day gave up its reign to a surprisingly warm evening. Chris brought his book to the front veranda and settled into the chair by the sofa, an unobtrusive surveillance spot.

Wine glasses and the plates of cheese and fruit were moved aside to clear the center of the dining table where the gang played Hearts. Peter teamed up with Jessie. His arm on the back of his girlfriend's seat, he picked out the cards from Jessie's hand. The couple was winning.

Luke munched on sweets. Valya sipped her tea.

"What do you call your cookies in Russian?" Debra asked.

"Don't name them, eat them," Luke advised.

Peter smirked. "How about 'Your diet just died'?"

What a perfect evening this could be, Chris thought. *Perfect, if Jessie's participation in the game was more than her death grip on a hand of cards; if Debra stopped pulling her cardigan tighter; if Peter didn't drink a whole bottle of wine.*

If Valya chose to speak to Chris instead of shunning him since his return from Kolieno.

He would have told her about the night-vision cameras Luke had installed upstairs. About the journal Peter had mailed home from a chaotic post office near Kolieno's main plaza, and about the messages to his half-brother, Kenny, sent from a bustling Internet café while Debra distracted Gregory.

"We can't trust Valya," Peter had said as he, Luke, and Chris stood by the electronics booth at the roofless bazaar. "She seems too confident we'll keep her secret. We might wake up tomorrow and remember nothing—or worse, considering what she did to Kenny."

"Maybe Valya doesn't even know she made your brother sick," Chris said.

Peter selected a gadget on the display. "Have you asked yourself why her childhood friends stay quiet about Vishenky? They know the locations of the occurrences. They could bring over the media. It doesn't add up, does it?"

"You're saying that somehow Valya forces them to stay quiet?" Chris asked.

"I drove Kenny to convulsions when I asked him about Valya." Peter paused, staring at Chris. "I suggest we keep it real. We know nothing about this woman, and we can't believe a word she says. I want to gather the proof the creatures exist and get the hell out of here before she messes up my brain."

I know her, Chris would have said if the statement reflected more than his gut feeling.

Hours later, he questioned the sentiment as he watched his students' contrived spectacle of an after-supper card game and Valya's eager partaking in the fake fun. She chatted, laughed, and flirted, clinging to the bogus normality with a blatant determination bordering on despair. Chris no longer saw the assertive, spirited woman who only a day ago fearlessly guided her guests through the preternatural terrain. Something shadowy and despondent clouded her emotions.

Chris didn't understand how he knew. Not a frown, not a single uncontrolled gesture betrayed Valya's distress. By instinct, by some zany reasoning, by magic, he perceived and recognized her anguish.

A monolith of self-control, Valya picked a cherry from the fruit plate, admired her selection, and bit into the juice-dripping ruby flesh.

What kind of an individual could exude such nonchalance when her emotions played tug of war with her every nerve?

The same person who can withstand daily encounters with horrid beasts. Peter was correct: Her emotions aside, Valya was a stranger. To what dangers did she expose herself? Why on this seemingly tranquil evening did the lioness turn into a fawn trapped in a wildfire?

Talk to me, Chris pleaded silently. *Your life, your choices aren't normal. If*

Vishenky's not a fairy tale, why do you have to endure its terrors?

Valya raised her eyes. They stopped on Chris, searing him as if he desecrated a monument.

Startled, he stared back. *You hear thoughts, don't you?*

"Do you want something to drink?" she asked, her tone light, playful.

Chris shook his head. *I'm becoming irrational.*

A loon yowled on the river. Valya checked the clock and put down her cards. "It's time."

"Let's do it." Peter pushed back his chair and stood up, his fervor the only sign of his inebriation. "This makes life worth living."

"Well said." Valya picked up the cheese plate. "Just give me a second to clear the table."

She hesitated in the doorway to the kitchen, looking back at Chris. "But sometimes I do wish that there were no monsters."

CHAPTER FIFTY-FOUR

Flakes of the moon overlay a strip of ripples on the river surface. For a moment I had the oddest feeling I had seen this before—black waters, Jessie pointing at something in the brush, and Debra's silhouette on the edge, wraithlike in her shimmering clear-plastic poncho.

The déjà vu passed. The unexplained sadness lingered.

As the day and my adrenaline wore out, shadows and dread seeped in. My peripheral vision caught shapes that weren't there. I imagined whispers in an empty room. By the time the first dewdrops of starlight sprinkled the sky, I was a pot of panic simmering on the hot oven of anguish. Dangers always stalked me as I pursued the paranormal creatures, adding zing to my quests, but this was different. Without an external outlet, emotional or physical, the energy of my affection for Chris found an unforeseen escape in fear.

I squeezed a tiny vial in my pocket. The potion induced the feeling of indifference. One sip and I'd be free. My tortured heart would stop pushing its jagged shards into my flesh with every beat.

But the cure remained hidden. I needed Chris so much that longing topped my common sense.

Looking like giant crystal bats, the guys tested their night-vision gear on Jess and Debra. Peter had purchased the iridescent hooded ponchos in Kolieno for everyone's protection. I didn't see a crumb of a chance to persuade the inquisitive lad to abandon his project. Jessie refused to wear her plastic garment—I figured it was to experience the paranormal universe more intimately. Chris had followed her example. I didn't want to know why.

I opted to stick with my flyswatter so I wouldn't lose an instant in mobility. Tucked under my belt behind my back, the flimsy weapon might look silly, but its swipes once held off an ogre the size of a rhinoceros. For everyone's sake, I needed to stay vigilant—a tough thing to do while walking with lungs full of paralyzing terror. I hated standing here, in the open, instead of taking cover behind the locked doors.

The panorama of the moonlit river awaiting its chimeras wasn't helping.

"You know what I'd like?" Chris asked me. "To go back inside, turn on all the lights, and wait for the morning."

"Tell this to Jess and Peter."

"They're not the problem. You are. You mingle too much with the monsters. Do you have self-discipline to walk away from all of this?"

I barely had self-discipline to pretend that I was okay, acting cool all evening long for the sake of his students. But Chris had been picking up on my distress.

"What do you usually worry about?" I asked him. "Mortgage payments? Gas prices?"

"Oh, I understand Vishenky's allure. Last night I was like a five-year-old his first time at a zoo. But now I see what you've taught yourself to ignore. You don't deserve to spend your life sorting out this horrendous mess."

"I don't deserve to be lectured by the man who'd rather spend his life hiding in a burrow."

"That was uncalled for," Chris said.

"I didn't ask for advice."

The look of an unjustly punished kid settled on his eyebrows and mouth. Could a few hurtful words break the bond between us?

I stretched a blade of grass along my thumbs and blew the primitive whistle. Its despondent shrieks fitted right in with the ethereal wisps of fog swirling above the water, a fallen tree bobbing in the current like a giant drowned insect, and my furtive, worthless remorse.

A bird answered from the willows on the other side of the river.

Debra migrated closer to Chris and me. "Just like in horror movies."

"A cry of loon," I said. "Nearby, a good sign. One nasty thing called Ostov patrols the area between the cemetery and the grove. If it strays from its grounds, I need to know." Out of all the monsters brought to Vishenky by July's moon, I dreaded the appearance of Ostov the most and knew how to hinder it the least.

"Isn't it what you like?" Chris asked. "Vicious creatures? The nastier the better?"

"Beats dealing with the humans," I informed him unenthusiastically. Sarcasm required resentment. I felt none.

To thwart his attempts to peruse my emotions, I went down the steps to the wooden platforms I used to do the laundry and dishes. My father built two square podiums, high and low, to accommodate rises and falls of the current. Just as I reached the bottom level, a colossal green bubble rose to the surface. Expanding, an extraterrestrial landscape emerged above the river like an enormous hologram.

Inside, a low shoreline framed a swampy lake, and a jade-green full moon hung in the starless sky. Half-reptiles, half-primates, whimsical creatures perched on floating mounds of grass. Everything glowed— rocks on the bottom, vegetation, scales, violet eyes, and exposed fangs.

I thrust my hand into the alien world. An olive sheen coated my skin. Violet charges began to crackle between my fingers. The comforting sense of recognition filled my body. My heart beat softer. The dread that tormented me until this moment evaporated like water drops on a hot stove burner. Enfolded in warm stillness, I savored the essence of the paranormal world, its sumptuous energy.

To walk away and give up this bliss? Substitute it with what, a bubble bath and scented candles? Champagne in a hot tub? An hour of massage? A day in a spa?

Poor Chris. He'd never understand the absurdity of his suggestion.

Sensing the intrusion, the creatures stirred. A lizard-like form slid into the water and snaked toward me.

Quick steps pounded the boards, and Jessie ventured on the platform. She put one arm around my shoulders as if not trusting her balance. She raised the other and stretched it parallel to mine. Instead of acquiring a ghostly luster, her hand turned black.

"You have no connection with that dimension," I informed her and looked back, searching for Debra. I wanted her, not Jessie, to place her hand inside the bubble. I assumed the Newt Spring had responded to her presence, but I needed to be sure.

Debra peeked at the supernatural fauna over Luke's shoulder. I was about to call her name, but a plaintive cry reverberated upstream where the river made a loop.

The scaly necks twisted. Dozens of unblinking eyes peered in the direction of the sound. The lizard swimming toward the platform changed its course.

Another mournful bawl cut the air. Just what I needed—an unexpected manifestation developing in front of my untrained, untested group. I pulled Jessie away from the portal. Luke and Debra retreated from the bank's edge. Now about twenty meters from the sphere, a fishing rowboat drifted in the middle of the slow-moving river, the blade tips of the oars floating lifelessly in the water. Age blackened the varnished wood.

A cute tuxedo cat darted back and forth between two bench seats as if trapped and knowing its fate but too afraid to jump off.

That little shapeshifter was good. Its performance of a feline in distress would convince any pet lover, though I knew that not everyone in the group observed the same animal. An iguana owner would see a magnificent lizard trying to escape the jaws of its paranormal counterparts. A koi lover would watch a showy fish flopping around in deathly panic.

I didn't have a pet. I saw the tabby because I was picking up someone else's tormenting illusion.

The next round of the cat's miserable squeaks stirred a wave of interest on the paranormal lake. Several slick forms circled the area where two bodies of water merged through the transparent luminous wall.

"Does anyone have a small pet?" I asked. "A cat? A bunny? Yorkie? Chihuahua?"

"A ferret," Luke said.

"A cat," Chris muttered. I should have known whose vision I was perceiving. He kicked off his sneakers. "I'll get this one out."

"No! This is not a real—"

Luke sprinted past us.

I caught him in mid-step and knocked him to the ground. He rolled, jumped up, and raced forward. Peter shoved the camera into his girlfriend's hands and darted to intercept his pal.

Luke pushed him back so forcefully that Peter fell, tearing off Luke's cloak. I'd have grabbed the maverick, but that would have been a mosquito's effort to carry off a moose. He dove into the river. I followed.

Cold water quickly peeled off my warmth. I tried to stand upright so I could wipe my face and clear my vision, but the bottom of the river, usually so shallow, was gone.

New screams reached my ears. This time the voice was Luke's. I breaststroked toward the pandemonium.

A tailless creature that in its appearance resembled lorises and tarsiers squatted on the stern, its teeth sunk into Luke's right forearm. He thrashed but couldn't free himself or pull the thing into the river. A tough cluster of thin limbs, the supernatural primate held on to the vessel like a liana to a tree.

Wilted flowers, pasty in the moonlight, covered the bottom of the boat. For food, the creature raided fresh graves. It wouldn't touch plastic forget-me-nots or artificial wreaths, but fresh-cut arrangements ended up in its stash.

Somewhere in the rotting pile lay a tuft of *volkanok's* fur, the one I had to replace yesterday. The shapeshifter's second weakness was to empty the lockets buried beside the victims' headstones. When the supernatural universe seeped into ours, its inhabitants had to adjust to their new environment. Once I saw the otherworldly primate, an omnivore, chewing on a bone of a goose killed by *volkanoks*. Every time one of the predators approached the creature, it thrust forward the bony front paw, offering its nemesis a tuft of fur for inspection—and was left alone, probably mistaken for another *volkanok*.

"What do we do?" Chris yelled into my ear. Startled, I glanced back. He effortlessly stayed afloat behind me.

"The bite's poisonous. Make sure he doesn't drown." Avoiding

Luke's ferocious swings, I strained to pull myself onto the boat. Chris grabbed the side to stabilize the cumbersome craft. The wooden rim dug into my stomach as I scrambled halfway in and seized the creature by the scruff.

Hissing, squirming, and spitting, the scrawny little devil released Luke's arm.

"Get him out of the water," I shouted to Chris.

I threw my knee over the side and rolled into the boat. My butt landed in the reeking soggy mass of the dead flowers.

Flexible in their sockets, the primate's limbs wrapped my arm up to my elbow. My wet sleeve provided a terrific grip for its hairy resilient fingers. The thing twisted its head in an attempt to bite me, mayhem and murder on its plum-sized brain.

Balancing the ten infuriated pounds on my outstretched arm, I rose to my feet. Meters ahead, the sphere was coming at me like an oceanic cruise ship.

Left with no time to mess with the flyswatter, I pulled at the thread around my neck. My locket reluctantly emerged from under the layers of my sodden clothes. Just as the prow was about to cross the line between the two dimensions, I snapped the jewelry open.

Like four serpents, the primate's lanky limbs disentangled from my arm and lunged toward my chest in their pursuit of *volkanok's* fur. I tossed the creature forward, into its native world, shut the locket, and leaped overboard.

The hushed, disorienting darkness ruled under the surface. Uninterrupted solitude. Cold slithering along my body. Thoughts, lightless and suffocating like this underwater world. *The panicky Luke has the weight and strength to drown Chris. Peter didn't get up after his buddy pushed him. The tumult could draw Ostov's attention, and Jessie isn't wearing the protective plastic garment.* I forced my way through the endless mass of water, wondering if I lost my direction and swam against the current instead of heading toward the bank. My heart, a chunk of heavy rubber, hammered in my rib cage until dull pain devoured my whole chest.

My fingers finally touched the sand. Out of breath, I coughed and fought to catch my balance on all fours in the shallows. If I could, I'd shake like an animal to get all this chilly wetness off my clothes.

Hands yanked me to my feet.

"If Luke dies...." Peter's onyx-black eyes finished his threat.

Well. At least Luke wasn't dead yet. I considered my next move. This probably wasn't the best moment to inform Peter about the parchment with the recipe that could save his friend. I had rescued it from the flooded old cellar, but the text had already suffered irreparable water damage.

CHAPTER FIFTY-FIVE

Valya sent Chris to change and find a portable space heater stored somewhere under the furniture in his bedroom. When he returned to the back veranda, sinus-clearing menthol replaced all the breathable air. The place resembled a doctor's office from the nineteen hundreds.

An assortment of glass test tubes lay scattered on the nightstand. Kneeling beside it, Peter held a bowl. A ring of a coffee-colored liquid stained its white enamel. For the moment, the crockery served as a wastebasket for the used chemical paraphernalia. Luke's soggy clothes and bloody cotton strips littered the floor. Valya crouched by his bed. She had taken off her soaked sweater and now sported a nude-colored bra, goose bumps, and a large bandage on her right shoulder.

The bruises Chris had inflicted were gone, but under the beige strip of plastic, he could see a blot that looked very much like caked blood. A new maggot of worries dug into his stomach. Her wrapped finger, which she refused to talk about, and her injured shoulder— Luke's bites were not the first wounds sustained within the group in the past forty-eight hours.

The hems of Valya's jeans dripped water, and her sock-clad feet left wet imprints on the linoleum-covered floor. Her hands flitted over a brown wooden medicine chest, the biggest Chris had ever seen. The bottom was divided into dozens of sections, each containing a vial plugged with a cork. Valya consulted the corresponding inscriptions in the squares on the lid as she mixed the remedies.

Her fingers fused in a white-knuckled clasp in her lap, Jessie froze by Luke's side. Debra stooped on Peter's bed, hugging his pillow.

Reluctantly, Chris moved closer to look at the victim. Luke lay on his back, his skin ashen and the slivers of the whites of his eyes gleaming between his eyelids. A thread of saliva seeped from the corner of his open mouth. He sucked in air in rapid, shallow gasps. The edges of his punctures had turned black.

Valya placed the opening of a test tube to the boy's lips, spilling some of its contents into his mouth. She then dribbled the maroon liquid over the necrosis on his forearm.

Peter took the glass cylinder from her trembling fingers and dropped it into the bowl. "How long do we have?"

Jessie checked her watch. "Six minutes."

Valya grabbed a clean test tube and a half-full vial from the nightstand. She selected a new solution from the chest. "Chris, don't just stand there, plug in the heater. It's freezing in here."

"Six minutes, and then what?" Chris asked.

"Nothing, if I find the right ingredients." She poured a few drops of each liquid into the test tube, capped it with her thumb, and vigorously shook the mixture. "Everything will be fine."

"And if you don't?"

Valya sniveled as if crying, but her eyes were dry. "Then Gregory will dump Luke's body into a portal and you'll report him missing."

"You mean, he could die?"

"Not if I make the antidote."

Chris pulled on the collar of his sweatshirt. The vacuum left by the dismal forecast was making it hard for him to breathe.

"You have no idea what you're doing, do you?" he asked the insane witch doctor.

"It will work," Valya snapped.

He spread his arms before the medicine chest. "But this gives you an infinite number of combinations!"

Valya pointed at the half-full vial in Peter's hand. "That's the first component, quaking-grass extract. The second one has 'r' in its name."

"Mr. Waller, she's Luke's only chance," Peter said. "Don't distract her."

"Deb, go wake up Gregory," Chris ordered. "We'll take Luke to the hospital. He needs antibiotics, not some herbal crap."

His cousin sobbed.

"Not herbal...." Valya studied the mixture she had just created. "Oh my God, that's it! The remedy is not herbal."

She tossed the test tube into the bowl. The glass cracked. She referred to the inscriptions on the chest's lid, pulled out a vial, and smashed it against the floorboards. Instead of an extract, it released an inch-long key.

"The first word was *kookooshki*." Valya lifted the chest and shoved it on top of the nightstand. The empty test tubes rolled toward the wall. "I thought it stood for the incomplete *kookooshkini slezki*, cuckoo's tears, quacking grass, but it's not. I'm supposed to use 'something of a cuckoo,' as in a real bird, which is a completely different recipe."

"Three minutes," Jessie whispered.

Luke wheezed and stopped breathing. Debra screamed.

"Jess, quick, keep his heart going," Valya said.

Jessie got on top of the motionless body. Her crossed flat palms glided over Luke's torso toward his heart as if she willed his dying organs to absorb her vitality. She started the rhythmic pumping.

"Say when you're tired," Peter rasped.

Valya inserted the key into the metal-encrusted hole on the bottom of the chest's front side. On her knees, she toiled to turn the key, moaning in her ferocious effort. The lock resisted her assault.

"Let me try," Chris said.

She scrambled backward. He took her spot.

A life depended on his success. His fingers versus the rusty mechanism.

The corrosion was winning.

"You need pliers," Debra squeaked behind his back, "or an ax."

"If we break the key or the bottles, Luke dies," Valya said.

"It's too small," Chris said. "I can't get a good grip."

"Wrap it." She handed him a cotton strip.

Just when he thought his fingertips would split, a grinding sound rose from the guts of the antique contraption. The upper drawer with all the vials came up and forward, exposing a hidden shelf and a row of six bottles. Valya snatched the first one on the left.

She covered her mouth, her face scrunched in disgust. "Cuckoo's eyes." The bottle was filled with a clear liquid, and several bead-looking globules rolled on the bottom.

She swiftly went through the remaining containers. "Only one with 'r.' *Roocheinik*. Larvae of an insect. They build sand tubes around their bodies and live in water."

"Caddisfly," Peter said.

"Whatever." Valya thrust the bottles into his hands. "You mix it. One eye, one larva. You have to squish them. Add a little bit of juice from each bottle, and shake it well. Apply to the bites, not internally."

"You should do it!" Peter said.

Valya touched her bandaged shoulder with her wrapped finger. "I just got injured by two supernatural animal cadavers. My immunity is compromised. Right now, I can't handle any more paranormal remains."

"But what if Luke—"

"Do it. This is only the first phase. I'll get us ready for tomorrow." Valya stepped over the squat heater Chris never plugged in and headed inside the main part of the house.

Chris knew better than to try to stop her. During the desperate seconds of their conquering the lock, his physical proximity to Valya placed him within the aura of her emotions. He'd be much happier without glimpsing what lay hidden under her pale but composed look.

CHAPTER FIFTY-SIX

Luke fell asleep. The quick whispers in Valya and Debra's bedroom had stopped, and only the drone of the space heater keeping the back veranda a few degrees warmer than the outdoors helped Chris stay awake. Still dressed, half-sitting, half-lying on his new bed, he tried to read in the weak light of a lamp.

His students didn't know why Valya had requested that he and Peter switch places for the night, but after she had dragged Luke back from the brink of death, it was preposterous to disobey her orders. Valya swore that if they took Luke to the hospital, his injury would only mystify the staff. To cure him and eliminate any possibility of complications, she needed some unearthly supplies that were inaccessible at that late hour. She was positive she could get them in the morning. Chris had no choice but to trust her expertise.

Under two heavy quilts he had found a springy mattress resting on a timber frame. A bare brick wall to which the back veranda was attached, a chipped plywood stool by the foot of each bed, cracked and faded linoleum on the floor—the simplicity of the room was beyond austere.

Living in a paranormal turmoil, Valya couldn't concern herself with home décor. Her mother, "the official owner of the house" as Valya had put it, didn't seem to care either. A minor detail considering that a dead bird's squished eye had just resuscitated his student, but Chris wondered what else went on under this roof. To what extent did the parents understand their unusual daughter? Did the family add a grain of normalcy to the young woman's life?

Maybe not. There was a reason why Valya had perfected her skill to hide the blowtorch of her emotions.

Luke mumbled in his sleep and turned away. Chris switched off the lamp. He saw the full moon through the old-fashioned straw blinds. Not a poetical beauty. An ominous harbinger.

Peter couldn't wait to tell the world about the mysterious village, Jessie had some personal stakes in the paranormal game, but Chris wished it would all go away—the creatures, the danger, the entire improbable reality and the very memory of it.

But not Valya. Not the woman whose mere presence in a room shook cobwebs off the broken clock that his spirit had become after his parents' death. The only woman whose hazel eyes, always intense—and gentle whenever Chris discovered he was the object of her furtive attention—had the power to restart his soul's gears. A wish to yank Valya from the abnormal milieu pulled him apart, unrelenting like the roots of an urban tree growing into asphalt.

Did he have the right or obligation or even a reason to do anything about Valya and Vishenky? Was there anything that could be done?

Chris held his breath. Yes, there it was again, a sound coming from the backyard, just a sigh louder than the humming of the fan, whispers like a prayer rustling in his ears.

Anticipation filled him, not the unnerving sense of threat but a hope for magic, for a fairy tale. Unsure what to make of it, Chris unlocked the outside door.

Paler than an apparition, Valya stood in the flowerbed by the veranda, facing the luminous moon, her arms reaching forward, hands opened as if in an appeal to the celestial body. In a white blouse with wide sleeves and a shin-length skirt, an ingenuous romance between the lace and ribbons, she looked like a peasant maiden from centuries ago. Eyes closed, wavy hair loose around her shoulders, she spoke in a strange language, unaware of his presence.

"What are you worshiping, pagan girl?" Chris asked.

Her arms fell along her body at the sound of his voice. In the curl of her unlocked lips, in her furrowing eyebrows, Chris saw what he'd been waiting for—a crash of Valya's rock-solid self-control, a splatter of emotions.

He opened his arms. "Come here."

Her flight toward him, and his optimism that she would listen to his concerns, lasted four energetic steps, a third of the space she had to traverse. Then Valya stopped. Her shoulders rose. She lowered her head.

Chris put one arm forward, palm up, as if her trust were a timid butterfly and it would land onto his hand if he stood still. Valya turned away and strode up the path.

"Oh, for the love of God." He chased after the pallid shape fleeing through the hushed garden.

The fugitive of his good intentions led him past the neglected orchard to the tall back fence. Chris heard a click of the deadbolt.

Valya left the heavy gate ajar. He took it as an invitation.

Behind the village stretched a narrow strip of pastures. A packed dirt road separated the uncultivated land from the rye fields. Gregory's grass was cut and hoarded in the neat haystacks. A meadow brushed against the back of Valya's property, a fragrant throw of the wildflowers and plumes glittering with dew.

The Russian runaway, poignantly romantic in her attire of moonlight and lace, left the path and walked into the knee-high vegetation.

She whispered words Chris didn't understand, and a cloud of lightning bugs emerged from the oak towering over Gregory's barn. Valya waved for Chris to come closer. Floating just above the ground, the swarm rolled leisurely toward them and stopped a few feet away.

The conjurer furled her fingers into a fist and released them in a single sprinkling motion. The flickering airborne amoeba broke apart. The fireflies alighted on the flowers. The meadow erupted in sparks of blue, pink, and lavender, like a festival of lights in a microcosm of elves and pixies.

Valya smiled at the result of her effort.

"You think I will applaud you?" Chris asked.

"*You think I will applaud you?*" Two voices, male and female, parroted his question, in sync, and coming from Valya's mouth.

Fear ripped through his stomach. Chris gasped. Her face turned blurry, as if he watched her through the air shimmering above an overheated highway. Laughing, the apparition jumped sideways, like a mischievous kid at play or a feline teasing its quarry.

He started backing away, wary of his footing in the tangled weeds. The creature followed, darting to the right and to the left with faster-than-the-eye-can-see swiftness.

Chris reached the path and ran. He plowed into the closed gate, his shoulder barely withstanding the collision. He ducked under the limbs of the unkempt fruit trees. His heart beat madly, not just from his shameless sprint. He expected fangs, talons, blades, or pitchforks to rip his back.

The back veranda was lit. On the last puff out of his stinging lungs, Chris burst through the unlocked half of the double door and blocked it with his body. On his bed, in jeans and a sweatshirt, with the book he had left, rested the real Valya.

She tossed the paperback aside. "What's out there?"

Chris tried to speak but ended up coughing, then laughing. The apparition had looked romantic. Her jaw set, fists clenched, the real woman was a soldier primed to act.

"Your perimeter is breached," he said. "The thing could go in and out."

"What thing?"

"It appeared...human."

"Just a shapeshifter," Valya said. "One of mine, trapped here. Not dangerous. Haven't seen him in years."

Him?

"Chris, it's okay. I'll deal with it. Where's the breach?"

"It's probably the back gate."

"Stay in."

She touched his shoulder, urging him to move from the door. His ability to read her had diminished, but the contact sent her emotions gushing through his nerves. One he had sensed before. It had frightened him into inaction earlier. Chris didn't know under what circumstances a person could experience such absolute, nearly maniacal resolve, other than while pressing the button to destroy the world.

There was something else, cold and pitiless, resembling hate but without its fury.

Alienation.

Her exposures to the supernatural world put Valya at odds with humanity. Chris saw her future. One night she'd cross the point of no return if left alone, and he'd lose the only woman who knew how to thaw the permafrost saturating his existence.

CHAPTER FIFTY-SEVEN

In the exact spot in the flowerbed where Chris had first seen Valya's replica, a slender man stood immersed in meditation, or moon tanning, his eyes closed, arms stretched forward, and his face ashen. He looked no older than twenty.

The fine lines of his nose and mouth, his high forehead and sculptured cheekbones reminded Chris of Peter. The man's hair was brown, too, but longer and with a slight wave. Though his attire boasted no lace, the fluffy cut of his white shirt bore the same medieval flair as the blouse of the previous manifestation.

Valya didn't stop to behold the ritual and its performer. She went straight to the apparition and shoved it. The man screamed as he fell, crushing peonies. Chris heard the thud of the skull hitting the border stones.

The assailant walked off without a glance at her victim. The ghostly form sprawled on the ground, wrapped in a green shine. Chris forced himself to look away.

"That will teach him," he called after the slim silhouette fleeing the scene. "Should I kick him for good measure?"

Valya made a 180-degree turn and raised her hand to her forehead in a paroxysm of heavy thinking.

"Come back," Chris urged. "If I get any louder, Luke will wake up."

Whether it was the likelihood he'd cross the boundary of plastic thus putting his life at risk or his threat to disturb the injured, Valya chose to return. She sat on the veranda's wooden stoop and hugged her knee, her other leg bent beneath her, the back of her head pressed against the locked half of the double door. Chris lowered himself on the boards, facing his opponent while every inch of his brain insisted that he turn and check the open space behind him.

For once, she seemed willing to listen. Chris stared in her eyes, his silence a glacial crevasse deepening between them.

What realistic plan could he propose? Valya should be taken away from Vishenky, offered a fresh start, shown another direction of existence. Suggesting anything less would be as incongruous as a fish head in a wedding cake. His egotistic, irrationally obsessive longing for Valya's company aside, did he seriously consider changing his life for a woman he had met two days ago?

Valya smiled and turned away, shaking her head as if aware of the fight between his heart and his logic. "In a few hours, Luke will be cured and you can leave," she said. "I promise that none of you will care if Vishenky exists."

"That's not what I want."

"What do you want?"

"Do you understand how this place affects you?" Chris glanced at the apparition's body bleeding green neon in the flowerbed. "You bottle up your emotions until they're beyond your control."

"It's a different world, and I play by different rules. Apparitions can get pesky. Call it necessary hostility."

Chris pointed at her shoulder where earlier he'd spotted a bandage slapped over dried blood. "How did you get hurt?"

He didn't mention her injured finger, but Valya hid it instinctively, curling her hands around her waist with the swiftness of an attacked hedgehog. "It won't happen again."

"Something else will."

"Don't concern yourself with problems that aren't yours."

Forget the black cat. In the proverbial dark room, he chased a timorous swallow with an injured wing. Was it even possible to separate her from the cursed village?

"I can't help it," Chris said. "I'm worried about your future."

"The future. Right. We'll be diving tomorrow. Even if you're a good swimmer, you'll need all your strength. Get some sleep."

"When was the last time you had a chance to show your real life to anyone? How often do you meet people like Debra and me, people who don't think you're crazy? People you can trust? People who can help?"

"For goodness' sake, Chris, what do you think you can do for me?"

A hot blush hit his face and neck. "Give you a different perspective on Vishenky? Tell me what's really going on. I need to know that you're safe."

Valya lowered her head, her hands steepled before her face, her index fingers pushing up the tips of her eyebrows.

"I care about you," Chris said. "Is that so difficult to believe?"

She straightened up. Her gaze consulted the moon, the willow by the fence, the steps, the landing she and Chris sat on, before she gathered her fortitude and looked at him. "Whatever you imagine you feel about me, these are not your genuine feelings. They're a side effect. You never got over some emotional trauma. I manipulated your emotions to start a healing process. As a result, you believe there's a connection between us." Her words were like slabs of ice carried by a fast, smooth, relentless river. Valya leaned forward and squeezed his wrist. "Don't be afraid to break it. You fear that without me you'll go back to your old bland existence. I promise, you won't. I erased all your melancholy for good. You don't need me to be happy."

Her palm felt warm through the fabric of his shirt. The young woman seemed so reachable, so sympathetic, yet Chris sat as motionless and silent as if encrusted in cement, squirming inside like a bug on a pin, alive but masterfully added to her collection of conquests. Dissected, labeled, and forgotten.

"This apparition"—he nodded over his shoulder—"who did it imitate?"

Her hand slid back into her lap. "No idea."

"Don't lie. You recognized him. My guess, your shapeshifter picks up on the observer's emotions and changes accordingly. Who was it?"

Valya wrapped her arms around her bent leg. Her forehead touched her knee. Her body rocked slightly from side to side.

"Must be an old boyfriend," Chris said.

"Don't be cruel."

"Did he break your heart?"

She set her chin to rest on her kneecap, her eyes glistening. "I lost a friend ten years ago." With the movements of her lower jaw constricted, her voice sounded childlike. "Every time I think I've gotten over it, this shapeshifter shows up. It gets older, only not as fast as a real person. Somehow that makes it more horrific—a dead friend who never dies."

"Oh my God. I'm so sorry. What happened?"

Valya shook her head, refusing or unable to speak. Her face was distorted by sadness so profound that it looked as though for all those years she had succeeded to bar the grief from her emotions, but it had managed to break through finally. Chris wanted to reach out, to touch her, but he willed himself to sit still, his elbow not leaving his knee, his hand dangling lifelessly in spite of his contracted bicep. She might be an expert on manifestations, a tamer of paranormal beasts, but sitting here stooped with the huge dark house behind her, Valya appeared small and defenseless, a child who'd painted an enchanted forest and been pulled into her own drawing. The fairy tale turned into a nightmare, but even confused, scared, and desperate, that child wouldn't take a stranger's hand to lead her out.

To lead her where?

"When was the last time you talked to somebody about him?" Chris asked.

Her body shrunk into a tighter ball. She stared sideways, her nostrils flaring in a fit of defensive stubbornness. "I'm okay. I don't need help."

"The shapeshifter shows up not because it wants to remind you of your friend. It's here because that loss is still on your mind. It might be painful, but you must, you absolutely must—"

"What? Confront my memories? You're not getting it." Her eyes flickered, narrowing for each curt sentence, as if Valya took aim to hit him with her every word. "Yes, I was thinking about Dimitry. You opened the door, you interacted with Prascovia, and now an entity identical to the one that killed him is lurking in the house. I've been through hell trying to keep you alive."

CHAPTER FIFTY-EIGHT

"You knew, and you never warned me?" Chris asked.

"I told you that you should leave." I spoke hastily in my defense.

A cryogenic chill induced by my betrayal had already purged the warmth Chris felt for me. Then I couldn't read him at all. Pushed so far, he plummeted into an emotional shutdown.

"How did your friend die?" he asked, his tone neutral, even. In that pleasantly courteous tenor he could be asking someone's grandmother in a retirement home about her day.

Dimitry killed himself. It took a while. I was a whisper away, I could have saved him, but with all my supernatural perception, I hadn't sensed a thing.

My legs shaky from the merciless memories—or was I picking up Chris's emotional state after all?—I stood up and raised my bandaged finger. "I've paid for your safety. It's late and we both are tired. Why don't you go to bed."

Chris was on his feet, coming at me, barging into my personal space. His palms slammed into the closed door and stayed there trapping me, almost touching my head. "No, let's talk," he suggested gently.

I flattened myself against the wood. I wasn't scared, just startled by his abruptness. His breath carried the scent of his mint toothpaste. How he controlled his voice was a puzzle, considering that his lungs pulled a doubled tempo to support his agitation.

I, on the other hand, calmed down and was comforted by the

physical nearness of the man to whom I was attracted.

"You put Peter in my room," Chris said. "Is this your idea of safety?"

"I moved you because Deb said you're a light sleeper. You'd hear if Luke was having trouble breathing." I was suddenly aware how much I resented the centimeters that separated our lips. "The entity won't go after Peter."

"How do you know?"

I itched to caress his cheek to reassure him. It took an effort to keep my fingers pressed to the wood behind me. "Prascovia doesn't give a damn about Peter. He's not a threat to my relationship with Vishenky."

"What do you mean?"

"I'm not in love with him."

We both fell silent, processing my reluctant confession. Then his hands enfolded my face. Our eyes locked.

What was I thinking? Somewhere overseas, a normal life, a predictable environment waited for this sweet, compassionate man. Too conventional, he wasn't cut out to handle my problems. I grew up accustomed to secrecy, self-reliant to a fault. No matter how much I craved it, I was unprepared to accept his affection.

My eyes welled with tears. I pressed my fists against his chest. "Chris, don't. Don't make this worse." *Don't tempt our infatuation with the intimacy of kisses.*

Did I really believe my halfhearted plea would stop the man who just found out that his advances were desired? Our lips met, and for a few breathtaking moments, nothing would convince our bodies that we were fooled by some supernatural conspiracy.

My mind knew better, and I found the strength to push Chris away.

He complied. His face glowed with tenderness. A happy smile played on his mouth as he lifted a strand of hair tickling my cheek and tucked it behind my ear.

I grabbed the doorknob. "Get some rest. It will be a tough morning." I opened the back veranda's door for him as if I was giving an indisputable order.

* * *

I walked around the house, unlocked the front veranda, and tiptoed into the kitchen and through the draped partition guarding Chris's quarters where I had relocated Peter.

My handsome target breathed evenly in his sleep, not sensing my uneasy presence. The tall metal-frame bed was wide enough to accommodate two people and I wouldn't be surprised to find Jessie in her boyfriend's arms, but he was alone.

I perched by his side. "Peter?"

He was half-sitting in a second, pushing off the comforter, his eyes still shut. "Is it Luke?"

"He's fine. How is your finger?"

"Healed. Jess talked me into using ribwort." Peter dropped back on his elbow, rubbing his face with his free hand. "What do you want?"

"I want to be your best friend."

He made a chuckling noise with his mouth closed. "All or nothing, huh?"

"Always."

Peter didn't ask why I needed a roll of plastic food wrap, or a shovel, or the basket with two eggs that I picked up in the tool shed. His curious squint added an ironic zest to his expression while he watched my fussing.

"This might take some time." I shut the shed's door. "That's why I left Chris with Luke."

Peter stared in the direction of the garden. "Not your best idea. Mr. Waller's running around your vegetables like he's mad, and I'm not sure what he's wearing."

I darted to see the picture. "That's not Chris," I said, both relieved and annoyed. "It's something that decided to imitate him for our amusement. A shapeshifter that got trapped when I laid a plastic barrier."

"Where's its portal? It should be somewhere here, on your property."

"Good question. If I ever find it, I'll throw a giant sheet of plastic over the spot and plug it forever."

Bad answer, I thought immediately.

Peter smirked. "You seem flustered. I'd be upset too if I were forced to watch Mr. Waller tramp all over my veggies. Why is it him?"

Because I let Chris kiss me. Because the damn shapeshifter senses who's on my mind.

"Surprised you, didn't it?" I replied with an unenthusiastic shrug.

"I can think of a quadrillion people whose materialization in your carrot patch would surprise me more."

Peter waited for me to defend my explanation. I didn't take the bait but followed the shapeshifter up the dew-soaked path.

It fled ahead of us toward the back of the garden, its fluffy white shirt easily detectable in the shadows of the orchard. I never figured out why its human imitations wore Renaissance garments. At least it didn't roam around naked.

The fake Chris squeezed through the crack-opened back gate and vanished. Its haste alarmed me. Rats leaving the ship? Or was I reading too much into the behavior of a mindless apparition?

Probably just wants its freedom. Great, one less reminder of Dimitry. *Or Chris.* I inspected the ground by the entrance and found a molehill. It had to be the critter's burrow that disrupted my safety perimeter.

Peter dug a shallow trench, I fixed the barrier, and then I took my new apprentice outside the property.

The fields, silvery in the moonlight, stretched out to the horizon. The sky looked overpowering. The familiar flash of blue we barely noticed in the daylight had unfolded into an agoraphobia-inducing hemisphere, the soot-black velvet sparkling with constellations. The village slouched below us like a sheepish pooch—head down but two glowing eyes, the lit windows in Prascovia's house, watching. I knew she couldn't see us, but I briskly moved through the meadow, stroking the handle of my flyswatter and looking for an angle where the trees would block her potential line of vision.

We stopped behind Gregory's barn. My diligent neighbor had gathered his hay in the loose stacks to prevent the night dew from dampening his harvest. I picked the heap closest to the field, climbed up, and pushed down its top to clear enough space for two people.

"Where's your skillet?" Peter asked. "I thought you were making me breakfast."

"Do you youngsters ever think of anything but food?" I patted a spot by my side. "You'd better come up here."

"Now, that's an offer a gentleman can't refuse." Touching the hay as if it consisted of steel needles, Peter clambered onto the stack.

The handle of the flyswatter was poking my stomach. I pulled my weapon from under my belt and laid it down between Peter and me.

"Uh-oh, the swords are drawn," he said. "Care to tell me what we're doing?"

"I hoped you'd be too proud to ask."

"Not when the flyswatter comes out."

"Prascovia put a spell on the eggs," I said. "Witchcraft. Not my area of expertise. No doubt something dangerous."

"You seem quite comfortable dealing with everything on your own, so why the sudden precautions?"

"I'm less capable handling hallucinogens. Strange things are known to happen when someone busts a hexed object. Watch me. If my responses become inadequate, take me home and stay with me until I fall asleep."

His lips executed their usual ironic curve. "Not sure if I feel honored or disposable."

"Scared?" I asked.

"Have you seen me scared before?"

"Only for your teammates. You've been reliably proactive in serious situations."

"Then you've made the right choice." Peter pointed toward the dark gardens and the village. "You shouldn't be doing any of this alone," he said, his voice filled with a sudden and strong emotion.

Beneath his business-like abrasiveness, he harbored a deep-seated concern—not only for Jessie, Luke, and Debra, but for me as well.

"Glad you're with me tonight. I wouldn't trust just anyone." I rose up on my knees and tossed the first egg into the field.

The stories hadn't prepared me for the effect. The sky erupted with the rattling of thousands wings. Black dragonflies filled the air, bumping into the haystack, diving into us like crazed kamikazes. Imaginary or not, the flying Furies delivered hits that stung. I ducked, instinctively covering my head. As Peter landed by my side, I felt a cover being thrown over me. He used his plastic poncho to shield us against the insects.

A straw tip dug into my cheek. I slid my palm under my face to protect it from the prickly assailant. "Care to break the other egg?"

Peter squirmed around, causing the stack to sway and making me wonder what he was doing. He came up with a cigarette-sized flashlight. "Maybe we should dig ourselves in instead of sitting on the top," he suggested as he examined the hay in the small circle of the yellow glow.

"I expected snakes or rats swarming on the ground," I said. "To scare us off. The eggs were meant for eating, not destruction."

Peter took the second egg from the basket and held it against the light. "A dark lump inside, like it's rotten." He peeked from under the poncho. "The coast is clear."

"Go for it."

He hurled the egg, and in an instant, the meadow was flooded with cats dashing by the stack and howling wildly. The hay seemed to float in a sea of fur. I hoped no one else witnessed this insanity but us, the frantic felines accumulating by Gregory's barn, all trying to get in through the open door, crawling on top of each other, shrieking, bawling.

Dizzy, I averted my eyes from the writhing mass and looked up. When I couldn't take the village any longer, the familiar patterns of the stars reminded me that I could have a different life, under the same sky but away from this lunacy.

Could I, really? My thoughts, like a flock of autumn leaves in a breeze, whirled through my Moscow apartment and the dark corridors of my college, touched my friends' faces, brought me to Chris, but didn't stay with him. Instead, the dazzling arc of the Milky Way whisked me into a world of better memories and hopes. A twelve-year old again, I smelled the smoke of a campfire, heard Dimitry's laughter, his soft voice asking me to hand him his guitar.

"I should have brought my camera." Peter's silky timbre blended into my daze.

The hay offered a haven too comfortable to leave, and my companion was in no hurry to return to bed. My imagination wasn't fooling me. Dimitry and he had a lot in common—brown eyes, velvety voices, the fascination with the village. At the time of Dimitry's death, I had been too young to desire more than his enthusiasm for my paranormal quests. My gaze turned to Peter, my contemplation not so innocent. If Dimitry had lived, what would it feel like to be with him tonight?

Peter shone the flashlight into my face. "Your pupils are dilated."

He took my wrist, his fingers on my pulse. I realized I was breathing through my mouth, quiet but greedy gulps of air moving hurriedly in and out of my chest.

My rationality fought to maintain its equilibrium. *The smell of campfire smoke.* It was real. Where did it come from on a warm summer night? Forcing myself to inhale slower, I pulled my hand from Peter's and rose up, scanning the landscape.

A thick column, pearly in the moonlight, levitated over Prascovia's house.

What was she doing? What was she doing to me?

I shook my head. We had broken the eggs. The energy had gone poof into dragonflies and cats. I felt fine, except for a few guilty thoughts and my habitual Prascovia-correlated paranoia.

I turned away from her chimney and leaned back on my elbows. Committed to his task, Peter watched me with grim concentration.

"Well, what are you waiting for?" I encouraged him. "Ask your questions."

"What's the point? You won't tell the truth."

"I might," I cajoled.

"All right. You said you wanted to meet Jess, but so far you spent with her, what, a whopping ten minutes?"

I shouldn't have touched the eggs. Adrift in the fluffy clouds of my flared-up nonchalance, I had just made Peter an offer I was already beginning to regret.

CHAPTER FIFTY-NINE

"Maybe Jessie and I use telepathy," I said.

"Or maybe you figured out she's not the one you're looking for."

"Good guess. She's not the one." Amused, I turned to my side and propped my head with my hand, ready to catch the opponent's slightest reaction. "Disappointed?"

"Trying to understand you." Peter stared back, the two disks of the moon brilliant in his pupils, his nostrils flaring in otherwise-concealed agitation. "Tell me, Valya, why show Vishenky to Kenny and then crush him? No one in his group met your requirements? Will this happen to us too? Because Jessie has failed to meet your expectations?"

"Allowing his group to come to the village was my mistake. I admit it. But I didn't crush Kenny. I just made him unwilling to remember what he saw. Kenny's much happier without memories of Vishenky. Not everyone can take the implications of its existence."

"If you understand that, then what are you trying to achieve by bringing in more people? How many lives are you willing to ruin before you find whoever you're looking for?" This time, Peter didn't hold back a single emotion, his eyes showering me with poisoned arrows, meteorites, and lightning.

"Don't be so dramatic," I said. "Let's hope none of you have Kenny's predisposition to crumble from a simple spell."

"I don't want to be turned into a nutcase. Let me keep my memories."

"They will ruin your life."

Peter's fingers twirled the flashlight. "Can you at least tell me who you're looking for?"

I dropped my eyes to stop the staring contest, my usual reservations surfacing like pop-up barriers.

Peter leaned forward, tilting his head as he tried to become my focal point. "Your childhood friends knew about the occurrences. As a kid, you felt comfortable to share your knowledge."

"Talk about a fundamental error."

"That's my point. They were an average crowd. Joe Shmoe can't handle Vishenky, but some of us can and want to. For me, it's a dream to be involved with something this unimaginable."

"So you can shout about it to the whole universe?"

"Say the word, and I'll never disclose a bit of what I've learned. I'd love keeping this gem to myself."

His arrogance aside, Peter had broached a murky subject, my obligations for revealing the village to all of humanity. Could the portals offer a cancer cure? Serve as an alternative energy source?

Sensing my hesitancy, he dropped on his elbow, his shoulders level with mine, his obsidian-black eyes impossible to avoid. "Do you ever talk to anybody about Vishenky?" he asked softly. "I'll bet there's lots of stuff you've never shared with anyone. It must be very trying to be you. Your darkest, scariest, most dismal, soul-wrenching secret—share it with me. Get it off your heart."

The organ Peter referred to accelerated its thumping.

Mole crickets lived underground in my garden. I didn't encounter them often, but I knew they were there, the unsightly nocturnal creatures. Just like some of my secrets, burrowed deeply in my soul. And this chitchat with Peter was my personal nighttime. Enticed by his infectious vehemence, a memory emerged, an ugly insect, and I couldn't block it.

A summer dusk a year ago. The front veranda. My good friend the flyswatter and I, ready to escape, blend with the night shadows and find a new adventure....

Trapped.

"Take your pills," my mother screamed, shaking a plastic container inches from my face. "Take your damn pills."

"I'm fine," I yelled back.

"You're sick."

"Only of your narrow-mindedness. What have you done with Leontina's diary?"

"That old filthy thing you keep under your pillow?"

"My whole life depends on it. How dare you touch what's mine!"

That's when it all came out. Her morbid revelation. The story of a stillborn my parents had brought to Vishenky to bury.

Mortified, I listened. My blood congealed, my lungs ossified, but I listened. How the moonlight fell on the baby's face. How she opened her eyes. They were glowing violet.

I stood in shock. I wanted to protest, to challenge my mother's tale. My mouth was parched and my throat shut as if I swallowed a big fat moth and its soft hairy body and wiggling legs stuffed my esophagus.

"You spent your first twenty-four hours in the morgue," my mother roared, droplets of her saliva airborne. "You're brain-damaged. That's why you're seeing monsters."

I dashed out and collapsed under the lilac bush, dry heaving. If the facts were accurate, my mother was right. I was damaged, but not in the sense that she thought.

To this day, I couldn't stand the lily-of-the-valley-sweet scent of the perfume she wore that evening. Nor could I concede that I, myself, was half-monster.

"God, what is it?" Peter touched my cheek. "You're cold and whiter than the moon."

I rolled to my stomach. A shovel blade's length apart, we froze in a standoff like two human-faced monitor lizards.

"What is it?" Peter whispered, his eyebrows twisted as if the man had nothing for me but compassion, oblivious that someone's secrets could be purgatory-black.

Lonelier than always, more insecure than I'd ever been, I struggled to produce words louder than my heartbeat. "What if someone told you that you were stillborn and brought back to life by a paranormal entity? Can you call yourself human if your every breath, every emotion, every desire is sustained by supernatural forces? Wouldn't you try anything to prove you're not an otherworldly creature?"

"On the contrary," Peter said. I expected horror, disdain, but his eyes glittered with a strange excitement. "Don't you get it? Your paranormal ties make you unique, extraordinary, a legacy of two worlds with phenomenal abilities. It's possible that you don't fully realize what you are."

I sat up. Peter mimicked my pose, no doubt some psychological trick. "With the system as complicated as Vishenky, you can't be certain you understand everything that's happening here," he said.

The looming invasion of the Violet Lights.

Peter's scrutinizing gaze picked up my internal debate. He squeezed my hand in his long warm fingers. "Whatever made you surface after all these years, whatever proof about yourself you're looking for, I can help you find it."

His tone was tender, lulling, almost seductive. My face burned. Since the possibility that I was a half-alien did nothing but excite Peter, should I trust this eager man to dissect the rest of my world?

"What will happen if you can't prove you're one hundred percent human?" Peter asked.

"Could be a death sentence," I said.

The facts followed, a trickle at first, but once I started, my reluctant consent to share the information became an urgent need. Juggling the timeline, infusing the improbable facts with my unreliable assumptions, I rambled on about Gretishnikoffs' history and my search for Debra; about *volkanoks* turning into man-eaters—the possible prelude to a brewing mayhem, an invasion of the Violet Lights; about Leontina's and Anna's disappearances that apparently stopped the attacks in the past. The only details that I wasn't ready to share were Dimitry's death and the reappearance of the entity.

As if afraid to miss a syllable, my listener turned into a blinking statue. I couldn't even see the movements of his ribcage.

"With everything I know, I have to assume that the Legend of an Unborn is true," I said. "One thing if I carry a mutated gene which allows me to draw the energy from the portals. But if I'm alive because some parasitic entity resides in my body and I might be next in line to—"

"Not parasitic. Symbiotic." Peter's head bobbled slowly to reinforce his suggestion. "Valya, listen. Your life is fused with the supernatural. That bond is tighter than the molecular connections in a diamond. The paranormal energy is a vital, inseparable, core part of you. You're stuck in denial if you still doubt who you are. It's the entity. It's a mutation in your DNA. I don't know what that makes you, but *Homo sapiens* you are not."

CHAPTER SIXTY

It mattered. Who I was? It mattered. My powers and knowledge had always set me apart from humanity, but from my standpoint, I was one of them. A human being—just different.

Until Peter's straightforward words cut the cord.

I thought I knew how the aloneness felt, but suddenly, Dimitry's death, my mother's hatred for her only daughter, my friends' betrayal—my life's worst issues, every devastating blow—were nothing, nada, a child's misplaced stuffed toy, compared to the Big Bang of Peter's verdict.

An endless frozen land spread before me. The cosmic solitude was withering my mind and whirling frigid winds blew across my soul. Cut by the crushing power of desolation, I let go. The starry sky, the meadow swirled around me in a sickening kaleidoscope of blue, black, and tarnished white. And I prayed that on the other side of this wormhole I'd find nothing. Not a thought. Not an emotion.

Peter pulled me into his arms. He pressed his face to the side of my head, whispering, "Easy...Easy...."

I needed that bodily contact, the confirmation that someone wasn't repulsed by my anomalous background. That someone wanted me. I turned my head and met his mouth. There was a second, a heartbeat of hesitation, but neither one of us had managed to stop what was about to happen.

* * *

I couldn't see where I had tossed my clothes, but Peter's burning body on top of mine warded off the night's damp chill. His lips glided across my face, barely touching my cheeks, forehead, and eyelids, while I grew acutely conscious that I lay naked in the arms of someone I didn't know or love.

He leaned back a little to look at me.

I sensed his guilt, but he was wrong to feel he'd broken my trust. The puffs of smoke from Prascovia's chimney still blurred part of the sky. What happened between Peter and me wasn't his fault. It was mine. I had underestimated my enemy.

"There's a good-sized portal opening not far from here," I said. "I need to replenish my energy."

"Should I go with you?"

"No. You'll be safer inside."

Peter eased away, the last scrap of our intimacy dissolving in awkwardness.

"If the world doesn't end by tomorrow morning," I said, "we'll keep this quiet, right?"

"You seriously care about appearances?" he asked, gathering his clothes.

"Hmm. Me and Jessie, having breakfast, 'Hey Jess, last night, your boyfriend and I, in a haystack....'"

"I'm not her boyfriend. The trip was coming up. Luke would drive Jess crazy wanting to comfort her, so we split up without an announcement."

"Sure," I said. "Let Luke enjoy his little drama. 'I'm secretly in love with my best buddy's girlfriend.'"

"Does any of this still matter?" Peter asked. "I'm going to write down everything you told me. I want to see your family tree. There are might be some patterns that you're subconsciously denying." He looked in the direction of my home. "One more thing, if I may. I'll keep it a secret what you told me about your birth. It's up to you if you let the others know, but I think you shouldn't."

"Why not?"

"They may turn out to be not as open-minded as you hope. Your life is complicated enough. I don't want you to get hurt."

His eyes were cold. Peter pressed his lips to mine, hard.

A seal?

A brand?

His clothes in his hand, he reached the gate and strode through the garden, his pale silhouette flickering between the cherry trees. The scent of his cologne clung to my clammy skin. I shut my eyes and waited. One minute. Two. Three. Should be enough for him to get inside. I grabbed my jeans and sweater.

The grass stubs poked my bare feet. The noise of grasshoppers pursued me like condemning hissing. I ran, slowing only to open and close the gates.

The river steamed in the cool air. Wispy forms glided over the surface. I dropped my stuff on the wooden platform and dove into the slow current. The silty bottom felt silken to my touch. The portal hadn't opened yet. Defying an urge to inhale, I held on to a sunken log to keep myself submerged.

Remorse clawed at my heart, an unforgiving punisher I couldn't reason with since I was guilty. My fling with Peter should have proven that Chris was nothing but a momentary infatuation. Whom was I kidding? I needed his acceptance more than anyone else's.

The wavering circle of the moon appeared green through the thickness of the water. A tall human shape materialized on the platform's edge. Wondering who the intruder into my despair was, I pushed myself from the bottom.

A stranger towered over me, and his double-barreled shotgun was pointed in my face.

CHAPTER SIXTY-ONE

My childhood companions and I once saw a man scouring the cemetery dump. He wore camouflage pants and a faded brown t-shirt. His scruffy beard was salt-and-pepper, which from the perspective of the eight- and nine-year-olds made him ancient. Bushy eyebrows, thin hooked nose—his owlish face was easy to remember. He pushed around discarded metal obelisks and empty paint cans, sorted through faded artificial flowers and wreaths.

We had enough sense to keep away from strangers, but I noticed what the man didn't see—a monkey perched on a metal cross meters away from the dump.

That's what someone whispered. "A monkey." A tailless animal with enormous round eyes and skeletal fingers looked like a caricature of the slender loris or spectral tarsier. The hideous thing watched the man as he went through the junk pile.

The oblivious stranger picked up a few weather-beaten wreaths and started walking. The creature followed him, jumping and freezing like a stalking cat.

We stayed close, hiding behind the headstones and vegetation. The man dragged his booty to the section of the cemetery where the last plot was filled over thirty years ago. He arranged the wreaths over a small mound, an abandoned grave without markings, and sat on his haunches, occasionally rubbing his face with the back of his hand. Then he headed to the earliest part of the cemetery.

The man crouched by a gravestone shaped like a sarcophagus. It rested on its side, half-sunk into the dirt. He began to dig with his hands like a dog, tossing layers of rotting leaves and moss. Shifting from knuckle to knuckle as it peeked through the weeds, the supernatural loris acted immensely interested in his activities. We hid in the undergrowth, hunkered down into a tight bundle, our eyes glued to the sight. And then someone's seven-year-old sister freaked out.

The man heard her cry of "I want to go ho-o-ome." He peered in our direction and saw the creature.

He yelped. His eyes turned wild. He barked, "Run!" We ran.

It wasn't until a few years later that I desperately tried to find the man. I had hit a passage in Leontina's diary describing how a locket with *volkanok's* fur prevented the victims' specters from wandering around, and some big-eyed creature with bony fingers stealing the fur from the graves. On a hunch, I returned to the location where we saw the stranger. I wouldn't have recognized the gravestone, except some dirt beneath it was recently disturbed. Sure enough, I found a buried locket. It stored fur darker than the one in my possession.

I spent three summers patrolling the cemetery to no avail, but convinced that even the faintest chance to befriend someone with the additional knowledge about the occurrences was worth my effort. I never expected that once the stranger and I had finally come across each other, his immediate intent would be to blow my head off.

Unable to look away from the two black holes of the muzzle, I felt faint, as if I stayed a minute too long under a shower a few degrees too hot. The barrel was within my reach. *Push it away and then dive under the platform. Yank it, pulling the assailant into the river.* My adrenaline against his reflexes. But I wasn't sure I had a single muscle in my body that would contract.

"*Shlyuha. Zaberemeneesh—ubyu.*" Instead of pulling the trigger, the man took a step backward. He slung the shotgun over his shoulder, turned around, and walked into the settling mist before I could reply.

He had called me a slut. He had also promised to kill me if I got pregnant.

My cheeks burned. My fright forgotten, I trembled in anger. Tears filled my eyes, blurring the world around me. This was unfair. Some pervert stalker didn't get to insult me when once in a millennium I succumbed to a simple human longing to be desired, touched.

Except, he disapproved of my morals, yes, but it wasn't extramarital sex for which he had threatened to kill me. What did he know about the fourth generations of Gretishnikoff women and their ability to conceive a child?

Leontina had left a daughter, but in her diary she was vague about some special circumstances she needed to have a baby.

What "special circumstances"?

The veil of fog broke and I looked at Prascovia's house, now immersed in darkness. *Special circumstances.* Like an entity identical to the one that had killed my first love being sent after someone I was smitten with for the past three days. My stomach began to quiver. What if, driven out of Chris, the lethal phantom didn't run out of energy and expired as I had assumed? What if it lingered in his room, the same room where for tonight I had relocated Peter?

I threw myself onto the lower platform, my arms barely having enough strength to pull my body from the water. The hexed eggs, the smell of smoke. I wasn't myself when I so eagerly sought comfort in Peter's embrace. If he had become the entity's new host and hence "the special circumstances" were met, then I might be....

I donned my sweater and squirmed on the ground to put on my jeans. Prascovia didn't need me as her successor. She wanted to save Andrey. She had no lever to make me cross a portal, but that would change if I had a child.

My teeth chattered and the spasms almost made me retch. I pulled my knees to my chest and rubbed my shins, a single aspiration pervading my mind.

Reclaiming my free will.

CHAPTER SIXTY-TWO

An untilled island of trees offered a refuge to the birds and wildlife halfway into the field. A colony of flowers called forest violets poked out of the grass in the moonlit clearing near the Dirge Birch. One of them, twice as tall and more robust than its sisters, was my salvation.

I broke the crispy stalk and retreated into the shadows. Leaning against the Dirge Birch, I brought the ivory-colored raceme to my lips.

The sweet fragrance of the nectar carried a tinge of decay. Holding my breath, I plucked a flower with my teeth and crushed the succulent petals between my tongue and palate. An explosion of bubbles tickled my mouth, as if I had taken a sip of fizzy soda. Leontina had used the forest violet to stop a couple of epidemics threatening the village. Some chemical component in a single blossom eliminated *nedoog*, an affliction, "that had entered a human body within an hour." Amazingly, her unorthodox method had never sparked off any accusations of witchcraft. Evaluating her accounts from a modern point of view, I understood that under the affliction she meant anything with genetic material. Viruses. Bacteria. Sperm.

The plant appeared more plump than usual after a rainy month. The active ingredient could be too diluted. If I ate another blossom—

* * *

Where am I?

Just a moment ago, I was on the front veranda, playing Hearts with my American visitors, but now everything was gone. Instead, the moon illuminated a small clearing. I sat under the Dirge Birch, clasping some droopy, broken plant in my sweaty palm.

A forest violet?

Two blossoms were missing from the stalk. I touched my tingling lips. No infection had ever snuck up on me in Vishenky; why would I medicate myself with an unexplored, untested remedy?

My hair was wet. I had been underwater.

The river.

The ghosts of memories began to thicken. Luke's bitten arm and the rush to save his life. The bearded stranger and his vehement threat to kill me. But what had happened in between my diving feats?

The eggs. We had disposed of Prascovia's hexed eggs. I shuddered, remembering the haystack and what had brought me to the secluded habitat of the forest violets.

I began to jog toward the village, terrified of another blackout. That's how Leontina had managed to cure her contemporaries without unsettling their superstitious minds. Her subjects simply forgot the treatment. The next time my memory might not recover. I needed to get home and write down my deductions about Prascovia's plan.

I was clutching the flower stalk in case I needed a reminder—

* * *

Why am I running?

I came to a stop at a crossroad, disoriented, my side aching and heart hammering. My sweater was soaked in sweat. What the hell?

A dirt road to my left disappeared into a field. Tall trees to my right marked the edge of a gully.

Panting, I walked back and forth to cool down. I recognized the spot. Every spring the aging willows harbored warbling nightingales, and later in the season gorgeous hardy geraniums thrived in the shade. I was three hundred meters away from my back gate. Not knowing how I had gotten there, barefooted and carrying a wilted plant, was beyond scary.

My bottom lip was tingling faintly. I touched it. A vision flashed through me. A strand of wavy hair, fallen across the forehead of a very handsome man. Green eyes. A joyful boyish smile. His hands, rising to my face. His mouth on mine.

I couldn't just imagine the moment of my profound, aching happiness. Who was he?

Chris. His name is Chris.

As I tried to chase the memory, an insight hit me like a twister. Kenny. Last summer, Prascovia saw us flirting and put an entity in him. Taken thousands of kilometers away from Vishenky, the phantom lived off the boy's energy. That's why Peter's brother was so sick.

My jaw dropped. Such specific information. A fact? A crucial guess? What else had I forgotten?

Something that Gregory had told me. *It wasn't Anna's turn. She couldn't complete the cycle.*

Dimitry. Kenny. And now, Chris and Peter. Another entity. My DNA. *Complete the cycle.* Why couldn't I connect the dots? So many facts, and yet something was missing from the picture.

I moaned in frustration.

A loon squealed its support from the waterlogged bottom of the gully. Then everything was quiet, too quiet for a summer night. I automatically brushed my hand against my waist and gasped. I wasn't carrying the flyswatter.

I tore a blade of grass and used a lungful of air to make it shriek. The bird didn't answer. Ostov lurked somewhere nearby.

The creature craved murder, and Leontina's manuscript was hazy on the subject of how to stop it. I expected fear to seize me, but I felt calm until I saw what was approaching to destroy me.

CHAPTER SIXTY-THREE

The time crept toward the dawn. Chris couldn't sleep. Twice he thought he heard some noise inside the house, but every time he checked, Valya's bed remained untouched.

"Where are you?" he whispered, peering into the dark bedroom. Maybe he should take a quick stroll to the back gate and see if she had fixed her plastic barrier. She could have returned but stayed on the front veranda.

Chris walked through the quiet house. The door between the veranda and the kitchen was closed. He tapped on the wood to announce his presence, then turned the doorknob.

The flame of a thick candle on the dining table wavered as he stepped over the threshold. The melted wax filled the ceramic holder and overflowed onto the oilcloth.

The door flung open. The lamp went on. Valya stood in the doorway, squinting.

"Finally," Chris said. "Where have you—"

"You're Chris," she informed him. Her pupils were enlarged. Her jittery movements made him think of somebody who hadn't slept for a couple of nights but kept going with the help of caffeine. She held a wilted flower stem in her hand.

"What's going on?" Chris asked.

"If you're hungry, snacks are on the upper shelves." Valya dropped the flower on the dining table and blew out the candle. She crouched in front of the cupboard, unlocked the bottom drawer, and studied the items in her secret depository with great concentration.

Chris peeked over her shoulder. Besides a bundle of bead bracelets, the front half contained sealed plastic bags and trial-size perfume vials. Skulls and crossed bones marked the contents, grayish powders and colorful liquids. Valya's strange shawl was stuffed in the back. The rooster's gaping beak lay on top like a creepy sentinel, guarding pages of papers stacked under the lace.

Valya rummaged through her chemical paraphernalia and then pulled a large sheet of tracing paper from under the shawl. The beak snapped but missed her fingers. She locked the drawer.

Folded up, the document appeared to be a pencil-drawn map. Valya spread it on the table. "Peter asked for my family tree. Do you know Peter?"

Chris didn't respond, his attention focused on ovals, arrows, and dates. His heart hit his chest like the spinning blades of an out-of-balance rotor.

We're here for a reason, Jessie had said.

The name in the left bottom corner, the only one written in English, stood out:

Debra Gretishnikoff Alley.

Portals into another dimension, the fight for Luke's life, and an unmatched emotional intimacy with a woman Chris had just met. A lifetime-worth of experiences crammed in three days, and then the sobering reality. Valya kept her true intentions a secret.

"Why did you bring Debra to Vishenky?" Chris asked. There wasn't a faintest chance for an innocent explanation of Valya's actions, yet he dared to hope for one.

Valya turned up her left palm. A red stripe ran from the tip of her index finger down to her wrist. "Who knew that Ostov could spit so far?"

"Something hurt you? Are you in a condition to talk?"

She rummaged through the cupboard's counter until she found a piece of scrap paper and a pencil. "Can you believe it?" she murmured, scribbling on the page. "You just saved my life."

"I can't believe anything you tell me," Chris said.

"I love you anyway." Valya rewarded him with the sweetest smile. She picked up the flower, smelled it, and placed the wilted stem on top of the family tree. "Do you know Peter? He needs this, but I don't know who he is."

Chris didn't try to stop her when she staggered inside the house. His mouth dry, he picked up the limp plant from the table. A sweet aroma trailed the unremarkable ivory blossoms. The dying cells added a hint of decay to the scent.

A feeling of drunkenness swept over him. Debra's name floated up in his mind like a colorful bubble and burst in a thousand odorous petals. Covering his nose and mouth with his sleeve, Chris carried the flower outside and tossed it into the bushes. He locked the front door and turned off the light. The family tree clutched in his hand, he waded through the swaying air into the kitchen.

The curtain leading to his room was drawn. He pulled it open. A man sat up in his bed.

"Sorry," Chris muttered, trying to remember the sleeping arrangements.

Somehow, he found his way to the back veranda. The frigid sheets shocked his body but his consciousness quickly drifted away.

CHAPTER SIXTY-FOUR

"Chris. Chris!"

Fear saturated Debra's voice. Chris couldn't get up. A hot and heavy shadow balanced on his chest, holding him down. Bony fingers dug into his shoulder. The pebbly ground hurt his back.

"He's not waking up either." Debra sounded frantic, on the verge of tears.

Who else, Luke? Chris wanted to ask but the ground beneath him split and he was thrashing in the river. The faceless adversary pushed him under. The water poured into his nostrils. The terror of dying burst out of his chest in a silent scream that ended in a coughing fit.

"Chris, please!" Debra squeaked.

He opened his eyes.

She clenched his shoulder, shaking him with all her might.

The back veranda looked bleak in the mixed lighting of the overhead lamp and the dawn barely germinating outside. His face was wet. The last droplets dribbled on the floor from an empty pitcher in Debra's hand.

Chris rose up on his elbows. The comforter clumped on his chest and a renegade spring in the mattress explained the rest of the nightmare.

He rubbed his face, groggy as if he had taken a sleeping pill. "What's going on?"

"Luke's running a fever," Debra said, "Valya looks like she's in a coma, and I thought you'd never wake up."

"Deb, you used up my water." Jessie sat on Luke's bed, pressing a towel to his forehead.

"I'll you get more." Debra dashed inside the house.

Chris planted his feet on the slick linoleum. "How is he?"

"Burning up," Jessie said.

"A towel's not enough. Wrap him in a wet sheet." Pulling on his jeans, Chris barely kept his balance.

"Are you okay? Everyone looks like shit this morning."

"Fine. What's wrong with Valya?"

"Sleeping." Jessie's tone implied the Russian couldn't have committed a nastier crime. "Peter's with her."

Chris walked into the girls' bedroom, worry clinging to him like sticky film.

The scratched pier table under the mismatched mirror, the chairs with the uniformly chewed-up armrests, the blond three-door closet, and the radio the size of a modern oven—suddenly he hated every piece of the shabby furniture that survived the seventies and ended up here. The faded chintz curtains, the tattered red rug on the floor—the room wasn't a cute time capsule but a hording-style memorial to the past. He, too, would seek a refuge in the supernatural world if he couldn't burn half of this clutter and make the space livable.

I'm looking for someone to blame for Valya's life choices, Chris realized.

Her ribcage expanded and fell in a healthy rhythm of someone deeply asleep, but she looked pallid against her matted curls spread on the pillow.

Peter hunched in the chair by her bed. "I shook her, slapped her. I tried CPR." The dark circles under his eyes were as prominent as Valya's.

The checkered blue-and-gray blanket left exposed her bare arms and shoulders. A set of tiny puncture wounds, in a shape of a rhomb, marked the spot that she kept hidden under a bandage the night before.

Chris crouched by Valya's side. "Has anybody checked her for injuries?"

"Externally, nothing new," Peter said.

"Are you sure?" Chris asked sharply, registering that Peter

volunteered no other noteworthy information, such as who had done the exam.

"I trust Deb not to miss any sticking-out bones or bleeding gashes. Don't you?"

Chris turned his eyes to Valya.

Debra hobbled from the kitchen with a full bucket of water. "Let's douse her."

"No. Take it to Jessie," Chris said.

Valya's arms stretched lifelessly along her body, but the fingers of her left hand curled as if concealing a small item.

Debra set the splashing bucket on the floor and pushed it closer to the bed.

"I said no." Chris cupped Valya's hand in his. Her fist tightened, but a tiny white cap peeked from under her thumb. He forced his own thumb under her fingers and slid the object free.

A vial of thick maroon liquid fell into his palm. Marked with a skull and crossed bones, the gooey brew oozing from one end of the container to the other looked gross, and somehow familiar.

Chris handed the vial to Debra. "Russian inscription. Can you read it?"

"*Protivoyadie ot slyuni ostova.*" His cousin consulted the ceiling, her eyebrows furrowed. "Antidote for skeleton's saliva." She uncapped it. "Smells like boiled cabbage."

"Give it to me," Chris said.

"I don't think you should start administering—"

"Luke may not have much time," Peter said. "Do it."

The vial changed shaky hands. Chris pressed the tip to Valya's bloodless lips and let the contents trickle into her mouth.

She gasped, whimpered as she exhaled, and stopped breathing.

Chris leaped on the bed. His crossed hands landed on Valya's chest, set to pump life back into her body.

"Wait." Peter leaned over the still woman. "She's holding her breath." He touched her forehead. "Valya? It's okay. It's just us."

She opened her eyes.

Chris jerked back his hands. Peter didn't move.

"Valya, sweetheart," Chris said. "Luke needs your help."

"English? Hmm." Under Chris's weight pinning down her legs, Valya pushed herself up with her elbows. "I'd love to hear who you people are."

CHAPTER SIXTY-FIVE

"Of course I remember how to treat the loris's bites." Valya's voice carried her usual I've-been-doing-this-forever conviction, but she couldn't hide from Chris the confusion in her eyes. Wrapped in her blue-and-gray blanket, she huddled up on top of her bed like a shipwreck survivor on a life raft, no land in sight, and sharks circling.

"In the left refrigerator, on the middle shelf, there's a pink jar, looks like facial cream," she instructed Debra. "Tell Tess to work the whole amount into Luke's skin. That should lower his temperature."

"It's Jess, not Tess," Peter said.

Valya clenched the edge of the blanket in a white-knuckled grip. "Put on your trunks and get your bicycles ready. We'll be harvesting medicinal mud for Luke. Now, if you will excuse me, I'd like to change."

"Wait," Peter said. "Remember breaking the eggs last night?"

"Let's take care of important things first, like saving your friend's life."

Peter's expression was hard to read, but it wasn't satisfaction with Valya's answer. "What eggs?" Chris asked.

"Two white shell-covered oval objects," Peter snapped. "Valya doesn't seem to recall."

"So we broke them," she said. "How did that go?"

"A swarm of dragonflies after the first one, and a stampede of cats after we busted the second one. Rings any bells?"

"Then what?" Valya asked.

"You decided to go to the river. Alone. I left a lit candle on the veranda before I went to bed."

"Did anybody hear me return?"

"I tried to wait up," Peter said. "I can't afford a sleepless night when so much is at stake."

I waited for you, too, Chris wanted to say. An instinct, a primeval sense of self-preservation told him to remain silent. No matter how much he scoured his brain, he couldn't remember how his wait for Valya had ended or when and how he had gotten to bed. But whatever had happened in that time frame had cast another cloud on his already bleak mood.

* * *

The day promised to be clear, its tranquility an utmost contrast to the night's shadowy dealings. A silvery coating of dew softened the colors of the meadows. In the quiet air, the river's surface was calm except for rare splashes of fish and the strikes of swallows drinking water in flight. The roosters crowed, but the village was asleep.

Ignoring the flashing red lights, Valya barely slowed down at the railroad crossing. Tired of constant uncertainty, Chris felt grateful for physical exercise, a chance to act.

Debra struggled with the ride. Jessie was a more apt bicyclist, but the guide had ordered her to stay with Luke.

"Do you really want to argue?" Valya asked when Chris had voiced his objections.

He couldn't shake off the crispiness of challenge in her tone. Chris was nothing more than an obstacle to her great paranormal venture. The idea of saving this woman was absurd. Healing Luke and going home looked like the only workable plan.

An unpaved road ran parallel to the tracks for about a mile, cut through a field, and finally brought the cavalcade to the forest. They left the bicycles in dense bushes. Valya picked a slight path. After fifteen minutes of a brisk hike between spruces and junipers, she turned and inspected her team, as if checking to see who got lost along the way.

"What's next?" Chris asked.

"Behold," she said and stepped aside.

Chris walked the last curve of the path.

It was a forest pond no wider than ten yards in diameter, but the black color of the water made it look deep. A liquid mirror, it reflected elms of respectable age growing on the banks, the thick canopies preventing sunlight from reaching the surface. On the damp, mossy ground, spectacular ferns rose here and there between the tree roots.

Valya took off her dress and smoothed the glossy fabric of her black two-piece swimsuit. Slender like Debra, barely touched by tan, she looked too delicate, too vulnerable, too exposed to deal with anything more hazardous that a teacup poodle.

Already shivering, Valya pulled a pint-sized glass jar from her linen bag. "The mud loses potency once it's out of this puddle." She dug deeper into the bag and came up with several bands of colorful plastic beads. "A portion every half-an-hour, four doses total. Might be overkill, but it's better than missing the right amount and starting all over."

"What can we do to help?" Peter asked.

"For now, stay away from the edge." Valya slipped the bands on her wrists and ankles.

She climbed onto a dead tree trunk, the foul-looking water gnawing on roots four feet below her, and fell in sideways. The surface evened out unnaturally fast, as if hurrying to cover up the intrusion.

No bubbles, Chris thought.

Debra touched his wrist. He realized he'd been soundlessly snapping his fingers.

"Twenty seconds," Peter said. "Thirty...thirty-five...."

"Shut up," Debra hissed.

A Russian black-and-gray crow screeched and landed in the canopies above, flapping its wings before settling on a branch. The pond's surface remained smooth like a pane of glass.

Peter kept his eyes on his watch. "One minute and ten seconds...and fifteen...and twenty."

A ladybug missed the bank by a yard. Debra picked up a long leafy twig. On all fours, she stretched her arm in an attempt to scoop up the insect without getting too close to the water.

"Get away from there," Chris said.

A brown form broke the surface. A foot-wide mouth, like the one of a large catfish, snatched the bug and jerked at the leaves, ripping the twig from Debra's hand. She screamed and scooted backward. The creature and its booty were gone.

"Oh shit," Peter muttered.

Breathing heavily through her nose, Debra scrambled to her feet.

"Two minutes." Peter removed his glasses and slipped them into his shirt's pocket. "I'm going in."

"Luke nearly killing himself is enough," Chris said. "Let Valya do her thing."

"And if you're wrong?" Peter asked.

"Just wait." Chris managed to stand rod-straight, his chin up, under Debra's anxious gaze.

"Two minutes and ten seconds," Peter said. "It might be too late."

"Hey, guys, over here."

Chris turned at the sound of Valya's voice.

Wincing, she squeezed through a thick growth of young spruces. Her bare feet treaded carefully on the forest floor. "I'm fine."

Gray streaks covered her swimsuit. A fresh scratch ran across her belly. She waved the glass jar. A brown jelly-like blob infused with golden speckles quivered inside. "The best healing mud lies in the middle of the underground tunnel between the two waterholes. This season it's just not wide enough to turn around. I had to push my way through six or seven yards of roots and debris."

"Shouldn't we wait for you by the other pool?" Peter asked.

"The brush is too dense," Valya said. "You're fine here."

"Did you see the fish?" Debra asked.

"You have no idea what's down there." Valya pulled at one of her bead bracelets and let the rubber band snap against her wrist. "Plastic. Seems to work." She handed the jar to Peter. "Go as fast as you can. I'll dive again in ten minutes. Chris will deliver the next dosage."

"I saw a housing development not far from the road," Peter said. "Deb can use her Russian to ask someone for a rope. She'll take the mud to Luke. I'll come back here. When you go in, you'll pull the rope through the tunnel. It should ease your remaining dives."

"A great idea," Chris said.

Valya crossed her arms. "That development was abandoned years ago. Peter, please, go. I'll be fine."

His face reddened. "Goddammit, Valya, if you get stuck in the fucking tunnel, you'll drown and Luke will die."

"Every second you stand here and argue the mud loses its effectiveness. You waste more time, I'll have to do an additional dive."

"This is just stupid." Peter gingerly lowered the jar into one of Valya's linen bags. He glanced at Debra and spun to face Valya as if stricken by a startling thought. "Are we saving Luke here?" he asked. "Or are you doing something else?"

Valya tilted her head. "Like what?"

"Like working on your original agenda. How much has your memory recovered so far?"

"Chris, would you please take the mud to Luke?" Valya asked, her gaze spearing Peter.

"Screw this," Peter said. His long legs promptly carried the frustrated man into the forest.

Foreboding, black and bottomless—like this pond, like Valya's pupils—filled Chris's stomach. *Debra.* Something about last night. A candle burning on the front veranda. Numbers. A page of numbers. Debra's name. *Yes, Debra's name.*

Valya knelt by her bag. Debra dropped a towel over her shoulders. Speaking softly, the Russian extracted from her stash a new bundle of beads.

Watching the two young women together, Deb at ease and utterly attentive to the guide's conduct, Chris felt a chill touching his arms and neck. What did he learn last night that made him so apprehensive about Valya's interaction with his cousin?

Debra fumbled with the knot of her beach wrap.

"What are you doing?" Chris asked.

"A bulky piece of debris obstructs the entrance to the tunnel," Valya said. "I can't move it by myself."

"I'll do it," Chris said. "I'm a better swimmer."

"Too narrow for you."

"Chris, don't worry, I won't go deep." Debra slid the bands on her wrists and ankles.

A page of numbers. Debra's name.

"I forbid you to go in the water," he said.

Valya's eyes zapped him with silent fury. She grabbed Debra's hand. "Come."

"Don't you dare—" Chris yelled, but he was too late. Valya dragged his cousin to the bank's edge. Debra screamed as the both women fell into the pool. The fluid darkness closed in over their heads.

Chris dove.

It wasn't the coldness of the water that took his breath away. He heard a melody. Unfamiliar yet coming from his past, the dulcet interlacing of guitars and violins unlocked vague memories. A tentative promise wavered on the edge of his consciousness. A revelation. A shy hope. The rest of his life depended on his ability to bring it to light, to comprehend what he was craving so desperately. The insight was getting warmer, closer. A few more seconds, and—

"Chris, get out of the water!"

The sword of Debra's voice slashed the billowing veil of his daze. The reality jumped back into place. The pond. The woods. Debra, alive and well, pulling on a gnarled root, and trying to haul her skinny butt up the slippery bank.

But something essential was lost. Something incredible. Something that he struggled to find his whole life. Probably, lost forever.

CHAPTER SIXTY-SIX

I winced when a branch brushed my bitten shoulder as I struggled through the undergrowth of evergreens. The beads around my ankles dug into my flesh. I remembered well the process of preparing the bracelets with my unsteady hands, while Peter applied cuckoo's eyes to Luke's wounds. Debra had thin limbs. I had made sure the plastic trinkets fit tightly. The next six hours of my whereabouts remained a mystery, a mystery that reeked of a dread worse than the haunted basement in a good horror movie.

Chris and Debra, wet, scared, and miserable, shivered under an elm. Huddled up under their towels, they looked like two sick orphaned baby chickens eyeballing an approaching cat. Chris hadn't taken off his soaked jeans or sneakers. Debra's legs protruded like two white sticks, her toes digging into her flip-flops.

The pitiful sight of her jolted me into seeing the truth. I was made of tungsten. Debra was made of porcelain. Even if she carried Gretishnikoffs' paranormal gene, I could never ask of her to become more than just an observer. This delicate china doll would shatter under pressure, especially in a scenario as challenging as my crossing between the two worlds.

A lump swelled in my throat.

I opened the jar that I had dragged with me through the tunnel. I shook out a blob of mud, slapped it onto the stinging spot on my shoulder, and wiped my hand on my stomach, treating the newly acquired scratch. I spilled a bit more mud into my palm and screwed the lid back, pressing the jar against my thigh.

"Who wants to take the mud to Luke?" I asked.

"Go," Chris told Debra, his voice flat.

Since I woke up, Chris and Peter had been acting so peculiarly that I began to wonder about their roles in my unexplained memory loss. Peter brooded as if I'd promised to marry him and instead gone on a date with a Gray Sniffer, but I wasn't worried about the younger man.

Debra accepted the container, keeping her eyes on mine. I resisted the temptation to gnash my teeth. She'd probably drop the precious mud.

The poor girl retreated behind the wall of spruces, all the while throwing anxious glances at Chris. I pulled off the soaked dressing from my right index finger and rubbed the mud, warmed up in my palm, over the scabs. Freshly extracted from the tunnel, it was already at work, its healing power incredible. My shoulder itched insanely. The skin punctured by the paranormal jaws must be regenerating like in a fast-forwarded film.

What would mend my soul?

The shape of the pond resembled a round diamond, its flat upper facet exposed, and the rest hidden below the ground. A green glow streamed from the conical bottom, making it beautiful down there, under the murky surface. Emerald lighting. Soft gurgles. Long whimsical shapes circling, graceful like flowing ribbons, maybe *Mosasaurs*, maybe dragons.

"This wasn't about helping you with debris," Chris said. "Why did you push her into the pond?"

"Deb is so slow on the bike, I thought I'd expose her to an open portal," I said without turning my head. "To see if it would give her some energy. How did she feel when she got out?"

"Scared out of her mind."

"Because I forced her to jump?"

"No. It's hard to believe, but that idiot still trusts you."

"It didn't look that way when I gave her the mud."

"When she hit the water," Chris said, "Deb saw a place. She'd never been there, but at the same time it looked intimately familiar."

"That frightened her?"

"Yes, because of how vivid it felt," Chris said. "It was as if seeing that town again was the most essential thing in her life. She wondered how you can withstand experiences like that over and over."

"I'm used to it. Did she feel stronger physically? Invigorated?"

"No. She felt drained, if anything. Why is this important?"

"The potency of the mud depends on the energy from the portal. Looks like it's weak," I said, my lie as smooth as hello and good-morning. The hitch was with Debra, not with the portal. "I better get the next portion."

"Wait."

Chris moved to sit closer to me, an empty jar in his hands and a frown on his face. "Deb's vision. What did it mean?"

"A premonition? A forgotten dream? The pond catches something vital in you and spirals it up. What did you see?"

"I heard music."

"Something familiar?" I asked.

"I wish I could tell."

"That's the problem with the supernatural, never knowing for sure. You collect data, you think you found logic and science in the occurrences, you bet your life on your neat theories, and one day you realize you're standing on the roof of a burning house."

"Maybe it's time to learn your lesson and quit."

I looked into his eyes.

The eyes of a stranger.

I longed to press my face to his shoulder, feel his warmth, his touch, I wanted Chris to like me, but the glorious side effect of my bids to protect him, the raw emotional closeness that had been pulsating between us, was gone.

I moistened my lips. "Speaking of quitting, something dangerous could have holed up in the house, and it might try to harm you."

"The entity," Chris said. "I know. You and I had a chat last night, but you don't remember."

"Must have been some chat. Forgive me if I'm repeating myself. I used Ostov's claw to repel the entity, then gave you my own energy to prevent it from coming back."

"I see."

"Most likely, you don't," I said. "Whatever happened to me last night reset my energy. It no longer protects you. As soon as Luke's strong enough, you should leave, hopefully tonight. I'll watch over you until then, but you'll be in the house on your own until I bring over the last batch of mud."

"You're coming straight home, right?"

"Absolutely. But promise that once you walk inside, you'll tell Debra not to let you out of her sight."

"How did your friend die?" Chris asked.

I stared at him, mute.

"Yes, you told me," he said.

"Sounds like we had a night of unnecessary revelations."

I pushed my hands into the luxurious memory foam of moss. Tickling my palms, the greedy little clumps began to suck the excess of the nourishing mud off my skin.

"Dimitry held a piece of green glass over a candle until it burst from the heat," I said. "He used the shards to slice his wrists. I guess he felt he wasn't bleeding out fast enough, so after several minutes he punctured his jugular vein." Unable to brave another look in Chris's eyes, I pulled the empty jar from his rigid fingers and launched myself, and my misery, into the pond's emerald realm.

CHAPTER SIXTY-SEVEN

"I'll push her through a portal myself." Jessie's whisper was loud enough for Chris to overhear her as he strode past the back veranda's open window. The conversation between the students stopped when he walked in.

Luke sat in his bed, propped with three pillows, his undivided attention focused on a bowl of cold borscht. His wounded arm smoothly delivered each spoonful to his mouth. The layers of gauze held the healing mud in place. Gray circles hung under Luke's eyes and his round face glittered with sweat, but as far as Chris could tell, the crisis was over.

"I know you're angry, but Luke's doing better," he said, handing the jar of fresh mud to Jessie. "Valya wants us to leave Vishenky tonight, and that's what we'll do. Where's Debra?"

"Why don't you sit down, and we'll tell you—"

"Deb's worn out after the ride," Peter interrupted her. "She wanted to lie down for a bit. She didn't tell us you both fell into the pond."

Chris patted his t-shirt. It was almost dry but muddy. His sneakers made squishy noises as he moved. "I'll go change."

Peter shifted on a wobbly plywood stool and looked pointedly at Chris's bed, which, caught in the earlier pandemonium and crisis, Chris had left a mess.

Valya's request to alert Deb played in his head as urgent as a tornado warning, but a drop of normalcy—making the bed so his tired student didn't have to perch on an uncomfortable seat—suddenly turned into the most imperative business of the moment.

A few seconds wouldn't make a difference. Chris tugged the comforter. A corner of trace paper folded like a map stuck out from under his pillow.

A page of numbers.

Debra's name.

Feeling his own heartbeat, Chris arranged the bedding then checked on his companions. Peter rubbed his unshaved face. His eyelids were heavy. Jessie began to change the application on Luke's arm.

Chris pulled the paper out. He slid it under his t-shirt, picked up his bag, and walked into Valya and Debra's bedroom.

The curtains were drawn. He flipped on the light switch. "You awake?"

Debra tossed off her throw. Her bare feet touched the tattered floor rug. "Is Valya back?" she asked.

"Not yet." Chris extracted the paper from under his t-shirt. He spread his trophy on the beat-up coffee table, painted black, gold, and red like Russian souvenir spoons, and serving as Debra's nightstand. "I found this under my pillow. If I hid it, I must have had a reason."

"You don't remember?"

"My memory is as blank as Valya's. Maybe this is a clue. I'll be right back."

The brick parts of the house held the night's chill. Without the comforting aromas of breakfast, the stale smell of soot pervaded the kitchen. Chris cracked open the window in his room to let in the warmth and breeze.

Hurrying, he stuck his sopping wet sneakers on the ledge and tossed his t-shirt over the back of a chair. He draped his damp jeans over a rung of the ladder in the kitchen. He looked up. The entrance to the second floor wasn't blocked.

It probably was cozy in there, the cheery sunrays shining through the east window, the view of the river and lush meadows spectacular. Chris just wanted a few minutes of peace, maybe to lie down on the couch under the red plaid throw and shut his eyes, let the shield of solitude hide him from the heartbreaking revelations and impossible decision-making. He'd dream of a faraway world, its colors verdant, as if seen through green glass, its stars—

A vehicle backfired next door. Chris gasped. He had climbed halfway up the ladder, no more aware of his actions than if he were sleepwalking.

The ladder jerked under his weight as he scurried down, nearly falling off after his foot became tangled in his jeans. He crushed through the doorways and stopped only when he reached the girls' bedroom.

Debra raised her head, her eyes wild, and patted the sofa. "Please, sit down. You won't believe this. Valya thinks she and I are related."

CHAPTER SIXTY-EIGHT

"This is me." Debra's finger traced the short lines between the ovals. "Dots and more dots above me—Mom, Grandma, and great-grandmother, but Valya obviously doesn't know their names. And this is my great-great-grandmother, Alexandra Gretishnikoff, the one who left Russia after the Revolution. Now, look to the left. Alexandra had a sister, Leontina Gretishnikoff. Down, down, down, and this is Leontina's offspring of the latest generation. Valenteena Gretishnikoff Svetlova."

Debra kneaded her naked elbows. Chris put his arm around the shivering girl.

"She kept it a secret," Debra muttered. "Why would she keep it a secret?"

Unable to come up with any words of comfort, Chris rubbed her shoulder, then pulled the wool throw from the sofa and put it over Debra's flimsy sleeveless blouse. He looked at the closed door. It was quiet on the back veranda, just the sick boy and his two friends. Valya hadn't returned from the pond.

Ten minutes between her dives. She would be slower on a bicycle than Chris. There was no reason to worry…yet.

Waiting. Worrying. With Valya, it had become a pattern. What did her mother think waking up at night and seeing her daughter's bed empty?

Valya didn't care. *Selfish, selfish, selfish.*

"Are you all right?" Debra asked.

"No. You're freezing. Let's go outside, in the sun."

"She'll be back any minute. This is our chance to figure out what's going on." She leaned over the coffee table, her lips moving. "Okay. See how every fourth generation is marked with a blue star?"

"Yes. Valya's name is, too."

"But with a question mark." Debra tapped at the beginning of the diagram. "Seventeenth century. There are two women on top, Antonina and her sister, Prascovia. There's no date of death for Prascovia." Her finger followed a vertical line of dots. "And it only shows her modern-time descendants, Anna and her son, Andrey. Recognize the handwriting?"

"What about it?"

"It's Valya's. Anna, Andrey, and my name. Someone else drew the tree. Prascovia's older sister, Antonina, died at thirty-six. The first blue star is her daughter, Lizaveta, who disappeared in her twenties. That's what it says, *propala*."

"Not too surprising, considering the period," Chris said. A bad feeling settled in the bottom of his stomach like a large jellyfish. He did not—absolutely did not—want to hear the rest.

Debra wiggled herself from under the throw, re-energized by the perspective to decipher the mystery of Valya Svetlova. "Look at the following fourth generations. If it's one blue star, only one child was born and it was always a female. The rest of the branches died out, and every time, that female vanished after childbirth."

"Are you sure you're getting this correctly?"

"*Propala*. The word itself could also be translated as 'perished,' but it's less likely it was used in that sense."

"What happened in the eighteen hundreds?" Chris asked. "I see three stars."

"This is the only time when three branches had survived. These are two cousins who were born in the same time frame and both lived into their sixties. The third branch produced another female, but her lifespan happened much later in the century. Guess what? She vanished at nineteen, without an offspring."

Chris pointed at the fourth name above Valya's. Like hers, it was marked with a blue star.

"Alexandra Gretishnikoff emigrated," Debra explained, "and Valya's great-great-grandmother, Leontina, disappeared, but look at Andrey's mother, Anna. *Propala*. That leaves Valya in her generation all alone."

Ovals, names, dates. A meticulous delineation of one family's chilling history. Blood pounded in his ears. Chris pressed his cold fingers to his throbbing temples.

Debra nudged him with her shoulder. "I know what you're thinking. Valya's name has a star. It takes two Gretishnikoff females to survive. She and I would be the third case of two girls of the same age group born in the fourth generation."

"She's in some serious, serious trouble."

"Chris, we have no idea where this tree came from. You know we can't believe it."

"What, you think Gregory made it up and stuck it under my pillow? Valya believes in it. No wonder she doesn't let anyone get emotionally close to her."

"Because she thinks she's predestined to disappear? Look, Vishenky is not some medieval village. Valya wasn't raised in the Dark Ages. She can stay in Moscow. She has a choice."

"Not exactly." Chris couldn't keep the thick bitterness out of his voice. "She made her choice. She chose Vishenky."

"You like her, don't you?" Debra asked.

"I did, but it's not just that. I know she exposed you to the portal in the pond. What else has she done to you?"

"I'm fine."

"And I'm scared...for both for you."

"Scared" was an understatement. Chris felt as though he were being forced to speed along a dark winding road with faulty brakes and headlights.

Debra touched his arm. "At least don't worry about me. The bottom line is Valya and I are not—"

The door burst open. Valenteena Gretishnikoff Svetlova walked in. Her gaze fell on the coffee table. "The family tree. Which one of you went snooping around?"

"You're a goddamn liar," Chris said. "I'll give you one minute to explain. Try telling the truth for a change."

"Shocking, huh?" Valya asked, her eyes fixed on his cousin.

"Not really," Debra said coolly. "The maiden name of my great-great-grandma was Efremoff. She married another Russian immigrant, Gretishnikoff, and took his name. You and I are not related."

Valya raised her eyebrows, pursed her lips, and bobbed her head unflappably, as if she just learned that Debra could wiggle her ears or would rather go hungry than eat catfish. "Glad we got that cleared up. Too bad. You'll never get to experience Vishenky the way I do. Listen, it's almost noon. Gregory will drive Luke to the hotel. He'll take your bags, too, to make your trip on the train easier. Whenever you're ready."

"Not even an apology?" Chris asked. "For all your lies?"

Valya's smile bore all the warmth of a snarling wolf. "For what? Does an owl feel sorry for killing a rabbit?"

CHAPTER SIXTY-NINE

I cooked chicken Tabaka for dinner, using a heavy stone and an antique iron—the kind that worked on coal—to press the lids down on the frying pans. Rubbed in salt and pepper, the birds acquired a mouth-watering crust.

The spicy smell and splattering noises promptly got Luke's attention. He poked his finger at the mini-boulder squashing his dinner. "It's time to sauté another delicious rock."

"Feeling better?" I asked. "Ready to explore Moscow?"

Luke put his hefty arm around me. "Not today, sweetie. You've got some explaining to do. We're waiting for you." He turned me toward the front veranda, where the discussion over my family tree went on for hours.

They were nothing to me, a bunch of strangers who accidentally ended up sleeping under my roof. I was alone again, and the worst part—I knew without a trace of a doubt that the Violet Lights were coming.

Having no desire to talk, I took my plate upstairs, to the unfinished second floor. There was no one to hassle me. No ghosts or humans. Only Peter's three cameras blinked their red indicator lights. I yanked at the cords to turn them off.

The worldwide invasion of the Violet Lights or just another peaceful evening in the village, dishwashing chores wouldn't take care of themselves. I carried a plastic container full of plates and cooking pans to the river.

Long shadows sprawled over the surface. I savored my favorite part of the day, the last hour before sunset, from the wooden steps that led to the water. The puckish deities that had pestered the land since morning, the breeze and the heat, had gone to torment other places and realms. Puffs of harmless gnats swirled in the quiet air, and the kids played badminton on the packed dirt road.

The finest afternoon of the season.

The darkest hours of my life.

I tried to imagine what I'd feel approaching a portal one final time, certain I could never return. What would happen to my body the moment I plunged into the glowing abysm? What would happen to my mind?

The river "bloomed." Inch-long translucent strips of algae abounded in each handful of water. I'd have to scald my tableware to ensure it was safe to use.

On the opposite bank, a plump light-brown animal sat on its hind legs, chewing grass.

"Nice, huh?" I asked the critter.

The little jaw stopped moving.

"And suddenly you have to throw your life away because it's up to you to save your species," I said. "What would you do?"

So close that I could reach it with my fingers, a blue dragonfly with velvety black wings hovered above the greenery, reluctant to settle. I turned to see what bothered the graceful insect.

Chris stood on the path.

"A brave man," I said. "Taking one for the team?"

"I was just nominated mediator of the week." He joined me on the steps. "Who were you talking to?"

I pointed at my furry listener. "*Ondatra*. A plain, real mammal."

"Muskrat," Chris said. Shadows circled his troubled eyes. This morning he hadn't been given time to shave, to have a cup of coffee. Looking at his pale, drawn face, I wondered if he had touched his lunch or dinner.

The critter sniffed the air, took another bite of sedge, and jumped into the current. It swam along the bank holding its nose above the water and carrying grass in its teeth. Then the muskrat dove under the exposed willow's roots.

"What's up?" I asked Chris, as if nothing was wrong, as if he came to find out where I kept my ping pong set, as if I didn't dally by the river because the haze of hopelessness smothered my aptitude to analyze and act.

"You can't avoid us forever," he said.

"Avoid? Two hours in the kitchen—I practically cooked you a feast."

"Yes, and Luke crunched every chicken bone. The problem is, we gave you space, but then you never joined us at the table."

Debating whether I should share my discovery with Chris, I slid my hand into my cardigan's pocket and touched the note I had found hidden in the heap of clothes I wore last night. It stated, in my rushed handwriting:

Whistling through a blade of grass attracts Ostov.

Gray Sniffers are people-friendly because I drink a potion to add the scent of acorns to my human scent. The same with the energy, human and otherworldly. I am the link. If I give in and enter the other dimension, Lights will recognize humans as a part of their kin and won't attack.

Prascovia can't let me go until she ensures her sister's uninterrupted lineage. She endows every prospective father with an entity, which appears to be a male counterpart of the paranormal energy that resurrected me. If not removed, it can turn deadly for the carrier. Peter should be warned about Kenny.

Prascovia's own family is her insurance. They can postpone the invasion, but only Antonina's descendants are powerful enough to stop it for nearly a century. I'm a fourth-generation Gretishnikoff. It is my turn.

What the hell happened to me last night? Reeking of finality, the note twisted me in an excruciating knot of options. I could wait for the impending strike of the Violet Lights and die with the rest of humanity, or I could say my goodbyes and sacrifice myself to save it.

I crumpled the paper and blurted out the damning truth, "Chris, I'm lost."

"I know. Lost, and scared, and that's why you push people away. You won't allow anyone to see you weak. But this time, you must let us in. Peter has found a way to stop the Violet Lights."

"When did that little anecdote become a common knowledge?"

"You were chatty last night, and Peter and I compared notes. He was livid that you didn't mention the entity to him." Chris slapped a mosquito trying to land on the back of his hand and flicked his finger to dispose of the squashed corpse. "You understand we don't have a choice; we must solve this?"

I felt chill, as if the frostiness in his quiet voice encrusted my world in a marble sarcophagus. "I'm not ready to do what you're asking of me."

"Can you hear me out before you start arguing?"

"No. Your only choice is to leave Vishenky. With you around, it's like fighting a dragon while holding a litter of puppies. I can't focus. Besides, my parents will be here tomorrow night. You think the end of the world is your worst nightmare? Wait till you meet my mother."

His frown deepened. "Parents. Right. That gives us twenty-four hours. Should be enough, but we can't proceed without your cooperation."

"And if I don't cooperate, then what?" I asked. "You'll push me into a portal?"

He met my glare with a soft smile, sad and short-lived. "You know, you're a different person today."

"Sorry I've become your infinite disappointment. Tell Peter his plan won't work. I make my own decisions. You can't force me to do anything. If any one of you tries to hurt me—"

"Jeez, Valya. No one wants to hurt you. Just answer a few questions and I'll leave you alone. Be reasonable. You don't gain anything by withholding information."

I paused, struck by his pained look. Unable to sense Chris's emotions and too engrossed in my own dilemma, I could have misread his objective. No menace lurked in his tired, regretful eyes. He was hurting, and I didn't know exactly why, but this wasn't a man willing to harm me for the sake of humankind.

"That's all you want?" I asked. "Information?"

"Yes."

"You already seem to know more than I ever intended to disclose," I said.

"Your friend's death," Chris said.

"*What?*"

"I know how difficult it must have been for you." He put his hand just above my knee. The gesture felt strangely impersonal. "Where did it happen?"

"In my home. On the second floor." My eyes were dry, my voice even.

"Why was he there alone?"

"Dimitry asked me for green glass and a candle and told me to stay in the kitchen." This wasn't difficult at all. Emotionally, I was a ghost.

"You're not someone who'd grant such a request without asking questions."

"It was an experiment."

"Go on. Why do you think his death was caused by the entity?" Chris asked.

"Did you notice a thicket of feathery shrubs in the garden just past the apple trees? Silver-green leaves?"

"Yes."

"Sea-buckthorns. The berries are tart if you eat them raw. I woke one night feeling like I just popped one in my mouth. A very bright fluorescent ball the size of a grapefruit hovered above my face. I poked it with my finger. The ball hit a window like a trapped bird and escaped the room through the hallway door."

I fell silent, remembering my initial thrill. A new manifestation to explore—what could be more exhilarating?

"Then what happened?" Chris asked.

"My friends and I used the second floor as our tree house. My parents didn't mind because that made it easier for them keep an eye on me. The day after I met the entity, Dimitry started having quick mood swings like sudden anger or unexplained loneliness. I tasted sea-buckthorn in my mouth every time he had a spell. He told me a strange thing—that the feelings weren't his."

Chris nodded grimly, as if too familiar with the sensation.

"Two days later, Dimitry came over alone. My parents were in Moscow. He asked for green glass and a candle. 'Wait here,' he said, 'it won't take long,' and climbed the ladder. I didn't check on him until he fell." I swallowed. "Blood was everywhere. So much blood."

Chris removed his hand from my trembling leg. "That's enough. Now pull yourself together. We must recreate the setting of Dimitry's death before it gets dark."

CHAPTER SEVENTY

"Don't argue, just listen." Chris shook his hands, fingers steepled, in front of his face. "Manifestations correspond with particular portals, right?"

"As far as I know," I muttered.

"We think Prascovia delivers the entity to your home when it gets lost because you have the only gateway it can use to go back and forth."

"In old times—maybe. But now I have plastic barriers around the house and our property. It wouldn't be able to cross them."

"We thought of that. The portal opens, and the entity rushes out like a dog through an electric fence that has just been installed. Then it's too scared to get back in. There must be something special about those entities, because every time one of them gets trapped on Earth, *volkanoks* start murdering humans as a misguided warning. They don't necessarily understand our world better than we know theirs. When the killings don't work, the whole army of the Violet Lights comes to the rescue."

Chris stopped, waiting for my reaction. I nodded. If I understood my reference to Kenny correctly, Prascovia put an entity in him last summer, and that would explain why in February *volkanoks* slaughtered Gregory's friend Terentey Malin.

"Peter analyzed your family tree," Chris said. "Normally, the portal opens once in every few decades. When did the village get the new power line?"

"Two years ago."

"It's less than a hundred yards from your house. He believes that's what could have triggered the portal to open again so quickly, out of the timetable. We need to find it, get rid of the entity, and plug the gateway with plastic. Then the Violet Lights won't come looking for their comrade."

The theory wasn't bad. After luxuriating in Chris, the entity would possess both energies, human and supernatural. Its homecoming would have pacified the Lights—except for one thing. To "complete the cycle," the human contribution had to come from Antonina's descendant.

Yet the seedling of hope sprouted in my chest, its feeble roots wrapping around my heart. What if I could make Chris's plan work? Somehow...someway. No more threat. No need for a sacrifice. I'd figure out how to deal with Prascovia later.

"I don't know for how long an entity can survive without a host," I said. "It's probably dead."

"I'm afraid you're wrong." His tone was casual, but I read too much resignation in his bearing, the way Chris lowered his head, his shoulders hunched.

"You think you are...."

"Infected. Yes." He pressed his lips together, but I saw his mouth quiver.

I slid my hand under his polo shirt and placed four fingers on his spine. My thumb dug into his side.

Chris didn't protest. He just looked at me, his eyes softened by the same tortured, mournful expression I'd noticed before.

I felt nothing at first, just the warmth of his skin. Then, like a stream of minuscule toppling dominoes, a current of his emotional energy tickled my palm and ran up my arm, spread throughout my body, and reached my scalp, toes, and the fingertips on my other hand. The surge was so intense, so turbulent, it jolted me into momentary confusion. As I tried to summon my focus, the astringent taste of sea-buckthorn berries filled my mouth.

"You're back," Chris whispered, his face lit up with hope. "I missed this...closeness."

Of course. Once he had experienced a supernaturally fueled affinity, he couldn't bear to lose it.

Neither could I. My heart tightened like a clenched hand.

"Tears of the Crying Tombstone," I said softly. "Antipathy potion. That's what you need. I'll find the vial."

"I don't want it."

"Without it you'll be in too much pain, but first, we'll go with Peter's plan. You're right. The entity is in you."

"I hate to look needy, but please don't let me die," Chris said.

I pressed my forehead to his shoulder and slid my hand around his waist, absorbing the fear that billowed under his casual tone. "The host doesn't have to die to send the entity back to its domain."

"That's how it worked with Dimitry."

It hadn't worked at all. Even if Dimitry had gotten rid of the entity, a week after his death Anna crossed the threshold into the other world, just like so many women of my bloodline had done before her. But it wouldn't be my turn. *Tears of the Crying Tombstone.* I had an idea how I could make Peter's plan succeed.

"Would you like me to find you some green glass?" I asked.

"Yes," Chris said with sudden enthusiasm. His face looked elated at a prospect I couldn't fathom. "How exciting."

Exciting indeed. If we both survived.

CHAPTER SEVENTY-ONE

Dust particles floated in slivers of light from the sun sinking behind the willows. The unfinished rooms of the second floor felt hotter than a sauna. The students stood in a semicircle, watching Chris like orderlies about to apprehend an out-of-control mental patient.

None of it was important.

"Green glass," Valya said.

Chris inspected the semi-transparent lump she placed in his palm. It must have melted in the village fires to acquire this misshapen form of an unidentifiable roadkill. The bulge in the middle contained some liquid. The bubbles rolled from side to side as he rotated the two-inch-thick piece.

Valya lit a pillar candle and carried it to a windowsill. She looked at Chris and her lips parted as if she was going to speak but instead she stepped aside. With the windows shut, the wick burned steadily in the unstirred air.

Chris held the glass over the flame.

The gorgeous, stunning candlelight shone through the green bubble. With the slightest movement of his hand, it pulsed, it danced, and it burst into a thousand twinkles. Nothing in the world could compare to its warmth and beauty. Nothing else could be so welcoming, so alluring. Chris feasted his eyes on the glow, wishing to be pulled in, wishing he could melt into the light, dissolve his thoughts, emotions, and his very soul in the majestic radiance.

"So, the portal must be this window," someone said. "How will we block it?"

"Don't worry about it," Valya said. "It's not the power line that triggers it. I'll make sure the entity never returns. Keep your eyes on Chris."

The moment approached, inevitable, long wished for. Chris had to make one last effort to overcome the gravity and the ballast of his brain. Then he could fly into the shine, into the magnificent green beacon, leaving behind the alien world where he had been stuck for too long.

The flame licked the bottom of the glass and stretched to his fingertips. Chris didn't move. Physical pain was the fair price for his freedom.

The liquid inside the bubble began to boil. A spider web of fissures spread over the thin top.

The glass burst. Its contents hit the flame, and the candle went out with a miniature mushroom cloud. Chris recoiled from the blast, dropping the pieces.

Someone shrieked his name.

Chris curled his fingers into fists. In his happiest moment, when he was about to cross the boundary, kissing the world with its yellow moon goodbye, a concrete wall fell in front of him, trapped him, and crushed all his hopes.

Hands grabbed his shoulders and pulled him backward. An arm tightened around his throat. Jerked out of balance, he couldn't free himself without hurting his captor. If he did, more humans would charge him before he chose his next move.

Debra darted in to snatch the broken glass. A sharp bit drew blood from her palm, showing Chris what might stop his suffering. He didn't want to go on. His lonely existence wasn't worth living if he was kept away from everything he craved.

"Luke, pay attention," Peter's voice barked. "We'll take him downstairs."

"Did it work?" Luke asked.

"No." Valya stared at Chris, apparently the only one who understood his predicament. Her feet apart, her arms relaxed along the sides of her body, she showed no intent to attack him. "Let him go and get out of here. All of you, get out. I know how to finish to this."

Chris waited. Debra had missed a large flake of glass stuck between two planks, thin and iridescent like a scale of some exotic fish. If his students believed in his compliance and left him in Valya's care, it would be easy to overpower the unsuspecting woman and get to the chip.

Peter's forearm slithered off Chris's throat. The students backed out of the room, their footsteps thumping on the loose boards.

Valya walked up to Chris and just stood there in silence, inches away but maybe realizing that they were two worlds apart. He hesitated to make his move, puzzled by her relaxed posture. Then she rose to her toes. Chris tensed, detesting the idea of a new loop of human arms around his neck. Instead, she pressed her lips to his, the only point of contact between them.

The Big Bang was nothing more than a strike of a matchstick. Millennia started and ended, universes sprouted and expired, the time unfurled and collapsed onto itself. In this eternal cacophony of nothingness and unimaginable matters, Chris held tight to the source, the core, the essence of his existence. The energy. The woman.

This isn't real, he thought. Another manifestation of the alien world. His frenzied, unearthly longing for Valya held no warmth, no euphoria of human affection. He had to pull them both from the cosmic vortex, before their minds disintegrated in the dimensions they couldn't grasp. His consciousness flickering like a streetlamp in a hurricane wind, Chris unlocked his embrace and ended the kiss. He thought he saw the violet glow in Valya's pupils. Then they were black.

She laughed, her nostrils flaring and teeth bared. "Did you feel it?"

He felt as though he just played five sets of tennis in the Virginian heat.

"It worked!" Valya ran to the ladder and rushed down into the chorus of voices below. Chris didn't follow her.

The indicator lights on Peter's cameras were dark. The plugs barely touched the sockets of the extension cords. Someone had sabotaged his student's effort to record the manifestations. Good. Chris didn't want anyone see the footage starring Valya and him.

It worked, she had said. The human race was saved. Chris survived. Life as usual awaited.

The loud argument downstairs spilled outside. No one, not even Debra thought of checking on Chris. Dizzy, too wiped out to talk, he was glad to be forgotten. Pincers of a headache clenched his temples.

A car door slammed. Chris walked to the wall facing Gregory's yard and leaned heavily on the windowsill, his forehead against the glass. In the waning light, he caught sight of Valya in the passenger seat of her neighbor's SUV. She looked straight ahead, ignoring the shouting students who surrounded the vehicle. Gregory sprinted to open the gate, pushed Luke aside, and jumped behind the wheel. The SUV slowly backed out. It sped off once on the street.

Life as usual. For Valya, new paranormal quests. For Chris, a chance for a future unaltered by the Vishenky adventure. Maybe he would feel happier about it tomorrow, after a good night's sleep.

Debra glanced around and then looked up as if it finally dawned on her that Chris had never left the second floor. She waved. He weakly raised his hand. She spoke to her teammates standing in Gregory's yard and strode toward Valya's front gate.

Chris brushed his palm across his face, wiping away tears running down his cheeks. He picked up the flake of green glass his cousin had missed.

CHAPTER SEVENTY-TWO

I called my trusted friend, Tamara Karpova, from the train station, the only place near Vishenky with cell phone reception. An hour later, the headlights of her train appeared on top of the hill. The bell began to ring at the crossing where Gregory and I sat waiting in his SUV. The gate went down. I opened the passenger-side door and climbed out.

"Please, just do what I asked," I told Gregory for the tenth time. "Take Tamara home. Then find Andrey and give him my message. Don't look for me. Don't follow the group. Don't even go near my house."

He grumbled about my rashness. I shut the door and ran to the platform.

In a sleek shimmery dress, all tiny pleats and lace, and to-die-for strap heels, Tamara got off the train like royalty stepping out of a carriage. A few unshaved elements who exited the adjacent car regarded us with curious glances but refrained from any loud comments. Mumbling to each other, they walked away with their heads down.

"Birthday party." Tamara twirled to show off the fabulously flowing skirt. "Nice restaurant."

"Sorry. And thank you." I led her to a wooden bench, took off my cardigan, and spread it over the weathered planks. "Don't want to ruin your dress."

Tamara unclasped her straps and placed her bare toes on the asphalt. She pointed to the gray figures at the end of the platform.

"You scared those dudes. Your eyes are flashing violet."

I frowned at the moon perched on top of a utility pole. "I'm running on two energies—the one that revived me after I was born and its male counterpart. For a human body it's over the top. I feel like I'm floating above the ground."

Tamara gave my forearm a firm squeeze, as if to keep me grounded.

"I figured out why Prascovia induces stillbirths," I said. "I'm the only progeny of her sister, Antonina. If tomorrow I walk into a portal and don't come back, what will happen?"

Still in a party mode, at least a couple cocktails away from my problems, Tamara blinked. "What?"

"Antonina's bloodline will end. How can Prascovia prevent that? By making sure that I have a baby."

"A baby," Tamara echoed. "So what if Antonina's bloodline dies out? Is Prascovia that sentimental?"

"We're her life support. Only Antonina's descendants can survive the presence of two energies in their bodies, and that's what Prascovia wants to harvest."

Tamara eyeballed me as if I were mentally ill and refused to take my meds. "How did you come up with all this hooey?"

"How else would the witch survive for hundreds of years?"

"Where does the second energy come from?" she asked.

"We can't conceive unless the father, just like the mother, is a carrier of a paranormal entity. I would be the mother. The father got infected four nights ago."

"Wait a minute. Are you—?"

"Not pregnant," I said. "I only kissed Chris. But because he's in love with me, his energy found mine irresistible. The hitch is, when the witch traps a 'male' entity and puts it in a prospective father, the Violet Lights come looking for it. I have to send it into its world."

Tamara's eyes darted around, unfocused, as if trying to snatch some elusive thought out of the air. Then she asked the most important question. "And Chris is—?"

"The mystery man at the hotel."

"What about Prascovia's own family? And the stories about inducing stillbirths in the village?"

"They are her insurance. When something goes wrong with Antonina's branch, Prascovia must send someone else who is a carrier to 'the other side.' The Violet Lights 'smell' the human energy, recognize humankind as family, and don't attack the Earth. Unlike in the old days, you won't find a lot of pregnant women in the village, so it gets trickier for Prascovia." I thought about my mother and her obsession with "fresh air." If only she had stayed in Moscow.... "But it's only Antonina's descendants, Gretishnikoffs, who can provide Prascovia with two energies. After the 'harvest,' we have just enough of the energy blend left in us to pacify the paranormal world. And it's easy to force the mother to go there because she wants her baby to live."

Tamara rubbed her lips together, her eyes thoughtful and her vibrant aura of gaiety gone. "How long before Prascovia tries to find you another mate?"

"It can only work with a man I like. I won't give Prascovia another chance."

Tamara slowly shook her head.

"Hey, I'm solving one problem at a time," I said. "Help me to stop the Violet Lights. Then I'll figure out my next step."

"What do you want me to do?"

"I know how to open a portal in my home and release the male entity into its dimension. I just need you to trick my guests to get out of the house and keep them away. The gypsy manifestation is tonight. Take the group to the ruins."

"What happens if both energies leave you? How will you survive?"

"A crucial question. I'm not a helpless infant, but to be safe, I'm going to try the antipathy potion. Tears of the Crying Tombstone. Once I end my crush on Chris, the energies should separate." I unfastened my locket with *volkanok's* fur and put it around her neck. "Gregory's waiting for you at the crossing. Take the group to see the gypsies."

"Why do you need to be alone?"

"Because at the slightest sign of trouble someone will interrupt the process. I can't risk it." I squeezed her forearm. "Please. Have fun, mesmerize them with your gypsy dance. That's all I ask."

"I hope you know what you're doing." Tamara stuck her feet back into her silvery straps.

"It will work," I said. "It will."

We hugged. She stomped down the platform. I peered into the fizzing night. I wanted Chris out of the house because once I opened the gateway he'd try to stop me from crossing over into it. I wasn't sure I should be stopped.

CHAPTER SEVENTY-THREE

Chris wanted some clarity. To know what was going on. To have his every question answered. *Just for once.*

An hour and a half after Valya took off in Gregory's SUV, he was on his third cup of coffee—black, freshly brewed, and strong—trying to shake off the daze of mental and physical fatigue, when this dumpy blonde, Tamara Karpova, knocked on the front door. Wobbly in her high heels and oozing sly grins, she assured him in her broken English that she was Valya Svetlova's best friend and would take the group to a spot outside the village where Valya would meet them.

"See?" Debra said to Chris. "I told you not to worry."

"And you were right." He raised his cup toward her and made an effort to smile.

"I have a bad feeling, too," Peter said quietly, watching Chris from across the dining table. "Valya's a problem solver, and her problems are never over."

"I really think we should torch the house," Jessie said. "Covering the window with plastic is not a permanent solution. What if her parents remove it?"

"You'll burn the whole village," Debra said.

"Might be a good idea."

"Valya said the power line doesn't open the portal."

"And you believed her?" Jessie asked.

"I believe her," Peter said. "I believe she's trying to finish this for good. I wish she'd let us help her."

Tamara emerged from Jessie's room boasting a floor-length colorful skirt, red shawl, and heavy coin necklace. "A dress of a gypsy," she explained. "Valya waits. Follow me."

Flirty but no less assertive than a cruise director, she battered her mascara-laden eyelashes at Luke, flashed toothy smiles at Peter, and then shepherded the group out of the house.

Not a bird, a frog, or even a cricket disturbed the night. Pus-colored moonlight seeped through a gauzy cloud. The group left the village behind and hiked along the riverbank. The path ended at the black mouth of a stone arch culvert cutting under the railroad embankment. The climb up the nearly vertical stairway was treacherous, the tall concrete steps offering little traction because of the gravel spilled from above them. They crossed the tracks. The descent was just as hazardous. When they reached the flat ground, Tamara headed into a sparse grove.

Their destination, the ruins of an old pump station, waited for them twenty yards ahead. Valya was nowhere to be seen.

The roof of the rectangular brick building had collapsed long ago. The flash from Jessie's camera lit up eerie landscapes of massive pipes disappearing into a concrete floor and the ghostly figures of her friends clad in clear-plastic ponchos. Tamara posed in an opening that used to be a window.

"Look around, be not afraid," she called out then spoke in Russian.

Debra clutched the ties of her protective garment at her throat. "During the time of the steam engines," she translated, "the station sent water from the river to Kolieno where the engines were refueled. Now it's abandoned and in ruins, but Gregory claims that the motor of the pump is still functional. Tonight—"

"I'm going back to the house," Chris said.

"No-no-no-no-no." Tamara waved her pudgy hand emphatically. "Valya—wait here. She arrives."

"When?" Chris asked. "When will she be here? Deb, can you explain to this idiot that we need to find Valya?"

"The word 'idiot' is about the same in Russian," Debra said in a lowered voice, "and I already asked her."

"Tamara wears Valya's locket," Jessie said. "She's telling us whatever Valya ordered her to say. Let's wait."

Perched on the brick carcass of the wall, Valya's best friend stared outside the ruins as if, to her, the conversation had no meaning.

Peter's eyes darted around the silent landscape. "What happened, Tamara lured us out of the house."

"Exactly what I'm thinking," Chris said.

"Let's split up then. You, Deb, and Luke should go back. Jess and I will wait here."

"I'd rather stay here, too." Luke stood half-upright with his butt pressed against the wall. His forehead glistened with perspiration.

"Buddy, you need to be in bed," Peter said.

"Wait." Tamara jumped down to the ground and tugged the hood of Debra's poncho. "*Perevodi.*"

Debra bent her head as she listened to the Russian's animated oration. "In 1905, the traveling gypsies picked this spot for their camp. The locals weren't particularly fond of them, blaming them for stealing chickens from the village. On that fateful day, several ducklings and a calf didn't return home. Someone saw the gypsies' campfire, so they got the blame. The events unravel again each year, probably because of the time when they took place, during the full moon in July."

"Good." Tamara pointed outside the dilapidated structure. "To the grass." She walked through the void of a doorway, motioning for the group to follow her into the meadow.

Jessie shrugged. "Whatever Valya's up to, she doesn't want us around." She sauntered after Tamara.

* * *

The sounds came first. Chris listened to loud voices speaking in unknown dialect, laughter, a dog barking, and the neigh of a horse somewhere very close. He caught himself holding his breath when a fire emerged in the middle of the clearing, getting brighter with every second. Then figures appeared, men, women, and children, having a late supper, going in and out of tents. The women wore distinctive clothes, similar to Tamara's outfit, full colorful skirts, shawls, and scarves covering their heads and tied at their napes.

Chris saw the camp so clearly it was hard for him to believe they weren't real gypsies going about their everyday lives. A train passed by on the hill, the illuminated golden band flashing through the trees, too far away to tell if the passengers noticed the bonfire in the meadow. The gypsies ignored the noisy locomotive.

A burly man with a long, bushy mustache brought out two guitars and handed one to a wispy-haired elder in a tattered vest. The latter's knotted fingers confidently scurried over the strings. These were the simple pleasures of the evening—a fire, a good meal, and a few women indulging in dancing. The older ones started the show, cheering each other in high-pitched voices. The young children jumped around with the music until their mothers made them go to their tents.

A woman stepped into the circle and the gypsies cheered. Her confident bearing showed she was accustomed to the attention.

Tamara strolled toward the fire, her right hand sending playful flutters through the hem of her skirt. A dance started, slow at first. Invisible to the gypsies, the living woman joined the ghost, their movements perfectly synchronized.

Debra spoke, but Chris didn't listen, absorbed in the incredible performance. The bonfire blazed higher, illuminating the dancers. A violin played along with the guitars. A tambourine struck a quickening rhythm, and Chris felt his pulse accelerating with the beat. The violin wept a passionate melody, the melody he had heard before, in another lifetime, in a never-never land, in some unfathomable dimension....

Chris grabbed Debra's shoulder. "This is what I heard at the pond."

The music stopped. No cheering erupted around the fire. The gypsies were staring at Tamara.

"They can see her," Jessie whispered.

The ghost dancer pulled out a short knife.

Tamara moved backward, one small step, then another. Her long skirt became tangled in the wet grass. She yelped as she fell.

Luke darted forward, Peter bent to pick something from the ground, and Chris swerved to avoid stepping on his student's hand. A sharp pain burst in his spine. He spun around. In the door of the pump station, a boy stood shaking his head and weighing in his hand a chunk of a broken brick. Chris recognized Gregory's kid, Andrey.

Luke reached Tamara and stuck his hands under her armpits. The gypsy advanced a couple of paces but stopped and watched in seeming confusion her quarry being dragged away by a hefty stranger muttering in foreign language.

"To the pump station, slowly," Chris said. From the corner of his eye, he saw a few shadows changing positions between the tree trunks on the edge of the clearing.

"They're trying to flank us," Jessie said.

"Those are not gypsies," Chris said. "They are the villagers. It's 1905."

Someone frightened the horses grazing on the far side of the meadow. They stampeded through the camp, some crashing into the tents and sending screaming women to take cover among the birches. The events of history fell into a predetermined pattern when a mob of peasants armed with clubs and pitchforks emerged from the grove. With the number of enemies comparable, the conflict evolved into hand-to-hand combat.

Inside the pump station's walls, Chris glanced around looking for Gregory's son. The boy crouched behind a pipe three yards away, where its wide mouth was cemented into the floor. Andrey brought his index finger to his lips then pointed it at Chris. *Valya*, the boy mouthed silently. He motioned in the direction of Vishenky, as if ordering Chris to go.

The meadow grew quiet. The end of the manifestation was nearing. The figures of the fighters began to fade. Chris didn't have much time to get away unnoticed. He retreated behind the pump station's breached walls, his eyes on Tamara and the students engrossed in the sight of the bloody clash. Then he raced back to the village with the grim images of what he might find in the house bombarding his mind.

CHAPTER SEVENTY-FOUR

Night distorted the character of Valya's home, turning it into a two-story-tall black mausoleum, formidable and menacing.

Chris bent in front of the entrance, coughing, with one hand on the door frame and the other on his aching side. His lungs burnt as if he had inhaled a fireball. He hadn't realized that he was so out of shape. When had he given up running? Why?

His sweat-soaked shirt clung to his back. He listened to the agitated chatter of crickets. The night flowers by the veranda's walls moved in the breeze like watchful eyes on invisible faces.

He savored the last gulp of the cool air and pulled at the door's handle. The veranda was unlocked. He went straight through to the kitchen, the floorboards creaking under his hurried steps.

He saw it right away, as soon as he walked into the stuffy space, still as a cemetery on a sweltering, windless day. A neon-green sheen. It was on a side of the brick stove, the washstand, on the hanging wire dish rack, and Valya's round cooking table. Chris could make out the fruit in the checkered pattern of the faded vinyl tablecloth. The ceiling was illuminated, too, but the partially drawn linen curtain that served as a partition between his bedroom and the kitchen shadowed the narrow strip of space to his left. The source of the glow was behind the thick fabric.

Chris moved forward, half-expecting to find another empty, deathly hushed room and a portal into the other world, the portal that Valya had crossed on her inconceivable quest. His stomach as stiff and heavy as if it had morphed into resin, he grabbed the curtain and swept the rings along the wire.

There was no mirror in the wooden frame above his bed. Instead, Chris was staring at a tunnel filled with swirling luminous fog. Like laser beams coming from the stage at a rock concert, thin rays cut through the mist. Her back rigid, Valya sat on his bed, cross-legged and facing the portal.

He breathed out. She was alive. She hadn't left *this* world.

Glass crunched under his step. Chris looked down. He had flattened an empty vial. Some barely discernible scent permeated the air, like lawn clippings ripening in a compost pile.

A low bench, painted black, gold, and red like Russian wooden spoons, stood on the bed in front of Valya. A two-inch-thick pillar candle burned on its lacquered top. Valya's hands rested on the shoulders of a plaster figurine, the shepherd boy with missing feet. Chris had seen it upstairs, in the crate with the antique bronze moose. Her lips moved in a silent monologue.

She wore a pair of leggings and a sleeveless tunic top, an outfit suitable for a yoga class, not for an encounter with supernatural perils. Her hair was gathered in a bun. In the ghostly lighting, Valya looked drained, pallid. Chris ran his fingertips over her naked arm. Her skin felt warm, but goose bumps sprouted in the wake of his caress.

Chris waved his hand in front of her face. She swayed to her left, keeping the portal in her sight. Her words acquired sound, droning like an unemotional recital.

He cupped her chin and turned her face toward his.

Valya closed her eyes and swung her head. Her frown exuded immense weariness, as though her escape from Chris's touch took a Herculean effort. Her voice lost its steadiness. She drew in air in shallow intakes, and swallowed after every few breaths. Her chant sounded like she was trying to talk after jogging uphill.

His fingers curled into fists. Blood pounded in his ears like faraway hammering on anvils. His common sense, age, experience, and worldliness should have given Chris an edge in swaying Valya's decisions, yet he had failed her. The ethereal rays spilling from the pits of the wicked realm were siphoning the last drops of the woman's strength.

For how long could she endure this trance?

Chris sat and put his arms around Valya. He pressed his nose to the side of her head. Whispered her name.

She tensed, pushing weakly against his embrace, trying to sit upright.

Chris leaned forward and blew out the candle.

The flame might have played a role in the initiating the séance, but quenching it did nothing to end the process. Holding the dazed woman close, Chris worked the candle loose from the puddle of melted wax collected in the cast-iron holder then flung it into the luminous fog.

Instead of disappearing in the tunnel, the candle bounced off with a thud. It hit the pillow, tumbled on the floor, and rolled under the table. Incredibly, it also fractured what Chris thought was an unobstructed opening between the two dimensions. A slight distortion was evident in every beam that brushed the invisible cracks in the otherwise imperceptible pane. The mirror was still there.

"How about we bust it?" Chris whispered. He freed the plaster shepherd boy from Valya's hands and hurled it into the center of the wooden frame.

CHAPTER SEVENTY-FIVE

Dr-r-r-r-r. The plaster boy's head rolled on the brim of his hat across the floorboards and under the bed. Then the silence coalesced with the stifling darkness.

With one arm wrapped around Valya's back, Chris pressed his hand to her stomach to support her if she collapsed.

Her ribcage wasn't moving.

"Please, wake up." He felt as if his heart was afraid to beat. Was she holding her breath? Or had the portal drained her life force?

"Valya, please. Wake up."

Another sliver of the smashed mirror came off the frame, bounced off the top of the bed frame, and landed on the pile of shards littering his pillow.

"I hate you," Valya said.

Chris shut his eyes.

"I hate you," she repeated as if to dismiss any doubts, his or her own. "Get your hands off me."

Chris got up, found by touch his way to the table, and turned on the lamp. He picked up his carry-on bag from the floor and dropped it on the chair. In the absence of a closet, his stuff lay on the spare bed.

He didn't turn to check on Valya. She could open another portal and dive right in. Helping her was like trying to transplant a tree clinging to a cliff with its roots lodged deeply in crevices. One more night inside these ugly soot-covered brick walls, and Chris would live the rest of his life as if the Beltway's rush-hour traffic was his biggest problem. An invasion of the Violet Lights? In the normal everyday surroundings, it would seem about as likely as a strike of a giant meteorite. He focused on refolding his shirts.

The doors opened and slammed, followed by a stampede of footsteps and excited voices. Yes, everything was marvelous. Valya's new glorious conquest. Total victory. The entity saga was over. The threat of the Violet Lights was history.

Chris finished packing and parked himself in the chair, an apathetic spectator wishing the participants of the senseless, tiresome drama would clear his sheets of the broken glass and the room of their exhausting presence. Tamara glanced in his direction, went to the kitchen, and reappeared with a trash bag.

She collected the sharp pieces, shooed Valya off the bed, and tossed the comforter and the pillow on the floor. "I will put new," she assured him. Then she pulled off her sandal and used it to gather the shards that had fallen through the gap between the bed and the wall. "Broken mirror must throw in water. Who goes with me?"

"You can't contaminate the river," Debra protested. "The bag will get broken, and somebody will get hurt."

"It's okay," Valya said. "Remember the newts? That's what they were. The shards of another mirror. Can you get me a paper towel from the kitchen?" She took the trash bag from Tamara. "I want to save a few pieces."

Too curious to resist seeing another paranormal manifestation, the students followed the Russians outside. Chris stayed in the chair. He looked at the sheet covering the mattress and the limp pile of bedding at his feet. He could replace the pillowcase with one of his t-shirts and use his windbreaker as a blanket. His physical exhaustion would let his mind sink into the blissful world of senseless dreams.

If only he could get up. He had no desire to move, his body sluggish as if his muscles were replaced with cotton balls.

Light steps rushed through the kitchen. Valya appeared by the room-dividing curtain. "The entity that was your buddy is gone. I don't think Prascovia will try to sneak in and bring another one while I'm around, but do you want to bet your life on it?"

"I want to go to bed." Chris kicked at the soft heap on the floor. "Do you by any chance have another blanket?"

"Chris, please, not now. I want you to join us, just for a few minutes."

"And I want you to leave me alone."

"You don't know the half of what's going on." An enraged bull pawing at the ground would appear more patient than Valya. "Andrey was supposed to watch over me. What happened? Why did he let you in?"

"He caught up with us at the pump station and sent me here."

"I want to strangle that little rat."

"He's what? Ten? Are you mad at him because he dared to ask an adult for help?"

Valya blew a puff of air through her lips. "Like Dracula would need your help." She paused and looked around the room. "Do you know anything about Kenny?"

"Kenny Ogden? Peter's half-brother? Debra mentioned something about his mental issues."

Valya shook her head. "It's another entity. I'll put a kit together to purge it. You held the green glass above the flame, but it should be placed between the candle and the mirror. You saw my setup. Peter might need your input."

"Sure, will be a hoot."

"Chris?"

"What? Invasion averted, Vishenky's yours again, life's good."

"Yea-yea-yea, everything's great in my domain." She shrugged, not a shadow of regret dimming her enthusiasm. "Listen. I used up my reserve of the antipathy potion. I need to tap the Crying Tombstone to get more. The secretion is sporadic and maddeningly slow, so the vial should be set up tonight if I want to collect enough before you leave Russia. It's all about giving you back your normal life. My only mission. Nothing else until it's done. We have to dispose of the mirror, but it makes me nervous leaving you in the house alone. So spare me from needless arguments. Please come with me."

"Giving me back my normal life?" Chris chuckled. "How about a blanket?"

"I'm trying to get you out of Vishenky alive, and you're bugging me about a blanket. What's next? A cup of warm milk?" She tilted her head and smiled—an instantaneous transformation from a crusader into a playful hostess.

Daring and lively, game to tease or fight for his life, she stood before Chris within his reach, the strangest woman he had ever met.

"What if *I* give *you* a normal life?" he asked.

Valya laughed. "Oh, Chris. Our concepts of normal are worlds apart." She inhaled deeply, arching her back, her face turned upward as if she were seeing the sky and the stars, feeling a breeze on her cheeks. "Gosh, only four days. Feels like forever. Please don't look at me like some feral beasts have ripped open your chest and mauled your heart."

"Is there a remedy for that?" Chris asked.

Valya rubbed her wrist. "Trust me, one application, and you won't miss me, not even my cooking." She sighed, an amiable smile softening the line of her mouth, but her eyes remained serious. "If you really want to go to bed, I'll send Tamara to guard you. Good night, my dear Chris. Goodbye."

And she was gone.

CHAPTER SEVENTY-SIX

His mood gloomy and the morning equally gray, Chris walked past the gooseberry bushes to the far end of the garden. A bird flew from a cherry tree into the gathering low clouds. Without the sun, light gusts of wind chilled him. He took cover by the solid wooden fence. The greenery blocked his view of the house, but the blue dome of the church towered above the grove on the hill.

Debra showed up on the path, lovely in a white safari dress, her lipstick bright, and her hand clutching the strap of her cross-body bag. She was ready for the city.

"I assume you've decided to stay?" she asked. "Because everyone else's loaded up and ready to go. Gregory will take the bags to the station."

Chris looked at the gray sky. "It's going to rain. Maybe we should wait."

"Once it starts, it'll drizzle all day long." Debra stretched out her arm offering him her hand. "Get up. She's not coming. She said her goodbyes last night."

* * *

The first raindrops threatened as the group emerged from the birch grove. Tamara headed to purchase the train tickets while Gregory helped them with their bags. Debra had money for him, but he refused to accept it. Passionate handshakes followed. Gregory waved to Tamara coming from the ticket window and drove off.

Chris nodded and mumbled politely at the right moments but felt numb inside. Everything appeared unreal, like a dull, endless dream.

The half-full train left the station. Luke went into an empty compartment and stuck his head out the window. Chris watched the railroad crossing, the birch grove and the church, the steel-gray strip of the river, and at last Vishenky passing by.

The rain intensified. Catching sprinkles, Tamara told Luke to shut the window. He did and sat alone in the compartment with their luggage.

An hour later Chris stood in the lobby of the great hotel staring into space with unseeing eyes and contemplating what would happen if he returned to the village and introduced himself to Valya's parents.

* * *

No escape. Anything Chris looked at seemed to spawn an immediate connection with Vishenky. Levitan's haunting landscapes drove him to tears, sending his mind back to the woman he left behind. It wasn't love or even affection, this relentless, obsessive, insanely raw drive to see Valya. Chris fought it, his will like an overstretched vibrating string, but the snare only tightened, a blinding force choking his emotions, stifling his common sense.

"Withdrawal," Jessie said. "It's tough for all of us, but in your case it's brutal because you experienced the energy first hand. That's why Valya will never leave Vishenky. It's her life force."

Peter listened to his girlfriend with his now-habitual oddly grim expression. He didn't comment.

On their last evening in Moscow, the group stood admiring the graceful lines of the Novodevichy Convent. The orange sun cast muted light on the red-and-white towers. Adding flavor to a dreamy setting, a black swan glided over the pond spread out under the ancient walls. Chris looked around at the people sitting on the benches, walking their dogs, and feeding breadcrumbs to the ducks. It wasn't the first time he caught himself hoping and aching to spot the familiar face, Valya's smiling eyes. That evening, returning to the hotel, Chris spotted a slim woman standing by a column, her wavy light-brown hair loose over her shoulders. As Chris headed in her direction, she turned her head, one of the city's eleven million strangers.

"Nope, not Valya," Peter commented with a malicious edge to his voice.

* * *

Their flight had been announced. The atmosphere of airports neither saddened nor agitated Chris, an inevitable hassle that would end the moment he was strapped in his seat. Debra, unfocused and nervous, checked the suitcases and counted the members of her team. She snapped at Jessie for stopping to take a picture. Chris felt mild curiosity watching the noisy, hectic crowds as the group made their way through the busy Sheremetyevo International.

There she was, waiting for them by the check-in line. Chris rushed over, dragging his suitcase and barely avoiding collisions between his luggage and other travelers.

"Valya, how are you?" he asked. "I'm so glad to see you."

"Did you all have a nice week in Moscow?" She didn't tilt her head, didn't squint mischievously before she smiled. Poised, cool, *worldly* in designer jeans and high-heel strappy wedges, with a touch of a makeup on her eyes and lips, Valya made small talk about their time in the city. Chris felt no connection to this impersonal Muscovite, as though they had never lived under one roof, never shared an adventure.

Saying goodbye, she offered Chris her hand, smiling with polite indifference. When their palms touched, her thumb brushed his wrist, leaving a moist, quickly evaporating trace. *Tears of the Crying Tombstone.* Chris met her eyes and Valya nodded.

By the time they reached the gate, Chris had awakened from a bad dream. Vishenky had never happened. Thoughts of Valya brought him an aftertaste of regret, but nothing strong enough to spoil the anticipation of going home, picking up his pets, and seeing his sister.

The plane was airborne. As it climbed through clouds that blocked the view of the ground, Luke annoyed Jessie, insisting that one of the villages they flew over had to be Vishenky because he saw a green glow around it.

Chris closed his eyes. *Goodbye, Valya,* he thought. *Good luck.*

CHAPTER SEVENTY-SEVEN

Chris spent the first week after his return on the usual needed chores. He mowed the lawn and revived the dried flowerbeds, shopped for groceries and took care of days' worth of mail. He received a call at the end of the week.

"Wolf Trap," a familiar voice said, "Sunday."

"Beth, Sunday is tomorrow."

"Gosh, it is," Beth Vogel said. "Were you out of town? I kept calling."

"Why?"

"I missed you."

"I was in Russia," Chris said. "I missed you, too."

* * *

Two hummingbirds hovered over the brilliant red flowers of the hibiscus in a glazed Malaysian pot. On the front porch, hanging baskets of fuchsia and a gigantic Boston fern placed on a stand in front of a Bird-of-Paradise created the tropical feel Beth favored.

Beth looked her best in a knee-long beige skirt and a silk sky-blue blouse that complimented her eyes and fair skin. When she greeted Chris with a kiss, the scent of her perfume brought a sense of keen familiarity.

"How is the real estate business?" he asked.

"Thriving but boring," Beth said. "What were you doing in

Russia?"

"Escorting Debra on a folklore tour."

She chuckled. "Was it as fulfilling as it sounds?"

"We survived," Chris said.

The restaurant was freezing. The steering wheel of his car, which was parked in the sun, burned his palms. A battle with Sunday's afternoon traffic stretched all the way from Arlington to Vienna. Yet Chris relished every drill of the Virginian summer, every bit of normality.

"As unoriginal as I might sound," he said to Beth as they walked toward the Barns, "it's worth going abroad just to be reminded how good it feels to come home."

"I thought you were easy on me yesterday. Now I know why."

"I'm glad you called."

She didn't answer, just pushed her fingers through his and gave his hand a squeeze.

* * *

The summer ended in heat waves and drought, and leaves took their autumn colors early. The exposed rocks of Great Falls looked majestic under the scalding sun as the Potomac River fell to an almost record low. The nights remained hot and muggy despite the calendar announcing the beginning of September.

Barbeque at Laurie's was a perfect ending to a perfect Labor Day weekend. A beer in his hand, Chris watched his sister and Beth bustle about in the kitchen, the counter filling up with salad bowls and hors d'oeuvres.

"How was the Bahamas?" Laurie asked.

"Windy," Beth replied. "But the cruise was fabulous. We stayed up past midnight dancing the night away."

"Wow. That doesn't sound like my brother."

"I'm a changed man." Chris toasted them with his drink.

Beth picked up a fruit plate and carried it to the patio where Laurie's husband, Mark, fended off his friends' advice on grilling.

Laurie slid the door closed. "Debra came over the other night."

"How is she?" Chris asked. "I haven't seen her in ages."

"Fine. She's dating the quarterback, but she sounded pretty angry when we talked about you.'"

"I can't wait to hear why."

Laurie stuck a spoon into the mountain of potato salad. "She said, quote-unquote, 'He left the love of his life in Russia.'"

"Argh." Chris tossed the empty bottle in the trash. "The love of my life is here with me tonight. As a matter of fact, I'm ready to propose."

"That's great, but...Chris? Don't rush it."

"I thought you liked Beth."

Laurie picked up her wine glass. "We get along. I also got along with Sheryl. Then she divorced you." She took a sip. "You never told me why Beth broke up with you last spring."

"I didn't want to go to the Bahamas."

"On the same cruise you just enjoyed so much?"

"What can I say? I see things differently these days."

"What happened in Russia?"

"Nothing worth mentioning. Nothing." Chris walked out to the patio into the heavenly smell of grilled meats.

Chris thought of Vishenky later that night, while driving on the empty beltway with Beth dozing comfortably in the passenger's seat. He remembered the rustic train station, the log bridge over the river, the old brick house, and the sweet-scented flowers by the front door, opening at dusk like tiny mauve stars. The pastoral images were clear in his head, as if he had left the place last week. But when he tried to visualize their fearless guide, Valya Svetlova—her face, her smile—his mind's eye went hopelessly blind. What bothered him more than anything was the fact that he was unhappy about it.

CHAPTER SEVENTY-EIGHT

Chris should have never said yes.

"You were a part of that tour and for the kids it won't be the same without you," Beth said. "Go, for Debra's sake. She's family."

The gang had gathered at Luke's house while his parents were having a night out.

"Don't step on my ferret," Luke warned Chris at the door.

"Why don't you put her in her cage?" Jessie yelled from the kitchen.

"I can't find her."

"Call her with a squeaky toy."

"She hid that, too," Luke said.

In the living room, Peter fidgeted with two remote controls. The TV screen remained blank.

Debra got up from the sectional sofa, rubbing her naked arms above her elbows, maybe feeling cold in her sleeveless blouse, maybe being jittery.

"Glad you could make it." She pecked Chris on the cheek.

From the moment he walked in, Chris thought he'd probably feel more at ease at a quilting party. He didn't want to talk about himself. He wasn't interested in the lives of his former fellow travelers. He saw no point in rehashing the torturous events of the trip.

Jessie stepped out from the kitchen. "Would you like beer or a glass of wine?" she offered.

Chris accepted a beer, hoping the alcohol would take care of his discomfort. The place smelled nice, something full of vanilla and cinnamon baking in the oven.

"Hey, Luke, is that how you make ends meet?" Debra pointed at a brown animal that dashed across the living room, dragging a small beige purse, and began to climb the stairs.

"No, Maggie!" Luke raced to catch his ferret. He tossed the purse to Debra.

"My wallet's missing," she said investigating the contents.

Chris chuckled. "How long did it take you to train her?" he asked Luke.

"That's what ferrets do, hide things," Luke said. "She has a stash of her goodies under my bed. C'mon, Mag, you're going into your cage."

Peter finally had the video going, the TV screen slowly presenting the 360-degree panoramic view filmed in front of Valya's home.

"Would you like to sit down?" Debra asked Chris.

He shook his head and took a swig of the beer.

Jessie showed up with a plate of cookies. "This is Valya's recipe. I think I got it right." She held her beautifully arranged sugar-powdered creation in front of him.

"No thanks."

She shrugged and moved to the sofa, leaving the plate on the coffee table before she sat. Peter and Debra didn't wait for her invitation to taste the treat.

Luke returned with Debra's wallet and a large framed photograph, someone's portrait. "Hey, guys, check this out." He placed the frame on the coffee table.

"And your girlfriends don't mind that you keep it in your room?" Debra asked. She pushed the picture with her finger so Chris could see it.

"Makes them jealous, sure," Luke said. "But I really like it. It has character."

The photograph was a shot of Valya in a field of daisies. Luke had managed to capture her perfectly, not posing, not smiling for the camera, but as if she had turned, ready to make one of her witty remarks.

A word popped into Chris's mind: *intervention*. That's what the silly kids were doing, trying to compel him to remember his brief and unfortunate romantic endeavor. No wonder every smile, every move seemed forced tonight. *I'm happy without memories of Vishenky, thank you very much*, Chris thought. Debra had never thawed out toward Beth. The gathering was her conscious or subconscious way to demonstrate her disapproval of his engagement.

Luke deftly picked a cookie, mimicking Debra's mannerism. "Sublime, *dahling*," he uttered with a full mouth. He shook the next cookie at the screen. "The cool stuff is coming up, the Gray Sniffers."

The shadows prowling among cattails, the fantastic animals feeding aggressively in the pond—Chris marveled at how quickly his perception had adjusted from "wow, unreal" to "sure, why not." You see a blobfish for the first time and you can't believe you're looking at an actual living marine creature, but when you stumble upon the hideous image again, your mind has already accepted the fact of its improbable existence.

"Now, look at this." Peter pointed at the spot in the upper left corner of the screen. "Something I discovered since we watched it last time."

Chris couldn't discern anything unusual, just some bog plants, and even those he had to guess at as the approaching twilight made the mottled picture blurry. Only when the spot changed position did it become obvious that what was mistaken for vegetation was actually an animal. Its greenish fur blended perfectly with the landscape.

"You know what I think it was?" Peter asked. "A *volkanok.*"

"Man, that's so cool," Luke raved.

"Yeah, so cool," Chris said. "You're lucky it didn't eat you."

"I don't see the whole pack," Peter said. "It was just one animal, and Valya wouldn't let it anywhere near us."

"She was clueless about the damn thing." Chris crushed the empty beer can in his hand.

"Wrong again. She saw it. Watch." Peter fast-forwarded the recording.

From the Gray Sniffers fighting at the pond, the camera panned to under the oak, where Chris was slumped against the trunk with his palms plastered to his temples. The lens found Valya. The flyswatter drawn, she stood on the slope staring in the direction of the *volkanok*. She then glanced back at the camera and moved forward, positioning herself exactly on the line between the group and the predator.

"Valya knew," Debra said.

"She did a hell of a job protecting us," Jessie said.

"Bullshit," Chris blurted out. "She risked our lives every single day. Did you forget what happened to Luke?"

"Luke's right here, gobbling up cookies," Jessie snapped back. "He's fine. Every one of us who went to Vishenky is fine, even Kenny."

"Considering how untested and unpredictable the environment was, and the level of danger, Valya's performance was remarkable." Peter turned back to the screen, now pitch-black.

"—scheming against us under the thick blanket of duckweed." In the guide's voice, coming from the impenetrable darkness, Chris sensed a smile. "We absorb this night with our eyes and hearts, and we're being absorbed into its misty depths and whispers…"

Unimpressed by her sentimental monologue, Chris went to the kitchen to get another beer. He looked out the window. The backyard was a jungle of dogwoods and magnolias.

The girls appeared in the kitchen after a hushed discussion in the living room. Debra settled on a stool by the counter. Jessie chose to stand. Chris set down his beer and folded his arms at his chest, his butt pressed against the sink's edge.

"You do know what happened to Valya's friend Dimitry, right?" Jessie asked.

"He killed himself," Chris said curtly.

"That's not the whole story. Dimitry was seventeen, the oldest in their crowd, everyone's favorite. When he died, Valya's closest friends blamed her for what happened. She was only thirteen, still a child. Instead of giving the grief-stricken girl support, they turned on her. Her parents had never been more than bystanders in Valya's life, so she turned to Vishenky."

"And your point is?" Chris asked and Debra winced.

Jessie's gaze didn't waver. "You blame her for the choices she made, but it's not that simple."

"You just don't get it, do you?" Chris asked. "I don't care. It is that simple. We stopped the Violet Lights and got out alive. It's over. I don't care what Valya does with her life. I just want to live mine as if the trip never happened. Stay in touch with her if you wish, or go back to Vishenky. I don't care. Leave me out of it."

"What has she done to you," Jessie muttered, shaking her head.

"You know what? Don't talk to me about her or the trip ever again." Chris headed for the door.

Debra slid off her seat and scurried to block his way.

"Not a word from Valya in three weeks," she said. Chris ignored her and she walked backward in front of him. "Her last message was a text: 'The threat of the Violet Lights will never go away unless I finish this for good. Thanks for everything.'"

Chris stopped. He touched his forehead, the spot where a weevil of headache began to burrow into his brow. "The summer is over. Valya's in Moscow."

"I have her landline number," Debra said. "No one's there."

"She found her ancestor's lost diary," Jessie said. "Valya wouldn't leave Vishenky until she finished deciphering it. She was looking for clues about that woman's disappearance."

"Sounds like a project Valya would thoroughly enjoy," Chris said.

"You don't understand," Debra said, her voice rising. "The full moon was three weeks ago. Peter's certain that she tried to open a portal and cross into the other world."

Chris smirked. "Well, if Peter is certain…."

"What if it's true?" Jessie asked. "How does her disappearance make you feel?"

"I'd be sorry she's gone, of course. On the other hand, I wouldn't be much surprised. She was headed in that direction. You all know that. So the question is, if Valya finally entered her personal heaven, why are you so worked up about it?"

"Because she had no choice." Peter stood in the arch separating the hallway and the living room. "If she crossed over, it wasn't on her own accord, and as long as there's a chance Valya's alive, I can't imagine you'd refuse helping us bring her back."

"I don't believe for a second she's a victim," Chris said, a spell of anger heating his face. "Nothing was more important for Valya than her paranormal world. It's her obsession. If she went there, she wouldn't want to be brought back."

"Mr. Waller, I can't explain everything to you," Peter said. "I gave Valya my word I'd keep certain aspects of her existence a secret. For her, living a normal life, whether she preferred that or not, just wasn't possible. Valya dreaded that one day she might find herself on the other side of a portal. Trust me when I'm telling you she had no desire to be trapped there. Why do you think she invited Debra to Vishenky? She was trying to secure a backup. Unfortunately, your cousin turned out to be a wrong Gretishnikoff."

"That leaves us with no one, *no one* who could secure Valya's return," Jessie said, staring at Chris. "Except you. After she gave you her energy, you shared this epic, stupefying supernatural connection. I remember how you two looked at each other. Do you?"

"Ah, Jess, I don't," Chris said softly.

"Well, you'd better start remembering," Debra snapped. "A few days ago, I had a message sent from Valya's cell phone number. It was a child's voice, most certainly Gregory's son. Here's the translation: 'Valya's not here and not there. I'll have to kill her if they try to take her. Where's the man to whom she gave so much energy? I'll put a hex on him if he doesn't come back.'"

Chris ran his fingers through his hair, shaking his head. "Deb, I wish I...I'd help if I could...I know what you're saying, Valya could be trapped, but the reality is the whole trip is a fog and I'm out of it, out of the loop, out of the whole Vishenky thing...I don't remember Valya at all."

"Luke, now!" Peter barked.

The sounds of the violin and guitar poured from the living room. Joyful, sorrowful, a whirlwind of moonlight slicing the pall of night, the gypsy music twirled around Chris like a flurry of spirits, getting closer, closer until it slammed him like a warm surf wave. The life he had led during the past three months shattered, the pieces falling down like the slivers of a broken mirror. July's memories flooded every corner of his brain.

"How will I know what to do?" he asked, as though it actually mattered, as though there definitely was some course of action if Valya had crossed over.

Debra shook her head and spread her arms, tears welling in her eyes. The end or the beginning, Chris was on his own. Slipping out the front door, he glanced back just in time to see the girls exchange a high-five.

CHAPTER SEVENTY-NINE

Everything that needed to be booked and requested had been taken care of—the flight, the hotel, his visa, the sick days from the college. Chris had told Beth the truth: He had met someone on the summer trip and was going back to Russia to search for that woman.

After he'd dropped off his cat and his golden retriever at Laurie's, Chris sat at his desk, the window shades drawn, the house quiet, and the electronic clock blinking away the minutes left before his ride to the airport. He had been running on autopilot during the past few days, impassively executing a string of simple tasks and avoiding pondering how he felt about giving up the tranquil, easy flow of life he had been drifting in since his return from Russia.

He stared at a streak of light that snuck in through the gap between the window shade and the wall and landed on his desk. His perception didn't acquire new depths and colors the moment Valya's protective shield had crumbled. He wasn't feeling more alive. Life didn't turn into a fabulous adventure. Instead, a painful emptiness, a paralyzing weakness struck him, along with an understanding that only a pilgrimage to Vishenky would close the throbbing gash. But the woman who could cure him had never missed a chance to profess how implicitly she belonged to the supernatural realm. There was a good chance she had been ultimately claimed by the unearthly forces.

It was time to go, and fear encircled Chris like an invisible malevolent presence. The pathway to his future led into a void.

CHAPTER EIGHTY

His overnight flight was only two-thirds full, and Chris went through customs in less than ten minutes after he disembarked. Because of rain and the heavy Friday traffic, he didn't get to the hotel until after four o'clock in the afternoon. He dialed Valya's landline and got no answer. As tired as he was, he couldn't make himself wait until morning. He boarded a train headed to Vishenky an hour later.

Raindrops covered the windows. Twilight had already settled despite the relatively early hour. Outside, the cheerless landscape passed by under pewter-gray sky.

The only passenger to step off the train, Chris saw a great contrast with the day of their first arrival when they had stood on the same platform enjoying a picturesque view of the fields and birch groves basking in the sun. Now the path ran across empty fields and heavy clouds swallowed the golden cross of the church.

She's not here, he thought crossing the bridge over the swollen river.

The village looked abandoned. Even the chickens avoided the rain, hiding somewhere in their sheds. A white-and-tan mutt barked at Chris but quickly lost interest.

The front gate of Valya's house boasted a padlock on a thick chain holding it tight against the fence. The curtains in the house were closed. Flowerbeds looked overgrown with weeds.

The damp, cold air made its way through Chris's heavy jacket. He should have stayed at the hotel until morning. He didn't know how long he would have to wait for the next train to Moscow, and, at best, it would take him a couple of hours to get back to the hotel. He counted the eleventh board from the gate. Holding a small flashlight between his teeth, he stepped on the logs and stuck his arm inside the fence. Nothing had changed since summer. The key for the gate still hung on the nail. He would stay in Vishenky overnight.

He picked up the spare house key from a hidden spot in the wall of the tool shed. Juggling his gloves and flashlight, he brushed the handle of the front door. It opened before Chris put the key in the lock.

His heart beat faster. The dark and silent house was left open for anybody to come in. If the sky cleared, the moon would shine in its full glory. The setting would be unsettling even under conventional circumstances. This was Vishenky.

Chris stepped inside calling out an obligatory "Hello?" No one answered. A strong herbal scent hit him as the humid air amplified the fragrance of Valya's dried bouquets hanging under the ceiling.

The veranda felt cooler than the outdoors, and he left the door open to let in the fresh air. He walked through the house flipping on all the light switches. The sound of rain gave Chris a feeling of connection with the outside world, but it was quiet in the bedrooms. The door to the back veranda was blocked with a wooden bar from the inside. Valya or her parents hadn't left security to chance, so it was even more troubling to find the front entrance unlocked.

Walking back into the kitchen, Chris was startled when one of the refrigerators suddenly turned on. Its usual purring sounded like a roar in the silence of the vacant house. He peeked inside. The well-stocked shelves offered an assortment of cheeses and cold cuts, and the packs looked sealed. Loafs of black and white bread filled the bottom shelf.

In the second refrigerator, tiny jars, hand-labeled in Russian, were lined up on the shelves. Chris opened one, thinking they were Valya's homemade jams. Suspicious green paste inside gave off a pleasant smell, like a spicy sauce of some kind. He wondered how it would taste on a piece of bread if he used it as a spread. He turned the jar as he twisted the lid back on and there was another sticker, a skull and cross bones hurriedly drawn with a black marker. Chris returned the substance to the shelf, hoping one whiff of the stuff hadn't harmed him.

A pile of wood sat in front of the brick stove. He locked the front and kitchen doors, figured out how to open the chimney, and found matches. Chris huddled under someone's oversize down coat in front of the open furnace, turning the burning logs and watching the flames, his spirits improving as the room slowly warmed up. The house was empty but not abandoned. Somebody was bound to show up for the upcoming weekend.

Bread and cheese seemed like the safest choice for supper. Chris located tea and sugar in the cupboard. An electric kettle quickly boiled water.

The taste of the brew reminded him of Laurie's flavored teas. Getting drowsy, Chris found a pillowcase and sheets in the closet. His last coherent thought for the evening was, *Should have set the wristwatch alarm.*

CHAPTER EIGHTY-ONE

The weather had changed overnight. The house cooled down, and it was freezing on the front veranda despite the sunny morning.

A shattered bottom-corner segment in the glass part of the front door contributed to the cold. Somebody had broken in.

Rust-colored blood smeared the shards remaining in the frame and scattered on the floor. Chris recalled that the front door wasn't secured when he'd arrived. Possibly, someone had picked the lock but got spooked when Chris showed up at the gate. Worn out, he had made the mistake of leaving the key in the keyhole. The trespasser smashed the glass, stuck his hand through the ruined section, and unlocked the door from the inside.

A trail of brown-red droplets led toward the door to the kitchen. The intruder intended to get further inside the house. If Chris hadn't used the deadbolt on the door between the kitchen and the front veranda, he would have been in trouble. He hadn't heard a thing after drinking Valya's tea.

At first glance, nothing appeared to be missing. The antique silver tray bearing the salt and pepper shakers still sat in the middle of the dining table. Chris checked the cupboard. The tableware looked intact. He tried the drawer where Valya stored her hoard of mysterious objects. It was unlocked. One thing that he remembered from his first visit but he didn't see now was Valya's lace shawl.

He cleaned the mess on the floor and fixed the broken section of the door with a piece of cardboard. He found eggs in the refrigerator and had breakfast. Prolonging his meal, he kept his eyes on the gate.

With the last sip of coffee, his self-imposed *any-moment-now* optimism cracked like an eggshell.

The train station was a short bicycle ride away and the frequent Saturday-morning arrivals would make his idle waiting more bearable. In case someone from Valya's family showed up without her, Chris wrote a note explaining that he was in Vishenky and hoped Valya was coming there for the weekend. He stuck it under the salt-and-pepper tray.

The nippy morning was turning into a gorgeous October day. Chris had never seen the color of the sky so vivid, and the red berries on the ash tree at the corner of the house sparkled against the blue. He secured the chain around the gate before he rode off.

He waited while several trains arrived and departed, every time bringing a slightly larger crowd. The majority of the passengers took the road leading to the church. Black scarves, grim faces, and flower arrangements indicated an upcoming funeral.

Chris told himself to be patient. Even if Valya didn't show up, maybe Gregory would, and Chris would find her whereabouts with the assistance of a dictionary.

Three hours passed before he gave up. The sky had turned gray. The autumn gloom began to settle upon the landscape, permeating Chris's mood. He stalled for time and took the road running behind the village, across vast fields—some harvested, some green with freshly planted grains. The chain was still in place when he got home....

But the front door creaked in the wind, wide open.

Chris tossed the bicycle aside and stormed in. His note lay torn in two on the table, pinned down with the salt and pepper shakers. He rushed through the house. Someone had removed the bar that blocked off the back veranda. The bed by the window that faced the street was made. An opened emergency kit and a leather-bound diary with a broken spine lay on the nightstand, and beside them...Chris closed his eyes, looked again, allowing himself a moment of triumphal cheer. Next to the kit and the diary sat Valya's favorite blue-and-gold porcelain cup, half full, coffee steaming.

His heartbeat echoing in his ears, his doubt and fear swept away by a surge of happy impatience, Chris burst through the door.

He froze on the back stoop.

CHAPTER EIGHTY-TWO

Valya was digging.

The yard sloped gently down toward the fence. She toiled only a few yards away from Chris, but not a single glance, word, smile, or nod indicated she was aware of his presence. She wore a flowing skirt and a tank top, both white, both too light, too flimsy for the weather. The lace shawl was wrapped around her throat, one end hanging loose and catching on the shovel's handle every time Valya bent to scoop a load of soil. Strands of her hair kept falling across her face. She mechanically brushed them back with her bandaged right hand and kept on digging. Like ugly black craters, foot-wide holes covered the lawn and flowerbeds as far as Chris could see, and clods of freshly dug dirt lay everywhere, even on the stoop.

"Valya," he called.

She dropped the shovel, her gaze fixed on the hole. Clutching the hem of her skirt, she crouched and scooped up a muddy ivory-colored globe.

She wiped it gingerly with her palms, inspecting the object as though it were a gold nugget or a truffle. She slid her hand along the folds of her skirt, fumbling for a hidden pocket and leaving a muddy trace on the white fabric in the process, and came up with an empty glass jar. She unscrewed the lid, pressed the globe against the opening, and squeezed it. The thing was a puff mushroom, Chris guessed, watching brown dust fill the container.

Behind his back, a gust of wind slammed the door shut like an angry poltergeist. Valya frowned. She stood and listened, staring past him, lips pressed together. Waves of fine sprinkles ran over the garden. Then the sun broke through low clouds, sparkling in the raindrops caught in Valya's hair. *She must be so cold*, Chris thought. He wanted to hug her, bring her inside, wrap a blanket over her wet shoulders, and put a cup of hot coffee into her hands.

"Valya," he called again.

She tossed the used-up mushroom back into the hole and tightened the lid. Then she headed in the direction of the veranda, walking straight at Chris yet not seeing him.

He stepped aside. Passing by, she slapped her neck as if stung by a bee.

She dropped the container and pulled at the shawl, trying to rip it off as though the lace was on fire. Chris caught the loose end and began to unwrap it over her head. Under the last layer, the familiar rooster's beak hung attached to her neck, its tiny teeth embedded in Valya's skin.

Chris yanked the beak out. He tossed the shawl on the ground and stomped on it, enjoying the crunch under his foot.

He removed Valya's hand from the bite. It didn't look bad, just a bunch of red dots lined up in a rhombus-shaped pattern. She promptly freed her wrist from his grip, her nostrils flaring. Before she tried to flee, he grabbed her shoulders and made her face him.

Her skin felt cold. She had lost weight. An unhealthy blush emphasized the pallor of her gaunt face.

"What happened?" he asked. "What have you done? Where are you?"

And suddenly there was the light of recognition in Valya's eyes. "Oh my God. Chris. I'm so close. So close. But they're coming. Don't let them take me."

CHAPTER EIGHTY-THREE

"They...who?" Chris asked, his heart pounding.

A silver SUV pulled to the fence. The driver killed the engine. Three people stepped out of the vehicle. Valya muttered in Russian, her voice loaded with seething incredulity, as if somebody just spilled coffee on her laptop.

Chris exhaled. An appearance of the Violet Lights would be a problem, but he could handle a few humans.

Valya strode up the path into the garden. The driver and the woman who had traveled shotgun noticed Chris and exchanged uneasy glances. The woman waited while the man went to the SUV's rising hatch, probably to get the luggage. The third person, Valya's friend Tamara Karpova, rushed to the gate, the heels of her over-the-knee boots sinking in the wet ground. Chris hurried to unlock the chain.

"Mother and uncle," Tamara informed him, skipping the greetings. "Want to take Valya to Moscow." She slammed the gate with too much force and pulled Chris toward the front veranda.

She wiped her feet on the rubber mat and then made a beeline for the cupboard. She searched the shelves, muttering and pushing things around and spilling the sugar in the process. Chris waited in the doorway, keeping an eye on Valya's uncle who fiddled with the uncooperative gate latch. Tamara found a shot glass and a flask-shaped bottle. She carried her booty to the dining table, flopped down into a chair, unscrewed the cap, poured, and tasted the amber-colored liquid.

"Cognac," she explained, unbuttoning her navy-blue trench coat. "Long ride. You must understand, in Moscow Valya will not live."

"Do you know what happened?" Chris asked.

"Opened portal in the river."

"Were you with her?"

"No. Andrey told me. Prascovia broke the mirror. Valya's mind trapped." Tamara tapped her forehead. "Half here, half there."

"She recognized me," Chris said.

"See? Not crazy. You stay here."

"But what can I do to help her?"

"She will open portal again. She cooked more green goo. From mushrooms. I pretended I will eat it, but she hit it from my hands. Not crazy."

"Green paste? In baby-food jars?" Chris spread his thumb and index finger to show her the size. "What does it do?"

Tamara energetically bobbed her head. "Opens portal. Knows what to do. Can't talk, but not crazy."

Valya's mother and uncle finally made it through the gate. The woman arrived to the village empty-handed, but her brother carried a leather briefcase. An innocuous object under ordinary circumstances, here it looked menacingly official, a cruel reminder that Chris lacked even a shadow of authority over Valya's fate.

"She needs time," Tamara said. "In village. You help us."

"They really don't know anything about Vishenky?" Chris asked, nodding slightly in the direction of the approaching pair.

Tamara focused on the shot glass in her fingers.

"We speak English," the man said, a generous smile cheery on his big mouth. "You must be one of her summer visitors." He offered Chris a handshake. "Anatoly, Valenteena's uncle. And this is Evgeniya, her mother."

Chris introduced himself. Evgeniya pointedly looked away. *Good cop, bad cop?* He stepped aside to let the pair in.

Youthful, fit, good-looking, the siblings wore jeans and leather bomber jackets. A set of twins, Chris realized. A team, an unshakable alliance. Dark hair barely touched by gray, bright-blue eyes, every facial feature angular and prominent, neither shared much of a family resemblance with Valya. There was one exception. All three had mastered the same intense, commanding stare.

Anatoly laid the briefcase on the dining table and pulled a chair for Evgeniya. She chose to stand by the cupboard, arms folded and legs crossed, swiping Tamara and Chris with frosty glances. He could visualize the ride to the village that sapped Tamara's outgoing disposition. The air conditioner would be on to keep the windows from fogging up, not a word spoken, an eternity-long symphony concert playing on the radio, the ambience about as warm as a cloud inversion, and the poor girl squirming in the back seat.

The uncle leaned forward and pulled the halves of Chris's note from under the salt and pepper shakers, put the pieces together, scanned it, smirked, crumpled the paper, and tossed it in the trashcan by the cupboard. He opened the briefcase. "Well, where's our patient?"

Chris forced himself to relax his grip on the door frame. "Tamara told me that Valya was unwell, but she didn't strike me as sick. Your niece saw you coming, and she told me she'd prefer to stay here."

"Oh, really? I've heard that last summer you fell for Valenteena's stories," Anatoly said. "Though I will be the first to admit, the girl knows how to be engaging and convincing. Where is she?"

"If Valya was under the weather, she's getting better now and taking her to Moscow will slow her recovery."

Anatoly's good-natured smile disappeared. "I don't know, and I'm not going to ask what you're doing here, Mr. Waller, but you can make yourself useful if you find Valenteena, bring her over, and assist me with sedating her. She's a strong girl. Better you than Evgeniya. We don't want to put a mother through it, do we?"

Chris stepped inside but remained in the strategic spot by the front door. He looked at Valya's mother. "Twenty-four hours. Please, let me help your daughter."

Evgeniya raised her chin.

"Just one day," Chris said. "Then I'll bring Valya to Moscow myself."

Anatoly's palm smacked the table, and the salt and pepper shakers jumped on the oilcloth. "Absolutely not. If you think I'd allow—"

Tamara pointed at the front windows. "She's coming."

Valya had just turned around the corner of the house.

"Oh, good." From the briefcase, Anatoly pulled out a flat black box. Its contents rattled when he set it on the table. "Let's get it over with."

He popped the lid and took a clear bag with blue markings into his hands. It had a disposable syringe inside. He ripped the wrapping apart.

"I won't let you take her," Chris said, panic rising to his throat in a nauseating swell.

"Really?" Anatoly poked the needle through a vial. "You will do what then, fight me?" he asked drawing sedative into the syringe. "What if you lose?"

There was casual confidence in the older man's voice.

Chris turned the key, pulled it from the lock, and stuck it into his jeans' pocket. If Valya wanted to come inside, she'd have to go around the house.

He leaned against the door. "Tamara, where's Gregory?"

"Ah. Of course." Anatoly shook his head, his mouth twisted in disdain. "Another knight in shining armor. That piece of shit was the one who convinced my sister and my brother-in-law to leave the girl here in the first place. I understand perfectly that no parent wants this for his or her daughter. But if Valenteena is not hospitalized, she'll never recover."

"Gregory should be in Vishenky on weekend," Tamara said.

"Find him," Chris ordered. "Go through the back veranda."

"A commendable move, Mr. Waller. To swallow your pride. To ask for another man's help." Anatoly handed the filled syringe to his sister, rose to his feet, sizing Chris up, removed his jacket, and began to roll up his shirt sleeves. "Won't do you any good, I'm afraid. I brought plenty of sedatives. I guess we should start with you."

"Tamara, go," Chris barked at the girl who froze in her seat like a frightened rabbit.

"Don't let her leave," Anatoly told his sister.

Evgeniya could have stepped in front of the door to the kitchen but she didn't move an inch, just said, "Stay," and her daughter's friend stayed, eyes wide open and mouth quivering.

Under the ash tree on the corner of the house, Valya stood like a faithful sentry, stoical in the drizzle and the wind, her right arm behind her back, her feet apart, and her shoulders straight. Her hair was a wet mess, and her skirt, soaked and muddy, hung plastered to her legs, but Chris was thankful that she was alert enough to avoid her pursuers, to conceal her bandaged hand.

"Look at her," Anatoly said. "It's ten degrees outside, and Valenteena's barely dressed. What is it in Fahrenheit?"

"Fifty," Evgeniya said.

"Fifty." Anatoly spread his arms and shook his head, the mocking regret profuse in his posture. "Still think we should leave her here on her own? You obviously care very little about her, Mr. Waller."

"How about you stop being a jerk?" Chris said. "Valya recognized me. She talked to me. Let me try again."

"You want me to leave her in the care of a stranger?" Anatoly asked. "In her condition? Maybe your ethics—"

"Enough," Evgeniya interrupted. "It worked."

"I don't see her coming in," Anatoly said.

"She's not running away either," his sister parried.

"What do you mean, 'it worked'?" Chris asked.

"Let's see what she does," Evgeniya said.

Valya slowly brought her right hand forward.

The bandage was gone. The handle of a rusty dagger rested in her open palm. The only shiny part, its tip reached the crease of her elbow, pointing at her bicep. Chris found this precarious arrangement troubling enough, but there was another object in Valya's possession, a thick metal coil the exact length of the dagger, wrapped around her forearm. The adornment looked like a gizmo in a scientific experiment. The tips were capped with inch-wide shiny balls, both in contact with the dagger. The mystery of its purpose alarmed Chris more that the sedative-filled syringe in Evgeniya's hands.

"What 'worked'?" he repeated.

"I'm sorry we used you as bait, Mr. Waller," Evgeniya said, not bothering to add a single decibel of sorry to her tone. "We tried to take my daughter home before. She senses our arrival and disappears. Gregory called, said you were here. He, too, worries about her. I predicted that if Anatoly pushed you hard enough, Valya would read your distress and rush to your rescue. Tamara's right, you matter a great deal to my daughter. Too bad that for her it's a clear-cut reason to reject you."

The woman wasn't lying and Chris felt her truth stabbing him. He had offered Valya a way out. She had chosen Vishenky.

"Should I try to approach her?" Anatoly asked his sister.

"I'll do it," Evgeniya said. "Mr. Waller, please understand, this is in Valya's best interest."

Chris nodded, embarrassed for the tears welling up in his eyes.

Valya closed her fingers over the dagger's handle and simultaneously brought her elbow to her side. The tip of the blade jabbed her flesh. Blood began to trickle.

"What the hell?" Anatoly whispered.

Chris chuckled. He knew the expression glowing on Valya's face. He knew this Valya: ruthless, unstoppable, victorious. No one was going to take this woman from Vishenky.

Luminous ping-pong-ball-sized spheres swarmed over her elbow. *Like wasps around a hummingbird feeder*, Chris thought. He could hear their buzzing.

"Entities. That's not good." Paler than an eggshell, Anatoly unbuttoned his collar, pulled out a cross, and leaned forward, clutching it in one hand, supporting himself against the table with the other.

The spheres hovered, fought, chased each other off, determined to land on Valya's blood-covered elbow. One finally settled on the coil's ball-shaped end.

Miniature lightning bolts shot in every direction. Valya raised her free hand to shield her eyes. Its buddies gone, the sphere fought to break free from the trap, shrieking, screeching, but whatever powers the coil, the dagger, and Valya's energy had generated, the entity was stuck.

"A short-circuit resulting in magnetic forces," Evgeniya muttered.

Anatoly shook a finger at his sister. "That's why Prascovia told you to smash the mirror."

"Why?" Chris asked.

"So my daughter wouldn't gain more power," Evgeniya said. "Do you see what she can now summon at will?"

Valya let the fireworks go on a few more seconds, then straightened her arm, hooked the tip of her left index finger under her thumb, took aim, and sent the sphere flying into the window.

Glass cracked as if hit by a bullet. Anatoly and Tamara jumped back. A web of fractures ran from the epicenter until it covered the whole panel.

"You show them, girl," Chris whispered.

Valya smiled, twirled the dagger in the air, caught it by the handle, tucked it in the waist of her skirt, and sauntered off.

Evgeniya tossed the syringe on the floor and stepped on it. She put her hand on Anatoly's shoulder. "We should go. This was just a threat, but she hates you and if we don't leave, she might actually harm you."

"The portals," Chris said, "Vishenky's energy. You knew all along."

"Of course I knew." Evgeniya pressed her white-knuckle fist under her chest. "Imagine what it's like, to raise a brilliant child who denies you any chance to be her parent."

"You should have tried harder."

She laughed, but she sounded tired, defeated. "Mr. Waller, my daughter's not a sweet soul lost in a tangle of unnatural events as you might foolishly believe, but good luck to you."

"Twenty-four hours," Anatoly snarled.

Minutes later, alone in the big, frigid house, Chris had no idea what he was going to do.

CHAPTER EIGHTY-FOUR

The padlock on the back gate was wrapped in plastic and appeared untouched. Chris searched the whole property, calling Valya's name, cursing the drenched tangles of weeds and dripping tree branches. He succeeded only in getting chilled, discouraged, and hungry. While Valya could keep going on puff mushrooms and rain, he needed warmth and food. Chris lit the fire for starters.

He was contemplating his dinner options when she entered the kitchen, quiet as a ghost, quick like a feline, wearing jeans, sneakers, and a fuzzy maroon sweater with a row of sparkling oversize buttons running down her shoulder. She looked around, moved to the stepladder but didn't climb, turned and leaned against it, one foot on the bottom rung. Then she stood still.

Her soundless arrival caught Chris off guard. Afraid to let her out of his sight, he stepped into his room, grabbed a towel, and rushed back to the kitchen. He approached Valya slowly, watching for any reaction. There was none.

He put the towel onto her head and ruffled her wet hair. "Glad I'm not your boyfriend. I'd go nuts."

Her hands found his. "You're giving me split ends."

He had no regrets about the past, no uncertainties about the future. The universe was no longer crushing around him. Chris felt nothing but the warmth of her palms for a long, delicious moment. Then Valya's eyes met his and the smile he had craved to see again, mischievous, genial, teasing, and sincere, curved her lips, and he surrendered to the all-consuming sense of closeness.

"You told me once that I wasn't, but I want to be a woman in your life," Valya said.

Chris kissed her, and the universe lost its importance altogether.

* * *

Valya pushed her ham and cheese sandwich around the plate, picked it up, and smelled the bread. She and Chris sat in the chairs in front of the burning brick stove, the logs crackling, steady rain droning on the roof, and dusk approaching fast.

"If the sky doesn't clear up, I'll lose the last night when the moon can be counted as full," Valya said.

"Are we opening another portal?" Chris asked.

"I am. What if I can't do that until a month from now? For how long are you going to stay?"

"I'm here until this is over. I'm not leaving you again."

Valya dropped her untouched sandwich on the plate. "You have to be realistic. For how long?"

"Let's see. My library books are due on Monday...."

"Please stop it. You have a job. You have a life. The last thing I want is to ruin it."

"Sure," Chris said. "You already tried to fix everything with the Tears of the Crying Stone. I could have been married to someone else by now. Just think how many problems that would have created."

"You don't understand certain things about me."

"Oh, I can bet on that. Always secrets, always—"

"I'm not one hundred percent human."

His eyes on the fire, he intertwined his fingers and straightened them, popping his joints. "I don't care if you're a space alien. I'm a million times happier here with you than I was back home. I'll do anything to get you out, because no matter what you believe, Vishenky is not your destiny. It can exist without you. I can't."

He looked at Valya. She watched him, her face unreadable.

Chris picked another log from the pile and tossed it into the furnace. It landed with a rustle. The sparks exploded and the flames began to lick the bark. "So tell me, why did you imagine that opening a portal would be such a swell idea?" he asked.

"Oh, God." Valya set her plate and her glass on the floor. "I'm a descendant of Antonina, Prascovia's sister. For centuries, the women in my lineage have served as incubators for the paranormal entities, which are the energy that allows Prascovia to stay alive. She harvests this energy from the fourth generations. After adding a Violet Light to the mix." Valya crossed her hands at the base of her throat. "I seek to purge the entity that resurrected me at birth. Otherwise, Prascovia will never leave me alone. That's why I opened a portal. Any questions so far?"

"Yes," Chris said. She wasn't defensive or falsely matter-of-fact while she recited her incredible tale, and he wanted to match her courage, her sincerity when he replied, but the pounding in his temples wouldn't wane and he couldn't bring his scattered thoughts into focus.

"We're on top of Vishenky's energy field," Valya said. "It's affecting you. Your emotions keep spiking and crushing. Way too much strain for a normal human being. Chris, darling, trains are still running tonight. I think it will be better if you go."

Her tone was silken and poignantly earnest...and so compelling. But there was something about her look. The way she leaned forward. The way her narrowed eyes were fixed on him, her face tilted to the right just slightly, her nostrils flared. The way her enlarged pupils reflected the fire.

"No," Chris said.

"It was so nice of you to drop everything and rush to my rescue. But you're not responsible for what happens next."

"Stop it."

"Don't feel obligated to be my savior. You've done so much. Now I can finish this on my own."

Any show of exasperation wouldn't earn him Valya's sympathy, but at least the ensuing adrenaline rush quenched his smoldering headache. He always let her win, but not this time. Chris slid to the edge of the chair and turned to face her, his instincts bellowing how the essence of the words he chose would determine Valya's future.

"That's exactly what frightens me," he said. "You're game to let me go. Just like last summer. I've been competing with supernatural forces for your attention, and they're always winning. You're addicted to this place. I feel helpless, because the life I'm offering may not be enough to pull you out. So tell me…." He took a deep breath to give his words a proper emphasis. "If you leave out your noble intent to preserve the way I lived my life before I met you, what do you really want me to do?"

"You fear I'm an addict," Valya said, "but you're not scared that emotionally I'm the Minotaur?"

"Of course not. Compared to my ex…? Gosh, no."

"You must be a magnet for challenging personalities."

"You finally figured me out." Chris smiled. He won. He saw it in Valya's eyes.

Now it was her turn.

"Explain to me the deal with the entities," Chris said. "Last summer I got infected, you opened a portal in the mirror, I broke it, and you declared that everything worked out."

"Yours was of a different kind." Valya picked up her glass from the floor, an inch of water sloshing on the bottom, and held it so Chris could see it. "A stillborn, revived by the first entity. What you need to understand is that entities are not self-contained units. They are energies."

She added a splash of black coffee from Chris's mug. "I wouldn't be able to conceive a child without the second entity from the baby's father. A Violet Light, like the one that was in you."

Valya dumped the brown mixture into her glass. "At conception, the Violet Light would blend with my entity and Prascovia would harvest both to prolong her life. Left with some residual paranormal energy, I was expected to walk through a portal after childbirth. It's like a smell. Part-human, part-paranormal. The Violet Lights would recognize humans as part of their tribe and wouldn't attack the Earth."

"You kissed me," Chris said, his memories swirling around the moment.

"Prascovia had high hopes we would do more than that, but she underestimated the level of our emotional intimacy. We kissed, and that was enough to persuade the entity to leave your body and enter mine. Then I used the antipathy potion and was able to get rid of it."

"What will happen if you open another portal tonight?"

"I'll try to disengage myself from the entity that brought me to life," she said.

"My head is spinning."

"I can imagine."

"If the entity keeps you alive," Chris said, "how will you survive without it?"

"*I* keep *it* alive. Technically, 'alive' is a wrong word. It's energy. Biologically, losing it shouldn't be a problem. Psychologically, reversing to ordinary human existence might get challenging." Valya hit the wooden chair armrest with her knuckles. "But it means freedom."

"Why can't you just leave this place for good?"

"Because the entity will always make me crave Vishenky's energy." She looked up. "Listen."

The fire crackled steadily in the stove, but no other sounds enlivened the house.

"I think the rain has stopped." Valya ran into his bedroom and pulled open the curtains. "The sky's clear. I'm going. You don't have to."

Chris watched her rushing around, gathering the things she needed. An oval bathroom mirror appeared from somewhere and ended up leaning against his chair. She checked a large black flashlight and placed it in his lap, then added a flyswatter. She found a canvas tote bag and began loading it with the baby-food jars from one of the refrigerators.

"I deciphered the diary of my predecessor, Leontina," Valya explained, clearing out the whole shelf. "In July, the river 'blooms'; water is full of algae and turns green. Something in that light spectrum upsets the balance between the two worlds and works as a catalyst for one specific portal." She held up a jar. "So I cooked the paste. In water, it produces microorganisms similar to algae."

"How did you find her diary?"

"Peter's idea. He suggested my parents wouldn't dare destroy an important family artifact. They'd take it away from me but keep it safe, kind of like a half-measure. I remembered my dad replacing the floorboards in the kitchen. They buried Leontina's diary in the crawlspace."

"You tried to open a portal on your own," Chris said. "What was your plan?"

Valya closed the refrigerator, put down the canvas bag, the jars clanking inside, and walked over to her chair. She lifted her empty glass from the floor and turned it upside down. One brown drop formed on the rim, but it didn't fall.

"The residual energy," Valya said. "What's left in Leontina— partially paranormal, but mostly human." She tapped her finger on the glass. The drop quivered but stayed on the rim. "Disengaging the paranormal component would be almost impossible. When you get too close to the portal, the pull from the other side is tremendous. Leontina stepped on the threshold, and the energy siphoned from her body was hers. She couldn't break away. I, on the other hand, planned to rid myself of the big plump entity before the supernatural dimension sucked me in." She brought her teacup to her glass and was about to tilt it to illustrate her point, but Chris waved that he understood the idea.

Valya knelt by his chair and touched his forearm. "You're scared."

"It's no longer something that we'll have to do some time in the future. It's now. You will open Pandora's Box in a few minutes. Something will go wrong. What if I can't save you?"

"Just Pandora's box? Not the Gates of Hell? Maybe you're not scared enough!" Valya grabbed the armrest, her face lit up with contagious excitement. "What went wrong last month had nothing to do with the physics of my plan. Prascovia disrupted the process. If I don't have a baby, she'll eventually lose her vitality and die. That's why the witch broke the mirror."

"It was your mother, per Prascovia's orders."

"Mother." Valya shook her head. "If you place a compass next to a magnet, the hand will dart in all directions. That's what her interference did to me. My brain went haywire, getting worse every time she came by, until you showed up and I could focus on you."

"Your mother's hurting. She's not a part of your life and has no idea how to reach you."

"You found a way."

"Because you finally let me," Chris said.

"Because you're the only person I trust." Valya grinned,

enthusiastic, certain. "One more night. My last portal. Tomorrow, we'll have only one thing to worry about: how quickly the embassy can issue my visa."

An addict. Chris cupped her face in his hands, flooded with an aching and foolish impulse to let down his guard and believe her.

CHAPTER EIGHTY-FIVE

The tattered edge of the departing storm stretched over the village. One-half of the sky was hidden behind the low wind-whipped clouds. The other half was cosmic-bright, blue-black, and starry. The crystalline moon shone high above the forested hillside across the river. The air smelled of autumn, an evocative and doleful mélange of wood smoke and fallen leaves and saturated earth.

Caught in a spasm of shivers, Chris regretted he had followed Valya's example and come to the river without his jacket. It was too late to retrieve it now; she had already opened the jars and tossed them into the flow, ever eager to start another supernatural event, too impatient for one more kiss or even a good-luck hug.

Standing on the muddy bottom step and holding onto the railing, Valya lowered the mirror onto the upper wooden platform used in the summer for laundry and dishwashing, but now submerged under three inches of rushing water. "I was worried the river would be too murky, but I can see the reflections," she said.

Across the river, the leafless willows dallied in the wind like some shady characters watching a crime scene from behind the police tape, whispering to each other and probably involved themselves. The single row of the village dwellings seemed to morph into a parade of somber monstrous heads staring at Chris with their empty sockets. Just two candles in Prascovia's windows glimmered like unholy pupils.

Valya took off her sneakers and socks.

"What are you doing?" Chris asked forcing his jaw to work.

"I have to be right on the threshold. That's what Leontina's notes said. Don't let anyone come close until you see me back on the solid ground." Valya stepped onto the mirror. She let go of the railing and straightened up, her arms flailing as she caught her balance.

"Dammit." Chris gripped the flyswatter's handle with both hands. "You'll freeze. You should have at least rolled up your jeans."

She turned, flashed a smile, and dove into the unquiet river.

"Valya!"

The current pushed her under the platforms, and Chris dashed along the bank expecting her to surface.

Then he saw the portal. A giant bubble was slowly emerging in the middle of the river.

Chris had forgotten how mesmerizing it was to witness a manifestation, a chilling dream from which you couldn't awake. The roiling vapors of phosphorescent mist limited his vision to glimpses of ash-colored mud eddying along the transparent membrane. The surface of the sludge flickered with rainbow splotches, an aurora-like effect, perhaps caused by glowing plankton. Whimsically shaped bubbles jumped out and fell down without bursting—gas or life forms or doomed spirits. An orb resembling a plasma ball darted in the fog. Its violet filaments probed the membrane, some breaking through but unable to penetrate the Earthly atmosphere more than a foot. And the sounds, their jungle hungriness, bone-chilling prehistoric ferocity— even muffled by the membrane, the distant roars made Chris covet a shelter. Bosch's paintings came to mind as he listened.

The contents of the semi-sphere rotated clockwise. If Valya had chosen the trajectory of her dive just right, and she would have considering her previous underwater antics, she'd have entered the portal on the downstream side; the inner current would carry her along the perimeter wall. Chris's leg muscles turned into quivering gelatin, and he waddled to the wooden steps to wait for the alien ecosystem to spin full circle, terrified of spotting Valya's lifeless body but unable to avert his eyes from the surreal caldron.

She was alive, comfortable even, carried by the languid current. Her mud-covered head and shoulders bobbed slowly above the surface.

Chris had no doubts the being was Valya. Her curls lay plastered to her scalp, and he could discern the oversize buttons on her sweater, but when she thrust her hand into the air, seemingly fascinated by the colorful flickers on her abnormally elongated fingers, her head twitched with animal abruptness.

She spun with the ease of a playful sea otter, bringing herself to the transparent wall. Her human face was gone, the nostrils reduced to the small holes in the mask of mud, her irises two deep-violet lights.

Suddenly she pulled back. An unearthly screech escaped her lipless mouth. The sound of rage? Despair? Before Chris could react, she swung her arm and tossed forward a handful of mud.

The lump broke into pieces when it went through the membrane, a pack of entities charging into the Earth's frigid air, each as bright as the light from a welding arc. They died out like fireworks before they reached him, but Chris instinctively ducked to his left.

A spear-like object pierced the space he occupied a moment ago. A crowbar, a straight and solid piece of metal used by Russians to break ice, penetrated the membrane, flew over Valya's head, and disappeared into the phosphorescent fog. Chris spun to see who had hurled the weapon.

A slim figure walking toward him looked unthreatening, a frail old woman in dark garb, her scarf-covered head lowered as if in grief. Her slender hands, clasped under her chest, appeared too delicate to lift and toss a crowbar with such strength.

"Prascovia?" Chris whispered.

She stopped, looked up, her mouth the lipless slit of an old woman. The brilliant October moon illuminated her sunken eyes. She then leapt at him, her arms stretched forward, her fingers a beast's appendages, each ending with a cluster of cat-like claws. The impact knocked Chris into the water.

The blue-black sky flashed over him. The cold was like a vise tightening around his whole body. The claws, a hundred merciless needles, pierced his back and stomach and pulled him down. The water closed in above his head. He kicked and thrashed, but it was too much, the stinging urge to take a breath, the paralyzing chill, the pangs in his ripped skin, all adding up to the sickening recognition of the nearing, inescapable end.

CHAPTER EIGHTY-SIX

When Prascovia raised the crowbar I tried to scream, but I had no voice.

I could taste the moonlight and touch the darkness. I could watch the sounds and listen to the colors, but I had no voice. I had become snakes' tongues, cats' whiskers, an array of sensory receptors unknown to the human mind. I just had no voice.

Then the humanoid being, who Chris thought was I, alerted him about the danger. The damning truth of what had happened hit me like a rockslide.

The entity had separated from me, but it held on to my emotions. It had managed to pull my soul, my essence, out of my body. Now, a lightning ball with violet tentacles, I was trapped inside the membrane without any means to let Chris know that I was the real Valya.

The witch dragged him under the surface. The other Valya, the one who currently possessed my morphed body, broke through the membrane and rushed to save him. I was left to throw myself against the impenetrable boundary.

Andrey appeared on the bank. He gazed straight at me while the waves of his screams ricocheted off the membrane. I wanted him to help me, help Chris, but the boy ran back toward his house. My anguish was so strong I thought I might explode from the terrible emotional buildup pulsing inside me. Then I understood Andrey's words: "Flee while you can. Don't let Grandma take you."

Of course. That's what happened to every Gretishnikoff female who disappeared. Once she crossed a portal, the paranormal energy left in her after childbirth yanked her soul out of her body. Bonus fuel for Prascovia: a human life force ready to be fetched and consumed. The witch had failed to make me produce an heir, so she decided she'd at least harvest my energy. Once she killed Chris, she'd push the soulless Valya back into the supernatural dimension. Without him, my corporeal counterpart would be trapped behind the membrane.

Soulless. I wondered what she felt and knew—the woman-creature in my physical body. Was she aware that she had lost her emotional essence? Or had my psyche simply split? That animalistic being wasn't completely without feelings. She went after Prascovia when the witch grabbed Chris.

Except, now none of my thousand new senses could locate him. What if this Valya wasn't as human as I had imagined? What if she deemed Chris a prey and rushed to catch him, competing with Prascovia?

Stuck helplessly under the transparent but unbreakable dome, I didn't know what to do. I hoped Valya would return and claim me. Collect her soul.

Andrey came back. His father was several paces behind him carrying an axe. An avid tree climber, the boy found an observation spot in the willow on the bank's edge. Gregory approached the wooden steps. He looked in my direction and shook his head resignedly then crouched and eyeballed the mirror.

My electric pulses pounded the membrane. *No, no, no*, I thought, thrashing in the agony of fear. *Don't close the portal. Don't leave me here.*

Then I spotted someone else walking across the meadow toward the river. My horror was so great that for a moment my violet plasma filaments went out.

CHAPTER EIGHTY-SEVEN

Moving his arms and legs required a Herculean effort, but Chris made it to the shore. Stiff and lightheaded, he crawled out of the river and dropped down onto the slippery weeds, the four-foot-high bank as unscalable as a castle wall. Behind him, the water whirled as if two mighty reptiles circled each other just under the surface. A child's shrill voice sounded in the close distance. About thirty feet upstream the semi-sphere glowed like a miniature sports dome, now almost opaque with the madly swirling mist. Violet filaments whipped the membrane's internal surface the way an angry sea creature would batter a specimen jar.

Chris slid his hand under his stomach to break a clump of soil that dug into his flesh, but he failed to grab it. Nearly fainting from the exertion, he dropped his forehead back on the dead grass. Violent shakes racked his body. He managed to push his torso up and free his hand. He stared at his bent, rigid fingers, coated in blood. His mind, though filled with terror, remained coherent, but numbness engulfed his chest as though a poison was taking over his body, immobilizing him and choking off his breathing.

Water licked his feet. Through pain and angst and a fatalistic desire to give up, Chris struggled to bring his elbows and shoulders over the bank's edge.

Staring at the dome intently, a man sat on his heels, one hand on the wooden railing, another on the knob of an axe handle.

His weapon would be worthless against the creatures. Valya's faithful pal and neighbor, Gregory, must have brought it along to close the portal. *Please wait*, Chris begged silently, too weak to call for help. *Don't break the mirror. We must know she's safe.*

Another person in camo pants and a jacket was moving swiftly across the meadow. The bushy beard. The hawkish nose. Chris had seen the elderly man on the river once before and thought he was a local hunter.

The bearded stranger slid a shotgun from his shoulder as he came up to Gregory.

"Watch out," Chris whispered, his mouth uncooperative.

The strike didn't look that powerful, but Gregory fell when the butt of the shotgun connected with the back of his head. The hunter took aim at the mirror.

CHAPTER EIGHTY-EIGHT

Out of nowhere, a skinny figure running at full speed rammed the man's side just as he pulled the trigger. The blast rang out, but the hunter missed the intended target.

Peppered with pellets, the membrane popped like a soap bubble. Its contents—the mud, the phosphorescent fog—collapsed into a giant opening in the middle of the river. Chris blinked to clear his vision. Above the promptly formed vortex, a single orb flew in erratic circles as if afraid to go in, violet streaks dying off in its wake.

Two beings leapt out of the water and dropped onto the dead weeds not far from Chris. The first one coughed, slapping the ground, her pallid face human, but the menacing violet dots shining in her eyes. The mane of her curly hair sparkled in the moonlight when Valya shook herself like a wet dog. She looked up at the approaching bearded stranger.

"Still loaded," Chris groaned, mindful of the double-barreled shotgun in the man's hands.

Valya nodded. The second being turned and hissed at her, baring yellow fangs.

"Prascovia?" the hunter asked uncertainly.

"*Ne lez ne v svoe delo, Ivan!*" the witch rasped.

"Go away, this is not your business," Valya translated in a whisper.

"You're back," Chris said. "Tell him to shoot the mirror. Close the portal."

His request seemed to stump her. Even now, with her appearance perfectly human, the violet lights no longer glowing in her pupils, Valya couldn't relinquish her ties with the other world. He should have never allowed himself to discount what he had witnessed all along: Valya's insatiable, outlandish longing for an everlasting bond with the supernatural. But after everything that had happened, everything she'd experienced and learned, everything she'd promised, what right did she have to cling to that malefic dimension?

Then the surge of anger was over and Chris was sprawled on the rough ground, defeated, crushed, and in too much agony to move. Another wave of pain swept through his body, bringing him to the brink of consciousness.

Valya made a step toward him, but the hunter raised the shotgun and barked a warning. She interrupted him in anger. Ivan responded, defensive notes clear in his tone, his husky voice breaking. Her face distorted, Valya spoke again, just a few words. Her outburst infuriated the armed man. He stomped forward, waving the shotgun between Valya and the portal, snarling orders, and Chris realized that he was threatening to kill her if she didn't start moving toward the vortex.

A warning shot over her head ripped through willow branches. Valya crouched beside Chris, her palms over her ears.

The attacker broke the shotgun to reload. Like an uncoiling spring, Gregory's son lunged at the hunter and grabbed the barrel. Ivan swung his weapon. A blow to the stomach brought the boy to the ground.

Prascovia's screech made Chris shudder. Defying gravity, she leaped on Ivan's back. Her clawed right hand slashed across his face.

Mournful squeals reverberated over the meadow. Chris recognized the sound: Andrey whistled through a blade of grass. Valya cursed in English, then in Russian, picked up a pebble, and tossed it in the boy's direction. The yowls stopped.

"Andrey just summoned Ostov," Valya said. Puffs of fog accompanied her words, but the frigid air didn't seem to bother her. "If that horror shows up, we're in trouble."

"I lost the flyswatter," Chris said apologetically.

"Prascovia can stop it. Ostov is her pet. It attacks indiscriminately, so she'll have to handle it to protect Andrey, but she might let it kill us first."

"*Babushka, ogni!*" Andrey yelled.

Prascovia released the screaming hunter. Valya turned to the river. A swarm of blindingly bright orbs were rising from the vortex. The one with the violet filaments seemed hesitant to join her brood; her solo flight continued a foot above the buzzing radiant cloud expanding between the banks.

"Chris, don't look at the Lights," Valya said. "They'll burn your retinas."

Ivan, crying like a hurt child, discarded the spent casings then blindly pushed the new shells into the barrel. Prascovia backed into the water, keeping an eye on the orbs.

"Get her," Chris whispered as though the paranormal swarm could understand him. His eyelids tingled. Every time he blinked, he toiled to open his eyes. Either the pain from spasms ripping his ribs and spine apart, or the poison, began to dull his brain. "Please get her. Drag her to Hell."

The orbs' humming rose in pitch. Then the whole cloud descended upon the woman. Prascovia dove, and so did the supernatural bees. Like a myriad of bites, tiny underwater sparks pushed her toward the abyss. Caught in the vortex, she screamed, and the gut-chilling sound lived several long seconds after she vanished from sight.

Chris exhaled. Clusters of stars drifted past him. Maybe they were molecules. They linked together, broke apart. They disappeared when he tried to follow individual specks. Their confusing motion was making him sick. He struggled to blow them away from his nose and mouth. Bitingly cold, they kept clinging to his face.

"Chris, stay awake." Valya touched his wrist, looking for a pulse. The standoffish orb with violet filaments buzzed around her like an annoying horsefly. Ivan's voice bellowed over the bank.

"It's hard to breathe," Chris said.

Valya swiped at the gleaming ball dancing around her. "Prascovia used Ostov's claws. That's a lot of the poison. Ivan got much less, but he's finished. You're alive because this wasn't your first time."

"What do you mean?" Chris asked.

Valya peeked over the bank's edge. "No sign of Ostov. Once Ivan's gone, I'll close the portal and get you inside the house."

Chris managed to raise his head. The doomed man swiveled to his right and left, shouting, his shotgun pointing in all directions. Just feet away from the blinded hunter, Andrey shook his father's shoulder, but Gregory remained unconscious.

A shadow bolted past Prascovia's windows.

"You might be wrong about Ostov," Chris said.

As exotic as they appeared, the creatures he had encountered in Vishenky could be counted as living, breathing animals, but not the thing that hopped over Prascovia's fence. As big as a Great Dane, the mummified carcass reached the river in a few leaps. It charged the screaming man and shook his body like a floppy dog toy. Chris averted his face from the slaughter.

Andrey sprinted through the shallows, collapsed onto the ground, and hid his face on Valya's stomach. She touched his head. The sobbing boy threw his arms around her neck and whispered into her ear. She listened as if awestruck, her eyes unblinking, frightened.

The creature finished the killing and rose to its hind legs. The enormous skull covered with brown parched skin turned searching for the next target. Gregory stirred, moaning, catching the monster's interest.

"Ay," Andrey snapped. He pried a clod of dirt from the hard ground and hurled it at the monster.

Ostov's body jerked. Andrey pulled Valya by the arm as if urging her to get up.

The creature reached them in two jumps. Ostov craned forward, the massive head towering over Chris. He stared into its empty nasal cavity.

"Okay," Valya said. She crawled away from Andrey and Chris. Ignoring the orb that hovered before her face, she climbed to her feet and straightened up.

Andrey tossed a rock. It rolled just past Ostov.

The creature pounced on the moving object. Valya slapped the orb and darted toward Gregory. The boy's ruse gave her time to grab the axe before Ostov spun in her direction. The rejected orb flew in circles above the monster's head.

"Hey, look at me, you big dumbo," Chris called. He tried to pull himself forward, to catch the creature's attention.

"Sh-h-h." Andrey put his hand on Chris's shoulder.

"*Ko mne.*" Valya patted her thigh as if calling a dog.

Its butt up in the air, Ostov lowered its chest to the ground, ready to leap. Valya raised the axe. Behind her, wobbly and confused, Gregory got up to his elbows.

A cloud of green formed between Valya and the monster. The specter took the appearance of a man, his lips whispering, eyes closed, his arms stretched toward the rapt Ostov. Astonished, Chris stared at his own doppelganger.

The apparition quivered, dimmed, and then came back as a different man, younger, with darker hair and a thinner face. The being's speech wasn't in sync with his lips. Two people were talking, and words were garbled. Then a female voice joined them. The image flickered again and turned into Valya. Even in a medieval peasant blouse and flowing skirt, with a strip of ribbon woven into a lock of hair, the specter looked chillingly real.

Frozen in mid-flight, the orb pulsed like a beating heart. *Love at first sight?* Chris almost laughed. Then the luminous ball charged the apparition.

Chris squeezed his eyes expecting an explosion—two otherworldly energies colliding. When there was no blast and he dared peek through his half-shut eyelids, the supernatural Valya looked a little brighter, as if illuminated by a parking lot lamp. She inched forward, speaking soothingly and smiling, the way a well-meaning person would approach a lost dog. Ostov lowered its skull, neck stretched, front legs spread.

Talking faster, she laid her palms on top of the creature's ugly mummified head. The insulted animal jumped to its hind legs like a bucking horse. The female apparition turned and sprinted down the steps, the beast in pursuit. Without slowing down, she leaped into the vortex. The creature followed. The real Valya fell to her knees, her shoulders slumped, out of steam, an ordinary human burned out by extraordinary events. At last.

Andrey slapped Chris's back and ran to Valya. The boy pried the unused weapon from her hands, dragged it down the steps, and puffed and grunted as he positioned it for a strike. He brought the axe head down onto the mirror.

* * *

The rest of the evening was a blur to Chris. First, he was moving across the meadow. Valya walked in front of him, and he didn't understand how he kept going without her assistance.

"*Davai, davai, davai,*" a voice shouted into his ear. Though he couldn't feel it, Chris saw his own arm wrapped around Gregory's neck.

Then he was lying on a pile of comforters in front of the blazing furnace. Some stinky brew boiled on the iron stove top, overflowing and sputtering. The pungent herbal scent tickled the back of his throat. He didn't remember how Valya stopped his bleeding and dressed the wounds. She never changed her soaked clothes. Instead of taking a moment to take care of herself, she fed the furnace with obsessive persistence. Chris understood what she was doing when he saw the ivory shawl with feathers and twigs disappear in the flames. Leontina's diary was next. Valya stood in front of the fire, staring darkly at the curling pages.

"Enough," Chris said.

She flinched at the sound of his voice and looked down at him as if she had forgotten about his presence. "This was my life," she replied curtly.

He could touch her ankle if he had the strength to move his arm. It didn't matter that physically Valya was within his reach. Emotionally, she was more distant than Polaris.

Through pain, Chris rose to his elbow, moved the blanket aside, and patted a spot before him. "Come here."

Valya peeled off the soggy clothes and knelt before the fire, letting the heat dry up her skin. She added wood and closed the furnace but left the bottom air vent open so everything would burn to ash. She slid under the covers, her body radiating warmth. Trying to avoid the twinges that accompanied his every move, Chris put his arm around her.

"I've done what I could," Valya muttered, still far away, still in her personal unreachable realm, still fighting some poignant inner battle. "One day, I'll forgive myself for all the mistakes I've made."

"You will." He touched her temple with his lips. "Until that day, remember: You have me. I love you unconditionally."

"Chris...." She closed her eyes. "I wouldn't have chosen this world if you felt differently."

* * *

Valya woke him before the sunrise. His wounds hurt, but Chris felt better than he expected.

"Who was the man with the shotgun?" he asked, grimacing as she stripped off the dressing on his stomach.

"He's been around since my childhood," Valya said. "I asked him last night whose grave he used to tend at the cemetery years ago. His daughter's grave. Stillborn in July. An opportunity for Prascovia, who played a midwife, to put an entity into a human baby. She could use it right away to pacify the Violet Lights if there was such a need, or harvest it a generation later for a little power gain. The child wasn't Gretishnikoff. She wouldn't be able draw the energy through the portals."

"What happened to the baby?" Chris asked.

"Prascovia ordered Ivan to take the dead newborn outside. Exposed to the full moon, the girl opened her eyes, and they were shining violet. He strangled his daughter. I told him that my parents were more merciful. He yelled that he was fed up with the supernatural. Feared I'd become the next Prascovia. You know the rest." She handed Chris an espresso cup filled with a white liquid. "Milk with honey. Hot. Sip it slowly."

Chris tasted the remedy and hated its syrupy sweetness. "It was so brave of you to step in front of Ostov," he said.

"Andrey swore that the shapeshifter would come to my rescue. It used to haunt my property. Andrey was absolutely certain that if it saved me from Ostov once before, it would do the same thing again."

"You put a lot of trust in his word."

"A leap of faith," Valya said, "but intuitively I knew he was right. All occurrences have a tendency to be repetitive. Something happened on the night when Luke got bitten and I lost my memory. The plastic barrier under the back gate was broken. The shapeshifter had a chance to escape."

"I remember," Chris said.

"And we know I had an encounter with Ostov that night and somehow survived."

"Did you see what happened to Prascovia? Could she be alive?"

"Her energy was her demise. She collected so much, and over such a long period of time, there's no way she could break away from it and escape. I mean, you saw how much 'my' entity wanted to reunite with me."

"The orb buzzing around you?"

"Good thing the pull from its own kind was stronger," Valya said. "It chose the shapeshifter that looked like me."

"How did you manage to get rid of it while you were on the other side?" Chris asked.

"Don't know. A human brain cannot comprehend that dimension. I remember the feeling of being there but no actual memories."

"How do you feel now?"

"Fine. Lost. No idea. Do you think there are portals in Virginia?"

"I almost wish I could say yes."

CHAPTER EIGHTY-NINE

Chris and I stood in front of the living-room window in my apartment. I was fortunate my grandmother had bequeathed the flat to me, not to my uncle. Anatoly pretended he didn't care. I was happy I no longer had to live with my parents. Chris had called them to reassure my mother that I was fine. I didn't want to talk to anyone.

The setting sun, a butter-yellow disk encircled in pink and periwinkle-blue, just touched the slender bell-tower of the Novodevichy Convent. A flock of pigeons flew off the roof, wings flapping, spiraling down in generous loops, and dissolved into the shadows.

The inescapable approach of the dusk tinged my mood with melancholy, the way the last day of summer would. No more warmth and colors. The end of a fairy tale.

"Two strangers, aren't we," I said.

"Not to me, no." Chris turned and crossed his arms over his chest. He leaned against the windowsill, his face dark in the waning light.

Just one idyllic, carefree day. That's all I wanted. Browse the streets, indulge in sightseeing, and take pleasure from each other's company. We really tried, but time after time, it felt as if we had just met on the Internet and gone on our first date. At least that's how it was for me.

"I should change my ticket," Chris said. "We'll spend a few more days together."

I shook my head, unable to speak, too close to tears. I wasn't going to complain, or cry, or blame him. No matter how wretched I felt, I wasn't going to tell him that it was only in his arms, only basking in his living energy, that I was myself again, strong, whole—but a step away, and I was crumbling. The only way to stop this slow, maddening torment was to set foot on the wicked grounds called Vishenky, let its sinfully delicious force mend me.

"I've done everything I can to help you," Chris said. "But it's never enough, is it?"

"My paranormal energy was a drug for your emotions," I parried apathetically. "How long will your affection last without it?"

He sighed and suddenly smiled. "I didn't fall in love with you because you were a creature straight out of Vishenky's folklore. I fell in love because you're so pretty."

I snorted.

"And because you're the bravest, most complicated, confident, and persevering human being I've ever met."

"I don't know how to be a human being," I muttered.

"Also the most resilient one." Serious again, he unlocked his arms and touched my cheek. "I know you'll start fantasizing about Vishenky the moment I board the plane. Don't go back. I'll return at Christmas. Will you fight for us?"

* * *

In the morning, they stopped at the hotel so Chris could pick up his luggage. Their late arrival at the airport left no time for a long farewell. His luggage was on the conveyor. Valya kissed him and told him not to worry. Chris did worry, but there was nothing left to do but summon his patience and wait.

CHAPTER NINETY

I squeezed the armrests and shut my eyes. The airplane's wheels touched the runway. We bounced up and down, decelerated, and were warned to remain in our seats. Chris was still asleep while we taxied to the gate.

Neither one of us had expected I'd be arriving with him to the United States just a few days before Christmas. The man who made changing my fate his life mission had been worried about the paperwork and our tickets, about meeting my parents, my frame of mind, and about a million other things while I had stepped back and let him take charge.

Then, suddenly, it was over. We had reached the cruising altitude. Chris, drained and relieved, had fallen asleep before the flight attendants had served us snacks.

I stayed alert. I had to, because I harbored a new dark secret. Last fall, every emotional experience I'd ever lived through had been ripped out of me. I could describe my friends and enemies, recount all my quests, all my triumphs and losses, discoveries and farewells, but I couldn't remember how the wealth of the events and people called "my life" was supposed to make me feel.

Today I stayed alert because I wanted to experience a transatlantic flight. I wanted to see the blanket of morning clouds beneath the airplane wings. I wanted to press my forehead to the shoulder of the sleeping man who said he loved me unconditionally.

The plane came to a stop. The passengers leapt to their feet. The cell phone conversations and the clicks of the opening overhead bins filled the cabin. Chris inhaled deeply, bent his neck back and forward, and stretched his arms.

He looked at me and smiled, his green eyes filled with tenderness and humor. "Are you ready for a new adventure?"

"Always." I unfastened my seatbelt and hesitated, watching him.

There was a sentiment that I had gained since my transformation into an ordinary human being, the only feeling that I didn't doubt. I leaned to Chris and whispered, "I love you."

EPILOGUE

Russia
1653

Another thrust of the dagger. And another. And another. Nothing was going as planned. Never before had the Dirge Birch stopped expelling poisonous juices, but on this breezy July night, no fluid came from the roots Prascovia scratched.

Expecting to be done in minutes, she had waited for nightfall to start digging. Her back hurt. Shoulders hurt. Palms hurt. She had become too lithe and slight after skipping so many meals. By the time she found a root that bled, her ears buzzed from dizziness. Prascovia pressed her tongue against the oozing gash in the wood, checking the poison's potency. Her mouth tingled. She spat out bits of mud, collected drops into a flask, and pushed some soil back into the hole. She rushed across the field, praying it wasn't too late.

A border of stones circled a spring in the grove next to the cemetery. The villagers favored the sediment-free flow over the chalky water from the wells of Vishenky. So did Ostov, the monster responsible for two recent deaths. Father Gerasim talked about piety and sins, and blamed wild boars for the carnage. Prascovia knew not to argue.

She jogged along the edge of the ravine until she reached the dirt-and-timber stairs leading to the spring. As she descended through the passageway between the walls of weeds, clouds snuffed out the moonlight.

Prascovia gripped the weather-worn pine railing and listened. The birches gossiped in whispers with the faint wind. Encouraged by darkness, the ferocious pests of her emotions bored holes in her composure. The idea of going home, curling under a thick blanket to block out sounds and lights and thoughts and fears was as tempting as a hot bowl of *kasha* on a rainy autumn day.

She picked a blade of grass, stretched it between her thumbs, and blew air through the gap. A whistle sliced the night. A loon would answer her call if nothing dangerous prowled around.

The bird responded, but from somewhere by the river, too far away to give her an idea about immediate danger.

She didn't have to do this. No one would know she gave up.

The memory of Father Gerasim's uneasy eyes, his voice dulled by distress, grinded her conscience like a sharp stone. Four boys, one of them Gerasim's son, Egor, had gone to Kolieno to see a wedding. They would return after midnight. Father Gerasim had chuckled nervously as he spoke about the hazards of the new town. Prascovia thought of perils lurking in their backyards. The path to the village ran footsteps from the well, and the boys would walk right by Ostov hanging around its waterhole.

Father Gerasim was a good man. He spoke with her as if she were a grownup. An illness had recently taken his wife, and Prascovia couldn't let him suffer another loss. Her grandmother taught her that the Dirge Birch's juices repelled Ostov.

Besides, she really liked Egor.

Her older sister, Antonina, liked him too; wanted to marry him.

Twinges of anger prickled Prascovia's chest like a weasel's fangs puncturing a mouse. Not because this morning her father chased her out of the house with a willow switch. Because her sister had convinced her to show Ostov's charcoal-drawn picture to their parents, promising they wouldn't get mad. But then Antonina mocked her and told Papa that Prascovia was a fool.

Fat, brainless wench. The time of Antonina's reckoning would come.

Riled up but quick and stealthy, Prascovia used a wooden bucket kept by the steps to empty the basin. When the water level fell low, she sprinkled the poison into the spring.

Voices and laughter sounded uphill. Prascovia crouched so fast, her knee bumped a stone. Sucking air through clenched teeth, she huddled against her pain. If somebody from the village caught her messing with the spring, she'd be in trouble, a tight-lipped twelve-year-old long-suspected for her involvement with magic. She crawled backward into the tall weeds. The scent of broken stems tickled her nose. The vegetation soaked her skirt. Her body was cooling off and her jaws drummed a quick rhythm.

A branch cracked in the bushes on the other side of the spring. Prascovia moved forward and peeked through the curtain of lacy plants. Ostov swayed its ugly head over the water, skimming the surface with its protruding teeth. Sensing the poison, the creature wasn't drinking. Then it looked up in the direction of the approaching voices.

"Guys, I'm thirsty," Egor was saying.

"It's going to rain," someone answered. "Let's get home."

"You go. I'll catch up with you."

Trembling, Prascovia rose to her feet. Ostov stared forward, aware of her, the closer target. A violet glow pulsed in its eye sockets.

From her skirt's pocket, Prascovia pulled a boiled egg, the only thing she had a chance to grab from the table when her father banned her from the morning meal. She had been saving it, not knowing when she would be forgiven.

She brought her arm back, inhaled, and hurled the egg into the monster.

Ostov caught the puny missile in its maw. The giant teeth crunched the eggshell. The creature swallowed.

Something sloshed through the mud at the bottom of the ravine. Ostov darted downhill, eager for a chase.

"Hey, who's there?" a voice called out from the top of the steps.

"I'll bet it's Prashka, Tonya's kid sister," Egor yelled on his way down. "Always skulking around in the dark. I'll take her home. Prashka, is it you?"

Prascovia inhaled the cool fragrant mist, the deepest breath her lungs could take. A roar of thunder rolled over the grove. Drops of rain fell on her face, washing off sweat and dirt. She waited for Egor to reach her and faked a whimper. "I fell into the spring. My foot hurts."

"Silly girl, you're freezing." He picked her up, his thirst forgotten. "How did this happen?"

"I tripped." Smiling demurely, she wrapped her arms around his neck. Her lips touched his ear. What was that love spell Grandma had taught her?

THE END

Thank you for reading! Find book two of the Auras of Night coming in 2017.

Please sign up for the City Owl Press newsletter for chances to win special subscriber-only contests and giveaways as well as receiving information on upcoming releases and special excerpts.

www.nataliabrothers.com

Facebook.com/NataliaBrothersAuthor

@ NataBrothers

All reviews are welcome and appreciated. Please consider leaving one on your favorite social media and book buying sites.

For books in the world of romance and speculative fiction that embody Innovation, Creativity, and Affordability, check out City Owl Press at www.cityowlpress.com.

ACKNOWLEDGEMENTS

It's a journey, it's a process, it's an electrifying succession of ups and downs, a sequence of tentative steps and exhilarating leaps forward. Writing a novel—I could never do this alone. I'm giving my thanks to my husband, who has read the first draft and never gets tired of answering my perpetual "Is it the, or a, or neither?" questions; to Laurie Jameson and Joel Q. Aaron for their infinite and unconditional support; to Kari Wainwright, Holly DeHerrera, and Debbie Maxwell Allen for their encouragement, brainstorming, and advice; to Sharon Platz for her essential input and friendship; and to Yelena Casale and Tina Moss for opening the door and helping me to take the ultimate step of turning the manuscript into a book.

Who else has helped me along the way? Caring critique groups, wonderful contest judges, and fantastic Pikes Peak Writers. The writing community — support, encouragement, patience, and knowledge. Thank you!

ABOUT THE AUTHOR

NATALIA BROTHERS was born in Moscow, growing up with the romance and magic of Russian fairy tales. She never imagined that one day she'd be swept off her feet by an American Marine. An engineer-physicist-chemist, Natalia realized that the powder metallurgy might not be her true calling when on a moonless summer night she was spooked by cries of a loon in a fog-wrapped meadow. What if, a writer's unrelenting muse, took hold of her. Natalia is an orchid expert and dark fantasy author.

www.nataliabrothers.com

ABOUT THE PUBLISHER

City Owl Press is a cutting edge indie publishing company, bringing the world of romance and speculative fiction to discerning readers.

www.cityowlpress.com